Praise for *The Book Thief*

"Thought-provoking, life-affirming, triumphant and tragic, this is a novel of breathtaking scope, masterfully told. It is an important piece of work, but also a wonderful page-turner."
—*The Guardian* (UK)

"This is a stunning book, seemingly channeled from a rare, artistic muse."
—*Seattle Post-Intelligencer*

"[A] haunting tale [that] will steal your heart."
—*The Miami Herald*

"One of the most highly anticipated young-adult books in years."
—*The Wall Street Journal*

"Intricate and extraordinary."
—*Newsday*

"An absorbing and searing narrative."
—*Orlando Sentinel*

"Lyrical and moving."
—*San Francisco Chronicle*

"This fabulous novel is rich, complicated and wise enough to satisfy a reader of any age."
—*The Atlanta Journal-Constitution*

"[B]oth gripping and touching, a work that kept me up late into the night feverishly reading the last 300 pages. You can't ask for much more than that."
—*The Plain Dealer* (Cleveland)

"A remarkable read."
—*The Sacramento Bee*

"This is a brilliant look at the wartime lives of ordinary decent people."
—*St. Louis Post-Dispatch*

"This is virtuoso work. Zusak exhibits the kind of mastery and peak power Kurt Vonnegut showed in his wartime tale 'Slaughterhouse-Five.'"
—*The Grand Rapids Press*

"It's the book to pick up for people who love to read."
—*The Florida Times-Union*

"Remarkable, just plain remarkable."
—*The Anniston Star*

"Subtle, simple, yet vividly imagined."
—*Teen Vogue*

★ "Beautiful and important."
—*Kirkus Reviews,* Starred

★ "Exquisitely written. . . . A tour de force to be not just read but inhabited."
—*The Horn Book Magazine,* Starred

★ "It's a book of greatness."
—*The Bulletin,* Starred

★ "An extraordinary narrative."
—*School Library Journal,* Starred

★ "An achievement."
—*Publishers Weekly,* Starred

Winner of the Book Sense Book of the Year Award
for Children's Literature

Winner of the Michael L. Printz Honor Book Award for Excellence
in Young Adult Literature

Winner of the National Jewish Book Award

Winner of the Association of Jewish Libraries Teen Book Award

A Quill Award Nominee

A *Publishers Weekly* Best Book of the Year

A *Kirkus Reviews* Editor's Choice

A *Horn Book* Fanfare

A *School Library Journal* Best Book of the Year

A *Booklist* Editors' Choice

A *Bulletin* Blue Ribbon Book

An ALA Notable Book

An ALA Top Ten Best Book for Young Adults

the book thief

the book thief

MARKUS ZUSAK

ILLUSTRATIONS BY TRUDY WHITE

ALFRED A. KNOPF
NEW YORK

This is a work of fiction. Names, characters, places, and incidents either are the
product of the author's imagination or are used fictitiously. Any resemblance
to actual persons, living or dead, events, or locales is entirely coincidental.

Text copyright © 2005 by Markus Zusak
Interior illustrations copyright © 2006 by Trudy White
Cover images copyright © 2013 by Twentieth Century Fox Film Corporation

All rights reserved. Published in the United States by Alfred A. Knopf, an
imprint of Random House Children's Books, a division of Random House LLC,
a Penguin Random House Company, New York. Previously published in the
United States in hardcover in 2006 and in paperback in 2007 by
Alfred A. Knopf, New York. Originally published in Australia in hardcover by
Picador, an imprint of Pan Macmillan Pty Ltd., Sydney, in 2005.

Knopf, Borzoi Books, and the colophon are registered trademarks of
Random House LLC.

Visit us on the Web! randomhouse.com

Educators and librarians, for a variety of teaching tools, visit us at
RHTeachersLibrarians.com

The Library of Congress has cataloged
the hardcover edition of this work as follows:
Zusak, Markus.
The book thief / by Markus Zusak.
p. cm.
Summary: Trying to make sense of the horrors of World War II,
Death relates the story of Liesel—a young German girl whose book-stealing
and story-telling talents help sustain her family and the Jewish man
they are hiding, as well as their neighbors.
ISBN 978-0-375-83100-3 (trade) — ISBN 978-0-375-93100-0 (lib. bdg.) —
ISBN 978-0-375-84220-7 (pbk.)
1. Germany—History—1933–1945—Juvenile fiction.
[1. Germany—History—1933–1945—Fiction. 2. Books and reading—Fiction.
3. Storytelling—Fiction. 4. Death—Fiction. 5. Jews—Germany—
History—1933–1945—Fiction. 6. World War, 1939–1945—Jews—
Rescue—Fiction.] I. Title.
PZ7.Z837Boo 2006 [Fic]—dc22 2005008942

ISBN 978-0-385-75472-9 (MTI pbk.)

Printed in the United States of America
10 9 8 7 6 5 4 3 2 1

Random House Children's Books supports the
First Amendment and celebrates the right to read.

For Elisabeth and Helmut Zusak,

with love and admiration

PROLOGUE

a mountain range of rubble

in which our narrator introduces:

himself—the colors—and the book thief

DEATH AND CHOCOLATE

First the colors.
Then the humans.
That's usually how I see things.
Or at least, how I try.

* * * HERE IS A SMALL FACT * * *
You are going to die.

I am in all truthfulness attempting to be cheerful about this whole topic, though most people find themselves hindered in believing me, no matter my protestations. Please, trust me. I most definitely *can* be cheerful. I can be amiable. Agreeable. Affable. And that's only the A's. Just don't ask me to be nice. Nice has nothing to do with me.

* * * REACTION TO THE * * *
AFOREMENTIONED FACT
Does this worry you?
I urge you — don't be afraid.
I'm nothing if not fair.

—Of course, an introduction.

A beginning.

Where are my manners?

I could introduce myself properly, but it's not really necessary. You will know me well enough and soon enough, depending on a diverse range of variables. It suffices to say that at some point in time, I will be standing over you, as genially as possible. Your soul will be in my arms. A color will be perched on my shoulder. I will carry you gently away.

At that moment, you will be lying there (I rarely find people standing up). You will be caked in your own body. There might be a discovery; a scream will dribble down the air. The only sound I'll hear after that will be my own breathing, and the sound of the smell, of my footsteps.

The question is, what color will everything be at that moment when I come for you? What will the sky be saying?

Personally, I like a chocolate-colored sky. Dark, dark chocolate. People say it suits me. I do, however, try to enjoy every color I see—the whole spectrum. A billion or so flavors, none of them quite the same, and a sky to slowly suck on. It takes the edge off the stress. It helps me relax.

∗ ∗ ∗ A SMALL THEORY ∗ ∗ ∗
People observe the colors of a day only at its beginnings and
ends, but to me it's quite clear that a day merges through a
multitude of shades and intonations, with each passing
moment. A single *hour* can consist of thousands of different
colors. Waxy yellows, cloud-spat blues. Murky darknesses.
In my line of work, I make it a point to notice them.

As I've been alluding to, my one saving grace is distraction. It keeps me sane. It helps me cope, considering the length of time I've been performing this job. The trouble is, who could ever replace me? Who could step in while I take a break in your stock-standard resort-style vacation destination, whether it be tropical or of the ski trip variety? The answer, of course, is nobody, which has prompted me to make a conscious, deliberate decision—to make distraction my vacation. Needless to say, I vacation in increments. In colors.

Still, it's possible that you might be asking, why does he even need a vacation? What does he need distraction *from*?

Which brings me to my next point.

It's the leftover humans.

The survivors.

They're the ones I can't stand to look at, although on many occasions I still fail. I deliberately seek out the colors to keep my mind off them, but now and then, I witness the ones who are left behind, crumbling among the jigsaw puzzle of realization, despair, and surprise. They have punctured hearts. They have beaten lungs.

Which in turn brings me to the subject I am telling you about tonight, or today, or whatever the hour and color. It's the story of one of those perpetual survivors—an expert at being left behind.

It's just a small story really, about, among other things:

* A girl
* Some words
* An accordionist
* Some fanatical Germans
* A Jewish fist fighter
* And quite a lot of thievery

I saw the book thief three times.

BESIDE THE RAILWAY LINE

First up is something white. Of the blinding kind.

Some of you are most likely thinking that white is not really a color and all of that tired sort of nonsense. Well, I'm here to tell you that it is. White is without question a color, and personally, I don't think you want to argue with me.

✳ ✳ ✳ A REASSURING ANNOUNCEMENT ✳ ✳ ✳
Please, be calm, despite that previous threat.
I am all bluster —
I am not violent.
I am not malicious.
I am a result.

Yes, it was white.

It felt as though the whole globe was dressed in snow. Like it had pulled it on, the way you pull on a sweater. Next to the train line, footprints were sunken to their shins. Trees wore blankets of ice.

As you might expect, someone had died.

. . .

They couldn't just leave him on the ground. For now, it wasn't such a problem, but very soon, the track ahead would be cleared and the train would need to move on.

There were two guards.

There was one mother and her daughter.

One corpse.

The mother, the girl, and the corpse remained stubborn and silent.

"Well, what else do you want me to do?"

The guards were tall and short. The tall one always spoke first, though he was not in charge. He looked at the smaller, rounder one. The one with the juicy red face.

"Well," was the response, "we can't just leave them like this, can we?"

The tall one was losing patience. "Why not?"

And the smaller one damn near exploded. He looked up at the tall one's chin and cried, "*Spinnst du?!* Are you stupid?!" The abhorrence on his cheeks was growing thicker by the moment. His skin widened. "Come on," he said, traipsing over the snow. "We'll carry all three of them back on if we have to. We'll notify the next stop."

As for me, I had already made the most elementary of mistakes. I can't explain to you the severity of my self-disappointment. Originally, I'd done everything right:

I studied the blinding, white-snow sky who stood at the window of the moving train. I practically *inhaled* it, but still, I wavered. I buckled—I became interested. In the girl. Curiosity got the better of me, and I resigned myself to stay as long as my schedule allowed, and I watched.

Twenty-three minutes later, when the train was stopped, I climbed out with them.

A small soul was in my arms.

I stood a little to the right.

The dynamic train guard duo made their way back to the mother, the girl, and the small male corpse. I clearly remember that my breath was loud that day. I'm surprised the guards didn't notice me as they walked by. The world was sagging now, under the weight of all that snow.

Perhaps ten meters to my left, the pale, empty-stomached girl was standing, frost-stricken.

Her mouth jittered.

Her cold arms were folded.

Tears were frozen to the book thief's face.

THE ECLIPSE

Next is a signature black, to show the poles of my versatility, if you like. It was the darkest moment before the dawn.

This time, I had come for a man of perhaps twenty-four years of age. It was a beautiful thing in some ways. The plane was still coughing. Smoke was leaking from both its lungs.

When it crashed, three deep gashes were made in the earth. Its wings were now sawn-off arms. No more flapping. Not for this metallic little bird.

* * * SOME OTHER SMALL FACTS * * *
Sometimes I arrive too early.
I rush,
and some people cling longer
to life than expected.

After a small collection of minutes, the smoke exhausted itself. There was nothing left to give.

A boy arrived first, with cluttered breath and what appeared to be a toolbox. With great trepidation, he approached the cockpit and watched the pilot, gauging if he was alive, at which point, he still was. The book thief arrived perhaps thirty seconds later.

Years had passed, but I recognized her.

She was panting.

From the toolbox, the boy took out, of all things, a teddy bear.

He reached in through the torn windshield and placed it on the pilot's chest. The smiling bear sat huddled among the crowded wreckage of the man and the blood. A few minutes later, I took my chance. The time was right.

I walked in, loosened his soul, and carried it gently away.

All that was left was the body, the dwindling smell of smoke, and the smiling teddy bear.

As the crowd arrived in full, things, of course, had changed. The horizon was beginning to charcoal. What was left of the blackness above was nothing now but a scribble, and disappearing fast.

The man, in comparison, was the color of bone. Skeleton-colored skin. A ruffled uniform. His eyes were cold and brown—like coffee stains—and the last scrawl from above formed what, to me, appeared an odd, yet familiar, shape. A signature.

The crowd did what crowds do.

As I made my way through, each person stood and played with the quietness of it. It was a small concoction of disjointed hand movements, muffled sentences, and mute, self-conscious turns.

When I glanced back at the plane, the pilot's open mouth appeared to be smiling.

A final dirty joke.

Another human punch line.

He remained shrouded in his uniform as the graying light arm-wrestled the sky. As with many of the others, when I began my journey away, there seemed a quick shadow again, a final moment of eclipse—the recognition of another soul gone.

You see, to me, for just a moment, despite all of the colors that touch and grapple with what I see in this world, I will often catch an eclipse when a human dies.

I've seen millions of them.

I've seen more eclipses than I care to remember.

THE FLAG

The last time I saw her was red. The sky was like soup, boiling and stirring. In some places, it was burned. There were black crumbs, and pepper, streaked across the redness.

Earlier, kids had been playing hopscotch there, on the street that looked like oil-stained pages. When I arrived, I could still hear the echoes. The feet tapping the road. The children-voices laughing, and the smiles like salt, but decaying fast.

Then, bombs.

This time, everything was too late.

The sirens. The cuckoo shrieks in the radio. All too late.

Within minutes, mounds of concrete and earth were stacked and piled. The streets were ruptured veins. Blood streamed till it was dried on the road, and the bodies were stuck there, like driftwood after the flood.

They were glued down, every last one of them. A packet of souls.

Was it fate?

Misfortune?

Is that what glued them down like that?

Of course not.

Let's not be stupid.

It probably had more to do with the hurled bombs, thrown down by humans hiding in the clouds.

Yes, the sky was now a devastating, home-cooked red. The small German town had been flung apart one more time. Snowflakes of ash fell so *lovelily* you were tempted to stretch out your tongue to catch them, taste them. Only, they would have scorched your lips. They would have cooked your mouth.

Clearly, I see it.

I was just about to leave when I found her kneeling there.

A mountain range of rubble was written, designed, erected around her. She was clutching at a book.

Apart from everything else, the book thief wanted desperately to go back to the basement, to write, or to read through her story one last time. In hindsight, I see it so obviously on her face. She was dying for it— the safety of it, the home of it—but she could not move. Also, the basement didn't even exist anymore. It was part of the mangled landscape.

Please, again, I ask you to believe me.

I wanted to stop. To crouch down.

I wanted to say:

"I'm sorry, child."

But that is not allowed.

I did not crouch down. I did not speak.

Instead, I watched her awhile. When she was able to move, I followed her.

She dropped the book.
    She knelt.
    The book thief howled.

Her book was stepped on several times as the cleanup began, and although orders were given only to clear the mess of concrete, the girl's most precious item was thrown aboard a garbage truck, at which point I was compelled. I climbed aboard and took it in my hand, not realizing that I would keep it and view it several thousand times over the years. I would watch the places where we intersect, and marvel at what the girl saw and how she survived. That is the best I can do— watch it fall into line with everything else I spectated during that time.

When I recollect her, I see a long list of colors, but it's the three in which I saw her in the flesh that resonate the most. Sometimes I manage to float far above those three moments. I hang suspended, until a septic truth bleeds toward clarity.
    That's when I see them formulate.

* * * THE COLORS * * *
RED: ■■ WHITE: O BLACK: ⌇

They fall on top of each other. The scribbled signature black, onto the blinding global white, onto the thick soupy red.
    Yes, often, I am reminded of her, and in one of my vast array of pockets, I have kept her story to retell. It is one of the small legion I carry, each one extraordinary in its own right. Each one an attempt—

an immense leap of an attempt—to prove to me that you, and your human existence, are worth it.

Here it is. One of a handful.

The Book Thief.

If you feel like it, come with me. I will tell you a story.

I'll show you something.

PART ONE

the grave digger's handbook

featuring:

himmel street — the art of *saumensch*ing — an ironfisted

woman — a kiss attempt — jesse owens —

sandpaper — the smell of friendship — a heavyweight

champion — and the mother of all *watschens*

ARRIVAL ON HIMMEL STREET

That last time.
   That red sky ...
   How does a book thief end up kneeling and howling and flanked by a man-made heap of ridiculous, greasy, cooked-up rubble?
   Years earlier, the start was snow.
   The time had come. For one.

   * * * A SPECTACULARLY TRAGIC MOMENT * * *
            A train was moving quickly.
            It was packed with humans.
      A six-year-old boy died in the third carriage.

The book thief and her brother were traveling down toward Munich, where they would soon be given over to foster parents. We now know, of course, that the boy didn't make it.

* * * HOW IT HAPPENED * * *
There was an intense spurt of coughing.
Almost an *inspired* spurt.
And soon after—nothing.

When the coughing stopped, there was nothing but the nothingness of life moving on with a shuffle, or a near-silent twitch. A suddenness found its way onto his lips then, which were a corroded brown color and peeling, like old paint. In desperate need of redoing.

Their mother was asleep.

I entered the train.

My feet stepped through the cluttered aisle and my palm was over his mouth in an instant.

No one noticed.

The train galloped on.

Except the girl.

With one eye open, one still in a dream, the book thief—also known as Liesel Meminger—could see without question that her younger brother, Werner, was now sideways and dead.

His blue eyes stared at the floor.

Seeing nothing.

Prior to waking up, the book thief was dreaming about the *Führer,* Adolf Hitler. In the dream, she was attending a rally at which he spoke, looking at the skull-colored part in his hair and the perfect square of his mustache. She was listening contentedly to the torrent of words spilling from his mouth. His sentences glowed in the light. In a quieter moment, he actually crouched down and smiled at her. She returned the smile and said, *"Guten Tag, Herr Führer. Wie geht's dir heut?"* She hadn't learned to speak too well, or even to read, as she had rarely frequented school. The reason for that she would find out in due course.

Just as the *Führer* was about to reply, she woke up.

It was January 1939. She was nine years old, soon to be ten.

Her brother was dead.

One eye open.

One still in a dream.

It would be better for a complete dream, I think, but I really have no control over that.

The second eye jumped awake and she caught me out, no doubt about it. It was exactly when I knelt down and extracted his soul, holding it limply in my swollen arms. He warmed up soon after, but when I picked him up originally, the boy's spirit was soft and cold, like ice cream. He started melting in my arms. Then warming up completely. Healing.

For Liesel Meminger, there was the imprisoned stiffness of movement and the staggered onslaught of thoughts. *Es stimmt nicht.* This isn't happening. This isn't happening.

And the shaking.

Why do they always shake them?

Yes, I know, I know, I assume it has something to do with instinct. To stem the flow of truth. Her heart at that point was slippery and hot, and loud, so loud so loud.

Stupidly, I stayed. I watched.

Next, her mother.

She woke her up with the same distraught shake.

If you can't imagine it, think clumsy silence. Think bits and pieces of floating despair. And drowning in a train.

• • •

Snow had been falling consistently, and the service to Munich was forced to stop due to faulty track work. There was a woman wailing. A girl stood numbly next to her.

In panic, the mother opened the door.

She climbed down into the snow, holding the small body.

What could the girl do but follow?

As you've been informed, two guards also exited the train. They discussed and argued over what to do. The situation was unsavory to say the least. It was eventually decided that all three of them should be taken to the next township and left there to sort things out.

This time, the train limped through the snowed-in country.

It hobbled in and stopped.

They stepped onto the platform, the body in her mother's arms.

They stood.

The boy was getting heavy.

Liesel had no idea where she was. All was white, and as they remained at the station, she could only stare at the faded lettering of the sign in front of her. For Liesel, the town was nameless, and it was there that her brother, Werner, was buried two days later. Witnesses included a priest and two shivering grave diggers.

* * * AN OBSERVATION * * *
A pair of train guards.
A pair of grave diggers.

When it came down to it, one of them called the shots.
The other did what he was told.
The question is, what if the *other* is a lot more than one?

Mistakes, mistakes, it's all I seem capable of at times.

For two days, I went about my business. I traveled the globe as always, handing souls to the conveyor belt of eternity. I watched them trundle passively on. Several times, I warned myself that I should keep a good distance from the burial of Liesel Meminger's brother. I did not heed my advice.

From miles away, as I approached, I could already see the small group of humans standing frigidly among the wasteland of snow. The cemetery welcomed me like a friend, and soon, I was with them. I bowed my head.

Standing to Liesel's left, the grave diggers were rubbing their hands together and whining about the snow and the current digging conditions. "So hard getting through all the ice," and so forth. One of them couldn't have been more than fourteen. An apprentice. When he walked away, after a few dozen paces, a black book fell innocuously from his coat pocket without his knowledge.

A few minutes later, Liesel's mother started leaving with the priest. She was thanking him for his performance of the ceremony.

The girl, however, stayed.

Her knees entered the ground. Her moment had arrived.

Still in disbelief, she started to dig. He couldn't be dead. He couldn't be dead. He couldn't—

Within seconds, snow was carved into her skin.

Frozen blood was cracked across her hands.

Somewhere in all the snow, she could see her broken heart, in two pieces. Each half was glowing, and beating under all that white. She realized her mother had come back for her only when she felt the boniness of a hand on her shoulder. She was being dragged away. A warm scream filled her throat.

* * * A SMALL IMAGE, PERHAPS * * *
TWENTY METERS AWAY
When the dragging was done, the mother and
the girl stood and breathed.
There was something black and rectangular
lodged in the snow.
Only the girl saw it.
She bent down and picked it up and
held it firmly in her fingers.
The book had silver writing on it.

They held hands.

A final, soaking farewell was let go of, and they turned and left the cemetery, looking back several times.

As for me, I remained a few moments longer.

I waved.

No one waved back.

Mother and daughter vacated the cemetery and made their way toward the next train to Munich.

Both were skinny and pale.

Both had sores on their lips.

Liesel noticed it in the dirty, fogged-up window of the train when they boarded just before midday. In the written words of the book thief herself, the journey continued like *everything* had happened.

When the train pulled into the *Bahnhof* in Munich, the passengers slid out as if from a torn package. There were people of every stature, but among them, the poor were the most easily recognized. The impoverished always try to keep moving, as if relocating might help. They ignore the reality that a new version of the same old problem will be waiting at the end of the trip—the relative you cringe to kiss.

I think her mother knew this quite well. She wasn't delivering her children to the higher echelons of Munich, but a foster home had apparently been found, and if nothing else, the new family could at least feed the girl and the boy a little better, and educate them properly.

The boy.

Liesel was sure her mother carried the memory of him, slung over her shoulder. She dropped him. She saw his feet and legs and body slap the platform.

How could that woman walk?

How could she move?

That's the sort of thing I'll never know, or comprehend—what humans are capable of.

She picked him up and continued walking, the girl clinging now to her side.

Authorities were met and questions of lateness and the boy raised their vulnerable heads. Liesel remained in the corner of the small, dusty office as her mother sat with clenched thoughts on a very hard chair.

There was the chaos of goodbye.

It was a goodbye that was wet, with the girl's head buried into the woolly, worn shallows of her mother's coat. There had been some more dragging.

Quite a way beyond the outskirts of Munich, there was a town called Molching, said best by the likes of you and me as "Molking." That's where they were taking her, to a street by the name of Himmel.

* * * A TRANSLATION * * *
Himmel = Heaven

Whoever named Himmel Street certainly had a healthy sense of irony. Not that it was a living hell. It wasn't. But it sure as hell wasn't heaven, either.

Regardless, Liesel's foster parents were waiting.

The Hubermanns.

They'd been expecting a girl and a boy and would be paid a small allowance for having them. Nobody wanted to be the one to tell Rosa Hubermann that the boy didn't survive the trip. In fact, no one ever really wanted to tell her anything. As far as dispositions go, hers wasn't really enviable, although she had a good record with foster kids in the past. Apparently, she'd straightened a few out.

For Liesel, it was a ride in a car.

She'd never been in one before.

There was the constant rise and fall of her stomach, and the futile hopes that they'd lose their way or change their minds. Among it all, her thoughts couldn't help turning toward her mother, back at the *Bahnhof,* waiting to leave again. Shivering. Bundled up in that useless coat. She'd be eating her nails, waiting for the train. The platform would be long and uncomfortable—a slice of cold cement. Would she keep an eye out for the approximate burial site of her son on the return trip? Or would sleep be too heavy?

The car moved on, with Liesel dreading the last, lethal turn.

The day was gray, the color of Europe.

Curtains of rain were drawn around the car.

"Nearly there." The foster care lady, Frau Heinrich, turned around and smiled. *"Dein neues Heim.* Your new home."

Liesel made a clear circle on the dribbled glass and looked out.

* * * A PHOTO OF HIMMEL STREET * * *
**The buildings appear to be glued together, mostly small houses
and apartment blocks that look nervous.
There is murky snow spread out like carpet.
There is concrete, empty hat-stand trees, and gray air.**

A man was also in the car. He remained with the girl while Frau Heinrich disappeared inside. He never spoke. Liesel assumed he was there to make sure she wouldn't run away or to force her inside if she gave them any trouble. Later, however, when the trouble did start, he simply sat there and watched. Perhaps he was only the last resort, the final solution.

After a few minutes, a very tall man came out. Hans Hubermann, Liesel's foster father. On one side of him was the medium-height Frau Heinrich. On the other was the squat shape of Rosa Hubermann, who looked like a small wardrobe with a coat thrown over it. There was a distinct waddle to her walk. Almost cute, if it wasn't for her face, which was like creased-up cardboard and annoyed, as if she was merely tolerating all of it. Her husband walked straight, with a cigarette smoldering between his fingers. He rolled his own.

• • •

The fact was this:

Liesel would not get out of the car.

"Was ist los mit dem Kind?" Rosa Hubermann inquired. She said it again. "What's wrong with this child?" She stuck her face inside the car and said, *"Na, komm. Komm."*

The seat in front was flung forward. A corridor of cold light invited her out. She would not move.

Outside, through the circle she'd made, Liesel could see the tall man's fingers, still holding the cigarette. Ash stumbled from its edge and lunged and lifted several times until it hit the ground. It took nearly fifteen minutes to coax her from the car. It was the tall man who did it.

Quietly.

There was the gate next, which she clung to.

A gang of tears trudged from her eyes as she held on and refused to go inside. People started to gather on the street until Rosa Hubermann swore at them, after which they reversed back, whence they came.

✳ ✳ ✳ A TRANSLATION OF ✳ ✳ ✳
ROSA HUBERMANN'S ANNOUNCEMENT
"What are you assholes looking at?"

Eventually, Liesel Meminger walked gingerly inside. Hans Hubermann had her by one hand. Her small suitcase had her by the other. Buried beneath the folded layer of clothes in that suitcase was a small black book, which, for all we know, a fourteen-year-old grave digger in a nameless town had probably spent the last few hours looking for. "I promise you," I imagine him saying to his boss, "I have no idea what happened to it. I've looked everywhere. *Everywhere!*" I'm sure he would never have suspected the girl, and yet, there it was—a black book with silver words written against the ceiling of her clothes:

* * * THE GRAVE DIGGER'S HANDBOOK * * *
A Twelve-Step Guide to
Grave-Digging Success
Published by the Bayern Cemetery Association

The book thief had struck for the first time—the beginning of an illustrious career.

GROWING UP A *SAUMENSCH*

Yes, an illustrious career.

I should hasten to admit, however, that there was a considerable hiatus between the first stolen book and the second. Another noteworthy point is that the first was stolen from snow and the second from fire. Not to omit that others were also given to her. All told, she owned fourteen books, but she saw her story as being made up predominantly of ten of them. Of those ten, six were stolen, one showed up at the kitchen table, two were made for her by a hidden Jew, and one was delivered by a soft, yellow-dressed afternoon.

When she came to write her story, she would wonder exactly when the books and the words started to mean not just something, but everything. Was it when she first set eyes on the room with shelves and shelves of them? Or when Max Vandenburg arrived on Himmel Street carrying handfuls of suffering and Hitler's *Mein Kampf*? Was it reading in the shelters? The last parade to Dachau? Was it *The Word Shaker*? Perhaps there would never be a precise answer as to when and where it occurred. In any case, that's getting ahead of myself. Before we make it to any of that, we first need to tour Liesel Meminger's beginnings on Himmel Street and the art of *saumensch*ing:

Upon her arrival, you could still see the bite marks of snow on her hands and the frosty blood on her fingers. Everything about her was undernourished. Wirelike shins. Coat hanger arms. She did not produce it easily, but when it came, she had a starving smile.

Her hair was a close enough brand of German blond, but she had dangerous eyes. Dark brown. You didn't really want brown eyes in Germany around that time. Perhaps she received them from her father, but she had no way of knowing, as she couldn't remember him. There was really only one thing she knew about her father. It was a label she did not understand.

✳ ✳ ✳ A STRANGE WORD ✳ ✳ ✳
Kommunist

She'd heard it several times in the past few years.

"Communist."

There were boardinghouses crammed with people, rooms filled with questions. And that word. That strange word was always there somewhere, standing in the corner, watching from the dark. It wore suits, uniforms. No matter where they went, there it was, each time her father was mentioned. She could smell it and taste it. She just couldn't spell or understand it. When she asked her mother what it meant, she was told that it wasn't important, that she shouldn't worry about such things. At one boardinghouse, there was a healthier woman who tried to teach the children to write, using charcoal on the wall. Liesel was tempted to ask her the meaning, but it never eventuated. One day, that woman was taken away for questioning. She didn't come back.

When Liesel arrived in Molching, she had at least some inkling that she was being saved, but that was not a comfort. If her mother loved her, why leave her on someone else's doorstep? Why? Why?

Why?

The fact that she knew the answer—if only at the most basic level—seemed beside the point. Her mother was constantly sick and there was never any money to fix her. Liesel knew that. But that didn't mean she had to accept it. No matter how many times she was told that she was loved, there was no recognition that the proof was in the abandonment. Nothing changed the fact that she was a lost, skinny child in another foreign place, with more foreign people. Alone.

The Hubermanns lived in one of the small, boxlike houses on Himmel Street. A few rooms, a kitchen, and a shared outhouse with neighbors. The roof was flat and there was a shallow basement for storage. It was supposedly not a basement of *adequate depth*. In 1939, this wasn't a problem. Later, in '42 and '43, it was. When air raids started, they always needed to rush down the street to a better shelter.

In the beginning, it was the profanity that made an immediate impact. It was so *vehement* and prolific. Every second word was either *Saumensch* or *Saukerl* or *Arschloch*. For people who aren't familiar with these words, I should explain. *Sau*, of course, refers to pigs. In the case of Sau*mensch,* it serves to castigate, berate, or plain humiliate a female. Sau*kerl* (pronounced "saukairl") is for a male. *Arschloch* can be translated directly into "asshole." That word, however, does not differentiate between the sexes. It simply is.

"*Saumensch, du dreckiges!*" Liesel's foster mother shouted that first evening when she refused to have a bath. "You filthy pig! Why won't you get undressed?" She was good at being furious. In fact, you could say that Rosa Hubermann had a face decorated with constant fury. That was how the creases were made in the cardboard texture of her complexion.

Liesel, naturally, was bathed in anxiety. There was no way she was getting into any bath, or into bed for that matter. She was twisted into one corner of the closetlike washroom, clutching for the nonexistent arms of the wall for some level of support. There was nothing but dry paint, difficult breath, and the deluge of abuse from Rosa.

"Leave her alone." Hans Hubermann entered the fray. His gentle voice made its way in, as if slipping through a crowd. "Leave her to me."

He moved closer and sat on the floor, against the wall. The tiles were cold and unkind.

"You know how to roll a cigarette?" he asked her, and for the next hour or so, they sat in the rising pool of darkness, playing with the to-bacco and the cigarette papers and Hans Hubermann smoking them.

When the hour was up, Liesel could roll a cigarette moderately well. She still didn't have a bath.

* * * SOME FACTS ABOUT * * *
HANS HUBERMANN
He loved to smoke.
The main thing he enjoyed about smoking
was the rolling.
He was a painter by trade and played the piano
accordion. This came in handy, especially in winter,
when he could make a little money playing in the pubs
of Molching, like the Knoller.
He had already cheated me in one world war but
would later be put into another (as a perverse

33

**kind of reward), where he would somehow
manage to avoid me again.**

To most people, Hans Hubermann was barely visible. An un-special person. Certainly, his painting skills were excellent. His musical ability was better than average. Somehow, though, and I'm sure you've met people like this, he was able to appear as merely part of the background, even if he was standing at the front of a line. He was always just *there*. Not noticeable. Not important or particularly valuable.

The frustration of that appearance, as you can imagine, was its complete misleadence, let's say. There most definitely *was* value in him, and it did not go unnoticed by Liesel Meminger. (The human child—so much cannier at times than the stupefyingly ponderous adult.) She saw it immediately.

His manner.

The quiet air around him.

When he turned the light on in the small, callous washroom that night, Liesel observed the strangeness of her foster father's eyes. They were made of kindness, and silver. Like soft silver, melting. Liesel, upon seeing those eyes, understood that Hans Hubermann was worth a lot.

* * * SOME FACTS ABOUT * * *
ROSA HUBERMANN
She was five feet, one inch tall and wore her
browny gray strands of elastic hair in a bun.
To supplement the Hubermann income, she did
the washing and ironing for five of the wealthier
households in Molching.
Her cooking was atrocious.

> She possessed the unique ability to aggravate
> almost anyone she ever met.
> But she *did* love Liesel Meminger.
> Her way of showing it just happened to be strange.
> It involved bashing her with wooden spoon and words
> at various intervals.

When Liesel finally had a bath, after two weeks of living on Himmel Street, Rosa gave her an enormous, injury-inducing hug. Nearly choking her, she said, "*Saumensch, du dreckiges*—it's about time!"

After a few months, they were no longer Mr. and Mrs. Hubermann. With a typical fistful of words, Rosa said, "Now listen, Liesel—from now on you call me Mama." She thought a moment. "What did you call your real mother?"

Liesel answered quietly. "*Auch Mama*—also Mama."

"Well, I'm Mama Number Two, then." She looked over at her husband. "And him over there." She seemed to collect the words in her hand, pat them together, and hurl them across the table. "That *Saukerl,* that filthy pig—you call him Papa, *verstehst?* Understand?"

"Yes," Liesel promptly agreed. Quick answers were appreciated in this household.

"Yes, *Mama,*" Mama corrected her. "*Saumensch.* Call me Mama when you talk to me."

At that moment, Hans Hubermann had just completed rolling a cigarette, having licked the paper and joined it all up. He looked over at Liesel and winked. She would have no trouble calling him Papa.

THE WOMAN WITH THE IRON FIST

Those first few months were definitely the hardest.

Every night, Liesel would nightmare.

Her brother's face.

Staring at the floor.

She would wake up swimming in her bed, screaming, and drowning in the flood of sheets. On the other side of the room, the bed that was meant for her brother floated boatlike in the darkness. Slowly, with the arrival of consciousness, it sank, seemingly into the floor. This vision didn't help matters, and it would usually be quite a while before the screaming stopped.

Possibly the only good to come out of these nightmares was that it brought Hans Hubermann, her new papa, into the room, to soothe her, to love her.

He came in every night and sat with her. The first couple of times, he simply stayed—a stranger to kill the aloneness. A few nights after that, he whispered, "Shhh, I'm here, it's all right." After three weeks, he held her. Trust was accumulated quickly, due primarily to the brute strength of the man's gentleness, his *thereness*. The girl knew from the outset that Hans Hubermann would always appear midscream, and he would not leave.

* * * A DEFINITION NOT FOUND * * *
IN THE DICTIONARY
Not leaving: an act of trust and love,
often deciphered by children

Hans Hubermann sat sleepy-eyed on the bed and Liesel would cry into his sleeves and breathe him in. Every morning, just after two o'clock, she fell asleep again to the smell of him. It was a mixture of dead cigarettes, decades of paint, and human skin. At first, she sucked it all in, then breathed it, until she drifted back down. Each morning, he was a few feet away from her, crumpled, almost halved, in the chair. He never used the other bed. Liesel would climb out and cautiously kiss his cheek and he would wake up and smile.

Some days Papa told her to get back into bed and wait a minute, and he would return with his accordion and play for her. Liesel would sit up and hum, her cold toes clenched with excitement. No one had ever given her music before. She would grin herself stupid, watching the lines drawing themselves down his face and the soft metal of his eyes—until the swearing arrived from the kitchen.

"STOP THAT NOISE, *SAUKERL!*"

Papa would play a little longer.

He would wink at the girl, and clumsily, she'd wink back.

A few times, purely to incense Mama a little further, he also brought the instrument to the kitchen and played through breakfast.

Papa's bread and jam would be half eaten on his plate, curled into the shape of bite marks, and the music would look Liesel in the face. I know it sounds strange, but that's how it felt to her. Papa's right hand strolled the tooth-colored keys. His left hit the buttons. (She especially loved to see him hit the silver, sparkled button—the C major.) The accordion's scratched yet shiny black exterior came back and forth as his arms squeezed the dusty bellows, making it suck in the air and throw it back out. In the kitchen on those mornings, Papa made the accordion live. I guess it makes sense, when you really think about it.

How do you tell if something's alive?

You check for breathing.

The sound of the accordion was, in fact, also the announcement of safety. Daylight. During the day, it was impossible to dream of her brother. She would miss him and frequently cry in the tiny washroom as quietly as possible, but she was still glad to be awake. On her first night with the Hubermanns, she had hidden her last link to him—*The Grave Digger's Handbook*—under her mattress, and occasionally she would pull it out and hold it. Staring at the letters on the cover and touching the print inside, she had no idea what any of it was saying. The point is, it didn't really matter what that book was about. It was what it meant that was more important.

* * * THE BOOK'S MEANING * * *
1. The last time she saw her brother.
2. The last time she saw her mother.

Sometimes she would whisper the word *Mama* and see her mother's face a hundred times in a single afternoon. But those were small mis-

38

eries compared to the terror of her dreams. At those times, in the enormous mileage of sleep, she had never felt so completely alone.

As I'm sure you've already noticed, there were no other children in the house.

The Hubermanns had two of their own, but they were older and had moved out. Hans Junior worked in the center of Munich, and Trudy held a job as a housemaid and child minder. Soon, they would both be in the war. One would be making bullets. The other would be shooting them.

School, as you might imagine, was a terrific failure.

Although it was state-run, there was a heavy Catholic influence, and Liesel was Lutheran. Not the most auspicious start. Then they discovered she couldn't read or write.

Humiliatingly, she was cast down with the younger kids, who were only just learning the alphabet. Even though she was thin-boned and pale, she felt gigantic among the midget children, and she often wished she was pale enough to disappear altogether.

Even at home, there wasn't much room for guidance.

"Don't ask *him* for help," Mama pointed out. "That *Saukerl*." Papa was staring out the window, as was often his habit. "He left school in fourth grade."

Without turning around, Papa answered calmly, but with venom, "Well, don't ask her, either." He dropped some ash outside. "She left school in *third* grade."

There were no books in the house (apart from the one she had secreted under her mattress), and the best Liesel could do was speak the alphabet under her breath before she was told in no uncertain terms to keep quiet. All that mumbling. It wasn't until later, when there was a bed-wetting incident midnightmare, that an extra reading education began. Unofficially, it was called the midnight class, even though it usually commenced at around two in the morning. More of that soon.

. . .

In mid-February, when she turned ten, Liesel was given a used doll that had a missing leg and yellow hair.

"It was the best we could do," Papa apologized.

"What are you talking about? She's lucky to have *that* much," Mama corrected him.

Hans continued his examination of the remaining leg while Liesel tried on her new uniform. Ten years old meant Hitler Youth. Hitler Youth meant a small brown uniform. Being female, Liesel was enrolled into what was called the BDM.

* * * EXPLANATION OF THE * * *
ABBREVIATION
It stood for *Bund Deutscher Mädchen* —
Band of German Girls.

The first thing they did there was make sure your "*heil* Hitler" was working properly. Then you were taught to march straight, roll bandages, and sew up clothes. You were also taken hiking and on other such activities. Wednesday and Saturday were the designated meeting days, from three in the afternoon until five.

Each Wednesday and Saturday, Papa would walk Liesel there and pick her up two hours later. They never spoke about it much. They just held hands and listened to their feet, and Papa had a cigarette or two.

The only anxiety Papa brought her was the fact that he was constantly leaving. Many evenings, he would walk into the living room (which doubled as the Hubermanns' bedroom), pull the accordion from the old cupboard, and squeeze past in the kitchen to the front door.

As he walked up Himmel Street, Mama would open the window and cry out, "Don't be home too late!"

"Not so loud," he would turn and call back.

"*Saukerl!* Lick my ass! I'll speak as loud as I want!"

The echo of her swearing followed him up the street. He never looked back, or at least, not until he was sure his wife was gone. On those evenings, at the end of the street, accordion case in hand, he would turn around, just before Frau Diller's corner shop, and see the figure who had replaced his wife in the window. Briefly, his long, ghostly hand would rise before he turned again and walked slowly on. The next time Liesel saw him would be at two in the morning, when he dragged her gently from her nightmare.

Evenings in the small kitchen were raucous, without fail. Rosa Hubermann was always talking, and when she was talking, it took the form of *schimpfen*. She was constantly arguing and complaining. There was no one to really argue with, but Mama managed it expertly every chance she had. She could argue with the entire world in that kitchen, and almost every evening, she did. Once they had eaten and Papa was gone, Liesel and Rosa would usually remain there, and Rosa would do the ironing.

A few times a week, Liesel would come home from school and walk the streets of Molching with her mama, picking up and delivering washing and ironing from the wealthier parts of town. Knaupt Strasse, Heide Strasse. A few others. Mama would deliver the ironing or pick up the washing with a dutiful smile, but as soon as the door was shut and she walked away, she would curse these rich people, with all their money and laziness.

"Too *g'schtinkerdt* to wash their own clothes," she would say, despite her dependence on them.

"Him," she accused Herr Vogel from Heide Strasse. "Made all his money from his father. He throws it away on women and drink. And washing and ironing, of course."

It was like a roll call of scorn.

Herr Vogel, Herr and Frau Pfaffelhürver, Helena Schmidt, the Weingartners. They were all guilty of *something*.

Apart from his drunkenness and expensive lechery, Ernst Vogel, according to Rosa, was constantly scratching his louse-ridden hair, licking his fingers, and then handing over the money. "I should wash it before I come home," was her summation.

The Pfaffelhürvers scrutinized the results. *"'Not one crease in these shirts, please,'"* Rosa imitated them. *"'Not one wrinkle in this suit.'* And then they stand there and inspect it all, right in front of me. Right under my nose! What a *G'sindel*—what trash."

The Weingartners were apparently stupid people with a constantly molting *Saumensch* of a cat. "Do you know how long it takes me to get rid of all that fur? It's everywhere!"

Helena Schmidt was a rich widow. "That old cripple—sitting there just wasting away. She's never had to do a day's work in all her life."

Rosa's greatest disdain, however, was reserved for 8 Grande Strasse. A large house, high on a hill, in the upper part of Molching.

"This one," she'd pointed out to Liesel the first time they went there, "is the mayor's house. That crook. His wife sits at home all day, too mean to light a fire—it's always freezing in there. She's crazy." She punctuated the words. "Absolutely. Crazy." At the gate, she motioned to the girl. "You go."

Liesel was horrified. A giant brown door with a brass knocker stood atop a small flight of steps. "What?"

Mama shoved her. "Don't you 'what' me, *Saumensch*. Move it."

Liesel moved it. She walked the path, climbed the steps, hesitated, and knocked.

A bathrobe answered the door.

Inside it, a woman with startled eyes, hair like fluff, and the posture of defeat stood in front of her. She saw Mama at the gate and handed the girl a bag of washing. "Thank you," Liesel said, but there was no reply. Only the door. It closed.

"You see?" said Mama when she returned to the gate. "This is what I have to put up with. These rich bastards, these lazy swine . . ."

Holding the washing as they walked away, Liesel looked back. The brass knocker eyed her from the door.

When she finished berating the people she worked for, Rosa Hubermann would usually move on to her other favorite theme of abuse. Her husband. Looking at the bag of washing and the hunched houses, she would talk, and talk, and talk. "If your papa was any good," she informed Liesel *every* time they walked through Molching, "I wouldn't have to do this." She sniffed with derision. "A painter! Why marry that *Arschloch*? That's what they told me—my family, that is." Their footsteps crunched along the path. "And here I am, walking the streets and slaving in my kitchen because that *Saukerl* never has any work. No real work, anyway. Just that pathetic accordion in those dirt holes every night."

"Yes, Mama."

"Is that all you've got to say?" Mama's eyes were like pale blue cutouts, pasted to her face.

They'd walk on.

With Liesel carrying the sack.

At home, it was washed in a boiler next to the stove, hung up by the fireplace in the living room, and then ironed in the kitchen. The kitchen was where the action was.

"Did you hear that?" Mama asked her nearly every night. The iron was in her fist, heated from the stove. Light was dull all through the house, and Liesel, sitting at the kitchen table, would be staring at the gaps of fire in front of her.

"What?" she'd reply. "What is it?"

"That was that Holtzapfel." Mama was already out of her seat. "That *Saumensch* just spat on our door again."

It was a tradition for Frau Holtzapfel, one of their neighbors, to spit on the Hubermanns' door every time she walked past. The front door was only meters from the gate, and let's just say that Frau Holtzapfel had the distance—and the accuracy.

The spitting was due to the fact that she and Rosa Hubermann were engaged in some kind of decade-long verbal war. No one knew the origin of this hostility. They'd probably forgotten it themselves.

Frau Holtzapfel was a wiry woman and quite obviously spiteful. She'd never married but had two sons, a few years older than the Hubermann offspring. Both were in the army and both will make cameo appearances by the time we're finished here, I assure you.

In the spiteful stakes, I should also say that Frau Holtzapfel was thorough with her spitting, too. She never neglected to *spuck* on the door of number thirty-three and say, "*Schweine!*" each time she walked past. One thing I've noticed about the Germans:

They seem very fond of pigs.

* * * A SMALL QUESTION AND * * *
ITS ANSWER
And who do you think was made to
clean the spit off the door each night?
Yes—you got it.

When a woman with an iron fist tells you to get out there and clean spit off the door, you do it. Especially when the iron's hot.

It was all just part of the routine, really.

Each night, Liesel would step outside, wipe the door, and watch the sky. Usually it was like spillage—cold and heavy, slippery and gray—but once in a while some stars had the nerve to rise and float, if only for a few minutes. On those nights, she would stay a little longer and wait.

"Hello, stars."

Waiting.

For the voice from the kitchen.

Or till the stars were dragged down again, into the waters of the German sky.

THE KISS

(A Childhood Decision Maker)

As with most small towns, Molching was filled with characters. A handful of them lived on Himmel Street. Frau Holtzapfel was only one cast member.

The others included the likes of these:

* Rudy Steiner—the boy next door who was obsessed with the black American athlete Jesse Owens.

* Frau Diller—the staunch Aryan corner-shop owner.

* Tommy Müller—a kid whose chronic ear infections had resulted in several operations, a pink river of skin painted across his face, and a tendency to twitch.

* A man known primarily as "Pfiffikus"—whose vulgarity made Rosa Hubermann look like a wordsmith and a saint.

On the whole, it was a street filled with relatively poor people, despite the apparent rise of Germany's economy under Hitler. Poor sides of town still existed.

As mentioned already, the house next door to the Hubermanns was rented by a family called Steiner. The Steiners had six children.

One of them, the infamous Rudy, would soon become Liesel's best friend, and later, her partner and sometime catalyst in crime. She met him on the street.

A few days after Liesel's first bath, Mama allowed her out, to play with the other kids. On Himmel Street, friendships were made outside, no matter the weather. The children rarely visited each other's homes, for they were small and there was usually very little in them. Also, they conducted their favorite pastime, like professionals, on the street. Soccer. Teams were well set. Garbage cans were used to mark out the goals.

Being the new kid in town, Liesel was immediately shoved between one pair of those cans. (Tommy Müller was finally set free, despite being the most useless soccer player Himmel Street had ever seen.)

It all went nicely for a while, until the fateful moment when Rudy Steiner was upended in the snow by a Tommy Müller foul of frustration.

"What?!" Tommy shouted. His face twitched in desperation. "What did I do?!"

A penalty was awarded by everyone on Rudy's team, and now it was Rudy Steiner against the new kid, Liesel Meminger.

He placed the ball on a grubby mound of snow, confident of the usual outcome. After all, Rudy hadn't missed a penalty in eighteen shots, even when the opposition made a point of booting Tommy Müller out of goal. No matter whom they replaced him with, Rudy would score.

On this occasion, they tried to force Liesel out. As you might imagine, she protested, and Rudy agreed.

"No, no." He smiled. "Let her stay." He was rubbing his hands together.

Snow had stopped falling on the filthy street now, and the muddy footprints were gathered between them. Rudy shuffled in, fired the shot, and Liesel dived and somehow deflected it with her elbow. She stood up grinning, but the first thing she saw was a snowball smashing into her face. Half of it was mud. It stung like crazy.

"How do you like that?" The boy grinned, and he ran off in pursuit of the ball.

"Saukerl," Liesel whispered. The vocabulary of her new home was catching on fast.

✳ ✳ ✳ SOME FACTS ABOUT RUDY STEINER ✳ ✳ ✳
He was eight months older than Liesel and had
bony legs, sharp teeth, gangly blue eyes,
and hair the color of a lemon.
One of six Steiner children, he was
permanently hungry.
On Himmel Street, he was considered a little crazy.
This was on account of an event that was rarely spoken about
but widely regarded as "The Jesse Owens Incident," in which he
painted himself charcoal black and ran the 100 meters at the
local playing field one night.

Insane or not, Rudy was always destined to be Liesel's best friend. A snowball in the face is surely the perfect beginning to a lasting friendship.

A few days after Liesel started school, she went along with the Steiners. Rudy's mother, Barbara, made him promise to walk with the new girl, mainly because she'd heard about the snowball. To Rudy's credit, he was happy enough to comply. He was not the junior misogynistic type of boy at all. He liked girls a lot, and he liked Liesel (hence, the snowball). In fact, Rudy Steiner was one of those auda-

48

cious little bastards who actually *fancied* himself with the ladies. Every childhood seems to have exactly such a juvenile in its midst and mists. He's the boy who refuses to fear the opposite sex, purely because everyone else embraces that particular fear, and he's the type who is unafraid to make a decision. In this case, Rudy had already made up his mind about Liesel Meminger.

On the way to school, he tried to point out certain landmarks in the town, or at least, he managed to slip it all in, somewhere between telling his younger siblings to shut their faces and the older ones telling him to shut his. His first point of interest was a small window on the second floor of an apartment block.

"That's where Tommy Müller lives." He realized that Liesel didn't remember him. "The twitcher? When he was five years old, he got lost at the markets on the coldest day of the year. Three hours later, when they found him, he was frozen solid and had an awful earache from the cold. After a while, his ears were all infected inside and he had three or four operations and the doctors wrecked his nerves. So now he twitches."

Liesel chimed in, "And he's bad at soccer."

"The worst."

Next was the corner shop at the end of Himmel Street. *Frau Diller's.*

✳ ✳ ✳ AN IMPORTANT NOTE ✳ ✳ ✳
ABOUT FRAU DILLER
She had one golden rule.

Frau Diller was a sharp-edged woman with fat glasses and a nefarious glare. She developed this evil look to discourage the very idea of stealing from her shop, which she occupied with soldierlike posture, a refrigerated voice, and even breath that smelled like *"heil* Hitler." The shop itself was white and cold, and completely bloodless. The small house compressed beside it shivered with a little more severity than the other buildings on Himmel Street. Frau Diller administered this feeling, dishing it out as the only free item from her premises. She lived for her shop and her shop lived for the Third Reich. Even when rationing started later in the year, she was known to sell certain hard-to-get items under the counter and donate the money to the Nazi Party. On the wall behind her usual sitting position was a framed photo of the *Führer*. If you walked into her shop and didn't say *"heil* Hitler," you wouldn't be served. As they walked by, Rudy drew Liesel's attention to the bulletproof eyes leering from the shop window.

"Say *'heil'* when you go in there," he warned her stiffly. "Unless you want to walk a little farther." Even when they were well past the shop, Liesel looked back and the magnified eyes were still there, fastened to the window.

Around the corner, Munich Street (the main road in and out of Molching) was strewn with slosh.

As was often the case, a few rows of troops in training came marching past. Their uniforms walked upright and their black boots further polluted the snow. Their faces were fixed ahead in concentration.

Once they'd watched the soldiers disappear, the group of Steiners and Liesel walked past some shop windows and the imposing town hall, which in later years would be chopped off at the knees and buried. A few of the shops were abandoned and still labeled with yellow stars and anti-Jewish slurs. Farther down, the church aimed itself at the sky, its rooftop a study of collaborated tiles. The street, overall, was a lengthy tube of gray—a corridor of dampness, people stooped in the cold, and the splashed sound of watery footsteps.

At one stage, Rudy rushed ahead, dragging Liesel with him.

He knocked on the window of a tailor's shop.

Had she been able to read the sign, she would have noticed that it belonged to Rudy's father. The shop was not yet open, but inside, a man was preparing articles of clothing behind the counter. He looked up and waved.

"My papa," Rudy informed her, and they were soon among a crowd of various-sized Steiners, each waving or blowing kisses at their father or simply standing and nodding hello (in the case of the oldest ones), then moving on, toward the final landmark before school.

✳ ✳ ✳ THE LAST STOP ✳ ✳ ✳
The road of yellow stars

It was a place nobody wanted to stay and look at, but almost everyone did. Shaped like a long, broken arm, the road contained several houses with lacerated windows and bruised walls. The Star of David was painted on their doors. Those houses were almost like lepers. At the very least, they were infected sores on the injured German terrain.

"Schiller Strasse," Rudy said. "The road of yellow stars."

At the bottom, some people were moving around. The drizzle made them look like ghosts. Not humans, but shapes, moving about beneath the lead-colored clouds.

"Come on, you two," Kurt (the oldest of the Steiner children) called back, and Rudy and Liesel walked quickly toward him.

At school, Rudy made a special point of seeking Liesel out during the breaks. He didn't care that others made noises about the new girl's stupidity. He was there for her at the beginning, and he would be there later on, when Liesel's frustration boiled over. But he wouldn't do it for free.

* * * THE ONLY THING WORSE THAN * * *
A BOY WHO HATES YOU
A boy who loves you.

In late April, when they'd returned from school for the day, Rudy and Liesel waited on Himmel Street for the usual game of soccer. They were slightly early, and no other kids had turned up yet. The one person they saw was the gutter-mouthed Pfiffikus.

"Look there." Rudy pointed.

* * * A PORTRAIT OF PFIFFIKUS * * *
He was a delicate frame.
He was white hair.
He was a black raincoat, brown pants, decomposing shoes, and
a mouth — and what a mouth it was.

"Hey, Pfiffikus!"

As the distant figure turned, Rudy started whistling.

The old man simultaneously straightened and proceeded to swear with a ferocity that can only be described as a talent. No one seemed to know the real name that belonged to him, or at least if they did, they never used it. He was only called Pfiffikus because you give that name to someone who likes to whistle, which Pfiffikus most definitely did. He was constantly whistling a tune called the Radetzky March, and all the kids in town would call out to him and duplicate that tune. At that precise moment, Pfiffikus would abandon his usual walking style (bent forward, taking large, lanky steps, arms behind his raincoated back) and erect himself to deliver abuse. It was then that any impression of serenity was violently interrupted, for his voice was brimming with rage.

On this occasion, Liesel followed Rudy's taunt almost as a reflex action.

"Pfiffikus!" she echoed, quickly adopting the appropriate cruelty that childhood seems to require. Her whistling was awful, but there was no time to perfect it.

He chased them, calling out. It started with *"Geh' scheissen!"* and deteriorated rapidly from there. At first, he leveled his abuse only at the boy, but soon enough, it was Liesel's turn.

"You little slut!" he roared at her. The words clobbered her in the back. "I've never seen you before!" Fancy calling a ten-year-old girl a slut. That was Pfiffikus. It was widely agreed that he and Frau Holtzapfel would have made a lovely couple. "Get back here!" were the last words Liesel and Rudy heard as they continued running. They ran until they were on Munich Street.

"Come on," Rudy said, once they'd recovered their breath. "Just down here a little."

He took her to Hubert Oval, the scene of the Jesse Owens incident, where they stood, hands in pockets. The track was stretched out in front of them. Only one thing could happen. Rudy started it. "Hundred meters," he goaded her. "I bet you can't beat me."

Liesel wasn't taking any of that. "I bet you I can."

"What do you bet, you little *Saumensch*? Have you got any money?"

"Of course not. Do you?"

"No." But Rudy had an idea. It was the lover boy coming out of him. "If I beat you, I get to kiss you." He crouched down and began rolling up his trousers.

Liesel was alarmed, to put it mildly. "What do you want to kiss *me* for? I'm filthy."

"So am I." Rudy clearly saw no reason why a bit of filth should get in the way of things. It had been a while between baths for both of them.

She thought about it while examining the weedy legs of her opposition. They were about equal with her own. There's no way he can beat me, she thought. She nodded seriously. This was business. "You can kiss me if you win. But if *I* win, I get out of being goalie at soccer."

Rudy considered it. "Fair enough," and they shook on it.

All was dark-skied and hazy, and small chips of rain were starting to fall.

The track was muddier than it looked.

Both competitors were set.

Rudy threw a rock in the air as the starting pistol. When it hit the ground, they could start running.

"I can't even see the finish line," Liesel complained.

"And *I* can?"

The rock wedged itself into the earth.

They ran next to each other, elbowing and trying to get in front. The slippery ground slurped at their feet and brought them down perhaps twenty meters from the end.

"Jesus, Mary, and Joseph!" yelped Rudy. "I'm covered in shit!"

"It's not shit," Liesel corrected him, "it's mud," although she had her doubts. They'd slid another five meters toward the finish. "Do we call it a draw, then?"

Rudy looked over, all sharp teeth and gangly blue eyes. Half his face was painted with mud. "If it's a draw, do I still get my kiss?"

"Not in a million years." Liesel stood up and flicked some mud off her jacket.

"I'll get you out of goalie."

"Stick your goalie."

As they walked back to Himmel Street, Rudy forewarned her. "One day, Liesel," he said, "you'll be dying to kiss me."

But Liesel knew.

She vowed.

As long as both she and Rudy Steiner lived, she would never kiss that miserable, filthy *Saukerl,* especially not *this* day. There were more important matters to attend to. She looked down at her suit of mud and stated the obvious.

"She's going to kill me."

She, of course, was Rosa Hubermann, also known as Mama, and she very nearly did kill her. The word *Saumensch* featured heavily in the administration of punishment. She made mincemeat out of her.

THE JESSE OWENS INCIDENT

As we both know, Liesel wasn't on hand on Himmel Street when Rudy performed his act of childhood infamy. When she looked back, though, it felt like she'd actually been there. In her memory, she had somehow become a member of Rudy's imaginary audience. Nobody else mentioned it, but Rudy certainly made up for that, so much that when Liesel came to recollect her story, the Jesse Owens incident was as much a part of it as everything she witnessed firsthand.

It was 1936. The Olympics. Hitler's games.

Jesse Owens had just completed the 4 × 100m relay and won his fourth gold medal. Talk that he was subhuman because he was black and Hitler's refusal to shake his hand were touted around the world. Even the most racist Germans were amazed with the efforts of Owens, and word of his feat slipped through the cracks. No one was more impressed than Rudy Steiner.

Everyone in his family was crowded together in their family room when he slipped out and made his way to the kitchen. He pulled some charcoal from the stove and gripped it in the smallness of his hands. "Now." There was a smile. He was ready.

He smeared the charcoal on, nice and thick, till he was covered in black. Even his hair received a once-over.

In the window, the boy grinned almost maniacally at his reflection, and in his shorts and tank top, he quietly abducted his older brother's bike and pedaled it up the street, heading for Hubert Oval. In one of his pockets, he'd hidden a few pieces of extra charcoal, in case some of it wore off later.

In Liesel's mind, the moon was sewn into the sky that night. Clouds were stitched around it.

The rusty bike crumbled to a halt at the Hubert Oval fence line and Rudy climbed over. He landed on the other side and trotted weedily up toward the beginning of the hundred. Enthusiastically, he conducted an awkward regimen of stretches. He dug starting holes into the dirt.

Waiting for his moment, he paced around, gathering concentration under the darkness sky, with the moon and the clouds watching, tightly.

"Owens is looking good," he began to commentate. "This could be his greatest victory ever. . . ."

He shook the imaginary hands of the other athletes and wished them luck, even though he knew. They didn't have a chance.

The starter signaled them forward. A crowd materialized around every square inch of Hubert Oval's circumference. They were all calling out one thing. They were chanting Rudy Steiner's name—and his name was Jesse Owens.

All fell silent.

His bare feet gripped the soil. He could feel it holding on between his toes.

At the request of the starter, he raised to crouching position—and the gun clipped a hole in the night.

For the first third of the race, it was pretty even, but it was only a matter of time before the charcoaled Owens drew clear and streaked away.

"Owens in front," the boy's shrill voice cried as he ran down the empty track, straight toward the uproarious applause of Olympic glory. He could even feel the tape break in two across his chest as he burst through it in first place. The fastest man alive.

It was only on his victory lap that things turned sour. Among the crowd, his father was standing at the finish line like the bogeyman. Or at least, the bogeyman in a suit. (As previously mentioned, Rudy's father was a tailor. He was rarely seen on the street without a suit and tie. On this occasion, it was only the suit and a disheveled shirt.)

"Was ist los?" he said to his son when he showed up in all his charcoal glory. "What the hell is going on here?" The crowd vanished. A breeze sprang up. "I was asleep in my chair when Kurt noticed you were gone. Everyone's out looking for you."

Mr. Steiner was a remarkably polite man under normal circumstances. Discovering one of his children smeared charcoal black on a summer evening was not what he considered normal circumstances. "The boy is crazy," he muttered, although he conceded that with six kids, something like this was bound to happen. At least one of them had to be a bad egg. Right now, he was looking at it, waiting for an explanation. "Well?"

Rudy panted, bending down and placing his hands on his knees. "I was being Jesse Owens." He answered as though it was the most natural thing on earth to be doing. There was even something implicit in his tone that suggested something along the lines of, "What the hell does it look like?" The tone vanished, however, when he saw the sleep deprivation whittled under his father's eyes.

"Jesse Owens?" Mr. Steiner was the type of man who was very wooden. His voice was angular and true. His body was tall and heavy, like oak. His hair was like splinters. "What about him?"

"You know, Papa, the Black Magic one."

"I'll give *you* black magic." He caught his son's ear between his thumb and forefinger.

Rudy winced. "Ow, that really hurts."

"Does it?" His father was more concerned with the clammy texture of charcoal contaminating his fingers. He covered everything, didn't he? he thought. It's even in his ears, for God's sake. "Come on."

On the way home, Mr. Steiner decided to talk politics with the boy as best he could. Only in the years ahead would Rudy understand it all—when it was too late to bother understanding anything.

* * * THE CONTRADICTORY POLITICS * * *
OF ALEX STEINER
Point One: He was a member of the Nazi Party, but he did not
hate the Jews, or anyone else for that matter.
Point Two: Secretly, though, he couldn't help feeling a
percentage of relief (or worse—gladness!) when
Jewish shop owners were put out of business—
propaganda informed him that it was only a matter of
time before a plague of Jewish tailors showed up
and stole his customers.
Point Three: But did that mean they should be driven
out completely?
Point Four: His family. Surely, he had to do whatever he

could to support them. If that meant being in the party,
it meant being in the party.
Point Five: Somewhere, far down, there was an itch in his
heart, but he made it a point not to scratch it. He was afraid of
what might come leaking out.

They walked around a few corners onto Himmel Street, and Alex
said, "Son, you can't go around painting yourself black, you hear?"

Rudy was interested, and confused. The moon was undone now,
free to move and rise and fall and drip on the boy's face, making him
nice and murky, like his thoughts. "Why not, Papa?"

"Because they'll take you away."

"Why?"

"Because you shouldn't want to be like black people or Jewish
people or anyone who is . . . not *us.*"

"Who are Jewish people?"

"You know my oldest customer, Mr. Kaufmann? Where we
bought your shoes?"

"Yes."

"Well, he's Jewish."

"I didn't know that. Do you have to pay to be Jewish? Do you
need a license?"

"No, Rudy." Mr. Steiner was steering the bike with one hand and
Rudy with the other. He was having trouble steering the conversation. He still hadn't relinquished the hold on his son's earlobe. He'd
forgotten about it. "It's like you're German or Catholic."

"Oh. Is Jesse Owens Catholic?"

"*I* don't know!" He tripped on a bike pedal then and released
the ear.

They walked on in silence for a while, until Rudy said, "I just wish
I was like Jesse Owens, Papa."

This time, Mr. Steiner placed his hand on Rudy's head and explained, "I know, son—but you've got beautiful blond hair and big, safe blue eyes. You should be happy with that; is that clear?"

But nothing was clear.

Rudy understood nothing, and that night was the prelude of things to come. Two and a half years later, the Kaufmann Shoe Shop was reduced to broken glass, and all the shoes were flung aboard a truck in their boxes.

THE OTHER SIDE OF SANDPAPER

People have defining moments, I suppose, especially when they're children. For some it's a Jesse Owens incident. For others it's a moment of bed-wetting hysteria:

It was late May 1939, and the night had been like most others. Mama shook her iron fist. Papa was out. Liesel cleaned the front door and watched the Himmel Street sky.

Earlier, there had been a parade.

The brown-shirted extremist members of the NSDAP (otherwise known as the Nazi Party) had marched down Munich Street, their banners worn proudly, their faces held high, as if on sticks. Their voices were full of song, culminating in a roaring rendition of *"Deutschland über Alles."* "Germany over Everything."

As always, they were clapped.

They were spurred on as they walked to who knows where.

People on the street stood and watched, some with straight-armed salutes, others with hands that burned from applause. Some kept faces that were contorted by pride and rally like Frau Diller, and then there were the scatterings of odd men out, like Alex Steiner, who stood like a human-shaped block of wood, clapping slow and dutiful. And beautiful. Submission.

On the footpath, Liesel stood with her papa and Rudy. Hans Hubermann wore a face with the shades pulled down.

✴ ✴ ✴ SOME CRUNCHED NUMBERS ✴ ✴ ✴
In 1933, 90 percent of Germans showed unflinching
support for Adolf Hitler.
That leaves 10 percent who didn't.
Hans Hubermann belonged to the 10 percent.
There was a reason for that.

In the night, Liesel dreamed like she always did. At first, she saw the brownshirts marching, but soon enough, they led her to a train, and the usual discovery awaited. Her brother was staring again.

When she woke up screaming, Liesel knew immediately that on this occasion, something had changed. A smell leaked out from under the sheets, warm and sickly. At first, she tried convincing herself that nothing had happened, but as Papa came closer and held her, she cried and admitted the fact in his ear.

"Papa," she whispered, "Papa," and that was all. He could probably smell it.

He lifted her gently from the bed and carried her into the washroom. The moment came a few minutes later.

"We take the sheets off," Papa said, and when he reached under and pulled at the fabric, something loosened and landed with a thud. A

black book with silver writing on it came hurtling out and landed on the floor, between the tall man's feet.

He looked down at it.

He looked at the girl, who timidly shrugged.

Then he read the title, with concentration, aloud: *"The Grave Digger's Handbook."*

So that's what it's called, Liesel thought.

A patch of silence stood among them now. The man, the girl, the book. He picked it up and spoke soft as cotton.

* * * A 2 A.M. CONVERSATION * * *
"Is this yours?"
"Yes, Papa."
"Do you want to read it?"
Again, "Yes, Papa."
A tired smile.
Metallic eyes, melting.
"Well, we'd better read it, then."

Four years later, when she came to write in the basement, two thoughts struck Liesel about the trauma of wetting the bed. First, she felt extremely lucky that it was Papa who discovered the book. (Fortunately, when the sheets had been washed previously, Rosa had made Liesel strip the bed and make it up. "And be quick about it, *Saumensch*! Does it look like we've got all day?") Second, she was clearly proud of Hans Hubermann's part in her education. *You wouldn't think it,* she wrote, *but it was not so much the school who helped me to read. It was Papa. People think he's not so smart, and it's true that he doesn't read too fast, but I would soon learn that words and writing actually saved his life once. Or at least, words and a man who taught him the accordion . . .*

"First things first," Hans Hubermann said that night. He washed the sheets and hung them up. "Now," he said upon his return. "Let's get this midnight class started."

The yellow light was alive with dust.

Liesel sat on cold clean sheets, ashamed, elated. The thought of bed-wetting prodded her, but she was going to read. She was going to read the book.

The excitement stood up in her.

Visions of a ten-year-old reading genius were set alight.

If only it was that easy.

"To tell you the truth," Papa explained upfront, "I am not such a good reader myself."

But it didn't matter that he read slowly. If anything, it might have helped that his own reading pace was slower than average. Perhaps it would cause less frustration in coping with the girl's lack of ability.

Still, initially, Hans appeared a little uncomfortable holding the book and looking through it.

When he came over and sat next to her on the bed, he leaned back, his legs angling over the side. He examined the book again and dropped it on the blanket. "Now why would a nice girl like you want to read such a thing?"

Again, Liesel shrugged. Had the apprentice been reading the complete works of Goethe or any other such luminary, that was what would have sat in front of them. She attempted to explain. "I — when . . . It was sitting in the snow, and —" The soft-spoken words fell off the side of the bed, emptying to the floor like powder.

Papa knew what to say, though. He always knew what to say.

He ran a hand through his sleepy hair and said, "Well, promise me one thing, Liesel. If I die anytime soon, you make sure they bury me right."

She nodded, with great sincerity.

"No skipping chapter six or step four in chapter nine." He laughed, as did the bed wetter. "Well, I'm glad that's settled. We can get on with it now."

He adjusted his position and his bones creaked like itchy floorboards. "The fun begins."

Amplified by the still of night, the book opened—a gust of wind.

Looking back, Liesel could tell exactly what her papa was thinking when he scanned the first page of *The Grave Digger's Handbook*. As he realized the difficulty of the text, he was clearly aware that such a book was hardly ideal. There were words in there that he'd have trouble with himself. Not to mention the morbidity of the subject. As for the girl, there was a sudden desire to read it that she didn't even attempt to understand. On some level, perhaps she wanted to make sure her brother was buried right. Whatever the reason, her hunger to read that book was as intense as any ten-year-old human could experience.

Chapter one was called "The First Step: Choosing the Right Equipment." In a short introductory passage, it outlined the kind of material to be covered in the following twenty pages. Types of shovels, picks, gloves, and so forth were itemized, as well as the vital need to properly maintain them. This grave digging was serious.

As Papa flicked through it, he could surely feel Liesel's eyes on him. They reached over and gripped him, waiting for something, anything, to slip from his lips.

"Here." He shifted again and handed her the book. "Look at this page and tell me how many words you can read."

She looked at it—and lied.

"About half."

"Read some for me." But of course, she couldn't. When he made her point out any words she could read and actually say them, there were only three—the three main German words for "the." The whole page must have had two hundred words on it.

This might be harder than I thought.

She caught him thinking it, just for a moment.

He lifted himself forward, rose to his feet, and walked out.

This time, when he came back, he said, "Actually, I have a better idea." In his hand, there was a thick painter's pencil and a stack of sandpaper. "Let's start from scratch." Liesel saw no reason to argue.

In the left corner of an upturned piece of sandpaper, he drew a square of perhaps an inch and shoved a capital *A* inside it. In the other corner, he placed a lowercase one. So far, so good.

"*A*," Liesel said.

"*A* for what?"

She smiled. "*Apfel.*"

He wrote the word in big letters and drew a misshapen apple under it. He was a housepainter, not an artist. When it was complete, he looked over and said, "Now for *B*."

As they progressed through the alphabet, Liesel's eyes grew larger. She had done this at school, in the kindergarten class, but this time was better. She was the only one there, and she was not gigantic. It was nice to watch Papa's hand as he wrote the words and slowly constructed the primitive sketches.

"Ah, come on, Liesel," he said when she struggled later on. "Something that starts with *S*. It's easy. I'm very disappointed in you."

She couldn't think.

"Come on!" His whisper played with her. "Think of Mama."

That was when the word struck her face like a slap. A reflex grin. "*SAUMENSCH!*" she shouted, and Papa roared with laughter, then quieted.

"Shhh, we have to be quiet." But he roared all the same and wrote the word, completing it with one of his sketches.

✳ ✳ ✳ A TYPICAL HANS HUBERMANN ✳ ✳ ✳
ARTWORK

"Papa!" she whispered. "I have no eyes!"

He patted the girl's hair. She'd fallen into his trap. "With a smile like that," Hans Hubermann said, "you don't need eyes." He hugged her and then looked again at the picture, with a face of warm silver. "Now for *T*."

With the alphabet completed and studied a dozen times, Papa leaned over and said, "Enough for tonight?"

"A few more words?"

He was definite. "Enough. When you wake up, I'll play accordion for you."

"Thanks, Papa."

"Good night." A quiet, one-syllable laugh. "Good night, *Saumensch*."

"Good night, Papa."

He switched off the light, came back, and sat in the chair. In the darkness, Liesel kept her eyes open. She was watching the words.

THE SMELL OF FRIENDSHIP

It continued.

Over the next few weeks and into summer, the midnight class began at the end of each nightmare. There were two more bed-wetting occurrences, but Hans Hubermann merely repeated his previous cleanup heroics and got down to the task of reading, sketching, and reciting. In the morning's early hours, quiet voices were loud.

On a Thursday, just after 3 p.m., Mama told Liesel to get ready to come with her and deliver some ironing. Papa had other ideas.

He walked into the kitchen and said, "Sorry, Mama, she's not going with you today."

Mama didn't even bother looking up from the washing bag. "Who asked you, *Arschloch*? Come on, Liesel."

"She's reading," he said. Papa handed Liesel a steadfast smile and a wink. "With me. I'm teaching her. We're going to the Amper—upstream, where I used to practice the accordion."

Now he had her attention.

Mama placed the washing on the table and eagerly worked herself up to the appropriate level of cynicism. "What did you say?"

"I think you heard me, Rosa."

Mama laughed. "What the hell could *you* teach her?" A cardboard grin. Uppercut words. "Like you could read so much, you *Saukerl*."

The kitchen waited. Papa counterpunched. "We'll take your ironing for you."

"You filthy—" She stopped. The words propped in her mouth as she considered it. "Be back before dark."

"We can't read in the dark, Mama," Liesel said.

"What was that, *Saumensch?*"

"Nothing, Mama."

Papa grinned and pointed at the girl. "Book, sandpaper, pencil," he ordered her, "and accordion!" once she was already gone. Soon, they were on Himmel Street, carrying the words, the music, the washing.

As they walked toward Frau Diller's, they turned around a few times to see if Mama was still at the gate, checking on them. She was. At one point, she called out, "Liesel, hold that ironing straight! Don't crease it!"

"Yes, Mama!"

A few steps later: "Liesel, are you dressed warm enough?!"

"What did you say?"

"*Saumensch dreckiges,* you never hear anything! Are you dressed warm enough? It might get cold later!"

Around the corner, Papa bent down to do up a shoelace. "Liesel," he said, "could you roll me a cigarette?"

Nothing would give her greater pleasure.

Once the ironing was delivered, they made their way back to the Amper River, which flanked the town. It worked its way past, pointing in the direction of Dachau, the concentration camp.

There was a wooden-planked bridge.

They sat maybe thirty meters down from it, in the grass, writing the words and reading them aloud, and when darkness was near,

Hans pulled out the accordion. Liesel looked at him and listened, though she did not immediately notice the perplexed expression on her papa's face that evening as he played.

* * * PAPA'S FACE * * *
It traveled and wondered,
but it disclosed no answers.
Not yet.

There had been a change in him. A slight shift.

She saw it but didn't realize until later, when all the stories came together. She didn't see him watching as he played, having no idea that Hans Hubermann's accordion was a story. In the times ahead, that story would arrive at 33 Himmel Street in the early hours of morning, wearing ruffled shoulders and a shivering jacket. It would carry a suitcase, a book, and two questions. A story. Story after story. Story *within* story.

For now, there was only the one as far as Liesel was concerned, and she was enjoying it.

She settled into the long arms of grass, lying back.

She closed her eyes and her ears held the notes.

There were, of course, some problems as well. A few times, Papa nearly yelled at her. "Come on, Liesel," he'd say. "You know this word; you know it!" Just when progress seemed to be flowing well, somehow things would become lodged.

When the weather was good, they'd go to the Amper in the afternoon. In bad weather, it was the basement. This was mainly on account of Mama. At first, they tried in the kitchen, but there was no way.

"Rosa," Hans said to her at one point. Quietly, his words cut through one of her sentences. "Could you do me a favor?"

She looked up from the stove. "What?"

"I'm asking you, I'm *begging* you, could you please shut your mouth for just five minutes?"

You can imagine the reaction.

They ended up in the basement.

There was no lighting there, so they took a kerosene lamp, and slowly, between school and home, from the river to the basement, from the good days to the bad, Liesel was learning to read and write.

"Soon," Papa told her, "you'll be able to read that awful graves book with your eyes closed."

"And I can get out of that midget class."

She spoke those words with a grim kind of ownership.

In one of their basement sessions, Papa dispensed with the sandpaper (it was running out fast) and pulled out a brush. There were few luxuries in the Hubermann household, but there was an oversupply of paint, and it became more than useful for Liesel's learning. Papa would say a word and the girl would have to spell it aloud and then paint it on the wall, as long as she got it right. After a month, the wall was recoated. A fresh cement page.

Some nights, after working in the basement, Liesel would sit crouched in the bath and hear the same utterances from the kitchen.

"You stink," Mama would say to Hans. "Like cigarettes and kerosene."

Sitting in the water, she imagined the smell of it, mapped out on her papa's clothes. More than anything, it was the smell of friendship, and she could find it on herself, too. Liesel loved that smell. She would sniff her arm and smile as the water cooled around her.

THE HEAVYWEIGHT CHAMPION
OF THE SCHOOL–YARD

The summer of '39 was in a hurry, or perhaps Liesel was. She spent her time playing soccer with Rudy and the other kids on Himmel Street (a year-round pastime), taking ironing around town with Mama, and learning words. It felt like it was over a few days after it began.

In the latter part of the year, two things happened.

* * * SEPTEMBER–NOVEMBER 1939 * * *
1. World War Two begins.
2. Liesel Meminger becomes the heavyweight
champion of the school-yard.

The beginning of September.

It was a cool day in Molching when the war began and my work-load increased.

The world talked it over.

Newspaper headlines reveled in it.

The *Führer*'s voice roared from German radios. We will not give up. We will not rest. We will be victorious. Our time has come.

The German invasion of Poland had begun and people were gathered everywhere, listening to the news of it. Munich Street, like every other main street in Germany, was alive with war. The smell, the voice. Rationing had begun a few days earlier—the writing on the wall—and now it was official. England and France had made their declaration on Germany. To steal a phrase from Hans Hubermann:

The fun begins.

The day of the announcement, Papa was lucky enough to have some work. On his way home, he picked up a discarded newspaper, and rather than stopping to shove it between paint cans in his cart, he folded it up and slipped it beneath his shirt. By the time he made it home and removed it, his sweat had drawn the ink onto his skin. The paper landed on the table, but the news was stapled to his chest. A tattoo. Holding the shirt open, he looked down in the unsure kitchen light.

"What does it say?" Liesel asked him. She was looking back and forth, from the black outlines on his skin to the paper.

"'Hitler takes Poland,'" he answered, and Hans Hubermann slumped into a chair. *"Deutschland über Alles,"* he whispered, and his voice was not remotely patriotic.

The face was there again—his accordion face.

That was one war started.

Liesel would soon be in another.

Nearly a month after school resumed, she was moved up to her rightful year level. You might think this was due to her improved reading, but it wasn't. Despite the advancement, she still read with great difficulty. Sentences were strewn everywhere. Words fooled her. The reason she was elevated had more to do with the fact that she became disruptive in the younger class. She answered questions directed to other children and called out. A few times, she was given what was known as a *Watschen* (pronounced "varchen") in the corridor.

✷ ✷ ✷ A DEFINITION ✷ ✷ ✷
Watschen = a good hiding

She was taken up, put in a chair at the side, and told to keep her mouth shut by the teacher, who also happened to be a nun. At the other end of the classroom, Rudy looked across and waved. Liesel waved back and tried not to smile.

At home, she was well into reading *The Grave Digger's Handbook* with Papa. They would circle the words she couldn't understand and take them down to the basement the next day. She thought it was enough. It was not enough.

Somewhere at the start of November, there were some progress tests at school. One of them was for reading. Every child was made to stand at the front of the room and read from a passage the teacher gave them. It was a frosty morning but bright with sun. Children scrunched their eyes. A halo surrounded the grim reaper nun, Sister Maria. (By the way—I like this human idea of the grim reaper. I like the scythe. It amuses me.)

In the sun-heavy classroom, names were rattled off at random.

"Waldenheim, Lehmann, Steiner."

They all stood up and did a reading, all at different levels of capability. Rudy was surprisingly good.

Throughout the test, Liesel sat with a mixture of hot anticipation and excruciating fear. She wanted desperately to measure herself, to find out once and for all how her learning was advancing. Was she up to it? Could she even come close to Rudy and the rest of them?

Each time Sister Maria looked at her list, a string of nerves tightened in Liesel's ribs. It started in her stomach but had worked its way up. Soon, it would be around her neck, thick as rope.

When Tommy Müller finished his mediocre attempt, she looked around the room. Everyone had read. She was the only one left.

"Very good." Sister Maria nodded, perusing the list. "That's everyone."

What?

"No!"

A voice practically appeared on the other side of the room. Attached to it was a lemon-haired boy whose bony knees knocked in his pants under the desk. He stretched his hand up and said, "Sister Maria, I think you forgot Liesel."

Sister Maria.

Was not impressed.

She plonked her folder on the table in front of her and inspected Rudy with sighing disapproval. It was almost melancholic. Why, she lamented, did she have to put up with Rudy Steiner? He simply couldn't keep his mouth shut. Why, God, why?

"No," she said, with finality. Her small belly leaned forward with the rest of her. "I'm afraid Liesel cannot do it, Rudy." The teacher looked across, for confirmation. "She will read for me later."

The girl cleared her throat and spoke with quiet defiance. "I can do it now, Sister." The majority of other kids watched in silence. A few of them performed the beautiful childhood art of snickering.

The sister had had enough. "No, you cannot! . . . What are you doing?"

—For Liesel was out of her chair and walking slowly, stiffly toward the front of the room. She picked up the book and opened it to a random page.

"All right, then," said Sister Maria. "You want to do it? Do it."

"Yes, Sister." After a quick glance at Rudy, Liesel lowered her eyes and examined the page.

When she looked up again, the room was pulled apart, then squashed back together. All the kids were mashed, right before her eyes, and in a moment of brilliance, she imagined herself reading the entire page in faultless, fluency-filled triumph.

* * * A KEY WORD * * *
Imagined

"Come on, Liesel!"

Rudy broke the silence.

The book thief looked down again, at the words.

Come on. Rudy mouthed it this time. Come on, Liesel.

Her blood loudened. The sentences blurred.

The white page was suddenly written in another tongue, and it didn't help that tears were now forming in her eyes. She couldn't even see the words anymore.

And the sun. That awful sun. It burst through the window—the glass was everywhere—and shone directly onto the useless girl. It shouted in her face. "You can steal a book, but you can't read one!"

It came to her. A solution.

Breathing, breathing, she started to read, but not from the book in front of her. It was something from *The Grave Digger's Handbook*. Chapter three: "In the Event of Snow." She'd memorized it from her papa's voice.

"In the event of snow," she spoke, "you must make sure you use a good shovel. You must dig deep; you cannot be lazy. You cannot cut corners." Again, she sucked in a large clump of air. "Of course, it is easier to wait for the warmest part of the day, when—"

It ended.

The book was snatched from her grasp and she was told. "Liesel—the corridor."

As she was given a small *Watschen,* she could hear them all laughing in the classroom, between Sister Maria's striking hand. She saw them. All those mashed children. Grinning and laughing. Bathed in sunshine. Everyone laughing but Rudy.

In the break, she was taunted. A boy named Ludwig Schmeikl came up to her with a book. "Hey, Liesel," he said to her, "I'm having trouble with this word. Could you read it for me?" He laughed—a ten-year-old, smugness laughter. "You *Dummkopf*—you idiot."

Clouds were filing in now, big and clumsy, and more kids were calling out to her, watching her seethe.

"Don't listen to them," Rudy advised.

"Easy for you to say. You're not the stupid one."

Nearing the end of the break, the tally of comments stood at nineteen. By the twentieth, she snapped. It was Schmeikl, back for more. "Come on, Liesel." He stuck the book under her nose. "Help me out, will you?"

Liesel helped him out, all right.

She stood up and took the book from him, and as he smiled over his shoulder at some other kids, she threw it away and kicked him as hard as she could in the vicinity of the groin.

Well, as you might imagine, Ludwig Schmeikl certainly buckled, and on the way down, he was punched in the ear. When he landed, he was set upon. When he was set upon, he was slapped and clawed and obliterated by a girl who was utterly consumed with rage. His skin was so warm and soft. Her knuckles and fingernails were so frighteningly tough, despite their smallness. "You *Saukerl.*" Her voice, too, was able to scratch him. "You *Arschloch.* Can you spell *Arschloch* for me?"

Oh, how the clouds stumbled in and assembled stupidly in the sky. Great obese clouds.

Dark and plump.

Bumping into each other. Apologizing. Moving on and finding room.

Children were there, quick as, well, quick as kids gravitating toward a fight. A stew of arms and legs, of shouts and cheers grew thicker around them. They were watching Liesel Meminger give Ludwig Schmeikl the hiding of a lifetime. "Jesus, Mary, and Joseph," a girl commentated with a shriek, "she's going to kill him!"

Liesel did not kill him.

But she came close.

In fact, probably the only thing that stopped her was the twitchingly pathetic, grinning face of Tommy Müller. Still crowded with adrenaline, Liesel caught sight of him smiling with such absurdity that she dragged him down and started beating *him* up as well.

"What are you doing?!" he wailed, and only then, after the third or fourth slap and a trickle of bright blood from his nose, did she stop.

On her knees, she sucked in the air and listened to the groans beneath her. She watched the whirlpool of faces, left and right, and she announced, "I'm not stupid."

No one argued.

It was only when everyone moved back inside and Sister Maria saw the state of Ludwig Schmeikl that the fight resumed. First, it was Rudy and a few others who bore the brunt of suspicion. They were always at each other. "Hands," each boy was ordered, but every pair was clean.

"I don't believe this," the sister muttered. "It can't be," because sure enough, when Liesel stepped forward to show her hands, Ludwig Schmeikl was all over them, rusting by the moment. "The corridor," she stated for the second time that day. For the second time that hour, actually.

This time, it was not a small *Watschen*. It was not an average one.

79

This time, it was the mother of all corridor *Watschens,* one sting of the stick after another, so that Liesel would barely be able to sit down for a week. And there was no laughter from the room. More the silent fear of listening in.

At the end of the school day, Liesel walked home with Rudy and the other Steiner children. Nearing Himmel Street, in a hurry of thoughts, a culmination of misery swept over her—the failed recital of *The Grave Digger's Handbook,* the demolition of her family, her nightmares, the humiliation of the day—and she crouched in the gutter and wept. It all led here.

Rudy stood there, next to her.

It began to rain, nice and hard.

Kurt Steiner called out, but neither of them moved. One sat painfully now, among the falling chunks of rain, and the other stood next to her, waiting.

"Why did he have to die?" she asked, but still, Rudy did nothing; he said nothing.

When finally she finished and stood herself up, he put his arm around her, best-buddy style, and they walked on. There was no request for a kiss. Nothing like that. You can love Rudy for that, if you like.

Just don't kick me in the eggs.

That's what he was thinking, but he didn't tell Liesel that. It was nearly four years later that he offered that information.

For now, Rudy and Liesel made their way onto Himmel Street in the rain.

He was the crazy one who had painted himself black and defeated the world.

She was the book thief without the words.

Trust me, though, the words were on their way, and when they arrived, Liesel would hold them in her hands like the clouds, and she would wring them out like the rain.

PART TWO

the shoulder shrug

featuring:

a girl made of darkness—the joy of cigarettes—

a town walker—some dead letters—hitler's birthday—

100 percent pure german sweat—the gates of thievery—

and a book of fire

A GIRL MADE OF DARKNESS

* * * SOME STATISTICAL INFORMATION * * *
First stolen book: January 13, 1939
Second stolen book: April 20, 1940
Duration between said stolen books: 463 days

If you were being flippant about it, you'd say that all it took was a little bit of fire, really, and some human shouting to go with it. You'd say that was all Liesel Meminger needed to apprehend her second stolen book, even if it smoked in her hands. Even if it lit her ribs.

The problem, however, is this:

This is no time to be flippant.

It's no time to be half watching, turning around, or checking the stove—because when the book thief stole her second book, not only were there many factors involved in her hunger to do so, but the act of stealing it triggered the crux of what was to come. It would provide her with a venue for continued book thievery. It would inspire Hans Huber-mann to come up with a plan to help the Jewish fist fighter. And it would show *me*, once again, that one opportunity leads directly to another, just as risk leads to more risk, life to more life, and death to more death.

In a way, it was destiny.

You see, people may tell you that Nazi Germany was built on anti-Semitism, a somewhat overzealous leader, and a nation of hate-fed bigots, but it would all have come to nothing had the Germans not loved one particular activity:

To burn.

The Germans loved to burn things. Shops, synagogues, Reichstags, houses, personal items, slain people, and of course, books. They enjoyed a good book-burning, all right—which gave people who were partial to books the opportunity to get their hands on certain publications that they otherwise wouldn't have. One person who *was* that way inclined, as we know, was a thin-boned girl named Liesel Meminger. She may have waited 463 days, but it was worth it. At the end of an afternoon that had contained much excitement, much beautiful evil, one blood-soaked ankle, and a slap from a trusted hand, Liesel Meminger attained her second success story. *The Shoulder Shrug.* It was a blue book with red writing engraved on the cover, and there was a small picture of a cuckoo bird under the title, also red. When she looked back, Liesel was not ashamed to have stolen it. On the contrary, it was pride that more re-sembled that small pool of felt *something* in her stomach. And it was anger and dark hatred that had fueled her desire to steal it. In fact, on April 20—the *Führer*'s birthday—when she snatched that book from beneath a steaming heap of ashes, Liesel was a girl made of darkness.

The question, of course, should be why?

What was there to be angry about?

What had happened in the past four or five months to culminate in such a feeling?

In short, the answer traveled from Himmel Street, to the *Führer,* to the unfindable location of her real mother, and back again.

Like most misery, it started with apparent happiness.

THE JOY OF CIGARETTES

Toward the end of 1939, Liesel had settled into life in Molching pretty well. She still had nightmares about her brother and missed her mother, but there were comforts now, too.

She loved her papa, Hans Hubermann, and even her foster mother, despite the abusages and verbal assaults. She loved and hated her best friend, Rudy Steiner, which was perfectly normal. And she loved the fact that despite her failure in the classroom, her reading and writing were definitely improving and would soon be on the verge of something respectable. All of this resulted in at least some form of contentment and would soon be built upon to approach the concept of *Being Happy*.

* * * THE KEYS TO HAPPINESS * * *
1. Finishing *The Grave Digger's Handbook*.
2. Escaping the ire of Sister Maria.
3. Receiving two books for Christmas.

• • •

December 17.

She remembered the date well, as it was exactly a week before Christmas.

As usual, her nightly nightmare interrupted her sleep and she was woken by Hans Hubermann. His hand held the sweaty fabric of her pajamas. "The train?" he whispered.

Liesel confirmed. "The train."

She gulped the air until she was ready, and they began reading from the eleventh chapter of *The Grave Digger's Handbook*. Just past three o'clock, they finished it, and only the final chapter, "Respecting the Graveyard," remained. Papa, his silver eyes swollen in their tiredness and his face awash with whiskers, shut the book and expected the leftovers of his sleep. He didn't get them.

The light was out for barely a minute when Liesel spoke to him across the dark.

"Papa?"

He made only a noise, somewhere in his throat.

"Are you awake, Papa?"

"*Ja.*"

Up on one elbow. "Can we finish the book, please?"

There was a long breath, the scratchery of hand on whiskers, and then the light. He opened the book and began. "'Chapter Twelve: Respecting the Graveyard.'"

They read through the early hours of morning, circling and writing the words she did not comprehend and turning the pages toward daylight. A few times, Papa nearly slept, succumbing to the itchy fatigue in his eyes and the wilting of his head. Liesel caught him out on each occasion, but she had neither the selflessness to allow him to sleep nor the hide to be offended. She was a girl with a mountain to climb.

Eventually, as the darkness outside began to break up a little, they finished. The last passage looked like this:

We at the Bayern Cemetery Association hope that we have in-formed and entertained you in the workings, safety measures, and duties of grave digging. We wish you every success with your career in the funerary arts and hope this book has helped in some way.

When the book closed, they shared a sideways glance. Papa spoke.

"We made it, huh?"

Liesel, half-wrapped in blanket, studied the black book in her hand and its silver lettering. She nodded, dry-mouthed and early-morning hungry. It was one of those moments of perfect tiredness, of having conquered not only the work at hand, but the night who had blocked the way.

Papa stretched with his fists closed and his eyes grinding shut, and it was a morning that didn't dare to be rainy. They each stood and walked to the kitchen, and through the fog and frost of the window, they were able to see the pink bars of light on the snowy banks of Himmel Street's rooftops.

"Look at the colors," Papa said. It's hard not to like a man who not only notices the colors, but speaks them.

Liesel still held the book. She gripped it tighter as the snow turned orange. On one of the rooftops, she could see a small boy, sit-ting, looking at the sky. "His name was Werner," she mentioned. The words trotted out, involuntarily.

Papa said, "Yes."

At school during that time, there had been no more reading tests, but as Liesel slowly gathered confidence, she did pick up a stray textbook before class one morning to see if she could read it without trouble. She could read every word, but she remained stranded at a much slower pace than that of her classmates. It's much easier, she realized, to be on the verge of something than to actually be it. This would still take time.

One afternoon, she was tempted to steal a book from the class bookshelf, but frankly, the prospect of another corridor *Watschen* at the hands of Sister Maria was a powerful enough deterrent. On top of that, there was actually no real desire in her to take the books from school. It was most likely the intensity of her November failure that caused this lack of interest, but Liesel wasn't sure. She only knew that it was there.

In class, she did not speak.

She didn't so much as look the wrong way.

As winter set in, she was no longer a victim of Sister Maria's frustrations, preferring to watch as others were marched out to the corridor and given their just rewards. The sound of another student struggling in the hallway was not particularly enjoyable, but the fact that it was *someone else* was, if not a true comfort, a relief.

When school broke up briefly for *Weihnachten,* Liesel even afforded Sister Maria a "merry Christmas" before going on her way. Knowing that the Hubermanns were essentially broke, still paying off debts and paying rent quicker than the money could come in, she was not expecting a gift of any sort. Perhaps only some better food. To her surprise, on Christmas Eve, after sitting in church at midnight with Mama, Papa, Hans Junior, and Trudy, she came home to find something wrapped in newspaper under the Christmas tree.

"From Saint Niklaus," Papa said, but the girl was not fooled. She hugged both her foster parents, with snow still laid across her shoulders.

Unfurling the paper, she unwrapped two small books. The first one, *Faust the Dog,* was written by a man named Mattheus Ottleberg. All told, she would read that book thirteen times. On Christmas Eve, she read the first twenty pages at the kitchen table while Papa and Hans Junior argued about a thing she did not understand. Something called politics.

Later, they read some more in bed, adhering to the tradition of circling the words she didn't know and writing them down. *Faust the Dog* also had pictures—lovely curves and ears and caricatures of a German Shepherd with an obscene drooling problem and the ability to talk.

The second book was called *The Lighthouse* and was written by a woman, Ingrid Rippinstein. That particular book was a little longer, so Liesel was able to get through it only nine times, her pace increasing ever so slightly by the end of such prolific readings.

It was a few days after Christmas that she asked a question regarding the books. They were eating in the kitchen. Looking at the spoonfuls of pea soup entering Mama's mouth, she decided to shift her focus to Papa. "There's something I need to ask."

At first, there was nothing.

"And?"

It was Mama, her mouth still half full.

"I just wanted to know how you found the money to buy my books."

A short grin was smiled into Papa's spoon. "You really want to know?"

"Of course."

From his pocket, Papa took what was left of his tobacco ration and began rolling a cigarette, at which Liesel became impatient.

"Are you going to tell me or not?"

Papa laughed. "But I *am* telling you, child." He completed the production of one cigarette, flipped it on the table, and began on another. "Just like this."

That was when Mama finished her soup with a clank, suppressed a cardboard burp, and answered for him. "That *Saukerl*," she said. "You know what he did? He rolled up all of his filthy cigarettes, went to the market when it was in town, and traded them with some gypsy."

"Eight cigarettes per book." Papa shoved one to his mouth, in triumph. He lit up and took in the smoke. "Praise the Lord for cigarettes, huh, Mama?"

Mama only handed him one of her trademark looks of disgust, followed by the most common ration of her vocabulary. *"Saukerl."*

Liesel swapped a customary wink with her papa and finished eating her soup. As always, one of her books was next to her. She could not deny that the answer to her question had been more than satisfactory. There were not many people who could say that their education had been paid for with cigarettes.

Mama, on the other hand, said that if Hans Hubermann was any good at all, he would trade some tobacco for the new dress she was in desperate need of or some better shoes. "But no . . ." She emptied the words out into the sink. "When it comes to me, you'd rather smoke a whole ration, wouldn't you? *Plus* some of next door's."

A few nights later, however, Hans Hubermann came home with a box of eggs. "Sorry, Mama." He placed them on the table. "They were all out of shoes."

Mama didn't complain.

She even sang to herself while she cooked those eggs to the brink of burndom. It appeared that there was great joy in cigarettes, and it was a happy time in the Hubermann household.

It ended a few weeks later.

THE TOWN WALKER

The rot started with the washing and it rapidly increased.

When Liesel accompanied Rosa Hubermann on her deliveries across Molching, one of her customers, Ernst Vogel, informed them that he could no longer afford to have his washing and ironing done. "The times," he excused himself, "what can I say? They're getting harder. The war's making things tight." He looked at the girl. "I'm sure you get an allowance for keeping the little one, don't you?"

To Liesel's dismay, Mama was speechless.

An empty bag was at her side.

Come on, Liesel.

It was not said. It was pulled along, rough-handed.

Vogel called out from his front step. He was perhaps five foot nine and his greasy scraps of hair swung lifelessly across his forehead. "I'm sorry, Frau Hubermann!"

Liesel waved at him.

He waved back.

Mama castigated.

"Don't wave to that *Arschloch*," she said. "Now hurry up."

That night, when Liesel had a bath, Mama scrubbed her

especially hard, muttering the whole time about that Vogel *Saukerl* and imitating him at two-minute intervals. "'You must get an allowance for the girl....'" She berated Liesel's naked chest as she scrubbed away. "You're not worth *that* much, *Saumensch*. You're not making me rich, you know."

Liesel sat there and took it.

Not more than a week after that particular incident, Rosa hauled her into the kitchen. "Right, Liesel." She sat her down at the table. "Since you spend half your time on the street playing soccer, you can make yourself useful out there. For a change."

Liesel watched only her own hands. "What is it, Mama?"

"From now on you're going to pick up and deliver the washing for me. Those rich people are less likely to fire us if *you're* the one standing in front of them. If they ask you where I am, tell them I'm sick. And look sad when you tell them. You're skinny and pale enough to get their pity."

"Herr Vogel didn't pity me."

"Well..." Her agitation was obvious. "The others *might*. So don't argue."

"Yes, Mama."

For a moment, it appeared that her foster mother would comfort her or pat her on the shoulder.

Good girl, Liesel. Good girl. Pat, pat, pat.

She did no such thing.

Instead, Rosa Hubermann stood up, selected a wooden spoon, and held it under Liesel's nose. It was a necessity as far as she was concerned. "When you're out on that street, you take the bag to each place and you bring it straight home, *with* the money, even though it's next to nothing. No going to Papa if he's actually working for once. No mucking around with that little *Saukerl*, Rudy Steiner. Straight. Home."

92

"Yes, Mama."

"And when you hold that bag, you hold it *properly*. You don't swing it, drop it, crease it, or throw it over your shoulder."

"Yes, Mama."

"Yes, Mama." Rosa Hubermann was a great imitator, and a fervent one. "You'd better not, *Saumensch*. I'll find out if you do; you know that, don't you?"

"Yes, Mama."

Saying those two words was often the best way to survive, as was doing what she was told, and from there, Liesel walked the streets of Molching, from the poor end to the rich, picking up and delivering the washing. At first, it was a solitary job, which she never complained about. After all, the very first time she took the sack through town, she turned the corner onto Munich Street, looked both ways, and gave it one enormous swing—a whole revolution—and then checked the contents inside. Thankfully, there were no creases. No wrinkles. Just a smile, and a promise never to swing it again.

Overall, Liesel enjoyed it. There was no share of the pay, but she was out of the house, and walking the streets without Mama was heaven in itself. No finger-pointing or cursing. No people staring at them as she was sworn at for holding the bag wrong. Nothing but serenity.

She came to like the people, too:

* The Pfaffelhürvers, inspecting the clothes and saying, *"Ja, ja, sehr gut, sehr gut."* Liesel imagined that they did everything twice.

* Gentle Helena Schmidt, handing the money over with an arthritic curl of the hand.

* The Weingartners, whose bent-whiskered cat always answered the door with them. Little Goebbels, that's what they called him, after Hitler's right-hand man.

* And Frau Hermann, the mayor's wife, standing fluffy-haired

and shivery in her enormous, cold-aired doorway. Always silent. Always alone. No words, not once.

Sometimes Rudy came along.

"How much money do you have there?" he asked one afternoon. It was nearly dark and they were walking onto Himmel Street, past the shop. "You've heard about Frau Diller, haven't you? They say she's got candy hidden somewhere, and for the right price . . ."

"Don't even think about it." Liesel, as always, was gripping the money hard. "It's not so bad for you—you don't have to face my mama."

Rudy shrugged. "It was worth a try."

In the middle of January, schoolwork turned its attention to letter writing. After learning the basics, each student was to write two letters, one to a friend and one to somebody in another class.

Liesel's letter from Rudy went like this:

> *Dear Saumensch,*
> *Are you still as useless at soccer as you were the last time we played? I hope so. That means I can run past you again just like Jesse Owens at the Olympics. . . .*

When Sister Maria found it, she asked him a question, very amiably.

* * * SISTER MARIA'S OFFER * * *
"Do you feel like visiting the corridor, Mr. Steiner?"

Needless to say, Rudy answered in the negative, and the paper was torn up and he started again. The second attempt was written to someone named Liesel and inquired as to what her hobbies might be.

At home, while completing a letter for homework, Liesel decided that writing to Rudy or some other *Saukerl* was actually ridiculous. It meant nothing. As she wrote in the basement, she spoke over to Papa, who was repainting the wall again.

Both he and the paint fumes turned around. *"Was wuistz?"* Now this was the roughest form of German a person could speak, but it was spoken with an air of absolute pleasantness. "Yeah, what?"

"Would I be able to write a letter to Mama?"

A pause.

"What do you want to write a letter to her for? You have to put up with her every day." Papa was *schmunzel*ing—a sly smile. "Isn't that bad enough?"

"Not *that* mama." She swallowed.

"Oh." Papa returned to the wall and continued painting. "Well, I guess so. You could send it to what's-her-name—the one who brought you here and visited those few times—from the foster people."

"Frau Heinrich."

"That's right. Send it to her. Maybe she can send it on to your mother." Even at the time, he sounded unconvincing, as if he wasn't telling Liesel something. Word of her mother had also been tight-lipped on Frau Heinrich's brief visits.

Instead of asking him what was wrong, Liesel began writing immediately, choosing to ignore the sense of foreboding that was quick to accumulate inside her. It took three hours and six drafts to perfect the letter, telling her mother all about Molching, her papa and his accordion, the strange but true ways of Rudy Steiner, and the exploits of Rosa Hubermann. She also explained how proud she was that she could now read and write a little. The next day, she posted it at Frau Diller's with a stamp from the kitchen drawer. And she began to wait.

The night she wrote the letter, she overheard a conversation between Hans and Rosa.

"What's she doing writing to her mother?" Mama was saying. Her voice was surprisingly calm and caring. As you can imagine, this worried the girl a great deal. She'd have preferred to hear them arguing. Whispering adults hardly inspired confidence.

"She asked me," Papa answered, "and I couldn't say no. How could I?"

"Jesus, Mary, and Joseph." Again with the whisper. "She should just forget her. Who knows where she is? Who knows what they've done to her?"

In bed, Liesel hugged herself tight. She balled herself up.

She thought of her mother and repeated Rosa Hubermann's questions.

Where was she?

What had they done to her?

And once and for all, who, in actual fact, were *they*?

DEAD LETTERS

Flash forward to the basement, September 1943.

A fourteen-year-old girl is writing in a small dark-covered book. She is bony but strong and has seen many things. Papa sits with the accordion at his feet.

He says, "You know, Liesel? I nearly wrote you a reply and signed your mother's name." He scratches his leg, where the plaster used to be. "But I couldn't. I couldn't bring myself."

Several times, through the remainder of January and the entirety of February 1940, when Liesel searched the mailbox for a reply to her letter, it clearly broke her foster father's heart. "I'm sorry," he would tell her. "Not today, huh?" In hindsight, she saw that the whole exercise had been pointless. Had her mother been in a position to do so, she would have already made contact with the foster care people, or directly with the girl, or the Hubermanns. But there had been nothing.

To lend insult to injury, in mid-February, Liesel was given a letter from another ironing customer, the Pfaffelhürvers, from Heide Strasse. The pair of them stood with great tallness in the doorway, giving her a melancholic regard. "For your mama," the man said, handing her the envelope. "Tell her we're sorry. Tell her we're sorry."

That was not a good night in the Hubermann residence.

Even when Liesel retreated to the basement to write her fifth letter to her mother (all but the first one yet to be sent), she could hear Rosa swearing and carrying on about those Pfaffelhürver *Arschlöcher* and that lousy Ernst Vogel.

"Feuer soll'n's brunzen für einen Monat!" she heard her call out. Translation: "They should all piss fire for a month!"

Liesel wrote.

When her birthday came around, there was no gift. There was no gift because there was no money, and at the time, Papa was out of tobacco.

"I told you." Mama pointed a finger at him. "I told you not to give her both books at Christmas. But no. Did you listen? Of *course* not!"

"I know!" He turned quietly to the girl. "I'm sorry, Liesel. We just can't afford it."

Liesel didn't mind. She didn't whine or moan or stamp her feet. She simply swallowed the disappointment and decided on one calculated risk—a present from herself. She would gather all of the accrued letters to her mother, stuff them into one envelope, and use just a tiny portion of the washing and ironing money to mail it. Then, of course, she would take the *Watschen,* most likely in the kitchen, and she would not make a sound.

Three days later, the plan came to fruition.

"Some of it's missing." Mama counted the money a fourth time, with Liesel over at the stove. It was warm there and it cooked the fast flow of her blood. "What happened, Liesel?"

She lied. "They must have given me less than usual."

"Did you count it?"

She broke. "I spent it, Mama."

Rosa came closer. This was not a good sign. She was very close to the wooden spoons. "You what?"

Before she could answer, the wooden spoon came down on Liesel Meminger's body like the gait of God. Red marks like footprints, and they burned. From the floor, when it was over, the girl actually looked up and explained.

There was pulse and yellow light, all together. Her eyes blinked. "I mailed my letters."

What came to her then was the dustiness of the floor, the feeling that her clothes were more next to her than on her, and the sudden realization that this would all be for nothing—that her mother would never write back and she would never see her again. The reality of this gave her a second *Watschen*. It stung her, and it did not stop for many minutes.

Above her, Rosa appeared to be smudged, but she soon clarified as her cardboard face loomed closer. Dejected, she stood there in all her plumpness, holding the wooden spoon at her side like a club. She reached down and leaked a little. "I'm sorry, Liesel."

Liesel knew her well enough to understand that it was not for the hiding.

The red marks grew larger, in patches on her skin, as she lay there, in the dust and the dirt and the dim light. Her breathing calmed, and a stray yellow tear trickled down her face. She could feel herself against the floor. A forearm, a knee. An elbow. A cheek. A calf muscle.

The floor was cold, especially against her cheek, but she was unable to move.

She would never see her mother again.

For nearly an hour, she remained, spread out under the kitchen table, till Papa came home and played the accordion. Only then did she sit up and start to recover.

When she wrote about that night, she held no animosity toward

Rosa Hubermann at all, or toward her mother for that matter. To her, they were only victims of circumstance. The only thought that continually recurred was the yellow tear. Had it been dark, she realized, that tear would have been black.

But it *was* dark, she told herself.

No matter how many times she tried to imagine that scene with the yellow light that she knew had been there, she had to struggle to visualize it. She was beaten in the dark, and she had remained there, on a cold, dark kitchen floor. Even Papa's music was the color of darkness.

Even Papa's music.

The strange thing was that she was vaguely comforted by that thought, rather than distressed by it.

The dark, the light.

What was the difference?

Nightmares had reinforced themselves in each, as the book thief began to truly understand how things were and how they would always be. If nothing else, she could prepare herself. Perhaps that's why on the *Führer*'s birthday, when the answer to the question of her mother's suffering showed itself completely, she was able to react, despite her perplexity and her rage.

Liesel Meminger was ready.

Happy birthday, Herr Hitler.

Many happy returns.

HITLER'S BIRTHDAY, 1940

Against all hopelessness, Liesel still checked the mailbox each afternoon, throughout March and well into April. This was despite a Hans-requested visit from Frau Heinrich, who explained to the Hubermanns that the foster care office had lost contact completely with Paula Meminger. Still, the girl persisted, and as you might expect, each day, when she searched the mail, there was nothing.

Molching, like the rest of Germany, was in the grip of preparing for Hitler's birthday. This particular year, with the development of the war and Hitler's current victorious position, the Nazi partisans of Molching wanted the celebration to be especially befitting. There would be a parade. Marching. Music. Singing. There would be a fire.

While Liesel walked the streets of Molching, picking up and delivering washing and ironing, Nazi Party members were accumulating fuel. A couple of times, Liesel was a witness to men and women knocking on doors, asking people if they had any material that they felt should be done away with or destroyed. Papa's copy of the *Molching Express* announced that there would be a celebratory fire in the town square, which would be attended by all local Hitler

Youth divisions. It would commemorate not only the *Führer*'s birthday, but the victory over his enemies and over the restraints that had held Germany back since the end of World War I. "Any materials," it requested, "from such times—newspapers, posters, books, flags—and any found propaganda of our enemies should be brought forward to the Nazi Party office on Munich Street." Even Schiller Strasse—the road of yellow stars—which was still awaiting its renovation, was ransacked one last time, to find something, anything, to burn in the name of the *Führer*'s glory. It would have come as no surprise if certain members of the party had gone away and published a thousand or so books or posters of poisonous moral matter simply to incinerate them.

Everything was in place to make April 20 magnificent. It would be a day full of burning and cheering.

And book thievery.

In the Hubermann household that morning, all was typical.

"That *Saukerl*'s looking out the window again," cursed Rosa Hubermann. "Every *day*," she went on. "What are you looking at this time?"

"Ohhh," moaned Papa with delight. The flag cloaked his back from the top of the window. "You should have a look at this woman I can see." He glanced over his shoulder and grinned at Liesel. "I might just go and run after her. She leaves you for dead, Mama."

"*Schwein!*" She shook the wooden spoon at him.

Papa continued looking out the window, at an imaginary woman and a very real corridor of German flags.

On the streets of Molching that day, each window was decorated for the *Führer*. In some places, like Frau Diller's, the glass was vigorously washed, and the swastika looked like a jewel on a red-and-white blanket. In others, the flag trundled from the ledge like washing hung out to dry. But it was there.

Earlier, there had been a minor calamity. The Hubermanns couldn't find their flag.

"They'll come for us," Mama warned her husband. "They'll come and take us away." They. "We have to find it!" At one point, it seemed like Papa might have to go down to the basement and paint a flag on one of his drop sheets. Thankfully, it turned up, buried behind the accordion in the cupboard.

"That infernal accordion, it was blocking my view!" Mama swiveled. "Liesel!"

The girl had the honor of pinning the flag to the window frame.

Hans Junior and Trudy came home for the afternoon eating, like they did at Christmas or Easter. Now seems like a good time to introduce them a little more comprehensively:

Hans Junior had the eyes of his father and the height. The silver in his eyes, however, wasn't warm, like Papa's—they'd been *Führer*ed. There was more flesh on his bones, too, and he had prickly blond hair and skin like off-white paint.

Trudy, or Trudel, as she was often known, was only a few inches taller than Mama. She had cloned Rosa Hubermann's unfortunate, waddlesome walking style, but the rest of her was much milder. Being a live-in housemaid in a wealthy part of Munich, she was most likely bored of children, but she was always capable of at least a few smiled words in Liesel's direction. She had soft lips. A quiet voice.

They came home together on the train from Munich, and it didn't take long for old tensions to rise up.

**✳ ✳ ✳ A SHORT HISTORY OF ✳ ✳ ✳
HANS HUBERMANN VS. HIS SON**

The young man was a Nazi; his father was not. In the opinion of
Hans Junior, his father was part of an old, decrepit Germany—
one that allowed everyone else to take it for the proverbial
ride while its own people suffered. As a teenager, he was aware
that his father had been called *"Der Juden Maler"*—the Jew
painter—for painting Jewish houses. Then came an incident I'll
fully present to you soon enough—the day Hans blew it, on the
verge of joining the party. Everyone knew you weren't supposed
to paint over slurs written on a Jewish shop front. Such behavior
was bad for Germany, and it was bad for the transgressor.

"So have they let you in yet?" Hans Junior was picking up where they'd
left off at Christmas.

"In what?"

"Take a guess—the party."

"No, I think they've forgotten about me."

"Well, have you even tried again? You can't just sit around waiting for the new world to take it with you. You have to go out and be
part of it—despite your past mistakes."

Papa looked up. "Mistakes? I've made many mistakes in my life,
but not joining the Nazi Party isn't one of them. They still have my
application—you know that—but I couldn't go back to ask. I just . . ."

That was when a great shiver arrived.

It waltzed through the window with the draft. Perhaps it was the
breeze of the Third Reich, gathering even greater strength. Or maybe
it was just Europe again, breathing. Either way, it fell across them as
their metallic eyes clashed like tin cans in the kitchen.

"You've never cared about this country," said Hans Junior. "Not enough, anyway."

Papa's eyes started corroding. It did not stop Hans Junior. He looked now for some reason at the girl. With her three books standing upright on the table, as if in conversation, Liesel was silently mouthing the words as she read from one of them. "And what trash is this girl reading? She should be reading *Mein Kampf.*"

Liesel looked up.

"Don't worry, Liesel," Papa said. "Just keep reading. He doesn't know what he's saying."

But Hans Junior wasn't finished. He stepped closer and said, "You're either for the *Führer* or against him—and I can see that you're against him. You always have been." Liesel watched Hans Junior in the face, fixated on the thinness of his lips and the rocky line of his bottom teeth. "It's pathetic—how a man can stand by and do nothing as a whole nation cleans out the garbage and makes itself great."

Trudy and Mama sat silently, scaredly, as did Liesel. There was the smell of pea soup, something burning, and confrontation.

They were all waiting for the next words.

They came from the son. Just two of them.

"You coward." He upturned them into Papa's face, and he promptly left the kitchen, and the house.

Ignoring futility, Papa walked to the doorway and called out to his son. "Coward? *I'm* the coward?!" He then rushed to the gate and ran pleadingly after him. Mama hurried to the window, ripped away the flag, and opened up. She, Trudy, and Liesel all crowded together, watching a father catch up to his son and grab hold of him, begging him to stop. They could hear nothing, but the manner in which Hans Junior shrugged loose was loud enough. The sight of Papa watching him walk away roared at them from up the street.

"Hansi!" Mama finally cried out. Both Trudy and Liesel flinched from her voice. "Come back!"

The boy was gone.

Yes, the boy was gone, and I wish I could tell you that everything worked out for the younger Hans Hubermann, but it didn't.

When he vanished from Himmel Street that day in the name of the *Führer,* he would hurtle through the events of another story, each step leading tragically to Russia.

To Stalingrad.

* * * SOME FACTS ABOUT STALINGRAD * * *
1. In 1942 and early '43, in that city, the sky was
bleached bedsheet-white each morning.
2. All day long, as I carried the souls across it,
that sheet was splashed with blood, until it was full
and bulging to the earth.
3. In the evening, it would be wrung out and bleached again,
ready for the next dawn.
4. And that was when the fighting was only during the day.

With his son gone, Hans Hubermann stood for a few moments longer. The street looked so big.

When he reappeared inside, Mama fixed her gaze on him, but no words were exchanged. She didn't admonish him at all, which, as you know, was highly unusual. Perhaps she decided he was injured enough, having been labeled a coward by his only son.

For a while, he remained silently at the table after the eating was finished. Was he really a coward, as his son had so brutally pointed out? Certainly, in World War I, he considered himself one. He attributed his survival to it. But then, is there cowardice in the acknowledgment of fear? Is there cowardice in being glad that you lived?

His thoughts crisscrossed the table as he stared into it.

"Papa?" Liesel asked, but he did not look at her. "What was he talking about? What did he mean when . . ."

"Nothing," Papa answered. He spoke quiet and calm, to the table. "It's nothing. Forget about him, Liesel." It took perhaps a minute for him to speak again. "Shouldn't you be getting ready?" He looked at her this time. "Don't you have a bonfire to go to?"

"Yes, Papa."

The book thief went and changed into her Hitler Youth uniform, and half an hour later, they left, walking to the BDM headquarters. From there, the children would be taken to the town square in their groups.

Speeches would be made.

A fire would be lit.

A book would be stolen.

100 PERCENT PURE GERMAN SWEAT

People lined the streets as the youth of Germany marched toward the town hall and the square. On quite a few occasions Liesel forgot about her mother and any other problem of which she currently held ownership. There was a swell in her chest as the people clapped them on. Some kids waved to their parents, but only briefly—it was an explicit instruction that they march straight and *don't look or wave* to the crowd.

When Rudy's group came into the square and was instructed to halt, there was a discrepancy. Tommy Müller. The rest of the regiment stopped marching and Tommy plowed directly into the boy in front of him.

"Dummkopf!" the boy spat before turning around.

"I'm sorry," said Tommy, arms held apologetically out. His face tripped over itself. "I couldn't hear." It was only a small moment, but it was also a preview of troubles to come. For Tommy. For Rudy.

At the end of the marching, the Hitler Youth divisions were allowed to disperse. It would have been near impossible to keep them all together as the bonfire burned in their eyes and excited them.

Together, they cried one united "*heil* Hitler" and were free to wander. Liesel looked for Rudy, but once the crowd of children scattered, she was caught inside a mess of uniforms and high-pitched words. Kids calling out to other kids.

By four-thirty, the air had cooled considerably.

People joked that they needed warming up. "That's all this trash is good for anyway."

Carts were used to wheel it all in. It was dumped in the middle of the town square and dowsed with something sweet. Books and paper and other material would slide or tumble down, only to be thrown back onto the pile. From further away, it looked like something volcanic. Or something grotesque and alien that had somehow landed miraculously in the middle of town and needed to be snuffed out, and fast.

The applied smell leaned toward the crowd, who were kept at a good distance. There were well in excess of a thousand people, on the ground, on the town hall steps, on the rooftops that surrounded the square.

When Liesel tried to make her way through, a crackling sound prompted her to think that the fire had already begun. It hadn't. The sound was kinetic humans, flowing, charging up.

They've started without me!

Although something inside told her that this was a crime—after all, her three books were the most precious items she owned—she was compelled to see the thing lit. She couldn't help it. I guess humans like to watch a little destruction. Sand castles, houses of cards, that's where they begin. Their great skill is their capacity to escalate.

The thought of missing it was eased when she found a gap in the bodies and was able to see the mound of guilt, still intact. It was prodded and splashed, even spat on. It reminded her of an unpopular child, forlorn and bewildered, powerless to alter its fate. No one liked it. Head down. Hands in pockets. Forever. Amen.

Bits and pieces continued falling to its sides as Liesel hunted for Rudy. Where is that *Saukerl*?

When she looked up, the sky was crouching.

A horizon of Nazi flags and uniforms rose upward, crippling her view every time she attempted to see over a smaller child's head. It was pointless. The crowd was itself. There was no swaying it, squeezing through, or reasoning with it. You breathed with it and you sang its songs. You waited for its fire.

Silence was requested by a man on a podium. His uniform was shiny brown. The iron was practically still on it. The silence began.

His first words: "*Heil* Hitler!"

His first action: the salute to the *Führer*.

"Today is a beautiful day," he continued. "Not only is it our great ·leader's birthday—but we also stop our enemies once again. We stop them reaching into our minds. . . ."

Liesel still attempted to fight her way through.

"We put an end to the disease that has been spread through Germany for the last twenty years, if not more!" He was performing now what is called a *Schreierei*—a consummate exhibition of passionate shouting—warning the crowd to be watchful, to be vigilant, to seek out and destroy the evil machinations plotting to infect the motherland with its deplorable ways. "The immoral! The *Kommunisten*!" That word again. That old word. Dark rooms. Suit-wearing men. "*Die Juden*—the Jews!"

Halfway through the speech, Liesel surrendered. As the word *communist* seized her, the remainder of the Nazi recital swept by, either side, lost somewhere in the German feet around her. Waterfalls of words. A girl treading water. She thought it again. *Kommunisten.*

Up until now, at the BDM, they had been told that Germany was the superior race, but no one else in particular had been mentioned. Of course, everyone knew about the Jews, as they were the main *offender* in regard to violating the German ideal. Not once, however, had the communists been mentioned until today, regardless of the fact that people of such political creed were also to be punished.

She had to get out.

In front of her, a head with parted blond hair and pigtails sat absolutely still on its shoulders. Staring into it, Liesel revisited those dark rooms of her past and her mother answering questions made up of one word.

She saw it all so clearly.

Her starving mother, her missing father. *Kommunisten.*

Her dead brother.

"And now we say goodbye to this trash, this poison."

Just before Liesel Meminger pivoted with nausea to exit the crowd, the shiny, brown-shirted creature walked from the podium. He received a torch from an accomplice and lit the mound, which dwarfed him in all its culpability. "*Heil* Hitler!"

The audience: "*Heil* Hitler!"

A collection of men walked from a platform and surrounded the heap, igniting it, much to the approval of everyone. Voices climbed over shoulders and the smell of pure German sweat struggled at first, then poured out. It rounded corner after corner, till they were all swimming in it. The words, the sweat. And smiling. Let's not forget the smiling.

Many jocular comments followed, as did another onslaught of "*heil* Hitlering." You know, it actually makes me wonder if anyone ever lost an eye or injured a hand or wrist with all of that. You'd only need to be facing the wrong way at the wrong time or stand marginally too close to another person. Perhaps people did get injured. Personally, I can only tell you that no one died from it, or at least, not physically.

There was, of course, the matter of forty million people I picked up by the time the whole thing was finished, but that's getting all metaphoric. Allow me to return us to the fire.

The orange flames waved at the crowd as paper and print dissolved inside them. Burning words were torn from their sentences.

On the other side, beyond the blurry heat, it was possible to see the brownshirts and swastikas joining hands. You didn't see people. Only uniforms and signs.

Birds above did laps.

They circled, somehow attracted to the glow—until they came too close to the heat. Or was it the humans? Certainly, the heat was nothing.

In her attempt to escape, a voice found her.

"Liesel!"

It made its way through and she recognized it. It was not Rudy, but she knew that voice.

She twisted free and found the face attached to it. Oh, no. Ludwig Schmeikl. He did not, as she expected, sneer or joke or make any conversation at all. All he was able to do was pull her toward him and motion to his ankle. It had been crushed among the excitement and was bleeding dark and ominous through his sock. His face wore a helpless expression beneath his tangled blond hair. An animal. Not a deer in lights. Nothing so typical or specific. He was just an animal, hurt among the melee of its own kind, soon to be trampled by it.

Somehow, she helped him up and dragged him toward the back. Fresh air.

They staggered to the steps at the side of the church. There was some room there and they rested, both relieved.

Breath collapsed from Schmeikl's mouth. It slipped down, over his throat. He managed to speak.

Sitting down, he held his ankle and found Liesel Meminger's face. "Thanks," he said, to her mouth rather than her eyes. More slabs of breath. "And . . ." They both watched images of school-yard antics, followed by a school-yard beating. "I'm sorry—for, you know."

Liesel heard it again.

Kommunisten.

She chose, however, to focus on Ludwig Schmeikl. "Me too."

They both concentrated on breathing then, for there was nothing more to do or say. Their business had come to an end.

The blood enlarged on Ludwig Schmeikl's ankle.

A single word leaned against the girl.

To their left, flames and burning books were cheered like heroes.

THE GATES OF THIEVERY

She remained on the steps, waiting for Papa, watching the stray ash and the corpse of collected books. Everything was sad. Orange and red embers looked like rejected candy, and most of the crowd had vanished. She'd seen Frau Diller leave (very satisfied) and Pfiffikus (white hair, a Nazi uniform, the same dilapidated shoes, and a triumphant whistle). Now there was nothing but cleaning up, and soon, no one would even imagine it had happened.

But you could smell it.

"What are you doing?"

Hans Hubermann arrived at the church steps.

"Hi, Papa."

"You were supposed to be in front of the town hall."

"Sorry, Papa."

He sat down next to her, halving his tallness on the concrete and taking a piece of Liesel's hair. His fingers adjusted it gently behind her ear. "Liesel, what's wrong?"

For a while, she said nothing. She was making calculations, despite already knowing. An eleven-year-old girl is many things, but she is not stupid.

* * * A SMALL ADDITION * * *
The word *communist* + a large bonfire + a collection of dead letters + the suffering of her mother + the death of her brother = the *Führer*

The *Führer*.

He was the *they* that Hans and Rosa Hubermann were talking about that evening when she first wrote to her mother. She knew it, but she had to ask.

"Is my mother a communist?" Staring. Straight ahead. "They were always asking her things, before I came here."

Hans edged forward a little, forming the beginnings of a lie. "I have no idea—I never met her."

"Did the *Führer* take her away?"

The question surprised them both, and it forced Papa to stand up. He looked at the brown-shirted men taking to the pile of ash with shovels. He could hear them hacking into it. Another lie was growing in his mouth, but he found it impossible to let it out. He said, "I think he might have, yes."

"I knew it." The words were thrown at the steps and Liesel could feel the slush of anger, stirring hotly in her stomach. "I hate the *Führer*," she said. "I *hate* him."

And Hans Hubermann?

What did he do?

What did he say?

Did he bend down and embrace his foster daughter, as he wanted to? Did he tell her that he was sorry for what was happening to her, to her mother, for what had happened to her brother?

Not exactly.

He clenched his eyes. Then opened them. He slapped Liesel Meminger squarely in the face.

"Don't *ever* say that!" His voice was quiet, but sharp.

As the girl shook and sagged on the steps, he sat next to her and held his face in his hands. It would be easy to say that he was just a tall man sitting poor-postured and shattered on some church steps, but he wasn't. At the time, Liesel had no idea that her foster father, Hans Hubermann, was contemplating one of the most dangerous dilemmas a German citizen could face. Not only that, he'd been facing it for close to a year.

"Papa?"

The surprise in her voice rushed her, but it also rendered her useless. She wanted to run, but she couldn't. She could take a *Watschen* from nuns and Rosas, but it hurt so much more from Papa. The hands were gone from Papa's face now and he found the resolve to speak again.

"You can say that in our house," he said, looking gravely at Liesel's cheek. "But you never say it on the street, at school, at the BDM, never!" He stood in front of her and lifted her by the triceps. He shook her. "Do you hear me?"

With her eyes trapped wide open, Liesel nodded her compliance.

It was, in fact, a rehearsal for a future lecture, when all of Hans Hubermann's worst fears arrived on Himmel Street later that year, in the early hours of a November morning.

"Good." He placed her back down. "Now, let us try . . ." At the bottom of the steps, Papa stood erect and cocked his arm. Forty-five degrees. "*Heil* Hitler."

Liesel stood up and also raised her arm. With absolute misery, she repeated it. "*Heil* Hitler." It was quite a sight—an eleven-year-old girl, trying not to cry on the church steps, saluting the *Führer* as the voices over Papa's shoulder chopped and beat at the dark shape in the background.

"Are we still friends?"

Perhaps a quarter of an hour later, Papa held a cigarette olive branch in his palm—the paper and tobacco he'd just received. Without a word, Liesel reached gloomily across and proceeded to roll it.

For quite a while, they sat there together.

Smoke climbed over Papa's shoulder.

After another ten minutes, the gates of thievery would open just a crack, and Liesel Meminger would widen them a little further and squeeze through.

* * * TWO QUESTIONS * * *
Would the gates shut behind her?
Or would they have the goodwill to let her back out?

As Liesel would discover, a good thief requires many things.

Stealth. Nerve. Speed.

More important than any of those things, however, was one final requirement.

Luck.

Actually.

Forget the ten minutes.

The gates open now.

BOOK OF FIRE

The dark came in pieces, and with the cigarette brought to an end, Liesel and Hans Hubermann began to walk home. To get out of the square, they would walk past the bonfire site and through a small side road onto Munich Street. They didn't make it that far.

A middle-aged carpenter named Wolfgang Edel called out. He'd built the platforms for the Nazi big shots to stand on during the fire and he was in the process now of pulling them down. "Hans Hubermann?" He had long sideburns that pointed to his mouth and a dark voice. "Hansi!"

"Hey, Wolfal," Hans replied. There was an introduction to the girl and a "*heil* Hitler." "Good, Liesel."

For the first few minutes, Liesel stayed within a five-meter radius of the conversation. Fragments came past her, but she didn't pay too much attention.

"Getting much work?"

"No, it's all tighter now. You know how it is, especially when you're not a member."

"You told me you were joining, Hansi."

"I tried, but I made a mistake—I think they're still considering."

. . .

Liesel wandered toward the mountain of ash. It sat like a magnet, like a freak. Irresistible to the eyes, similar to the road of yellow stars.

As with her previous urge to see the mound's ignition, she could not look away. All alone, she didn't have the discipline to keep a safe distance. It sucked her toward it and she began to make her way around.

Above her, the sky was completing its routine of darkening, but far away, over the mountain's shoulder, there was a dull trace of light.

"Pass auf, Kind," a uniform said to her at one point. "Look out, child," as he shoveled some more ash onto a cart.

Closer to the town hall, under a light, some shadows stood and talked, most likely exulting in the success of the fire. From Liesel's position, their voices were only sounds. Not words at all.

For a few minutes, she watched the men shoveling up the pile, at first making it smaller at the sides to allow more of it to collapse. They came back and forth from a truck, and after three return trips, when the heap was reduced near the bottom, a small section of living material slipped from inside the ash.

* * * THE MATERIAL * * *
**Half a red flag, two posters advertising a Jewish poet,
three books, and a wooden sign with something written
on it in Hebrew**

Perhaps they were damp. Perhaps the fire didn't burn long enough to fully reach the depth where they sat. Whatever the reason, they were huddled among the ashes, shaken. Survivors.

"Three books." Liesel spoke softly and she looked at the backs of the men.

"Come on," said one of them. "Hurry up, will you, I'm starving."

They moved toward the truck.

The threesome of books poked their noses out.

Liesel moved in.

The heat was still strong enough to warm her when she stood at the foot of the ash heap. When she reached her hand in, she was bitten, but on the second attempt, she made sure she was fast enough. She latched onto the closest of the books. It was hot, but it was also wet, burned only at the edges, but otherwise unhurt.

It was blue.

The cover felt like it was woven with hundreds of tightly drawn strings and clamped down. Red letters were pressed into those fibers. The only word Liesel had time to read was *Shoulder*. There wasn't enough time for the rest, and there was a problem. The smoke.

Smoke lifted from the cover as she juggled it and hurried away. Her head was pulled down, and the sick beauty of nerves proved more ghastly with each stride. There were fourteen steps till the voice.

It propped itself up behind her.

"Hey!"

That was when she nearly ran back and tossed the book onto the mound, but she was unable. The only movement at her disposal was the act of turning.

"There are some things here that didn't burn!" It was one of the cleanup men. He was not facing the girl, but rather, the people standing by the town hall.

"Well, burn them again!" came the reply. "And *watch* them burn!"

"I think they're wet!"

"Jesus, Mary, and Joseph, do I have to do everything myself?" The sound of footsteps passed by. It was the mayor, wearing a black coat over his Nazi uniform. He didn't notice the girl who stood absolutely still only a short distance away.

∗ ∗ ∗ A REALIZATION ∗ ∗ ∗
A statue of the book thief stood in the courtyard. . . .
It's very rare, don't you think, for a statue to appear
before its subject has become famous.

She sank.

The thrill of being ignored!

The book felt cool enough now to slip inside her uniform. At first, it was nice and warm against her chest. As she began walking, though, it began to heat up again.

By the time she made it back to Papa and Wolfgang Edel, the book was starting to burn her. It seemed to be igniting.

Both men looked at her.

She smiled.

Immediately, when the smile shrank from her lips, she could feel something else. Or more to the point, *someone* else. There was no mistaking the watched feeling. It was all over her, and it was confirmed when she dared to face the shadows over at the town hall. To the side of the collection of silhouettes, another one stood, a few meters removed, and Liesel realized two things.

∗ ∗ ∗ A FEW SMALL PIECES ∗ ∗ ∗
OF RECOGNITION
1. The shadow's identity and
2. The fact that it had seen everything

The shadow's hands were in its coat pockets.

It had fluffy hair.

If it had a face, the expression on it would have been one of injury.

"Gottverdammt," Liesel said, only loud enough for herself. "God-damn it."

"Are we ready to go?"

In the previous moments of stupendous danger, Papa had said goodbye to Wolfgang Edel and was ready to accompany Liesel home.

"Ready," she answered.

They began to leave the scene of the crime, and the book was well and truly burning her now. *The Shoulder Shrug* had applied itself to her rib cage.

As they walked past the precarious town hall shadows, the book thief winced.

"What's wrong?" Papa asked.

"Nothing."

Quite a few things, however, were most definitely wrong:

Smoke was rising out of Liesel's collar.

A necklace of sweat had formed around her throat.

Beneath her shirt, a book was eating her up.

PART THREE

mein kampf

featuring:

the way home — a broken woman — a struggler —

a juggler — the attributes of summer —

an aryan shopkeeper — a snorer — two tricksters —

and revenge in the shape of mixed candy

THE WAY HOME

Mein Kampf.

The book penned by the *Führer* himself.

It was the third book of great importance to reach Liesel Meminger; only this time, she did not steal it. The book showed up at 33 Himmel Street perhaps an hour after Liesel had drifted back to sleep from her obligatory nightmare.

Some would say it was a miracle that she ever owned that book at all.

Its journey began on the way home, the night of the fire.

They were nearly halfway back to Himmel Street when Liesel could no longer take it. She bent over and removed the smoking book, allowing it to hop sheepishly from hand to hand.

When it had cooled sufficiently, they both watched it a moment, waiting for the words.

Papa: "What the hell do you call that?"

He reached over and grabbed hold of *The Shoulder Shrug*. No explanation was required. It was obvious that the girl had stolen it from the fire. The book was hot and wet, blue and red—embarrassed—and Hans Hubermann opened it up. Pages thirty-eight and thirty-nine. "Another one?"

Liesel rubbed her ribs.

Yes.

Another one.

"Looks like," Papa suggested, "I don't need to trade any more cigarettes, do I? Not when you're stealing these things as fast as I can buy them."

Liesel, by comparison, did not speak. Perhaps it was her first realization that criminality spoke best for itself. Irrefutable.

Papa studied the title, probably wondering exactly what kind of threat this book posed to the hearts and minds of the German people. He handed it back. Something happened.

"Jesus, Mary, and Joseph." Each word fell away at its edges. It broke off and formed the next.

The criminal could no longer resist. "What, Papa? What is it?"

"Of course."

Like most humans in the grip of revelation, Hans Hubermann stood with a certain numbness. The next words would either be shouted or would not make it past his teeth. Also, they would most likely be a repetition of the last thing he'd said, only moments earlier.

"Of course."

This time, his voice was like a fist, freshly banged on the table.

The man was seeing something. He was watching it quickly, end to end, like a race, but it was too high and too far away for Liesel to see. She begged him. "Come on, Papa, what is it?" She fretted that he would tell Mama about the book. As humans do, this was all about her. "Are you going to tell?"

"Sorry?"

"You know. Are you going to tell Mama?"

Hans Hubermann still watched, tall and distant. "About what?"

She raised the book. "This." She brandished it in the air, as if waving a gun.

Papa was bewildered. "Why would I?"

She hated questions like that. They forced her to admit an ugly truth, to reveal her own filthy, thieving nature. "Because I stole again."

Papa bent himself to a crouching position, then rose and placed his hand on her head. He stroked her hair with his rough, long fingers and said, "Of course not, Liesel. You are safe."

"So what are you going to do?"

That was the question.

What marvelous act was Hans Hubermann about to produce from the thin Munich Street air?

Before I show you, I think we should first take a look at what he was seeing prior to his decision.

* * * PAPA'S FAST-PACED VISIONS * * *
First, he sees the girl's books: *The Grave Digger's Handbook,*
Faust the Dog, The Lighthouse,* and now *The Shoulder Shrug.
Next is a kitchen and a volatile Hans Junior, regarding those
books on the table, where the girl often reads. He speaks:
"And what trash is this girl reading?" His son repeats
the question three times, after which he makes his
suggestion for more appropriate reading material.

"Listen, Liesel." Papa placed his arm around her and walked her on. "This is our secret, this book. We'll read it at night or in the basement, just like the others—but you have to promise me something."

"Anything, Papa."

The night was smooth and still. Everything listened. "If I ever ask you to keep a secret for me, you will do it."

"I promise."

"Good. Now come on. If we're any later, Mama will kill us, and we don't want that, do we? No more book stealing then, huh?"

Liesel grinned.

What she didn't know until later was that within the next few days, her foster father managed to trade some cigarettes for another book, although this one was not for her. He knocked on the door of the Nazi Party office in Molching and took the opportunity to ask about his membership application. Once this was discussed, he proceeded to give them his last scraps of money and a dozen cigarettes. In return, he received a used copy of *Mein Kampf*.

"Happy reading," said one of the party members.

"Thank you." Hans nodded.

From the street, he could still hear the men inside. One of the voices was particularly clear. "He will never be approved," it said, "even if he buys a hundred copies of *Mein Kampf*." The statement was unanimously agreed upon.

Hans held the book in his right hand, thinking about postage money, a cigaretteless existence, and the foster daughter who had given him this brilliant idea.

"Thank you," he repeated, to which a passerby inquired as to what he'd said.

With typical affability, Hans replied, "Nothing, my good man, nothing at all. *Heil* Hitler," and he walked down Munich Street, holding the pages of the *Führer*.

There must have been a good share of mixed feelings at that moment, for Hans Hubermann's idea had not only sprung from Liesel, but from his son. Did he already fear he'd never see him again? On the other hand, he was also enjoying the ecstasy of an idea, not daring just yet to envision its complications, dangers, and vicious absurdities. For now, the idea was enough. It was indestructible. Transforming it into reality, well, that was something else altogether. For now, though, let's let him enjoy it.

We'll give him seven months.

Then we come for him.

And oh, how we come.

THE MAYOR'S LIBRARY

Certainly, something of great magnitude was coming toward 33 Himmel Street, to which Liesel was currently oblivious. To distort an overused human expression, the girl had more immediate fish to fry:

She had stolen a book.

Someone had seen her.

The book thief reacted. Appropriately.

Every minute, every hour, there was worry, or more to the point, paranoia. Criminal activity will do that to a person, especially a child. They envision a prolific assortment of *caughtoutedness*. Some examples: People jumping out of alleys. Schoolteachers suddenly being aware of every sin you've ever committed. Police showing up at the door each time a leaf turns or a distant gate slams shut.

For Liesel, the paranoia itself became the punishment, as did the dread of delivering some washing to the mayor's house. It was no mistake, as I'm sure you can imagine, that when the time came, Liesel conveniently overlooked the house on Grande Strasse. She delivered to the arthritic Helena Schmidt and picked up at the cat-loving

Weingartner residence, but she ignored the house belonging to *Bürgermeister* Heinz Hermann and his wife, Ilsa.

✳ ✳ ✳ ANOTHER QUICK TRANSLATION ✳ ✳ ✳
Bürgermeister = mayor

On the first occasion, she stated that she simply forgot about that place—a poor excuse if ever I've heard one—as the house straddled the hill, overlooking the town, and it was unforgettable. When she went back and still returned empty-handed, she lied that there was no one home.

"No one home?" Mama was skeptical. Skepticism gave her an itch for the wooden spoon. She waved it at Liesel and said, "Get back over there now, and if you don't come home with the washing, don't come home at all."

"Really?"

That was Rudy's response when Liesel told him what Mama had said. "Do you want to run away together?"

"We'll starve."

"I'm starving anyway!" They laughed.

"No," she said, "I have to do it."

They walked the town as they usually did when Rudy came along. He always tried to be a gentleman and carry the bag, but each time, Liesel refused. Only she had the threat of a *Watschen* loitering over her head, and therefore only she could be relied upon to carry the bag correctly. Anyone else was more likely to manhandle it, twist it, or mistreat it in even the most minimal way, and it was not worth the risk. Also, it was likely that if she allowed Rudy to carry it for her, he would expect a kiss for his services, and that was not an option. Besides, she was accustomed to its burden. She would swap the bag from shoulder to shoulder, relieving each side every hundred steps or so.

Liesel walked on the left, Rudy the right. Rudy talked most of the time, about the last soccer match on Himmel Street, working in his father's shop, and whatever else came to mind. Liesel tried to listen but failed. What she heard was the dread, chiming through her ears, growing louder the closer they stepped toward Grande Strasse.

"What are you doing? Isn't this it?"

Liesel nodded that Rudy was right, for she had tried to walk past the mayor's house to buy some time.

"Well, go on," the boy hurried her. Molching was darkening. The cold was climbing out of the ground. "Move it, *Saumensch*." He remained at the gate.

After the path, there were eight steps up to the main entrance of the house, and the great door was like a monster. Liesel frowned at the brass knocker.

"What are you waiting for?" Rudy called out.

Liesel turned and faced the street. Was there any way, any way at all, for her to evade this? Was there another story, or let's face it, another lie, that she'd overlooked?

"We don't have all day." Rudy's distant voice again. "What the hell are you waiting for?"

"Will you shut your trap, Steiner?" It was a shout delivered as a whisper.

"What?"

"I said shut up, you stupid *Saukerl*...."

With that, she faced the door again, lifted back the brass knuckle, and tapped it three times, slowly. Feet approached from the other side.

At first, she didn't look at the woman but focused on the washing bag in her hand. She examined the drawstring as she passed it over. Money was handed out to her and then, nothing. The mayor's wife, who never spoke, simply stood in her bathrobe, her soft fluffy hair tied back into a short tail. A draft made itself known. Something like the imagined breath of a corpse. Still there were no words, and when Liesel found the courage to face her, the woman wore an expression not of reproach, but utter distance. For a moment, she looked over Liesel's shoulder at the boy, then nodded and stepped back, closing the door.

For quite a while, Liesel remained, facing the blanket of upright wood.

"Hey, *Saumensch!*" No response. "Liesel!"

Liesel reversed.

Cautiously.

She took the first few steps backward, calculating.

Perhaps the woman hadn't seen her steal the book after all. It had been getting dark. Perhaps it was one of those times when a person appears to be looking directly at you when, in fact, they're contentedly watching something else or simply daydreaming. Whatever the answer, Liesel didn't attempt any further analysis. She'd gotten away with it and that was enough.

She turned and handled the remainder of the steps normally, taking the last three all at once.

"Let's go, *Saukerl.*" She even allowed herself a laugh. Eleven-year-old paranoia was powerful. Eleven-year-old relief was euphoric.

* * * A LITTLE SOMETHING TO * * *
DAMPEN THE EUPHORIA
She had gotten away with nothing.
The mayor's wife had seen her, all right.
She was just waiting for the right moment.

. . .

A few weeks passed.

Soccer on Himmel Street.

Reading *The Shoulder Shrug* between two and three o'clock each morning, post-nightmare, or during the afternoon, in the basement.

Another benign visit to the mayor's house.

All was lovely.

Until.

When Liesel next visited, minus Rudy, the opportunity presented itself. It was a pickup day.

The mayor's wife opened the door and she was not holding the bag, like she normally would. Instead, she stepped aside and motioned with her chalky hand and wrist for the girl to enter.

"I'm just here for the washing." Liesel's blood had dried inside of her. It crumbled. She almost broke into pieces on the steps.

The woman said her first word to her then. She reached out, cold-fingered, and said, "*Warte*—wait." When she was sure the girl had steadied, she turned and walked hastily back inside.

"Thank God," Liesel exhaled. "She's getting it." *It* being the washing.

What the woman returned with, however, was nothing of the sort.

When she came and stood with an impossibly frail steadfastness, she was holding a tower of books against her stomach, from her navel to the beginnings of her breasts. She looked so vulnerable in the monstrous doorway. Long, light eyelashes and just the slightest twinge of expression. A suggestion.

Come and see, it said.

She's going to torture me, Liesel decided. She's going to take me inside, light the fireplace, and throw me in, books and all. Or she'll lock me in the basement without any food.

For some reason, though—most likely the lure of the books—she found herself walking in. The squeaking of her shoes on the wooden floorboards made her cringe, and when she hit a sore spot, inducing the wood to groan, she almost stopped. The mayor's wife was not deterred. She only looked briefly behind and continued on, to a chestnut-colored door. Now her face asked a question.

Are you ready?

Liesel craned her neck a little, as if she might see over the door that stood in her way. Clearly, that was the cue to open it.

"Jesus, Mary . . ."

She said it out loud, the words distributed into a room that was full of cold air and books. Books everywhere! Each wall was armed with overcrowded yet immaculate shelving. It was barely possible to see the paintwork. There were all different styles and sizes of lettering on the spines of the black, the red, the gray, the every-colored books. It was one of the most beautiful things Liesel Meminger had ever seen.

With wonder, she smiled.

That such a room existed!

Even when she tried to wipe the smile away with her forearm, she realized instantly that it was a pointless exercise. She could feel the eyes of the woman traveling her body, and when she looked at her, they had rested on her face.

There was more silence than she ever thought possible. It extended like an elastic, dying to break. The girl broke it.

"Can I?"

The two words stood among acres and acres of vacant, wooden-floored land. The books were miles away.

The woman nodded.

Yes, you can.

• • •

Steadily, the room shrank, till the book thief could touch the shelves within a few small steps. She ran the back of her hand along the first shelf, listening to the shuffle of her fingernails gliding across the spinal cord of each book. It sounded like an instrument, or the notes of running feet. She used both hands. She raced them. One shelf against the other. And she laughed. Her voice was sprawled out, high in her throat, and when she eventually stopped and stood in the middle of the room, she spent many minutes looking from the shelves to her fingers and back again.

How many books had she touched?

How many had she *felt*?

She walked over and did it again, this time much slower, with her hand facing forward, allowing the dough of her palm to feel the small hurdle of each book. It felt like magic, like beauty, as bright lines of light shone down from a chandelier. Several times, she almost pulled a title from its place but didn't dare disturb them. They were too perfect.

To her left, she saw the woman again, standing by a large desk, still holding the small tower against her torso. She stood with a delighted crookedness. A smile appeared to have paralyzed her lips.

"Do you want me to—?"

Liesel didn't finish the question but actually performed what she was going to ask, walking over and taking the books gently from the woman's arms. She then placed them into the missing piece in the shelf, by the slightly open window. The outside cold was streaming in.

For a moment, she considered closing it, but thought better of it. This was not her house, and the situation was not to be tampered with. Instead, she returned to the lady behind her, whose smile gave the appearance now of a bruise and whose arms were hanging slenderly at each side. Like girls' arms.

What now?

An awkwardness treated itself to the room, and Liesel took a final, fleeting glance at the walls of books. In her mouth, the words fidgeted, but they came out in a rush. "I should go."

It took three attempts to leave.

She waited in the hallway for a few minutes, but the woman didn't come, and when Liesel returned to the entrance of the room, she saw her sitting at the desk, staring blankly at one of the books. She chose not to disturb her. In the hallway, she picked up the washing.

This time, she avoided the sore spot in the floorboards, walking the long length of the corridor, favoring the left-hand wall. When she closed the door behind her, a brass clank sounded in her ear, and with the washing next to her, she stroked the flesh of the wood. "Get going," she said.

At first, she walked home dazed.

The surreal experience with the roomful of books and the stunned, broken woman walked alongside her. She could see it on the buildings, like a play. Perhaps it was similar to the way Papa had his *Mein Kampf* revelation. Wherever she looked, Liesel saw the mayor's wife with the books piled up in her arms. Around corners, she could hear the shuffle of her own hands, disturbing the shelves. She saw the open window, the chandelier of lovely light, and she saw herself leaving, without so much as a word of thanks.

Soon, her sedated condition transformed to harassment and self-loathing. She began to rebuke herself.

"You said nothing." Her head shook vigorously, among the hurried footsteps. "Not a 'goodbye.' Not a 'thank you.' Not a 'that's the most beautiful sight I've ever seen.' Nothing!" Certainly, she was a book thief, but that didn't mean she should have no manners at all. It didn't mean she couldn't be polite.

She walked a good few minutes, struggling with indecision.

On Munich Street, it came to an end.

Just as she could make out the sign that said STEINER—
SCHNEIDERMEISTER, she turned and ran back.

This time, there was no hesitation.

She thumped the door, sending an echo of brass through the wood.

Scheisse!

It was not the mayor's wife, but the mayor himself who stood
before her. In her hurry, Liesel had neglected to notice the car that
sat out front, on the street.

Mustached and black-suited, the man spoke. "Can I help you?"

Liesel could say nothing. Not yet. She was bent over, short of air,
and fortunately, the woman arrived when she'd at least partially recovered. Ilsa Hermann stood behind her husband, to the side.

"I forgot," Liesel said. She lifted the bag and addressed the
mayor's wife. Despite the forced labor of breath, she fed the words
through the gap in the doorway—between the mayor and the frame—
to the woman. Such was her effort to breathe that the words escaped
only a few at a time. "I forgot . . . I mean, I just . . . wanted," she said,
"to . . . thank you."

The mayor's wife bruised herself again. Coming forward to stand
beside her husband, she nodded very faintly, waited, and closed the
door.

It took Liesel a minute or so to leave.

She smiled at the steps.

ENTER THE STRUGGLER

Now for a change of scenery.

We've both had it too easy till now, my friend, don't you think? How about we forget Molching for a minute or two?

It will do us some good.

Also, it's important to the story.

We will travel a little, to a secret storage room, and we will see what we see.

* * * A GUIDED TOUR OF SUFFERING * * *
To your left,
perhaps your right,
perhaps even straight ahead,
you find a small black room.
In it sits a Jew.
He is scum.
He is starving.
He is afraid.
Please—try not to look away.

A few hundred miles northwest, in Stuttgart, far from book thieves, mayors' wives, and Himmel Street, a man was sitting in the dark. It was the best place, they decided. It's harder to find a Jew in the dark.

He sat on his suitcase, waiting. How many days had it been now?

He had eaten only the foul taste of his own hungry breath for what felt like weeks, and still, nothing. Occasionally voices wandered past and sometimes he longed for them to knuckle the door, to open it, to drag him out, into the unbearable light. For now, he could only sit on his suitcase couch, hands under his chin, his elbows burning his thighs.

There was sleep, starving sleep, and the irritation of half awakeness, and the punishment of the floor.

Ignore the itchy feet.

Don't scratch the soles.

And don't move too much.

Just leave everything as it is, at all cost. It might be time to go soon. Light like a gun. Explosive to the eyes. It might be time to go. It might be time, so wake up. Wake up now, Goddamn it! Wake up.

The door was opened and shut, and a figure was crouched over him. The hand splashed at the cold waves of his clothes and the grimy currents beneath. A voice came down, behind it.

"Max," it whispered. "Max, wake up."

His eyes did not do anything that shock normally describes. No snapping, no slapping, no jolt. Those things happen when you wake from a bad dream, not when you wake *into* one. No, his eyes dragged themselves open, from darkness to dim. It was his body that reacted, shrugging upward and throwing out an arm to grip the air.

The voice calmed him now. "Sorry it's taken so long. I think people have been watching me. And the man with the identity card took longer than I thought, but—" There was a pause. "It's yours now. Not great quality, but hopefully good enough to get you there if it comes to that." He crouched down and waved a hand at the suitcase. In his other hand, he held something heavy and flat. "Come on—off." Max obeyed, standing and scratching. He could feel the tightening of his bones. "The card is in this." It was a book. "You should put the map in here, too, and the directions. And there's a key—taped to the inside cover." He clicked open the case as quietly as he could and planted the book like a bomb. "I'll be back in a few days."

He left a small bag filled with bread, fat, and three small carrots. Next to it was a bottle of water. There was no apology. "It's the best I could do."

Door open, door shut.

Alone again.

What came to him immediately then was the sound.

Everything was so desperately noisy in the dark when he was alone. Each time he moved, there was the sound of a crease. He felt like a man in a paper suit.

The food.

Max divided the bread into three parts and set two aside. The one in his hand he immersed himself in, chewing and gulping, forcing it down the dry corridor of his throat. The fat was cold and hard, scaling its way down, occasionally holding on. Big swallows tore them away and sent them below.

Then the carrots.

Again, he set two aside and devoured the third. The noise was astounding. Surely, the *Führer* himself could hear the sound of the orange crush in his mouth. It broke his teeth with every bite. When he drank, he was quite positive that he was swallowing them. Next time, he advised himself, drink first.

Later, to his relief, when the echoes left him and he found the courage to check with his fingers, each tooth was still there, intact. He tried for a smile, but it didn't come. He could only imagine a meek attempt and a mouthful of broken teeth. For hours, he felt at them.

He opened the suitcase and picked up the book.

He could not read the title in the dark, and the gamble of striking a match seemed too great right now.

When he spoke, it was the taste of a whisper.

"Please," he said. "Please."

He was speaking to a man he had never met. As well as a few other important details, he knew the man's name. Hans Hubermann. Again, he spoke to him, to the distant stranger. He pleaded.

"Please."

THE ATTRIBUTES OF SUMMER

So there you have it.

You're well aware of exactly what was coming to Himmel Street by the end of 1940.

I know.

You know.

Liesel Meminger, however, cannot be put into that category.

For the book thief, the summer of that year was simple. It consisted of four main elements, or attributes. At times, she would wonder which was the most powerful.

✳ ✳ ✳ AND THE NOMINEES ARE . . . ✳ ✳ ✳
1. Advancing through *The Shoulder Shrug* every night.
2. Reading on the floor of the mayor's library.
3. Playing soccer on Himmel Street.
4. The seizure of a different stealing opportunity.

The Shoulder Shrug, she decided, was excellent. Each night, when she calmed herself from her nightmare, she was soon pleased that she was awake and able to read. "A few pages?" Papa asked her, and Liesel would nod. Sometimes they would complete a chapter the next afternoon, down in the basement.

The authorities' problem with the book was obvious. The protagonist was a Jew, and he was presented in a positive light. Unforgivable. He was a rich man who was tired of letting life pass him by—what he referred to as the shrugging of the shoulders to the problems and pleasures of a person's time on earth.

In the early part of summer in Molching, as Liesel and Papa made their way through the book, this man was traveling to Amsterdam on business, and the snow was shivering outside. The girl loved that— the shivering snow. "That's exactly what it does when it comes down," she told Hans Hubermann. They sat together on the bed, Papa half asleep and the girl wide awake.

Sometimes she watched Papa as he slept, knowing both more and less about him than either of them realized. She often heard him and Mama discussing his lack of work or talking despondently about Hans going to see their son, only to discover that the young man had left his lodging and was most likely already on his way to war.

"*Schlaf gut,* Papa," the girl said at those times. "Sleep well," and she slipped around him, out of bed, to turn off the light.

The next attribute, as I've mentioned, was the mayor's library.

To exemplify that particular situation, we can look to a cool day in late June. Rudy, to put it mildly, was incensed.

Who did Liesel Meminger think she was, telling him she had to take the washing and ironing alone today? Wasn't he good enough to walk the streets with her?

"Stop complaining, *Saukerl*," she reprimanded him. "I just feel bad. You're missing the game."

He looked over his shoulder. "Well, if you put it like that." There was a *Schmunzel*. "You can stick your washing." He ran off and wasted no time joining a team. When Liesel made it to the top of Himmel Street, she looked back just in time to see him standing in front of the nearest makeshift goals. He was waving.

"*Saukerl*," she laughed, and as she held up her hand, she knew completely that he was simultaneously calling her a *Saumensch*. I think that's as close to love as eleven-year-olds can get.

She started to run, to Grande Strasse and the mayor's house.

Certainly, there was sweat, and the wrinkled pants of breath, stretching out in front of her.

But she was reading.

The mayor's wife, having let the girl in for the fourth time, was sitting at the desk, simply watching the books. On the second visit, she had given permission for Liesel to pull one out and go through it, which led to another and another, until up to half a dozen books were stuck to her, either clutched beneath her arm or among the pile that was climbing higher in her remaining hand.

On this occasion, as Liesel stood in the cool surrounds of the room, her stomach growled, but no reaction was forthcoming from the mute, damaged woman. She was in her bathrobe again, and although she observed the girl several times, it was never for very long. She usually paid more attention to what was next to her, to something missing. The window was opened wide, a square cool mouth, with occasional gusty surges.

Liesel sat on the floor. The books were scattered around her.

After forty minutes, she left. Every title was returned to its place.

"Goodbye, Frau Hermann." The words always came as a shock. "Thank you." After which the woman paid her and she left. Every movement was accounted for, and the book thief ran home.

As summer set in, the roomful of books became warmer, and with every pickup or delivery day the floor was not as painful. Liesel would sit with a small pile of books next to her, and she'd read a few paragraphs of each, trying to memorize the words she didn't know, to ask Papa when she made it home. Later on, as an adolescent, when Liesel wrote about those books, she no longer remembered the titles. Not one. Perhaps had she stolen them, she would have been better equipped.

What she did remember was that one of the picture books had a name written clumsily on the inside cover:

* * * THE NAME OF A BOY * * *
Johann Hermann

Liesel bit down on her lip, but she could not resist it for long. From the floor, she turned and looked up at the bathrobed woman and made an inquiry. "Johann Hermann," she said. "Who is that?"

The woman looked beside her, somewhere next to the girl's knees.

Liesel apologized. "I'm sorry. I shouldn't be asking such things. . . ." She let the sentence die its own death.

The woman's face did not alter, yet somehow she managed to speak. "He is nothing now in this world," she explained. "He was my . . ."

* * * THE FILES OF RECOLLECTION * * *
Oh, yes, I definitely remember him.
The sky was murky and deep like quicksand.
There was a young man parceled up in barbed wire,
like a giant crown of thorns. I untangled him and carried him
out. High above the earth, we sank together,
to our knees. It was just another day, 1918.

"Apart from everything else," she said, "he froze to death." For a moment, she played with her hands, and she said it again. "He froze to death, I'm sure of it."

The mayor's wife was just one of a worldwide brigade. You have seen her before, I'm certain. In your stories, your poems, the screens you like to watch. They're everywhere, so why not here? Why not on a shapely hill in a small German town? It's as good a place to suffer as any.

The point is, Ilsa Hermann had decided to make suffering her triumph. When it refused to let go of her, she succumbed to it. She embraced it.

She could have shot herself, scratched herself, or indulged in other forms of self-mutilation, but she chose what she probably felt was the weakest option—to at least endure the discomfort of the weather. For all Liesel knew, she prayed for summer days that were cold and wet. For the most part, she lived in the right place.

When Liesel left that day, she said something with great uneasiness. In translation, two giant words were struggled with, carried on her shoulder, and dropped as a bungling pair at Ilsa Hermann's feet. They fell off sideways as the girl veered with them and could no longer sustain their weight. Together, they sat on the floor, large and loud and clumsy.

✳ ✳ ✳ TWO GIANT WORDS ✳ ✳ ✳
I'M SORRY

Again, the mayor's wife watched the space next to her. A blank-page face.

"For what?" she asked, but time had elapsed by then. The girl was already well out of the room. She was nearly at the front door. When she heard it, Liesel stopped, but she chose not to go back, preferring to make her way noiselessly from the house and down the steps. She took in the view of Molching before disappearing down into it, and she pitied the mayor's wife for quite a while.

At times, Liesel wondered if she should simply leave the woman alone, but Ilsa Hermann was too interesting, and the pull of the books was too strong. Once, words had rendered Liesel useless, but now, when she sat on the floor, with the mayor's wife at her husband's desk, she felt an innate sense of power. It happened every time she deciphered a new word or pieced together a sentence.

She was a girl.

In Nazi Germany.

How fitting that she was discovering the power of words.

And how awful (and yet exhilarating!) it would feel many months later, when she would unleash the power of this newfound discovery the very moment the mayor's wife let her down. How quickly the pity would leave her, and how quickly it would spill over into something else completely. . . .

Now, though, in the summer of 1940, she could not see what lay ahead, in more ways than one. She was witness only to a sorrowful woman with a roomful of books whom she enjoyed visiting. That was all. It was part two of her existence that summer.

Part three, thank God, was a little more lighthearted—Himmel Street soccer.

Allow me to play you a picture:

Feet scuffing road.

The rush of boyish breath.

Shouted words: "Here! This way! *Scheisse!*"

The coarse bounce of ball on road.

• • •

All were present on Himmel Street, as well as the sound of apologies, as summer further intensified.

The apologies belonged to Liesel Meminger.

They were directed at Tommy Müller.

By the start of July, she finally managed to convince him that she wasn't going to kill him. Since the beating she'd handed him the previous November, Tommy was still frightened to be around her. In the soccer meetings on Himmel Street, he kept well clear. "You never know when she might snap," he'd confided in Rudy, half twitching, half speaking.

In Liesel's defense, she never gave up on trying to put him at ease. It disappointed her that she'd successfully made peace with Ludwig Schmeikl and not with the innocent Tommy Müller. He still cowered slightly whenever he saw her.

"How could I know you were smiling *for* me that day?" she asked him repeatedly.

She'd even put in a few stints as goalie for him, until everyone else on the team begged him to go back in.

"Get back in there!" a boy named Harald Mollenhauer finally ordered him. "You're useless." This was after Tommy tripped him up as he was about to score. He would have awarded himself a penalty but for the fact that they were on the same side.

Liesel came back out and would somehow always end up opposing Rudy. They would tackle and trip each other, call each other names. Rudy would commentate: "She can't get around him *this* time, the stupid *Saumensch Arschgrobbler*. She hasn't got a hope." He seemed to enjoy calling Liesel an ass scratcher. It was one of the joys of childhood.

Another of the joys, of course, was stealing. Part four, summer 1940.

In fairness, there were many things that brought Rudy and Liesel

together, but it was the stealing that cemented their friendship completely. It was brought about by one opportunity, and it was driven by
one inescapable force—Rudy's hunger. The boy was permanently dying for something to eat.

On top of the rationing situation, his father's business wasn't doing
so well of late (the threat of Jewish competition was taken away, but so
were the Jewish customers). The Steiners were scratching things together to get by. Like many other people on the Himmel Street side of
town, they needed to trade. Liesel would have given him some food
from her place, but there wasn't an abundance of it there, either. Mama
usually made pea soup. On Sunday nights she cooked it—and not just
enough for one or two repeat performances. She made enough pea soup
to last until the following Saturday. Then on Sunday, she'd cook another
one. Pea soup, bread, sometimes a small portion of potatoes or meat.
You ate it up and you didn't ask for more, and you didn't complain.

At first, they did things to try to forget about it.

Rudy wouldn't be hungry if they played soccer on the street. Or if
they took bikes from his brother and sister and rode to Alex Steiner's
shop or visited Liesel's papa, if he was working that particular day.
Hans Hubermann would sit with them and tell jokes in the last light
of afternoon.

With the arrival of a few hot days, another distraction was learning to swim in the Amper River. The water was still a little too cold,
but they went anyway.

"Come on," Rudy coaxed her in. "Just here. It isn't so deep here."
She couldn't see the giant hole she was walking into and sank straight
to the bottom. Dog-paddling saved her life, despite nearly choking on
the swollen intake of water.

"You *Saukerl,*" she accused him when she collapsed onto the
riverbank.

Rudy made certain to keep well away. He'd seen what she did to
Ludwig Schmeikl. "You can swim now, can't you?"

Which didn't particularly cheer her up as she marched away. Her hair was pasted to the side of her face and snot was flowing from her nose.

He called after her. "Does this mean I don't get a kiss for teaching you?"

"*Saukerl!*"

The nerve of him!

It was inevitable.

The depressing pea soup and Rudy's hunger finally drove them to thievery. It inspired their attachment to an older group of kids who stole from the farmers. Fruit stealers. After a game of soccer, both Liesel and Rudy learned the benefits of keeping their eyes open. Sitting on Rudy's front step, they noticed Fritz Hammer—one of their older counterparts—eating an apple. It was of the *Klar* variety—ripening in July and August—and it looked magnificent in his hand. Three or four more of them clearly bulged in his jacket pockets. They wandered closer.

"Where did you get those?" Rudy asked.

The boy only grinned at first. "Shhh," and he stopped. He then proceeded to pull an apple from his pocket and toss it over. "Just look at it," he warned them. "Don't eat it."

The next time they saw the same boy wearing the same jacket, on a day that was too warm for it, they followed him. He led them toward the upstream section of the Amper River. It was close to where Liesel sometimes read with her papa when she was first learning.

A group of five boys, some lanky, a few short and lean, stood waiting.

There were a few such groups in Molching at the time, some with members as young as six. The leader of this particular outfit was an agreeable fifteen-year-old criminal named Arthur Berg. He looked around and saw the two eleven-year-olds dangling off the back. *"Und?"* he asked. "And?"

"I'm starving," Rudy replied.

"And he's fast," said Liesel.

Berg looked at her. "I don't recall asking for your opinion." He was teenage tall and had a long neck. Pimples were gathered in peer groups on his face. "But I like you." He was friendly, in a smart-mouth adolescent way. "Isn't this the one who beat up your brother, Anderl?" Word had certainly made its way around. A good hiding transcends the divides of age.

Another boy—one of the short, lean ones—with shaggy blond hair and ice-colored skin, looked over. "I think so."

Rudy confirmed it. "It is."

Andy Schmeikl walked across and studied her, up and down, his face pensive before breaking into a gaping smile. "Great work, kid." He even slapped her among the bones of her back, catching a sharp piece of shoulder blade. "I'd get whipped for it if I did it myself."

Arthur had moved on to Rudy. "And you're the Jesse Owens one, aren't you?"

Rudy nodded.

"Clearly," said Arthur, "you're an idiot—but you're our kind of idiot. Come on."

They were in.

When they reached the farm, Liesel and Rudy were thrown a sack. Arthur Berg gripped his own burlap bag. He ran a hand through his mild strands of hair. "Either of you ever stolen before?"

"Of course," Rudy certified. "All the time." He was not very convincing.

Liesel was more specific. "I've stolen two books," at which Arthur laughed, in three short snorts. His pimples shifted position.

"You can't eat books, sweetheart."

From there, they all examined the apple trees, who stood in long, twisted rows. Arthur Berg gave the orders. "One," he said. "Don't get caught on the fence. You get caught on the fence, you get left behind. Understood?" Everyone nodded or said yes. "Two. One in the tree, one below. Someone has to collect." He rubbed his hands together. He was enjoying this. "Three. If you see someone coming, you call out loud enough to wake the dead—and we all run. *Richtig?*"

"*Richtig.*" It was a chorus.

✻ ✻ ✻ TWO DEBUTANT APPLE THIEVES, ✻ ✻ ✻
WHISPERING
"Liesel—are you sure? Do you still want to do this?"
"Look at the barbed wire, Rudy. It's so high."
"No, no, look, you throw the sack on. See? Like them."
"All right."
"Come on then!"
"I can't!" Hesitation. "Rudy, I—"
"Move it, *Saumensch!*"

He pushed her toward the fence, threw the empty sack on the wire, and they climbed over, running toward the others. Rudy made his way up the closest tree and started flinging down the apples. Liesel stood below, putting them into the sack. By the time it was full, there was another problem.

"How do we get back over the fence?"

The answer came when they noticed Arthur Berg climbing as close to a fence post as possible. "The wire's stronger there." Rudy pointed. He threw the sack over, made Liesel go first, then landed beside her on the other side, among the fruit that spilled from the bag.

Next to them, the long legs of Arthur Berg stood watching in amusement.

"Not bad," landed the voice from above. "Not bad at all."

When they made it back to the river, hidden among the trees, he took the sack and gave Liesel and Rudy a dozen apples between them.

"Good work," was his final comment on the matter.

That afternoon, before they returned home, Liesel and Rudy consumed six apples apiece within half an hour. At first, they entertained thoughts of sharing the fruit at their respective homes, but there was considerable danger in that. They didn't particularly relish the opportunity of explaining just where the fruit had come from. Liesel even thought that perhaps she could get away with only telling Papa, but she didn't want him thinking that he had a compulsive criminal on his hands. So she ate.

On the riverbank where she learned to swim, each apple was disposed of. Unaccustomed to such luxury, they knew it was likely they'd be sick.

They ate anyway.

"*Saumensch!*" Mama abused her that night. "Why are you vomiting so much?"

"Maybe it's the pea soup," Liesel suggested.

"That's right," Papa echoed. He was over at the window again. "It must be. I feel a bit sick myself."

"Who asked you, *Saukerl?*" Quickly, she turned back to face the vomiting *Saumensch*. "Well? What is it? What is it, you filthy pig?"

But Liesel?

She said nothing.

The apples, she thought happily. The apples, and she vomited one more time, for luck.

THE ARYAN SHOPKEEPER

They stood outside Frau Diller's, against the whitewashed wall.

A piece of candy was in Liesel Meminger's mouth.

The sun was in her eyes.

Despite these difficulties, she was still able to speak and argue.

* * * ANOTHER CONVERSATION * * *
BETWEEN RUDY AND LIESEL
"Hurry up, *Saumensch,* that's ten already."
"It's not, it's only eight—I've got two to go."
"Well, hurry up, then. I told you we should have gotten a knife
and sawn it in half. . . . Come on, that's two."
"All right. Here. And don't swallow it."
"Do I look like an idiot?"
[A short pause]
"This is great, isn't it?"
"It sure is, *Saumensch.*"

At the end of August and summer, they found one pfennig on the ground. Pure excitement.

It was sitting half rotten in some dirt, on the washing and ironing route. A solitary corroded coin.

"Take a look at that!"

Rudy swooped on it. The excitement almost stung as they rushed back to Frau Diller's, not even considering that a single pfennig might not be the *right price*. They burst through the door and stood in front of the Aryan shopkeeper, who regarded them with contempt.

"I'm waiting," she said. Her hair was tied back and her black dress choked her body. The framed photo of the *Führer* kept watch from the wall.

"*Heil* Hitler," Rudy led.

"*Heil* Hitler," she responded, straightening taller behind the counter. "And you?" She glared at Liesel, who promptly gave her a "*heil* Hitler" of her own.

It didn't take Rudy long to dig the coin from his pocket and place it firmly on the counter. He looked straight into Frau Diller's spectacled eyes and said, "Mixed candy, please."

Frau Diller smiled. Her teeth elbowed each other for room in her mouth, and her unexpected kindness made Rudy and Liesel smile as well. Not for long.

She bent down, did some searching, and came back. "Here," she said, tossing a single piece of candy onto the counter. "Mix it yourself."

Outside, they unwrapped it and tried biting it in half, but the sugar was like glass. Far too tough, even for Rudy's animal-like choppers. Instead, they had to trade sucks on it until it was finished. Ten sucks for Rudy. Ten for Liesel. Back and forth.

"This," Rudy announced at one point, with a candy-toothed grin, "is the good life," and Liesel didn't disagree. By the time they were finished, both their mouths were an exaggerated red, and as they walked home, they reminded each other to keep their eyes peeled, in case they found another coin.

Naturally, they found nothing. No one can be that lucky twice in one year, let alone a single afternoon.

Still, with red tongues and teeth, they walked down Himmel Street, happily searching the ground as they went.

The day had been a great one, and Nazi Germany was a wondrous place.

THE STRUGGLER, CONTINUED

We move forward now, to a cold night struggle. We'll let the book thief catch up later.

It was November 3, and the floor of the train held on to his feet. In front of him, he read from the copy of *Mein Kampf.* His savior. Sweat was swimming out of his hands. Fingermarks clutched the book.

* * * BOOK THIEF PRODUCTIONS * * *
OFFICIALLY PRESENTS
Mein Kampf
(My Struggle)
by
Adolf Hitler

Behind Max Vandenburg, the city of Stuttgart opened its arms in mockery.

He was not welcome there, and he tried not to look back as the stale bread disintegrated in his stomach. A few times, he shifted again and watched the lights become only a handful and then disappear altogether.

Look proud, he advised himself. You cannot look afraid. Read the book. Smile at it. It's a great book—the greatest book you've ever read. Ignore that woman on the other side. She's asleep now anyway. Come on, Max, you're only a few hours away.

As it had turned out, the promised return visit in the room of darkness didn't take days; it had taken a week and a half. Then another week till the next, and another, until he lost all sense of the passing of days and hours. He was relocated once more, to another small storage room, where there was more light, more visits, and more food. Time, however, was running out.

"I'm leaving soon," his friend Walter Kugler told him. "You know how it is—the army."

"I'm sorry, Walter."

Walter Kugler, Max's friend from childhood, placed his hand on the Jew's shoulder. "It could be worse." He looked his friend in his Jewish eyes. "I could be you."

That was their last meeting. A final package was left in the corner, and this time, there was a ticket. Walter opened *Mein Kampf* and slid it inside, next to the map he'd brought with the book itself. "Page thirteen." He smiled. "For luck, yes?"

"For luck," and the two of them embraced.

When the door shut, Max opened the book and examined the ticket. *Stuttgart to Munich to Pasing.* It left in two days, in the night, just in time to make the last connection. From there, he would walk. The map was already in his head, folded in quarters. The key was still taped to the inside cover.

He sat for half an hour before stepping toward the bag and opening it. Apart from food, a few other items sat inside.

* * * THE EXTRA CONTENTS OF * * *
WALTER KUGLER'S GIFT
One small razor.
A spoon — the closest thing to a mirror.
Shaving cream.
A pair of scissors.

When he left it, the storeroom was empty but for the floor.

"Goodbye," he whispered.

The last thing Max saw was the small mound of hair, sitting casually against the wall.

Goodbye.

With a clean-shaven face and lopsided yet neatly combed hair, he had walked out of that building a new man. In fact, he walked out German. Hang on a second, he *was* German. Or more to the point, he *had* been.

In his stomach was the electric combination of nourishment and nausea.

He walked to the station.

He showed his ticket and identity card, and now he sat in a small box compartment of the train, directly in danger's spotlight.

"Papers."

That was what he dreaded to hear.

It was bad enough when he was stopped on the platform. He knew he could not withstand it twice.

The shivering hands.

The smell — no, the stench — of guilt.

He simply couldn't bear it again.

Fortunately, they came through early and only asked for the ticket, and now all that was left was a window of small towns, the congregations of lights, and the woman snoring on the other side of the compartment.

For most of the journey, he made his way through the book, trying never to look up.

The words lolled about in his mouth as he read them.

Strangely, as he turned the pages and progressed through the chapters, it was only two words he ever tasted.

Mein Kampf. My struggle —

The title, over and over again, as the train prattled on, from one German town to the next.

Mein Kampf.

Of all the things to save him.

TRICKSTERS

You could argue that Liesel Meminger had it easy. She *did* have it easy compared to Max Vandenburg. Certainly, her brother practically died in her arms. Her mother abandoned her.

But anything was better than being a Jew.

In the time leading up to Max's arrival, another washing customer was lost, this time the Weingartners. The obligatory *Schimpferei* occurred in the kitchen, and Liesel composed herself with the fact that there were still two left, and even better, one of them was the mayor, the wife, the books.

As for Liesel's other activities, she was still causing havoc with Rudy Steiner. I would even suggest that they were polishing their wicked ways.

They made a few more journeys with Arthur Berg and his friends, keen to prove their worth and extend their thieving repertoire. They took potatoes from one farm, onions from another. Their biggest victory, however, they performed alone.

As witnessed earlier, one of the benefits of walking through town was the prospect of finding things on the ground. Another was noticing people, or more important, the *same* people, doing identical things week after week.

A boy from school, Otto Sturm, was one such person. Every Friday afternoon, he rode his bike to church, carrying goods to the priests.

For a month, they watched him, as good weather turned to bad, and Rudy in particular was determined that one Friday, in an abnormally frosty week in October, Otto wouldn't quite make it.

"All those priests," Rudy explained as they walked through town. "They're all too fat anyway. They could do without a feed for a week or so." Liesel could only agree. First of all, she wasn't Catholic. Second, she was pretty hungry herself. As always, she was carrying the washing. Rudy was carrying two buckets of cold water, or as he put it, two buckets of future ice.

Just before two o'clock, he went to work.

Without any hesitation, he poured the water onto the road in the exact position where Otto would pedal around the corner.

Liesel had to admit it.

There was a small portion of guilt at first, but the plan was perfect, or at least as close to perfect as it could be. At just after two o'clock every Friday, Otto Sturm turned onto Munich Street with the produce in his front basket, at the handlebars. On this particular Friday, that was as far as he would travel.

The road was icy as it was, but Rudy put on the extra coat, barely able to contain a grin. It ran across his face like a skid.

"Come on," he said, "that bush there."

After approximately fifteen minutes, the diabolical plan bore its fruit, so to speak.

Rudy pointed his finger into a gap in the bush. "There he is."

Otto came around the corner, dopey as a lamb.

He wasted no time in losing control of the bike, sliding across the ice, and lying facedown on the road.

When he didn't move, Rudy looked at Liesel with alarm. "Crucified Christ," he said, "I think we might have *killed* him!" He crept slowly out, removed the basket, and they made their getaway.

"Was he breathing?" Liesel asked, farther down the street.

"Keine Ahnung," Rudy said, clinging to the basket. He had no idea.

From far down the hill, they watched as Otto stood up, scratched his head, scratched his crotch, and looked everywhere for the basket.

"Stupid *Scheisskopf.*" Rudy grinned, and they looked through the spoils. Bread, broken eggs, and the big one, *Speck*. Rudy held the fatty ham to his nose and breathed it gloriously in. "Beautiful."

As tempting as it was to keep the victory to themselves, they were overpowered by a sense of loyalty to Arthur Berg. They made their way to his impoverished lodging on Kempf Strasse and showed him the produce. Arthur couldn't hold back his approval.

"Who did you steal this from?"

It was Rudy who answered. "Otto Sturm."

"Well," he nodded, "whoever that is, I'm grateful to him." He walked inside and returned with a bread knife, a frying pan, and a jacket, and the three thieves walked the hallway of apartments. "We'll get the others," Arthur Berg stated as they made it outside. "We might be criminals, but we're not totally immoral." Much like the book thief, he at least drew the line somewhere.

A few more doors were knocked on. Names were called out to apartments from streets below, and soon, the whole conglomerate of Arthur Berg's fruit-stealing troop was on its way to the Amper. In the clearing on the other side, a fire was lit and what was left of the eggs was salvaged and fried. The bread and *Speck* were cut. With hands and knives, every last piece of Otto Sturm's delivery was eaten. No priest in sight.

It was only at the end that an argument developed, regarding the basket. The majority of boys wanted to burn it. Fritz Hammer and Andy Schmeikl wanted to keep it, but Arthur Berg, showing his incongruous moral aptitude, had a better idea.

"You two," he said to Rudy and Liesel. "Maybe you should take it back to that Sturm character. I'd say that poor bastard probably deserves that much."

"Oh, come on, Arthur."

"I don't want to hear it, Andy."

"Jesus Christ."

"*He* doesn't want to hear it, either."

The group laughed and Rudy Steiner picked up the basket. "I'll take it back and hang it on their mailbox."

He had walked only twenty meters or so when the girl caught up. She would be home far too late for comfort, but she was well aware that she had to accompany Rudy Steiner through town, to the Sturm farm on the other side.

For a long time, they walked in silence.

"Do you feel bad?" Liesel finally asked. They were already on the way home.

"About what?"

"You know."

"Of course I do, but I'm not hungry anymore, and I bet *he's* not hungry, either. Don't think for a second that the priests would get food if there wasn't enough to go around at home."

"He just hit the ground so hard."

"Don't remind me." But Rudy Steiner couldn't resist smiling. In years to come, he would be a giver of bread, not a stealer—proof again of the contradictory human being. So much good, so much evil. Just add water.

Five days after their bittersweet little victory, Arthur Berg emerged again and invited them on his next stealing project. They ran into him on Munich Street, on the way home from school on a Wednesday. He was already in his Hitler Youth uniform. "We're going again tomorrow afternoon. You interested?"

They couldn't help themselves. "Where?"

"The potato place."

Twenty-four hours later, Liesel and Rudy braved the wire fence again and filled their sack.

The problem showed up as they made their getaway.

"Christ!" shouted Arthur. "The farmer!" It was his next word, however, that frightened. He called it out as if he'd already been attacked with it. His mouth ripped open. The word flew out, and the word was *ax*.

Sure enough, when they turned around, the farmer was running at them, the weapon held aloft.

The whole group ran for the fence line and made their way over. Rudy, who was farthest away, caught up quickly, but not quickly enough to avoid being last. As he pulled his leg up, he became entangled.

"Hey!"

The sound of the stranded.

The group stopped.

Instinctively, Liesel ran back.

"Hurry up!" Arthur called out. His voice was far away, as if he'd swallowed it before it exited his mouth.

White sky.

The others ran.

Liesel arrived and started pulling at the fabric of his pants. Rudy's eyes were opened wide with fear. "Quick," he said, "he's coming."

Far off, they could still hear the sound of deserting feet when an extra hand grabbed the wire and reefed it away from Rudy Steiner's pants. A piece was left on the metallic knot, but the boy was able to escape.

"Now move it," Arthur advised them, not long before the farmer arrived, swearing and struggling for breath. The ax held on now, with force, to his leg. He called out the futile words of the robbed:

"I'll have you arrested! I'll find you! I'll find out who you are!"

That was when Arthur Berg replied.

"The name is Owens!" He loped away, catching up to Liesel and Rudy. "Jesse Owens!"

When they made it to safe ground, fighting to suck the air into their lungs, they sat down and Arthur Berg came over. Rudy wouldn't look at him. "It's happened to all of us," Arthur said, sensing the disappointment. Was he lying? They couldn't be sure and they would never find out.

A few weeks later, Arthur Berg moved to Cologne.

They saw him once more, on one of Liesel's washing delivery rounds. In an alleyway off Munich Street, he handed Liesel a brown paper bag containing a dozen chestnuts. He smirked. "A contact in the roasting industry." After informing them of his departure, he managed to proffer a last pimply smile and to cuff each of them on the forehead. "Don't go eating all those things at once, either," and they never saw Arthur Berg again.

As for me, I can tell you that I most definitely saw him.

* * * A SMALL TRIBUTE TO ARTHUR BERG, * * *
A STILL-LIVING MAN
The Cologne sky was yellow and rotting,
flaking at the edges.
He sat propped against a wall with a child
in his arms. His sister.

When she stopped breathing, he stayed with her,
and I could sense he would hold her for hours.
There were two stolen apples in his pocket.

This time, they played it smarter. They ate one chestnut each and sold the rest of them door to door.

"If you have a few pfennig to spare," Liesel said at each house, "I have chestnuts." They ended up with sixteen coins.

"Now," Rudy grinned, "revenge."

That same afternoon, they returned to Frau Diller's, "*heil* Hitlered," and waited.

"Mixed candy again?" She *schmunzel*ed, to which they nodded. The money splashed the counter and Frau Diller's smile fell slightly ajar.

"Yes, Frau Diller," they said in unison. "Mixed candy, please."

The framed *Führer* looked proud of them.

Triumph before the storm.

THE STRUGGLER, CONCLUDED

The juggling comes to an end now, but the struggling does not. I have Liesel Meminger in one hand, Max Vandenburg in the other. Soon, I will clap them together. Just give me a few pages.

The struggler:

If they killed him tonight, at least he would die alive.

The train ride was far away now, the snorer most likely tucked up in the carriage she'd made her bed, traveling on. Now there were only footsteps between Max and survival. Footsteps and thoughts, and doubts.

He followed the map in his mind, from Pasing to Molching. It was late when he saw the town. His legs ached terribly, but he was nearly there—the most dangerous place to be. Close enough to touch it.

Just as it was described, he found Munich Street and made his way along the footpath.

Everything stiffened.

Glowing pockets of streetlights.

Dark, passive buildings.

The town hall stood like a giant ham-fisted youth, too big for his age. The church disappeared in darkness the farther his eyes traveled upward.

It all watched him.

He shivered.

He warned himself. "Keep your eyes open."

(German children were on the lookout for stray coins. German Jews kept watch for possible capture.)

In keeping with the usage of number thirteen for luck, he counted his footsteps in groups of that number. Just thirteen foot-steps, he would tell himself. Come on, just thirteen more. As an esti-mate, he completed ninety sets, till at last, he stood on the corner of Himmel Street.

In one hand, he held his suitcase.

The other was still holding *Mein Kampf*.

Both were heavy, and both were handled with a gentle secretion of sweat.

Now he turned on to the side street, making his way to number thirty-three, resisting the urge to smile, resisting the urge to sob or even imagine the safety that might be awaiting him. He reminded himself that this was no time for hope. Certainly, he could almost touch it. He could feel it, somewhere just out of reach. Instead of ac-knowledging it, he went about the business of deciding again what to do if he was caught at the last moment or if by some chance the wrong person awaited him inside.

Of course, there was also the scratchy feeling of sin.

How could he do this?

How could he show up and ask people to risk their lives for him? How could he be so selfish?

Thirty-three.

They looked at each other.

· · ·

The house was pale, almost sick-looking, with an iron gate and a brown spit-stained door.

From his pocket, he pulled out the key. It did not sparkle but lay dull and limp in his hand. For a moment, he squeezed it, half expecting it to come leaking toward his wrist. It didn't. The metal was hard and flat, with a healthy set of teeth, and he squeezed it till it pierced him.

Slowly, then, the struggler leaned forward, his cheek against the wood, and he removed the key from his fist.

PART FOUR

the standover man

featuring:

the accordionist — a promise keeper — a good girl —

a jewish fist fighter — the wrath of rosa — a lecture —

a sleeper — the swapping of nightmares —

and some pages from the basement

THE ACCORDIONIST
(The Secret Life of Hans Hubermann)

There was a young man standing in the kitchen. The key in his hand
felt like it was rusting into his palm. He didn't speak anything like
hello, or please help, or any other such expected sentence. He asked
two questions.

* * * QUESTION ONE * * *
"Hans Hubermann?"

* * * QUESTION TWO * * *
"Do you still play the accordion?"

As he looked uncomfortably at the human shape before him, the
young man's voice was scraped out and handed across the dark like it
was all that remained of him.

Papa, alert and appalled, stepped closer.

To the kitchen, he whispered, "Of course I do."
It all dated back many years, to World War I.

They're strange, those wars.

Full of blood and violence—but also full of stories that are equally difficult to fathom. "It's true," people will mutter. "I don't care if you don't believe me. It was that fox who saved my life," or, "They died on either side of me and I was left standing there, the only one without a bullet between my eyes. Why me? Why me and not them?"

Hans Hubermann's story was a little like that. When I found it within the book thief's words, I realized that we passed each other once in a while during that period, though neither of us scheduled a meeting. Personally, I had a lot of work to do. As for Hans, I think he was doing his best to avoid me.

The first time we were in the vicinity of each other, Hans was twenty-two years old, fighting in France. The majority of young men in his platoon were eager to fight. Hans wasn't so sure. I had taken a few of them along the way, but you could say I never even came close to touching Hans Hubermann. He was either too lucky, or he deserved to live, or there was a good reason for him to live.

In the army, he didn't stick out at either end. He ran in the middle, climbed in the middle, and he could shoot straight enough so as not to affront his superiors. Nor did he excel enough to be one of the first chosen to run straight at me.

✳ ✳ ✳ A SMALL BUT NOTEWORTHY NOTE ✳ ✳ ✳
I've seen so many young men
over the years who think they're
running at other young men.

They are not.
They're running at me.

He'd been in the fight for almost six months when he ended up in France, where, at face value, a strange event saved his life. Another perspective would suggest that in the nonsense of war, it made perfect sense.

On the whole, his time in the Great War had astonished him from the moment he entered the army. It was like a serial. Day after day after day. After day:

The conversation of bullets.

Resting men.

The best dirty jokes in the world.

Cold sweat—that malignant little friend—outstaying its welcome in the armpits and trousers.

He enjoyed the card games the most, followed by the few games of chess, despite being thoroughly pathetic at it. And the music. Always the music.

It was a man a year older than himself—a German Jew named Erik Vandenburg—who taught him to play the accordion. The two of them gradually became friends due to the fact that neither of them was terribly interested in fighting. They preferred rolling cigarettes to rolling in snow and mud. They preferred shooting craps to shooting bullets. A firm friendship was built on gambling, smoking, and music, not to mention a shared desire for survival. The only trouble with this was that Erik Vandenburg would later be found in several pieces on a grassy hill. His eyes were open and his wedding ring was stolen. I shoveled up his soul with the rest of them and we drifted away. The horizon was the color of milk. Cold and fresh. Poured out among the bodies.

All that was really left of Erik Vandenburg was a few personal items and the fingerprinted accordion. Everything but the instrument was sent home. It was considered too big. Almost with self-reproach, it sat on his makeshift bed at the base camp and was given to his friend, Hans Hubermann, who happened to be the only man to survive.

* * * HE SURVIVED LIKE THIS * * *
He didn't go into battle that day.

For that, he had Erik Vandenburg to thank. Or more to the point, Erik Vandenburg and the sergeant's toothbrush.

That particular morning, not too long before they were leaving, Sergeant Stephan Schneider paced into the sleeping quarters and called everyone to attention. He was popular with the men for his sense of humor and practical jokes, but more so for the fact that he never followed anyone into the fire. He always went first.

On certain days, he was inclined to enter the room of resting men and say something like, "Who comes from Pasing?" or, "Who's good with mathematics?" or, in the fateful case of Hans Hubermann, "Who's got neat handwriting?"

No one ever volunteered, not after the first time he did it. On that day, an eager young soldier named Philipp Schlink stood proudly up and said, "Yes, sir, I come from Pasing." He was promptly handed a toothbrush and told to clean the shit house.

When the sergeant asked who had the best penmanship, you can surely understand why no one was keen to step forward. They thought they might be first to receive a full hygiene inspection or scrub an eccentric lieutenant's shit-trampled boots before they left.

"Now come on," Schneider toyed with them. Slapped down with oil, his hair gleamed, though a small piece was always upright and vigilant at the apex of his head. "At least *one* of you useless bastards must be able to write properly."

In the distance, there was gunfire.

It triggered a reaction.

"Look," said Schneider, "this isn't like the others. It will take all morning, maybe longer." He couldn't resist a smile. "Schlink was polishing that shit house while the rest of you were playing cards, but this time, you're going out *there*."

Life or pride.

He was clearly hoping that one of his men would have the intelligence to take life.

Erik Vandenburg and Hans Hubermann glanced at each other. If someone stepped forward now, the platoon would make his life a living hell for the rest of their time together. No one likes a coward. On the other hand, if someone was to be nominated . . .

Still no one stepped forward, but a voice stooped out and ambled toward the sergeant. It sat at his feet, waiting for a good kicking. It said, "Hubermann, sir." The voice belonged to Erik Vandenburg. He obviously thought that today wasn't the appropriate time for his friend to die.

The sergeant paced up and down the passage of soldiers.

"Who said that?"

He was a superb pacer, Stephan Schneider—a small man who spoke, moved, and acted in a hurry. As he strode up and down the two lines, Hans looked on, waiting for the news. Perhaps one of the nurses was sick and they needed someone to strip and replace bandages on the infected limbs of injured soldiers. Perhaps a thousand envelopes were to be licked and sealed and sent home with death notices in them.

At that moment, the voice was put forward again, moving a few others to make themselves heard. "Hubermann," they echoed. Erik even said, "Immaculate handwriting, sir, *immaculate*."

"It's settled, then." There was a circular, small-mouthed grin. "Hubermann. You're it."

The gangly young soldier made his way forward and asked what his duty might be.

The sergeant sighed. "The captain needs a few dozen letters written for him. He's got terrible rheumatism in his fingers. Or arthritis. You'll be writing them for him."

This was no time to argue, especially when Schlink was sent to clean the toilets and the other one, Pflegger, nearly killed himself licking envelopes. His tongue was infection blue.

"Yes, sir." Hans nodded, and that was the end of it. His writing ability was dubious to say the least, but he considered himself lucky. He wrote the letters as best he could while the rest of the men went into battle.

None of them came back.

That was the first time Hans Hubermann escaped me. The Great War.

A second escape was still to come, in 1943, in Essen.

Two wars for two escapes.

Once young, once middle-aged.

Not many men are lucky enough to cheat me twice.

He carried the accordion with him during the entirety of the war.

When he tracked down the family of Erik Vandenburg in Stuttgart upon his return, Vandenburg's wife informed him that he could keep it. Her apartment was littered with them, and it upset her too much to look at that one in particular. The others were reminder enough, as was her once-shared profession of teaching it.

"He taught me to play," Hans informed her, as though it might help.

Perhaps it did, for the devastated woman asked if he could play it for her, and she silently wept as he pressed the buttons and keys of a clumsy "Blue Danube Waltz." It was her husband's favorite.

"You know," Hans explained to her, "he saved my life." The light in the room was small, and the air restrained. "He—if there's anything you ever need." He slid a piece of paper with his name and address on it across the table. "I'm a painter by trade. I'll paint your apartment for free, whenever you like." He knew it was useless compensation, but he offered anyway.

The woman took the paper, and not long after, a small child wandered in and sat on her lap.

"This is Max," the woman said, but the boy was too young and shy to say anything. He was skinny, with soft hair, and his thick, murky eyes watched as the stranger played one more song in the heavy room. From face to face, he looked on as the man played and the woman wept. The different notes handled her eyes. Such sadness.

Hans left.

"You never told me," he said to a dead Erik Vandenburg and the Stuttgart skyline. "You never told me you had a son."

After a momentary, head-shaken stoppage, Hans returned to Munich, expecting never to hear from those people again. What he didn't know was that his help would most definitely be needed, but not for painting, and not for another twenty years or so.

There were a few weeks before he started painting. In the good-weather months, he worked vigorously, and even in winter, he often said to Rosa that business might not be pouring, but it would at least drizzle now and again.

For more than a decade, it all worked.

Hans Junior and Trudy were born. They grew up making visits to their papa at work, slapping paint on walls and cleaning brushes.

When Hitler rose to power in 1933, though, the painting business fell slightly awry. Hans didn't join the NSDAP like the majority of people did. He put a lot of thought into his decision.

* * * THE THOUGHT PROCESS OF * * *
HANS HUBERMANN
He was not well-educated or political, but if
nothing else, he was a man who appreciated
fairness. A Jew had once saved his life and
he couldn't forget that. He couldn't join a
party that antagonized people in such a way.
Also, much like Alex Steiner, some of his
most loyal customers were Jewish. Like many
of the Jews believed, he didn't think the
hatred could last, and it was a conscious
decision not to follow Hitler. On many
levels, it was a disastrous one.

Once the persecution began, his work slowly dried up. It wasn't too bad to begin with, but soon enough, he was losing customers. Handfuls of quotes seemed to vanish into the rising Nazi air.

He approached an old faithful named Herbert Bollinger—a man with a hemispheric waistline who spoke *Hochdeutsch* (he was from Hamburg)—when he saw him on Munich Street. At first, the man looked down, past his girth, to the ground, but when his eyes returned to the painter, the question clearly made him uncomfortable. There was no reason for Hans to ask, but he did.

"What's going on, Herbert? I'm losing customers quicker than I can count."

Bollinger didn't flinch anymore. Standing upright, he delivered the fact as a question of his own. "Well, Hans. Are you a member?"

"Of what?"

But Hans Hubermann knew exactly what the man was talking about.

"Come on, Hansi," Bollinger persisted. "Don't make me spell it out."

The tall painter waved him away and walked on.

As the years passed by, the Jews were being terrorized at random throughout the country, and in the spring of 1937, almost to his shame, Hans Hubermann finally submitted. He made some inquiries and applied to join the Party.

After lodging his form at the Nazi headquarters on Munich Street, he witnessed four men throw several bricks into a clothing store named Kleinmann's. It was one of the few Jewish shops that were still in operation in Molching. Inside, a small man was stuttering about, crushing the broken glass beneath his feet as he cleaned up. A star the color of mustard was smeared to the door. In sloppy lettering, the words JEWISH FILTH were spilling over at their edges. The movement inside tapered from hurried to morose, then stopped altogether.

Hans moved closer and stuck his head inside. "Do you need some help?"

Mr. Kleinmann looked up. A dust broom was fixed powerlessly to his hand. "No, Hans. Please. Go away." Hans had painted Joel Kleinmann's house the previous year. He remembered his three children. He could see their faces but couldn't recall their names.

"I will come tomorrow," he said, "and repaint your door."

Which he did.

It was the second of two mistakes.

The first occurred immediately after the incident.

He returned to where he'd come from and drove his fist onto the door and then the window of the NSDAP. The glass shuddered but no one replied. Everyone had packed up and gone home. A last member was walking in the opposite direction. When he heard the rattle of the glass, he noticed the painter.

He came back and asked what was wrong.

"I can no longer join," Hans stated.

The man was shocked. "Why not?"

Hans looked at the knuckles of his right hand and swallowed. He could already taste the error, like a metal tablet in his mouth. "Forget it." He turned and walked home.

Words followed him.

"You just think about it, Herr Hubermann. Let us know what you decide."

He did not acknowledge them.

The following morning, as promised, he rose earlier than usual, but not early enough. The door at Kleinmann's Clothing was still moist with dew. Hans dried it. He managed to match the color as close as humanly possible and gave it a good solid coat.

Innocuously, a man walked past.

"*Heil* Hitler," he said.

"*Heil* Hitler," Hans replied.

✳ ✳ ✳ THREE SMALL BUT ✳ ✳ ✳
IMPORTANT FACTS
1. The man who walked past was Rolf Fischer, one of

Molching's greatest Nazis.
2. A new slur was painted on the door
within sixteen hours.
3. Hans Hubermann was not granted
membership in the Nazi Party.
Not yet, anyway.

For the next year, Hans was lucky that he didn't revoke his membership application officially. While many people were instantly approved, he was added to a waiting list, regarded with suspicion. Toward the end of 1938, when the Jews were cleared out completely after Kristallnacht, the Gestapo visited. They searched the house, and when nothing or no one suspicious was found, Hans Hubermann was one of the fortunate:

He was allowed to stay.

What probably saved him was that people knew he was at least *waiting* for his application to be approved. For this, he was tolerated, if not endorsed as the competent painter he was.

Then there was his other savior.

It was the accordion that most likely spared him from total ostracism. Painters there were, from all over Munich, but under the brief tutorage of Erik Vandenburg and nearly two decades of his own steady practice, there was no one in Molching who could play exactly like him. It was a style not of perfection, but warmth. Even mistakes had a good feeling about them.

He "*heil* Hitlered" when it was asked of him and he flew the flag on the right days. There was no apparent problem.

Then, on June 16, 1939 (the date was like cement now), just over six months after Liesel's arrival on Himmel Street, an event occurred that altered the life of Hans Hubermann irreversibly.

It was a day in which he had some work.

He left the house at 7 a.m. sharp.

He towed his paint cart behind him, oblivious to the fact that he was being followed.

When he arrived at the work site, a young stranger walked up to him. He was blond and tall, and serious.

The pair watched each other.

"Would you be Hans Hubermann?"

Hans gave him a single nod. He was reaching for a paintbrush. "Yes, I would."

"Do you play the accordion, by any chance?"

This time, Hans stopped, leaving the brush where it was. Again, he nodded.

The stranger rubbed his jaw, looked around him, and then spoke with great quietness, yet great clarity. "Are you a man who likes to keep a promise?"

Hans took out two paint cans and invited him to sit down. Before he accepted the invitation, the young man extended his hand and introduced himself. "My name's Kugler. Walter. I come from Stuttgart."

They sat and talked quietly for fifteen minutes or so, arranging a meeting for later on, in the night.

A GOOD GIRL

In November 1940, when Max Vandenburg arrived in the kitchen of 33 Himmel Street, he was twenty-four years old. His clothes seemed to weigh him down, and his tiredness was such that an itch could break him in two. He stood shaking and shaken in the doorway.

"Do you still play the accordion?"

Of course, the question was really, "Will you still help me?"

Liesel's papa walked to the front door and opened it. Cautiously, he looked outside, each way, and returned. The verdict was "nothing."

Max Vandenburg, the Jew, closed his eyes and drooped a little further into safety. The very idea of it was ludicrous, but he accepted it nonetheless.

Hans checked that the curtains were properly closed. Not a crack could be showing. As he did so, Max could no longer bear it. He crouched down and clasped his hands.

The darkness stroked him.

His fingers smelled of suitcase, metal, *Mein Kampf,* and survival.

It was only when he lifted his head that the dim light from the hallway reached his eyes. He noticed the pajamaed girl, standing there, in full view.

"Papa?"

Max stood up, like a struck match. The darkness swelled now, around him.

"Everything's fine, Liesel," Papa said. "Go back to bed."

She lingered a moment before her feet dragged from behind. When she stopped and stole one last look at the foreigner in the kitchen, she could decipher the outline of a book on the table.

"Don't be afraid," she heard Papa whisper. "She's a good girl."

For the next hour, the good girl lay wide awake in bed, listening to the quiet fumbling of sentences in the kitchen.

One wild card was yet to be played.

A SHORT HISTORY OF
THE JEWISH FIST FIGHTER

Max Vandenburg was born in 1916.

He grew up in Stuttgart.

When he was younger, he grew to love nothing more than a good fistfight.

He had his first bout when he was eleven years old and skinny as a whittled broom handle.

Wenzel Gruber.

That's who he fought.

He had a smart mouth, that Gruber kid, and wire-curly hair. The local playground demanded that they fight, and neither boy was about to argue.

They fought like champions.

For a minute.

Just when it was getting interesting, both boys were hauled away by their collars. A watchful parent.

A trickle of blood was dripping from Max's mouth.

He tasted it, and it tasted good.

• • •

Not many people who came from his neighborhood were fighters, and if they were, they didn't do it with their fists. In those days, they said the Jews preferred to simply stand and take things. Take the abuse quietly and then work their way back to the top. Obviously, every Jew is not the same.

He was nearly two years old when his father died, shot to pieces on a grassy hill.

When he was nine, his mother was completely broke. She sold the music studio that doubled as their apartment and they moved to his uncle's house. There he grew up with six cousins who battered, annoyed, and loved him. Fighting with the oldest one, Isaac, was the training ground for his fist fighting. He was trounced almost every night.

At thirteen, tragedy struck again when his uncle died.

As percentages would suggest, his uncle was not a hothead like Max. He was the type of person who worked quietly away for very little reward. He kept to himself and sacrificed everything for his family—and he died of something growing in his stomach. Something akin to a poison bowling ball.

As is often the case, the family surrounded the bed and watched him capitulate.

Somehow, between the sadness and loss, Max Vandenburg, who was now a teenager with hard hands, blackened eyes, and a sore tooth, was also a little disappointed. Even disgruntled. As he watched his uncle sink slowly into the bed, he decided that he would never allow himself to die like that.

The man's face was so accepting.

So yellow and tranquil, despite the violent architecture of his skull—the endless jawline, stretching for miles; the pop-up cheekbones; and the pothole eyes. So calm it made the boy want to ask something.

Where's the fight? he wondered.

Where's the will to hold on?

Of course, at thirteen, he was a little excessive in his harshness. He had not looked something like *me* in the face. Not yet.

With the rest of them, he stood around the bed and watched the man die—a safe merge, from life to death. The light in the window was gray and orange, the color of summer's skin, and his uncle appeared relieved when his breathing disappeared completely.

"When death captures me," the boy vowed, "he will feel my fist on his face."

Personally, I quite like that. Such stupid gallantry.

Yes.

I like that a lot.

From that moment on, he started to fight with greater regularity. A group of die-hard friends and enemies would gather down at a small reserve on Steber Street, and they would fight in the dying light. Archetypal Germans, the odd Jew, the boys from the east. It didn't matter. There was nothing like a good fight to expel the teenage energy. Even the enemies were an inch away from friendship.

He enjoyed the tight circles and the unknown.

The bittersweetness of uncertainty:

To win or to lose.

It was a feeling in the stomach that would be stirred around until he thought he could no longer tolerate it. The only remedy was to move forward and throw punches. Max was not the type of boy to die thinking about it.

• • •

His favorite fight, now that he looked back, was Fight Number Five against a tall, tough, rangy kid named Walter Kugler. They were fifteen. Walter had won all four of their previous encounters, but this time, Max could feel something different. There was new blood in him—the blood of victory—and it had the capability to both frighten and excite.

As always, there was a tight circle crowded around them. There was grubby ground. There were smiles practically wrapped around the onlooking faces. Money was clutched in filthy fingers, and the calls and cries were filled with such vitality that there was nothing else but this.

God, there was such joy and fear there, such brilliant commotion.

The two fighters were clenched with the intensity of the moment, their faces loaded up with expression, exaggerated with the stress of it. The wide-eyed concentration.

After a minute or so of testing each other out, they began moving closer and taking more risks. It was a street fight after all, not an hour-long title fight. They didn't have all day.

"Come on, Max!" one of his friends was calling out. There was no breath between any of the words. "Come on, Maxi Taxi, you've got him now, you've got him, Jew boy, you've got him, you've got him!"

A small kid with soft tufts of hair, a beaten nose, and swampy eyes, Max was a good head shorter than his opposition. His fighting style was utterly graceless, all bent over, nudging forward, throwing fast punches at the face of Kugler. The other boy, clearly stronger and more skillful, remained upright, throwing jabs that constantly landed on Max's cheeks and chin.

Max kept coming.

Even with the heavy absorption of punches and punishment, he continued moving forward. Blood discolored his lips. It would soon be dried across his teeth.

There was a great roar when he was knocked down. Money was almost exchanged.

Max stood up.

He was beaten down one more time before he changed tactics, luring Walter Kugler a little closer than he'd wanted to come. Once he was there, Max was able to apply a short, sharp jab to his face. It stuck. Exactly on the nose.

Kugler, suddenly blinded, shuffled back, and Max seized his chance. He followed him over to the right and jabbed him once more and opened him up with a punch that reached into his ribs. The right hand that ended him landed on his chin. Walter Kugler was on the ground, his blond hair peppered with dirt. His legs were parted in a V. Tears like crystal floated down his skin, despite the fact that he was not crying. The tears had been bashed out of him.

The circle counted.

They always counted, just in case. Voices and numbers.

The custom after a fight was that the loser would raise the hand of the victor. When Kugler finally stood up, he walked sullenly to Max Vandenburg and lifted his arm into the air.

"Thanks," Max told him.

Kugler proffered a warning. "Next time I kill you."

Altogether, over the next few years, Max Vandenburg and Walter Kugler fought thirteen times. Walter was always seeking revenge for that first victory Max took from him, and Max was looking to emulate his moment of glory. In the end, the record stood at 10–3 for Walter.

They fought each other until 1933, when they were seventeen. Grudging respect turned to genuine friendship, and the urge to fight left them. Both held jobs until Max was sacked with the rest of the Jews at the Jedermann Engineering Factory in '35. That wasn't long after the Nuremberg Laws came in, forbidding Jews to have German citizenship and for Germans and Jews to intermarry.

"Jesus," Walter said one evening, when they met on the small corner where they used to fight. "That was a time, wasn't it? There was none of this around." He gave the star on Max's sleeve a back-handed slap. "We could never fight like that now."

Max disagreed. "Yes we could. You can't marry a Jew, but there's no law against fighting one."

Walter smiled. "There's probably a law *rewarding* it—as long as you win."

For the next few years, they saw each other sporadically at best. Max, with the rest of the Jews, was steadily rejected and repeatedly trodden upon, while Walter disappeared inside his job. A printing firm.

If you're the type who's interested, yes, there were a few girls in those years. One named Tania, the other Hildi. Neither of them lasted. There was no time, most likely due to the uncertainty and mounting pressure. Max needed to scavenge for work. What could he offer those girls? By 1938, it was difficult to imagine that life could get any harder.

Then came November 9. Kristallnacht. The night of broken glass.

It was the very incident that destroyed so many of his fellow Jews, but it proved to be Max Vandenburg's moment of escape. He was twenty-two.

Many Jewish establishments were being surgically smashed and looted when there was a clatter of knuckles on the apartment door. With his aunt, his mother, his cousins, and their children, Max was crammed into the living room.

"*Aufmachen!*"

The family watched each other. There was a great temptation to scatter into the other rooms, but apprehension is the strangest thing. They couldn't move.

Again. "Open up!"

Isaac stood and walked to the door. The wood was alive, still humming from the beating it had just been given. He looked back at the faces naked with fear, turned the lock, and opened the door.

As expected, it was a Nazi. In uniform.

"Never."

That was Max's first response.

He clung to his mother's hand and that of Sarah, the nearest of his cousins. "I won't leave. If we all can't go, I don't go, either."

He was lying.

When he was pushed out by the rest of his family, the relief struggled inside him like an obscenity. It was something he didn't want to feel, but nonetheless, he felt it with such gusto it made him want to throw up. How could he? How could he?

But he did.

"Bring nothing," Walter told him. "Just what you're wearing. I'll give you the rest."

"Max." It was his mother.

From a drawer, she took an old piece of paper and stuffed it in his jacket pocket. "If ever . . ." She held him one last time, by the elbows. "This could be your last hope."

He looked into her aging face and kissed her, very hard, on the lips.

"Come on." Walter pulled at him as the rest of the family said their goodbyes and gave him money and a few valuables. "It's chaos out there, and chaos is what we need."

They left, without looking back.

It tortured him.

If only he'd turned for one last look at his family as he left the apartment. Perhaps then the guilt would not have been so heavy. No final goodbye.

No final grip of the eyes.

Nothing but goneness.

For the next two years, he remained in hiding, in an empty store-room. It was in a building where Walter had worked in previous years. There was very little food. There was plenty of suspicion. The remaining Jews with money in the neighborhood were emigrating. The Jews without money were also trying, but without much success. Max's family fell into the latter category. Walter checked on them occasionally, as inconspicuously as he could. One afternoon, when he visited, someone else opened the door.

When Max heard the news, his body felt like it was being screwed up into a ball, like a page littered with mistakes. Like garbage.

Yet each day, he managed to unravel and straighten himself, disgusted and thankful. Wrecked, but somehow not torn into pieces.

Halfway through 1939, just over six months into the period of hiding, they decided that a new course of action needed to be taken. They examined the piece of paper Max was handed upon his desertion. That's right—his desertion, not only his escape. That was how he viewed it, amid the grotesquerie of his relief. We already know what was written on that piece of paper:

✳ ✳ ✳ ONE NAME, ONE ADDRESS ✳ ✳ ✳
Hans Hubermann
Himmel Street 33, Molching

"It's getting worse," Walter told Max. "Anytime now, they could find us out." There was much hunching in the dark. "We don't know what might happen. I might get caught. You might need to find that place. . . . I'm too scared to ask anyone for help here. They might put me in." There was only one solution. "I'll go down there and find this man. If he's turned into a Nazi—which is very likely—I'll just turn around. At least we know then, *richtig*?"

Max gave him every last pfennig to make the trip, and a few days later, when Walter returned, they embraced before he held his breath. "And?"

Walter nodded. "He's good. He still plays that accordion your mother told you about—your father's. He's not a member of the party. He gave me money." At this stage, Hans Hubermann was only a list. "He's fairly poor, he's married, and there's a kid."

This sparked Max's attention even further. "How old?"

"Ten. You can't have everything."

"Yes. Kids have big mouths."

"We're lucky as it is."

They sat in silence awhile. It was Max who disturbed it.

"He must already hate me, huh?"

"I don't think so. He gave me the money, didn't he? He said a promise is a promise."

A week later, a letter came. Hans notified Walter Kugler that he would try to send things to help whenever he could. There was a one-page map of Molching and Greater Munich, as well as a direct route from Pasing (the more reliable train station) to his front door. In his letter, the last words were obvious.

Be careful.

Midway through May 1940, *Mein Kampf* arrived, with a key taped to the inside cover.

The man's a genius, Max decided, but there was still a shudder

195

when he thought about traveling to Munich. Clearly, he wished, along with the other parties involved, that the journey would not have to be made at all.

You don't always get what you wish for.

Especially in Nazi Germany.

Again, time passed.

The war expanded.

Max remained hidden from the world in another empty room.

Until the inevitable.

Walter was notified that he was being sent to Poland, to continue the assertion of Germany's authority over both the Poles and Jews alike. One was not much better than the other. The time had come.

Max made his way to Munich and Molching, and now he sat in a stranger's kitchen, asking for the help he craved and suffering the condemnation he felt he deserved.

Hans Hubermann shook his hand and introduced himself.

He made him some coffee in the dark.

The girl had been gone quite a while, but now some more footsteps had approached arrival. The wildcard.

In the darkness, all three of them were completely isolated. They all stared. Only the woman spoke.

THE WRATH OF ROSA

Liesel had drifted back to sleep when the unmistakable voice of Rosa Hubermann entered the kitchen. It shocked her awake.

"Was ist los?"

Curiosity got the better of her then, as she imagined a tirade thrown down from the wrath of Rosa. There was definite movement and the shuffle of a chair.

After ten minutes of excruciating discipline, Liesel made her way to the corridor, and what she saw truly amazed her, because Rosa Hubermann was at Max Vandenburg's shoulder, watching him gulp down her infamous pea soup. Candlelight was standing at the table. It did not waver.

Mama was grave.

Her plump figure glowed with worry.

Somehow, though, there was also a look of triumph on her face, and it was not the triumph of having saved another human being from persecution. It was something more along the lines of, See? At least *he's* not complaining. She looked from the soup to the Jew to the soup.

When she spoke again, she asked only if he wanted more.

Max declined, preferring instead to rush to the sink and vomit. His back convulsed and his arms were well spread. His fingers gripped the metal.

"Jesus, Mary, and Joseph," Rosa muttered. "Another one."

Turning around, Max apologized. His words were slippery and small, quelled by the acid. "I'm sorry. I think I ate too much. My stomach, you know, it's been so long since . . . I don't think it can handle such—"

"Move," Rosa ordered him. She started cleaning up.

When she was finished, she found the young man at the kitchen table, utterly morose. Hans was sitting opposite, his hands cupped above the sheet of wood.

Liesel, from the hallway, could see the drawn face of the stranger, and behind it, the worried expression scribbled like a mess onto Mama.

She looked at both her foster parents.

Who were these people?

LIESEL'S LECTURE

Exactly what kind of people Hans and Rosa Hubermann were was not the easiest problem to solve. Kind people? Ridiculously ignorant people? People of questionable sanity?

What was easier to define was their predicament.

* * * THE SITUATION OF HANS AND * * *
ROSA HUBERMANN
Very sticky indeed.
In fact, *frightfully* sticky.

When a Jew shows up at your place of residence in the early hours of morning, in the very birthplace of Nazism, you're likely to experience extreme levels of discomfort. Anxiety, disbelief, paranoia. Each plays its part, and each leads to a sneaking suspicion that a less than heavenly consequence awaits. The fear is shiny. Ruthless in the eyes.

The surprising point to make is that despite this iridescent fear glowing as it did in the dark, they somehow resisted the urge for hysteria.

Mama ordered Liesel away.

"Bett, Saumensch." The voice calm but firm. Highly unusual.

Papa came in a few minutes later and lifted the covers on the vacant bed.

"*Alles gut,* Liesel? Is everything good?"

"Yes, Papa."

"As you can see, we have a visitor." She could only just make out the shape of Hans Hubermann's tallness in the dark. "He'll sleep in here tonight."

"Yes, Papa."

A few minutes later, Max Vandenburg was in the room, noiseless and opaque. The man did not breathe. He did not move. Yet, somehow, he traveled from the doorway to the bed and was under the covers.

"Everything good?"

It was Papa again, talking this time to Max.

The reply floated from his mouth, then molded itself like a stain to the ceiling. Such was his feeling of shame. "Yes. Thank you." He said it again, when Papa made his way over to his customary position in the chair next to Liesel's bed. "Thank you."

Another hour passed before Liesel fell asleep.

She slept hard and long.

A hand woke her just after eight-thirty the next morning.

The voice at the end of it informed her that she would not be attending school that day. Apparently, she was sick.

When she awoke completely, she watched the stranger in the bed opposite. The blanket showed only a nest of lopsided hair at the top, and there was not a sound, as if he'd somehow trained himself even to sleep more quietly. With great care, she walked the length of him, following Papa to the hall.

For the first time ever, the kitchen and Mama were dormant. It was a kind of bemused, inaugural silence. To Liesel's relief, it lasted only a few minutes.

There was food and the sound of eating.

Mama announced the day's priority. She sat at the table and said, "Now listen, Liesel. Papa's going to tell you something today." This was serious—she didn't even say *Saumensch*. It was a personal feat of abstinence. "He'll talk to you and you have to listen. Is that clear?"

The girl was still swallowing.

"Is that clear, *Saumensch?*"

That was better.

The girl nodded.

When she reentered the bedroom to fetch her clothes, the body in the opposite bed had turned and curled up. It was no longer a straight log but a kind of Z shape, reaching diagonally from corner to corner. Zigzagging the bed.

She could see his face now, in the tired light. His mouth was open and his skin was the color of eggshells. Whiskers coated his jaw and chin, and his ears were hard and flat. He had a small but misshapen nose.

"Liesel!"

She turned.

"Move it!"

She moved, to the washroom.

Once changed and in the hallway, she realized she would not be traveling far. Papa was standing in front of the door to the basement. He smiled very faintly, lit the lamp, and led her down.

Among the mounds of drop sheets and the smell of paint, Papa told her to make herself comfortable. Ignited on the walls were the painted words, learned in the past. "I need to tell you some things."

Liesel sat on top of a meter-tall heap of drop sheets, Papa on a fifteen-liter paint can. For a few minutes, he searched for the words. When they came, he stood to deliver them. He rubbed his eyes.

"Liesel," he said quietly, "I was never sure if any of this would happen, so I never told you. About me. About the man upstairs." He walked from one end of the basement to the other, the lamplight magnifying his shadow. It turned him into a giant on the wall, walking back and forth.

When he stopped pacing, his shadow loomed behind him, watching. Someone was always watching.

"You know my accordion?" he said, and there the story began.

He explained World War I and Erik Vandenburg, and then the visit to the fallen soldier's wife. "The boy who came into the room that day is the man upstairs. *Verstehst?* Understand?"

The book thief sat and listened to Hans Hubermann's story. It lasted a good hour, until the moment of truth, which involved a very obvious and necessary lecture.

"Liesel, you must listen." Papa made her stand up and held her hand.

They faced the wall.

Dark shapes and the practice of words.

Firmly, he held her fingers.

"Remember the *Führer*'s birthday—when we walked home from the fire that night? Remember what you promised me?"

The girl concurred. To the wall, she said, "That I would keep a secret."

"That's right." Between the hand-holding shadows, the painted words were scattered about, perched on their shoulders, resting on their heads, and hanging from their arms. "Liesel, if you tell anyone about the man up there, we will all be in big trouble." He walked the fine line of scaring her into oblivion and soothing her enough to keep her calm. He fed her the sentences and watched with his metallic eyes. Desperation and placidity. "At the very least, Mama and I will be taken away." Hans was clearly worried that he was on the verge of frightening her too much, but he calculated the risk, preferring to err on the side of too much fear rather than not enough. The girl's compliance had to be an absolute, immutable fact.

Toward the end, Hans Hubermann looked at Liesel Meminger and made certain she was focused.

He gave her a list of consequences.

"If you tell anyone about that man . . ."

Her teacher.

Rudy.

It didn't matter whom.

What mattered was that all were punishable.

"For starters," he said, "I will take each and every one of your books—and I will burn them." It was callous. "I'll throw them in the stove or the fireplace." He was certainly acting like a tyrant, but it was necessary. "Understand?"

The shock made a hole in her, very neat, very precise.

Tears welled.

"Yes, Papa."

"Next." He had to remain hard, and he needed to strain for it. "They'll take you away from me. Do you want that?"

She was crying now, in earnest. *"Nein."*

"Good." His grip on her hand tightened. "They'll drag that man up there away, and maybe Mama and me, too—and we will never, ever come back."

And that did it.

The girl began to sob so uncontrollably that Papa was dying to pull her into him and hug her tight. He didn't. Instead, he squatted down and watched her directly in the eyes. He unleashed his quietest words so far. *"Verstehst du mich?"* Do you understand me?"

The girl nodded. She cried, and now, defeated, broken, her papa held her in the painted air and the kerosene light.

"I understand, Papa, I do."

Her voice was muffled against his body, and they stayed like that for a few minutes, Liesel with squashed breath and Papa rubbing her back.

Upstairs, when they returned, they found Mama sitting in the kitchen, alone and pensive. When she saw them, she stood and beckoned Liesel to come over, noticing the dried-up tears that streaked her. She brought the girl into her and heaped a typically rugged embrace around her body. *"Alles gut, Saumensch?"*

She didn't need an answer.

Everything was good.

But it was awful, too.

THE SLEEPER

Max Vandenburg slept for three days.

In certain excerpts of that sleep, Liesel watched him. You might say that by the third day it became an obsession, to check on him, to see if he was still breathing. She could now interpret his signs of life, from the movement of his lips, his gathering beard, and the twigs of hair that moved ever so slightly when his head twitched in the dream state.

Often, when she stood over him, there was the mortifying thought that he had just woken up, his eyes splitting open to view her—to watch her watching. The idea of being caught out plagued and enthused her at the same time. She dreaded it. She invited it. Only when Mama called out to her could she drag herself away, simultaneously soothed and disappointed that she might not be there when he woke.

Sometimes, close to the end of the marathon of sleep, he spoke.

There was a recital of murmured names. A checklist.

Isaac. Aunt Ruth. Sarah. Mama. Walter. Hitler.

Family, friend, enemy.

They were all under the covers with him, and at one point, he appeared to be struggling with himself. *"Nein,"* he whispered. It was repeated seven times. "No."

Liesel, in the act of watching, was already noticing the similarities between this stranger and herself. They both arrived in a state of agitation on Himmel Street. They both nightmared.

When the time came, he awoke with the nasty thrill of disorientation. His mouth opened a moment after his eyes and he sat up, right-angled.

"Ay!"

A patch of voice escaped his mouth.

When he saw the upside-down face of a girl above him, there was the fretful moment of unfamiliarity and the grasp for recollection—to decode exactly where and when he was currently sitting. After a few seconds, he managed to scratch his head (the rustle of kindling) and he looked at her. His movements were fragmented, and now that they were open, his eyes were swampy and brown. Thick and heavy.

As a reflex action, Liesel backed away.

She was too slow.

The stranger reached out, his bed-warmed hand taking her by the forearm.

"Please."

His voice also held on, as if possessing fingernails. He pressed it into her flesh.

"Papa!" Loud.

"Please!" Soft.

It was late afternoon, gray and gleaming, but it was only dirty-colored light that was permitted entrance into the room. It was all the fabric of the curtains allowed. If you're optimistic, think of it as bronze.

When Papa came in, he first stood in the doorway and witnessed Max Vandenburg's gripping fingers and his desperate face. Both held on to Liesel's arm. "I see you two have met," he said.

Max's fingers started cooling.

THE SWAPPING OF NIGHTMARES

Max Vandenburg promised that he would never sleep in Liesel's room again. What was he thinking that first night? The very idea of it mortified him.

He rationalized that he was so bewildered upon his arrival that he allowed such a thing. The basement was the only place for him as far as he was concerned. Forget the cold and the loneliness. He was a Jew, and if there was one place he was destined to exist, it was a basement or any other such hidden venue of survival.

"I'm sorry," he confessed to Hans and Rosa on the basement steps. "From now on I will stay down here. You will not hear from me. I will not make a sound."

Hans and Rosa, both steeped in the despair of the predicament, made no argument, not even in regard to the cold. They heaved blankets down and topped up the kerosene lamp. Rosa admitted that there could not be much food, to which Max fervently asked her to bring only scraps, and only when they were not wanted by anyone else.

"Na, na," Rosa assured him. "You will be fed, as best I can."

They also took the mattress down, from the spare bed in Liesel's room, replacing it with drop sheets—an excellent trade.

• • •

Downstairs, Hans and Max placed the mattress beneath the steps and built a wall of drop sheets at the side. The sheets were high enough to cover the whole triangular entrance, and if nothing else, they were easily moved if Max was in dire need of extra air.

Papa apologized. "It's quite pathetic. I realize that."

"Better than nothing," Max assured him. "Better than I deserve—thank you."

With some well-positioned paint cans, Hans actually conceded that it did simply look like a collection of junk gathered sloppily in the corner, out of the way. The one problem was that a person needed only to shift a few cans and remove a drop sheet or two to smell out the Jew.

"Let's just hope it's good enough," he said.

"It has to be." Max crawled in. Again, he said it. "Thank you."

Thank you.

For Max Vandenburg, those were the two most pitiful words he could possibly say, rivaled only by *I'm sorry.* There was a constant urge to speak both expressions, spurred on by the affliction of guilt.

How many times in those first few hours of awakeness did he feel like walking out of that basement and leaving the house altogether? It must have been hundreds.

Each time, though, it was only a twinge.

Which made it even worse.

He wanted to walk out—Lord, how he wanted to (or at least he *wanted* to want to)—but he knew he wouldn't. It was much the same as the way he left his family in Stuttgart, under a veil of fabricated loyalty.

To live.

Living was living.

The price was guilt and shame.

. . .

For his first few days in the basement, Liesel had nothing to do with him. She denied his existence. His rustling hair, his cold, slippery fingers.

His tortured presence.

Mama and Papa.

There was such gravity between them, and a lot of failed decision-making.

They considered whether they could move him.

"But where?"

No reply.

In this situation, they were friendless and paralyzed. There was nowhere else for Max Vandenburg to go. It was them. Hans and Rosa Hubermann. Liesel had never seen them look at each other so much, or with such solemnity.

It was they who took the food down and organized an empty paint can for Max's excrement. The contents would be disposed of by Hans as prudently as possible. Rosa also took him some buckets of hot water to wash himself. The Jew was filthy.

Outside, a mountain of cold November air was waiting at the front door each time Liesel left the house.

Drizzle came down in spades.

Dead leaves were slumped on the road.

Soon enough, it was the book thief's turn to visit the basement. They made her.

She walked tentatively down the steps, knowing that no words were required. The scuffing of her feet was enough to rouse him.

In the middle of the basement, she stood and waited, feeling more like she was standing in the center of a great dusky field. The sun was setting behind a crop of harvested drop sheets.

When Max came out, he was holding *Mein Kampf*. Upon his arrival, he'd offered it back to Hans Hubermann but was told he could keep it.

Naturally, Liesel, while holding the dinner, couldn't take her eyes off it. It was a book she had seen a few times at the BDM, but it hadn't been read or used directly in their activities. There were occasional references to its greatness, as well as promises that the opportunity to study it would come in later years, as they progressed into the more senior Hitler Youth division.

Max, following her attention, also examined the book.

"Is?" she whispered.

There was a queer strand in her voice, planed off and curly in her mouth.

The Jew moved only his head a little closer. "*Bitte?* Excuse me?"

She handed him the pea soup and returned upstairs, red, rushed, and foolish.

"Is it a good book?"

She practiced what she'd wanted to say in the washroom, in the small mirror. The smell of urine was still about her, as Max had just used the paint can before she'd come down. *So ein G'schtank,* she thought. What a stink.

No one's urine smells as good as your own.

The days hobbled on.

Each night, before the descent into sleep, she would hear Mama and Papa in the kitchen, discussing what had been done, what they were doing now, and what needed to happen next. All the while, an image of Max hovered next to her. It was always the injured, thankful expression on his face and the swamp-filled eyes.

Only once was there an outburst in the kitchen.

Papa.

"I know!"

His voice was abrasive, but he brought it back to a muffled whisper in a hurry.

"I have to keep going, though, at least a few times a week. I can't be here all the time. We need the money, and if I quit playing there, they'll get suspicious. They might wonder why I've stopped. I told them you were sick last week, but now we have to do everything like we always have."

Therein lay the problem.

Life had altered in the wildest possible way, but it was imperative that they act as if nothing at all had happened.

Imagine smiling after a slap in the face. Then think of doing it twenty-four hours a day.

That was the business of hiding a Jew.

As days turned into weeks, there was now, if nothing else, a beleaguered acceptance of what had transpired—all the result of war, a promise keeper, and one piano accordion. Also, in the space of just over half a year, the Hubermanns had lost a son and gained a replacement of epically dangerous proportions.

What shocked Liesel most was the change in her mama. Whether it was the calculated way in which she divided the food, or the considerable muzzling of her notorious mouth, or even the gentler expression on her cardboard face, one thing was becoming clear.

* * * AN ATTRIBUTE OF ROSA HUBERMANN * * *
She was a good woman for a crisis.

Even when the arthritic Helena Schmidt canceled the washing and ironing service, a month after Max's debut on Himmel Street, she simply sat at the table and brought the bowl toward her. "Good soup tonight."

The soup was terrible.

Every morning when Liesel left for school, or on the days she ventured out to play soccer or complete what was left of the washing round, Rosa would speak quietly to the girl. "And remember, Liesel . . ." She would point to her mouth and that was all. When Liesel nodded, she would say, "Good girl, *Saumensch*. Now get going."

True to Papa's words, and even Mama's now, she was a good girl. She kept her mouth shut everywhere she went. The secret was buried deep.

She town-walked with Rudy as she always did, listening to his jabbering. Sometimes they compared notes from their Hitler Youth divisions, Rudy mentioning for the first time a sadistic young leader named Franz Deutscher. If Rudy wasn't talking about Deutscher's intense ways, he was playing his usual broken record, providing renditions and re-creations of the last goal he scored in the Himmel Street soccer stadium.

"I *know*," Liesel would assure him. "I was *there*."

"So what?"

"So I saw it, *Saukerl*."

"How do I know that? For all I know, you were probably on the ground somewhere, licking up the mud I left behind when I scored."

Perhaps it was Rudy who kept her sane, with the stupidity of his talk, his lemon-soaked hair, and his cockiness.

He seemed to resonate with a kind of confidence that life was still nothing but a joke—an endless succession of soccer goals, trickery, and a constant repertoire of meaningless chatter.

Also, there was the mayor's wife, and reading in her husband's library. It was cold in there now, colder with every visit, but still Liesel could not stay away. She would choose a handful of books and read small segments of each, until one afternoon, she found one she could not put down. It was called *The Whistler*. She was originally drawn to it because of her sporadic sightings of the whistler of Himmel Street— Pfiffikus. There was the memory of him bent over in his coat and his appearance at the bonfire on the *Führer*'s birthday.

The first event in the book was a murder. A stabbing. A Vienna street. Not far from the Stephansdom—the cathedral in the main square.

* * * A SMALL EXCERPT FROM * * *
THE WHISTLER
She lay there, frightened, in a pool of
blood, a strange tune singing in her
ear. She recalled the knife, in and
out, and a smile. As always, the
whistler had smiled as he ran away,
into a dark and murderous night. . . .

Liesel was unsure whether it was the words or the open window that caused her to tremble. Every time she picked up or delivered from the mayor's house, she read three pages and shivered, but she could not last forever.

Similarly, Max Vandenburg could not withstand the basement much longer. He didn't complain—he had no right—but he could slowly feel himself deteriorating in the cold. As it turned out, his rescue owed itself to some reading and writing, and a book called *The Shoulder Shrug*.

"Liesel," said Hans one night. "Come on."

Since Max's arrival, there had been a considerable hiatus in the reading practice of Liesel and her papa. He clearly felt that now was a good time to resume. *"Na, komm,"* he told her. "I don't want you slacking off. Go and get one of your books. How about *The Shoulder Shrug?"*

The disturbing element in all of this was that when she came back, book in hand, Papa was motioning that she should follow him down to their old workroom. The basement.

"But, Papa," she tried to tell him. "We can't—"

"What? Is there a monster down there?"

It was early December and the day had been icy. The basement became unfriendlier with each concrete step.

"It's too cold, Papa."

"That never bothered you before."

"Yes, but it was never *this* cold. . . ."

When they made their way down, Papa whispered to Max, "Can we borrow the lamplight, please?"

With trepidation, the sheets and cans moved and the light was passed out, exchanging hands. Looking at the flame, Hans shook his head and followed it with some words. *"Es ist ja Wahnsinn, net?* This is crazy, no?" Before the hand from within could reposition the sheets, he caught it. "Bring yourself, too. Please, Max."

Slowly then, the drop sheets were dragged aside and the emaciated body and face of Max Vandenburg appeared. In the moist light, he stood with a magic discomfort. He shivered.

Hans touched his arm, to bring him closer.

"Jesus, Mary, and Joseph. You cannot stay down here. You'll freeze to death." He turned. "Liesel, fill up the tub. Not too hot. Make it just like it is when it starts cooling down."

Liesel ran up.

"Jesus, Mary, and Joseph."

She heard it again when she reached the hallway.

When he was in the pint-sized bath, Liesel listened at the washroom door, imagining the tepid water turning to steam as it warmed his iceberg body. Mama and Papa were at the climax of debate in the combined bedroom and living room, their quiet voices trapped inside the corridor wall.

"He'll die down there, I promise you."

"But what if someone sees in?"

"No, no, he only comes up at night. In the day, we leave everything open. Nothing to hide. And we use this room rather than the kitchen. Best to keep away from the front door."

Silence.

Then Mama. "All right . . . Yes, you're right."

"If we gamble on a Jew," said Papa soon after, "I would prefer to gamble on a live one," and from that moment, a new routine was born.

Each night, the fire was lit in Mama and Papa's room, and Max would silently appear. He would sit in the corner, cramped and perplexed, most likely by the kindness of the people, the torment of survival, and overriding all of it, the brilliance of the warmth.

With the curtains clamped tight, he would sleep on the floor with a cushion beneath his head, as the fire slipped away and turned to ash.

In the morning, he would return to the basement.

A voiceless human.

The Jewish rat, back to his hole.

Christmas came and went with the smell of extra danger. As expected, Hans Junior did not come home (both a blessing and an ominous disappointment), but Trudy arrived as usual, and fortunately, things went smoothly.

* * * THE QUALITIES OF SMOOTHNESS * * *
Max remained in the basement.
Trudy came and went without
any suspicion.

215

It was decided that Trudy, despite her mild demeanor, could not be trusted.

"We trust only the people we have to," Papa stated, "and that is the three of us."

There was extra food and the apology to Max that this was not his religion, but a ritual nonetheless.

He didn't complain.

What grounds did he have?

He explained that he was a Jew in upbringing, in blood, but also that Jewry was now more than ever a label—a ruinous piece of the dumbest luck around.

It was then that he also took the opportunity to say he was sorry that the Hubermanns' son had not come home. In response, Papa told him that such things were out of their control. "After all," he said, "you should know it yourself—a young man is still a boy, and a boy sometimes has the right to be stubborn."

They left it at that.

For the first few weeks in front of the fire, Max remained wordless. Now that he was having a proper bath once a week, Liesel noticed that his hair was no longer a nest of twigs, but rather a collection of feathers, flopping about on his head. Still shy of the stranger, she whispered it to her papa.

"His hair is like feathers."

"What?" The fire had distorted the words.

"I said," she whispered again, leaning closer, "his hair is like feathers. . . ."

Hans Hubermann looked across and nodded his agreement. I'm sure he was wishing to have eyes like the girl. They didn't realize that Max had heard everything.

Occasionally he brought the copy of *Mein Kampf* and read it next to the flames, seething at the content. The third time he brought it, Liesel finally found the courage to ask her question.

"Is it—good?"

He looked up from the pages, forming his fingers into a fist and then flattening them back out. Sweeping away the anger, he smiled at her. He lifted the feathery fringe and dumped it toward his eyes. "It's the best book ever." Looking at Papa, then back at the girl. "It saved my life."

The girl moved a little and crossed her legs. Quietly, she asked it. "How?"

So began a kind of storytelling phase in the living room each night. It was spoken just loud enough to hear. The pieces of a Jewish fist-fighting puzzle were assembled before them all.

Sometimes there was humor in Max Vandenburg's voice, though its physicality was like friction—like a stone being gently rubbed across a large rock. It was deep in places and scratched apart in others, sometimes breaking off altogether. It was deepest in regret, and broken off at the end of a joke or a statement of self-deprecation.

"Crucified Christ" was the most common reaction to Max Vandenburg's stories, usually followed by a question.

* * * QUESTIONS LIKE * * *
How long did you stay in that room?
Where is Walter Kugler now?
Do you know what happened to your family?
Where was the snorer traveling to?
A 10–3 losing record!
Why would you keep fighting him?

When Liesel looked back on the events of her life, those nights in the living room were some of the clearest memories she had. She could see the burning light on Max's eggshell face and even taste the human flavor of his words. The course of his survival was related, piece by piece, as if he were cutting each part out of him and presenting it on a plate.

"I'm so selfish."

When he said that, he used his forearm to shield his face. "Leaving people behind. Coming here. Putting all of you in danger . . ." He dropped everything out of him and started pleading with them. Sorrow and desolation were clouted across his face. "I'm sorry. Do you believe me? I'm so sorry, I'm so sorry, I'm—!"

His arm touched the fire and he snapped it back.

They all watched him, silent, until Papa stood and walked closer. He sat next to him.

"Did you burn your elbow?"

One evening, Hans, Max, and Liesel were sitting in front of the fire. Mama was in the kitchen. Max was reading *Mein Kampf* again.

"You know something?" Hans said. He leaned toward the fire. "Liesel's actually a good little reader herself." Max lowered the book. "And she has more in common with you than you might think." Papa checked that Rosa wasn't coming. "She likes a good fistfight, too."

"Papa!"

Liesel, at the high end of eleven, and still rake-skinny as she sat against the wall, was devastated. "I've never been in a fight!"

"Shhh," Papa laughed. He waved at her to keep her voice down and tilted again, this time to the girl. "Well, what about the hiding you gave Ludwig Schmeikl, huh?"

"I never—" She was caught. Further denial was useless. "How did you find out about that?"

"I saw his papa at the Knoller."

Liesel held her face in her hands. Once uncovered again, she asked the pivotal question. "Did you tell Mama?"

"Are you kidding?" He winked at Max and whispered to the girl, "You're still alive, aren't you?"

That night was also the first time Papa played his accordion at home for months. It lasted half an hour or so until he asked a question of Max.

"Did you learn?"

The face in the corner watched the flames. "I did." There was a considerable pause. "Until I was nine. At that age, my mother sold the music studio and stopped teaching. She kept only the one instrument but gave up on me not long after I resisted the learning. I was foolish."

"No," Papa said. "You were a boy."

During the nights, both Liesel Meminger and Max Vandenburg would go about their other similarity. In their separate rooms, they would dream their nightmares and wake up, one with a scream in drowning sheets, the other with a gasp for air next to a smoking fire.

Sometimes, when Liesel was reading with Papa close to three o'clock, they would both hear the waking moment of Max. "He dreams like you," Papa would say, and on one occasion, stirred by the sound of Max's anxiety, Liesel decided to get out of bed. From listening to his history, she had a good idea of what he saw in those dreams, if not the exact part of the story that paid him a visit each night.

She made her way quietly down the hallway and into the living and bedroom.

"Max?"

The whisper was soft, clouded in the throat of sleep.

To begin with, there was no sound of reply, but he soon sat up and searched the darkness.

With Papa still in her bedroom, Liesel sat on the other side of the fireplace from Max. Behind them, Mama loudly slept. She gave the snorer on the train a good run for her money.

The fire was nothing now but a funeral of smoke, dead and dying, simultaneously. On this particular morning, there were also voices.

* * * THE SWAPPING OF NIGHTMARES * * *
The girl: "Tell me. What do you see
when you dream like that?"
The Jew: ". . . I see myself turning
around, and waving goodbye."
The girl: "I also have nightmares."
The Jew: "What do you see?"
The girl: "A train, and my dead brother."
The Jew: "Your brother?"
The girl: "He died when I moved
here, on the way."
The girl and the Jew, together: "*Ja*—yes."

It would be nice to say that after this small breakthrough, neither Liesel nor Max dreamed their bad visions again. It would be nice but untrue. The nightmares arrived like they always did, much like the best player in the opposition when you've heard rumors that he might be injured or sick—but there he is, warming up with the rest of them, ready to take the field. Or like a timetabled train, arriving at a nightly platform, pulling the memories behind it on a rope. A lot of dragging. A lot of awkward bounces.

The only thing that changed was that Liesel told her papa that she should be old enough now to cope on her own with the dreams.

For a moment, he looked a little hurt, but as always with Papa, he gave the right thing to say his best shot.

"Well, thank God." He halfway grinned. "At least now I can get some proper sleep. That chair was killing me." He put his arm around the girl and they walked to the kitchen.

As time progressed, a clear distinction developed between two very different worlds—the world inside 33 Himmel Street, and the one that resided and turned outside it. The trick was to keep them apart.

In the outside world, Liesel was learning to find some more of its uses. One afternoon, when she was walking home with an empty washing bag, she noticed a newspaper poking out of a garbage can. The weekly edition of the *Molching Express*. She lifted it out and took it home, presenting it to Max. "I thought," she told him, "you might like to do the crossword to pass the time."

Max appreciated the gesture, and to justify her bringing it home, he read the paper from cover to cover and showed her the puzzle a few hours later, completed but for one word.

"Damn that seventeen down," he said.

In February 1941, for her twelfth birthday, Liesel received another used book, and she was grateful. It was called *The Mud Men* and was about a very strange father and son. She hugged her mama and papa, while Max stood uncomfortably in the corner.

"Alles Gute zum Geburtstag." He smiled weakly. "All the best for your birthday." His hands were in his pockets. "I didn't know, or else I could have given you something." A blatant lie—he had nothing to give, except maybe *Mein Kampf,* and there was no way he'd give such propaganda to a young German girl. That would be like the lamb handing a knife to the butcher.

There was an uncomfortable silence.

She had embraced Mama and Papa.

Max looked so alone.

Liesel swallowed.

And she walked over and hugged him for the first time. "Thanks, Max."

At first, he merely stood there, but as she held on to him, gradually his hands rose up and gently pressed into her shoulder blades.

Only later would she find out about the helpless expression on Max Vandenburg's face. She would also discover that he resolved at that moment to give her something back. I often imagine him lying awake all that night, pondering what he could possibly offer.

As it turned out, the gift was delivered on paper, just over a week later.

He would bring it to her in the early hours of morning, before retreating down the concrete steps to what he now liked to call home.

PAGES FROM THE BASEMENT

For a week, Liesel was kept from the basement at all cost. It was Mama and Papa who made sure to take down Max's food.

"No, *Saumensch*," Mama told her each time she volunteered. There was always a new excuse. "How about you do something useful in *here* for a change, like finish the ironing? You think carrying it around town is so special? Try ironing it!" You can do all manner of underhanded nice things when you have a caustic reputation. It worked.

During that week, Max had cut out a collection of pages from *Mein Kampf* and painted over them in white. He then hung them up with pegs on some string, from one end of the basement to the other. When they were all dry, the hard part began. He was educated well enough to get by, but he was certainly no writer, and no artist. Despite this, he formulated the words in his head till he could recount them without error. Only then, on the paper that had bubbled and humped under the stress of drying paint, did he begin to write the story. It was done with a small black paintbrush.

The Standover Man.

He calculated that he needed thirteen pages, so he painted forty, expecting at least twice as many slipups as successes. There were practice versions on the pages of the *Molching Express,* improving his basic, clumsy artwork to a level he could accept. As he worked, he heard the whispered words of a girl. "His hair," she told him, "is like feathers."

When he was finished, he used a knife to pierce the pages and tie them with string. The result was a thirteen-page booklet that went like this:

All my life,

I've been scared

of men standing over me.

I suppose my first standover man was my father,

but he vanished before I could remember him.

For some reason, when I was a boy, I liked to fight. A lot of the time, I lost. Another boy, sometimes with blood falling from his nose, would be standing over me.

Many years later, I needed to hide. I tried not to sleep because I was afraid of who might be there when I woke up.

But I was lucky. It was always my friend.

When I was hiding, I dreamed of a certain man. The hardest was when I traveled to find him.

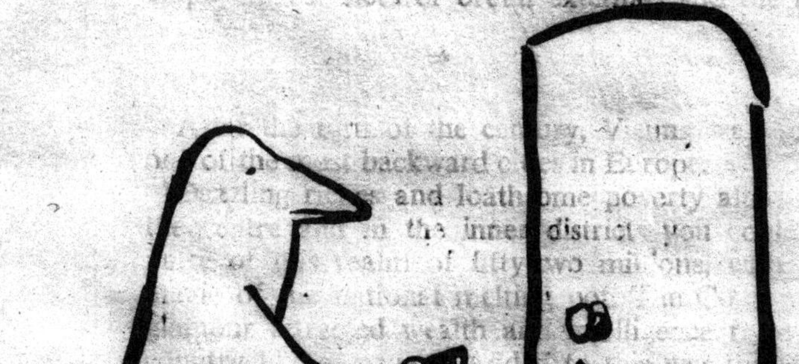

Out of sheer luck and many footsteps, I made it.

I slept there for a long time. Three days, they told me... and what did I find when I woke up? Not a man, but someone else, standing over me.

KARL, headwaiter, b. July 26, 1897

KARL, student of engineering, b. October

KURT, valet, b. March 27, 1899

LAUS VON, businessman, b. August 1904

STEN, THEODOR VON DER, County Court Coun-
VON, May 14, 197

EN, TIERS, JOHANN, retired Cavalry Captain, b. May

BNER-RICHTER, MAX ERWIN VON, Doctor
engineering, b. July 9, 1884

eer, b. March
14, 1889

WOLF, WILHELM, businessman, b. October 19, 1898

So-called national authorities heroes a
common grave.

Therefore memory, the first
volume work. As its blood witnesses, may they shine
forever glowing example to the followers of our movement.

ADOLF HITLER

Landsberg am Lech
Fortress Prison
October 16, 1924

States which do not serve this purpose are misbegotten,

But there is one strange thing.

life must never base ourselves on so-called 'accepted facts' and false ones at that. If we did, we would not be the champions of a new idea, but the copyists of the present-day vessel and the race as its content. This vessel has meaning only if it can preserve and protect the content; otherwise it is useless.

Thus, the highest purpose of a folkish state is concern for the preservation of those original racial elements which bestow culture and create the beauty and dignity of a higher mankind. We, as Aryans, can conceive of the state only as the living organism of a nationality which not only assures the preservation of this nationality, but by the development of its spiritual and ideal abilities leads it to the highest freedom.

But what they try to palm off on us as a state today is usually nothing but a monstrosity born of deepest human error, error with untold suffering as a consequence.

We National Socialists know that with this conception we stand as revolutionaries in the world of today and are branded as such. But our thoughts and actions must in no way be determined by the approval or disapproval of our time, but by the binding obligation to a truth which we have recognized. Then we may be convinced that the higher insight of posterity will not only understand our actions of today, but will also confirm their correctness and exalt them.

The girl says I look like something else.

From this, we National Socialists derive a standard for the evaluation of a state. This value will be relative from the standpoint of the individual nationality, absolute from that of humanity as such. This means, in other words:

The quality of a state cannot be evaluated according to the cultural level or the power of this state in the frame of the outside world, but solely and exclusively by the degree of this institution's goodness for the nationality involved in each specific case.

358

Now I live in a basement.
Bad dreams still live in
my sleep.

One night, after my usual
nightmare, a shadow stood above
me. She said, "Tell me what you
dream of." So I did.

In return, she explained
what her own dreams
were made of.

Now I think we are friends, this girl and me. On her birthday, it was she who gave a gift - to me.

It makes me understand that the best standover man I've ever known is not a man at all...

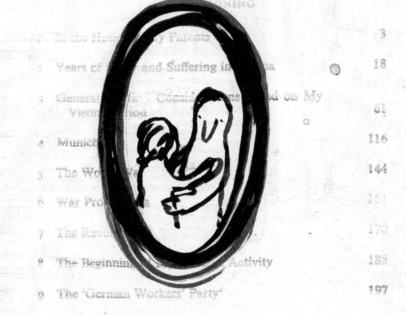

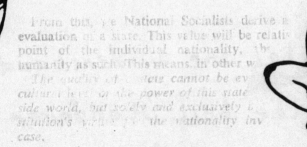

In late February, when Liesel woke up in the early hours of morning, a figure made its way into her bedroom. Typical of Max, it was as close as possible to a noiseless shadow.

Liesel, searching through the dark, could only vaguely sense the man coming toward her.

"Hello?"

There was no reply.

There was nothing but the near silence of his feet as he came closer to the bed and placed the pages on the floor, next to her socks. The pages crackled. Just slightly. One edge of them curled into the floor.

"Hello?"

This time there was a response.

She couldn't tell exactly where the words came from. What mattered was that they reached her. They arrived and kneeled next to the bed.

"A late birthday gift. Look in the morning. Good night."

For a while, she drifted in and out of sleep, not sure anymore whether she'd dreamed of Max coming in.

In the morning, when she woke and rolled over, she saw the pages sitting on the floor. She reached down and picked them up, listening to the paper as it rippled in her early-morning hands.

All my life, I've been scared of men standing over me. . . .

As she turned them, the pages were noisy, like static around the written story.

Three days, they told me . . . and what did I find when I woke up?

There were the erased pages of *Mein Kampf*, gagging, suffocating under the paint as they turned.

It makes me understand that the best standover man I've ever known . . .

Liesel read and viewed Max Vandenburg's gift three times, noticing a different brush line or word with each one. When the third reading was finished, she climbed as quietly as she could from her bed and walked to Mama and Papa's room. The allocated space next to the fire was vacant.

As she thought about it, she realized it was actually appropriate, or even better—perfect—to thank him where the pages were made.

She walked down the basement steps. She saw an imaginary framed photo seep into the wall—a quiet-smiled secret.

No more than a few meters, it was a long walk to the drop sheets and the assortment of paint cans that shielded Max Vandenburg. She removed the sheets closest to the wall until there was a small corridor to look through.

The first part of him she saw was his shoulder, and through the slender gap, she slowly, painfully, inched her hand in until it rested there. His clothing was cool. He did not wake.

She could feel his breathing and his shoulder moving up and down ever so slightly. For a while, she watched him. Then she sat and leaned back.

Sleepy air seemed to have followed her.

The scrawled words of practice stood magnificently on the wall by the stairs, jagged and childlike and sweet. They looked on as both the hidden Jew and the girl slept, hand to shoulder.

They breathed.

German and Jewish lungs.

Next to the wall, *The Standover Man* sat, numb and gratified, like a beautiful itch at Liesel Meminger's feet.

PART FIVE

the whistler

featuring:

a floating book—the gamblers—a small ghost—

two haircuts—rudy's youth—losers and sketches—

a whistler and some shoes—three acts of stupidity—

and a frightened boy with frozen legs

THE FLOATING BOOK (Part I)

A book floated down the Amper River.

A boy jumped in, caught up to it, and held it in his right hand. He grinned.

He stood waist-deep in the icy, Decemberish water.

"How about a kiss, *Saumensch*?" he said.

The surrounding air was a lovely, gorgeous, nauseating cold, not to mention the concrete ache of the water, thickening from his toes to his hips.

How about a kiss?

How about a kiss?

Poor Rudy.

* * * A SMALL ANNOUNCEMENT * * *
ABOUT RUDY STEINER
He didn't deserve to die the way he did.

In your visions, you see the sloppy edges of paper still stuck to his fingers. You see a shivering blond fringe. Preemptively, you conclude, as

I would, that Rudy died that very same day, of hypothermia. He did not. Recollections like those merely remind me that he was not deserving of the fate that met him a little under two years later.

On many counts, taking a boy like Rudy was robbery—so much life, so much to live for—yet somehow, I'm certain he would have loved to see the frightening rubble and the swelling of the sky on the night he passed away. He'd have cried and turned and smiled if only he could have seen the book thief on her hands and knees, next to his decimated body. He'd have been glad to witness her kissing his dusty, bomb-hit lips.

Yes, I know it.

In the darkness of my dark-beating heart, I know. He'd have loved it, all right.

You see?

Even death has a heart.

THE GAMBLERS
(A SEVEN-SIDED DIE)

Of course, I'm being rude. I'm spoiling the ending, not only of the entire book, but of this particular piece of it. I have given you two events in advance, because I don't have much interest in building mystery. Mystery bores me. It chores me. I know what happens and so do you. It's the machinations that wheel us there that aggravate, perplex, interest, and astound me.

There are many things to think of.

There is much story.

Certainly, there's a book called *The Whistler,* which we really need to discuss, along with exactly how it came to be floating down the Amper River in the time leading up to Christmas 1941. We should deal with all of that first, don't you think?

It's settled, then.

We will.

It started with gambling. Roll a die by hiding a Jew and this is how you live. This is how it looks.

Life was at least starting to mimic normality with more force:

Hans and Rosa Hubermann were arguing in the living room, even if it was much quieter than it used to be. Liesel, in typical fashion, was an onlooker.

The argument originated the previous night, in the basement, where Hans and Max were sitting with paint cans, words, and drop sheets. Max asked if Rosa might be able to cut his hair at some stage. "It's getting me in the eyes," he'd said, to which Hans had replied, "I'll see what I can do."

Now Rosa was riffling through the drawers. Her words were shoved back to Papa with the rest of the junk. "Where are those damn scissors?"

"Not in the one below?"

"I've been through that one already."

"Maybe you missed them."

"Do I look blind?" She raised her head and bellowed. "Liesel!"

"I'm right here."

Hans cowered. "Goddamn it, woman, deafen me, why don't you!"

"Quiet, *Saukerl*." Rosa went on riffling and addressed the girl. "Liesel, where are the scissors?" But Liesel had no idea, either. "*Saumensch*, you're useless, aren't you?"

"Leave her out of it."

More words were delivered back and forth, from elastic-haired woman to silver-eyed man, till Rosa slammed the drawer. "I'll probably make a lot of mistakes on him anyway."

"Mistakes?" Papa looked ready to tear his own hair out by that stage, but his voice became a barely audible whisper. "Who the hell's going to *see* him?" He motioned to speak again but was distracted by the feathery appearance of Max Vandenburg, who stood politely, embarrassed, in the doorway. He carried his own scissors and came forward, handing them not to Hans or Rosa but to the twelve-year-old girl. She was the calmest option. His mouth quivered a moment before he said, "Would you?"

Liesel took the scissors and opened them. They were rusty and shiny in different areas. She turned to Papa, and when he nodded, she followed Max down to the basement.

The Jew sat on a paint can. A small drop sheet was wrapped around his shoulders. "As many mistakes as you want," he told her.

Papa parked himself on the steps.

Liesel lifted the first tufts of Max Vandenburg's hair.

As she cut the feathery strands, she wondered at the sound of scissors. Not the snipping noise, but the grinding of each metal arm as it cropped each group of fibers.

When the job was done, a little severe in places, a little crooked in others, she walked upstairs with the hair in her hands and fed it into the stove. She lit a match and watched as the clump shriveled and sank, orange and red.

Again, Max was in the doorway, this time at the top of the basement steps. "Thanks, Liesel." His voice was tall and husky, with the sound in it of a hidden smile.

No sooner had he spoken than he disappeared again, back into the ground.

 The Newspaper: Early May

"There's a Jew in my basement."

"There's a Jew. In my basement."

Sitting on the floor of the mayor's roomful of books, Liesel Meminger heard those words. A bag of washing was at her side and the ghostly figure of the mayor's wife was sitting hunch-drunk over at the desk. In front of her, Liesel read *The Whistler,* pages twenty-two and twenty-three. She looked up. She imagined herself walking over, gently tearing some fluffy hair to the side, and whispering in the woman's ear:

"There's a Jew in my basement."

As the book quivered in her lap, the secret sat in her mouth. It made itself comfortable. It crossed its legs.

"I should be getting home." This time, she actually spoke. Her hands were shaking. Despite a trace of sunshine in the distance, a gentle breeze rode through the open window, coupled with rain that came in like sawdust.

When Liesel placed the book back into position, the woman's chair stubbed the floor and she made her way over. It was always like this at the end. The gentle rings of sorrowful wrinkles swelled a moment as she reached across and retrieved the book.

She offered it to the girl.

Liesel shied away.

"No," she said, "thank you. I have enough books at home. Maybe another time. I'm rereading something else with my papa. You know, the one I stole from the fire that night."

The mayor's wife nodded. If there was one thing about Liesel Meminger, her thieving was not gratuitous. She only stole books on what she felt was a need-to-have basis. Currently, she had enough. She'd gone through *The Mud Men* four times now and was enjoying her reacquaintance with *The Shoulder Shrug.* Also, each night before bed, she would open a fail-safe guide to grave digging. Buried deep inside it, *The Standover Man* resided. She mouthed the words and touched the birds. She turned the noisy pages, slowly.

"Goodbye, Frau Hermann."

She exited the library, walked down the floorboard hall and out the monstrous doorway. As was her habit, she stood for a while on the steps, looking at Molching beneath her. The town that afternoon was covered in a yellow mist, which stroked the rooftops as if they were pets and filled up the streets like a bath.

When she made it down to Munich Street, the book thief swerved in and out of the umbrellaed men and women—a rain-cloaked girl who made her way without shame from one garbage can to another. Like clockwork.

"There!"

She laughed up at the coppery clouds, celebrating, before reaching in and taking the mangled newspaper. Although the front and back pages were streaked with black tears of print, she folded it neatly in half and tucked it under her arm. It had been like this each Thursday for the past few months.

Thursday was the only delivery day left for Liesel Meminger now, and it was usually able to provide some sort of dividend. She could never dampen the feeling of victory each time she found a *Molching Express* or any other publication. Finding a newspaper was a good day. If it was a paper in which the crossword wasn't done, it was a great day. She would make her way home, shut the door behind her, and take it down to Max Vandenburg.

"Crossword?" he would ask.

"Empty."

"Excellent."

The Jew would smile as he accepted the package of paper and started reading in the rationed light of the basement. Often, Liesel would watch him as he focused on reading the paper, completed the crossword, and then started to reread it, front to back.

With the weather warming, Max remained downstairs all the time. During the day, the basement door was left open to allow the small bay of daylight to reach him from the corridor. The hall itself was not exactly bathed in sunshine, but in certain situations, you take what you can get. Dour light was better than none, and they needed

247

to be frugal. The kerosene had not yet approached a dangerously low level, but it was best to keep its usage to a minimum.

Liesel would usually sit on some drop sheets. She would read while Max completed those crosswords. They sat a few meters apart, speaking very rarely, and there was really only the noise of turning pages. Often, she also left her books for Max to read while she was at school. Where Hans Hubermann and Erik Vandenburg were ultimately united by music, Max and Liesel were held together by the quiet gathering of words.

"Hi, Max."

"Hi, Liesel."

They would sit and read.

At times, she would watch him. She decided that he could best be summed up as a picture of pale concentration. Beige-colored skin. A swamp in each eye. And he breathed like a fugitive. Desperate yet soundless. It was only his chest that gave him away for something alive.

Increasingly, Liesel would close her eyes and ask Max to quiz her on the words she was continually getting wrong, and she would swear if they still escaped her. She would then stand and paint those words to the wall, anywhere up to a dozen times. Together, Max Vandenburg and Liesel Meminger would take in the odor of paint fumes and cement.

"Bye, Max."

"Bye, Liesel."

In bed, she would lie awake, imagining him below, in the basement. In her bedtime visions, he always slept fully clothed, shoes included, just in case he needed to flee again. He slept with one eye open.

 The Weatherman: Mid-May

Liesel opened the door and her mouth simultaneously.

On Himmel Street, her team had trounced Rudy's 6–1, and triumphant, she burst into the kitchen, telling Mama and Papa all about the goal she'd scored. She then rushed down to the basement to describe it blow by blow to Max, who put down his newspaper and intently listened and laughed with the girl.

When the story of the goal was complete, there was silence for a good few minutes, until Max looked slowly up. "Would you do something for me, Liesel?"

Still excited by her Himmel Street goal, the girl jumped from the drop sheets. She did not say it, but her movement clearly showed her intent to provide exactly what he wanted.

"You told me all about the goal," he said, "but I don't know what sort of day it is up there. I don't know if you scored it in the sun, or if the clouds have covered everything." His hand prodded at his short-cropped hair, and his swampy eyes pleaded for the simplest of simple things. "Could you go up and tell me how the weather looks?"

Naturally, Liesel hurried up the stairs. She stood a few feet from the spit-stained door and turned on the spot, observing the sky.

When she returned to the basement, she told him.

"The sky is blue today, Max, and there is a big long cloud, and it's stretched out, like a rope. At the end of it, the sun is like a yellow hole. . . ."

Max, at that moment, knew that only a child could have given him a weather report like that. On the wall, he painted a long, tightly knotted rope with a dripping yellow sun at the end of it, as if you could dive right into it. On the ropy cloud, he drew two figures—a thin girl and a withering Jew—and they were walking, arms balanced, toward that dripping sun. Beneath the picture, he wrote the following sentence.

* * * THE WALL-WRITTEN WORDS * * *
OF MAX VANDENBURG
It was a Monday, and they walked
on a tightrope to the sun.

For Max Vandenburg, there was cool cement and plenty of time to spend with it.

The minutes were cruel.

Hours were punishing.

Standing above him at all moments of awakeness was the hand of time, and it didn't hesitate to wring him out. It smiled and squeezed and let him live. What great malice there could be in allowing something to live.

At least once a day, Hans Hubermann would descend the basement steps and share a conversation. Rosa would occasionally bring a spare crust of bread. It was when Liesel came down, however, that Max found himself most interested in life again. Initially, he tried to resist, but it was harder every day that the girl appeared, each time with a new weather report, either of pure blue sky, cardboard clouds, or a sun that had broken through like God sitting down after he'd eaten too much for his dinner.

When he was alone, his most distinct feeling was of disappearance. All of his clothes were gray—whether they'd started out that way or not—from his pants to his woolen sweater to the jacket that dripped from him now like water. He often checked if his skin was flaking, for it was as if he were dissolving.

What he needed was a series of new projects. The first was exercise. He started with push-ups, lying stomach-down on the cool basement floor, then hoisting himself up. It felt like his arms snapped at each elbow, and he envisaged his heart seeping out of him and dropping pathetically to the ground. As a teenager in Stuttgart, he could reach fifty push-ups at a time. Now, at the age of twenty-four, perhaps fifteen pounds lighter than his usual weight, he could barely make it to ten. After a week, he was completing three sets each of sixteen push-ups and twenty-two sit-ups. When he was finished, he would sit against the basement wall with his paint-can friends, feeling his pulse in his teeth. His muscles felt like cake.

He wondered at times if pushing himself like this was even worth it. Sometimes, though, when his heartbeat neutralized and his body became functional again, he would turn off the lamp and stand in the darkness of the basement.

He was twenty-four, but he could still fantasize.

"In the blue corner," he quietly commentated, "we have the champion of the world, the Aryan masterpiece—the *Führer*." He breathed and turned. "And in the red corner, we have the Jewish, rat-faced challenger—Max Vandenburg."

Around him, it all materialized.

White light lowered itself into a boxing ring and a crowd stood and murmured—that magical sound of many people talking all at once. How could every person there have so much to say at the same time? The ring itself was perfect. Perfect canvas, lovely ropes. Even the stray hairs of each thickened string were flawless, gleaming in the tight white light. The room smelled like cigarettes and beer.

Diagonally across, Adolf Hitler stood in the corner with his entourage. His legs poked out from a red-and-white robe with a black swastika burned into its back. His mustache was knitted to his face. Words were whispered to him from his trainer, Goebbels. He bounced foot to foot, and he smiled. He smiled loudest when the ring announcer listed his many achievements, which were all vociferously applauded by the adoring crowd. "Undefeated!" the ringmaster proclaimed. "Over many a Jew, and over any other threat to the German ideal! Herr *Führer*," he concluded, "we salute you!" The crowd: mayhem.

Next, when everyone had settled down, came the challenger.

The ringmaster swung over toward Max, who stood alone in the challenger's corner. No robe. No entourage. Just a lonely young Jew with dirty breath, a naked chest, and tired hands and feet. Naturally, his shorts were gray. He too moved from foot to foot, but it was kept at a minimum to conserve energy. He'd done a lot of sweating in the gym to make the weight.

"The challenger!" sang the ringmaster. "Of," and he paused for effect, "*Jew*ish blood." The crowd oohed, like human ghouls. "Weighing in at . . ."

The rest of the speech was not heard. It was overrun with the abuse from the bleachers, and Max watched as his opponent was derobed and came to the middle to hear the rules and shake hands.

"*Guten Tag,* Herr Hitler." Max nodded, but the *Führer* only showed him his yellow teeth, then covered them up again with his lips.

"Gentlemen," a stout referee in black pants and a blue shirt began. A bow tie was fixed to his throat. "First and foremost, we want a good clean fight." He addressed only the *Führer* now. "Unless, of course, Herr Hitler, you begin to lose. Should this occur, I will be quite willing to turn a blind eye to any unconscionable tactics you might employ to grind this piece of Jewish stench and filth into the canvas." He nodded, with great courtesy. "Is that clear?"

The *Führer* spoke his first word then. "Crystal."

To Max, the referee extended a warning. "As for you, my Jewish chum, I'd watch my step very closely if I were you. Very closely indeed," and they were sent back to their respective corners.

A brief quiet ensued.

The bell.

First out was the *Führer,* awkward-legged and bony, running at Max and jabbing him firmly in the face. The crowd vibrated, the bell still in their ears, and their satisfied smiles hurdled the ropes. The smoky breath of Hitler steamed from his mouth as his hands bucked at Max's face, collecting him several times, on the lips, the nose, the chin—and Max had still not ventured out of his corner. To absorb the punishment, he held up his hands, but the *Führer* then aimed at his ribs, his kidneys, his lungs. Oh, the eyes, the *Führer*'s eyes. They were so deliciously brown—like Jews' eyes—and they were so determined that even Max stood transfixed for a moment as he caught sight of them between the healthy blur of punching gloves.

There was only one round, and it lasted hours, and for the most part, nothing changed.

The *Führer* pounded away at the punching-bag Jew.

Jewish blood was everywhere.

Like red rain clouds on the white-sky canvas at their feet.

Eventually, Max's knees began to buckle, his cheekbones silently moaned, and the *Führer*'s delighted face still chipped away, chipped away, until depleted, beaten, and broken, the Jew flopped to the floor.

First, a roar.

Then silence.

The referee counted. He had a gold tooth and a plethora of nostril hair.

Slowly, Max Vandenburg, the Jew, rose to his feet and made himself upright. His voice wobbled. An invitation. "Come on, *Führer*," he said, and this time, when Adolf Hitler set upon his Jewish counterpart, Max stepped aside and plunged him into the corner. He punched him seven times, aiming on each occasion for only one thing.

The mustache.

With the seventh punch, he missed. It was the *Führer*'s chin that sustained the blow. All at once, Hitler hit the ropes and creased forward, landing on his knees. This time, there was no count. The referee flinched in the corner. The audience sank down, back to their beer. On his knees, the *Führer* tested himself for blood and straightened his hair, right to left. When he returned to his feet, much to the approval of the thousand-strong crowd, he edged forward and did something quite strange. He turned his back on the Jew and took the gloves from his fists.

The crowd was stunned.

"He's given up," someone whispered, but within moments, Adolf Hitler was standing on the ropes, and he was addressing the arena.

"My fellow Germans," he called, "you can see something here tonight, can't you?" Bare-chested, victory-eyed, he pointed over at Max. "You can see that what we face is something far more sinister and powerful than we ever imagined. Can you see that?"

They answered. "Yes, *Führer*."

"Can you see that this enemy has found its ways—its despicable ways—through our armor, and that clearly, I cannot stand up here alone and fight him?" The words were visible. They dropped from his mouth like jewels. "Look at him! Take a good look." They looked. At the bloodied Max Vandenburg. "As we speak, he is plotting his way into your neighborhood. He's moving in next door. He's infesting you with his family and he's about to take you over. He—" Hitler glanced at him a moment, with disgust. "He will soon own you, until it is he who stands not at the counter of your grocery shop, but sits in the back, smoking his pipe. Before you know it, you'll be working for him at minimum wage while he can hardly walk from the weight in his pockets. Will you simply stand there and let him do this? Will you stand by as your leaders did in the past, when they gave your land to everybody else, when they sold your country for the price of a few signatures? Will you stand out there, powerless? Or"—and now he stepped one rung higher—"will you climb up into this ring with me?"

Max shook. Horror stuttered in his stomach.

Adolf finished him. "Will you climb in here so that we can defeat this enemy together?"

In the basement of 33 Himmel Street, Max Vandenburg could feel the fists of an entire nation. One by one they climbed into the ring and beat him down. They made him bleed. They let him suffer. Millions of them—until one last time, when he gathered himself to his feet . . .

He watched the next person climb through the ropes. It was a girl, and as she slowly crossed the canvas, he noticed a tear torn down her left cheek. In her right hand was a newspaper.

"The crossword," she gently said, "is empty," and she held it out to him.

Dark.

Nothing but dark now.

Just basement. Just Jew.

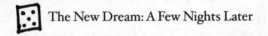 The New Dream: A Few Nights Later

It was afternoon. Liesel came down the basement steps. Max was halfway through his push-ups.

She watched awhile, without his knowledge, and when she came and sat with him, he stood up and leaned back against the wall. "Did I tell you," he asked her, "that I've been having a new dream lately?"

Liesel shifted a little, to see his face.

"But I dream this when I'm awake." He motioned to the glowless kerosene lamp. "Sometimes I turn out the light. Then I stand here and wait."

"For what?"

Max corrected her. "Not for what. For whom."

For a few moments, Liesel said nothing. It was one of those conversations that require some time to elapse between exchanges. "Who do you wait for?"

Max did not move. "The *Führer*." He was very matter-of-fact about this. "That's why I'm in training."

"The push-ups?"

"That's right." He walked to the concrete stairway. "Every night, I wait in the dark and the *Führer* comes down these steps. He walks down and he and I, we fight for hours."

Liesel was standing now. "Who wins?"

At first, he was going to answer that no one did, but then he noticed the paint cans, the drop sheets, and the growing pile of newspapers in the periphery of his vision. He watched the words, the long cloud, and the figures on the wall.

"I do," he said.

It was as though he'd opened her palm, given her the words, and closed it up again.

Under the ground, in Molching, Germany, two people stood and spoke in a basement. It sounds like the beginning of a joke:

"There's a Jew and a German standing in a basement, right? . . ."

This, however, was no joke.

 The Painters: Early June

Another of Max's projects was the remainder of *Mein Kampf*. Each page was gently stripped from the book and laid out on the floor to receive a coat of paint. It was then hung up to dry and replaced between the front and back covers. When Liesel came down one day after school, she found Max, Rosa, and her papa all painting the various pages. Many of them were already hanging from a drawn-out string with pegs, just as they must have done for *The Standover Man*.

All three people looked up and spoke.

"Hi, Liesel."

"Here's a brush, Liesel."

"About time, *Saumensch*. Where have you been so long?"

As she started painting, Liesel thought about Max Vandenburg fighting the *Führer,* exactly as he'd explained it.

✳ ✳ ✳ BASEMENT VISIONS, JUNE 1941 ✳ ✳ ✳
Punches are thrown, the crowd climbs out of
the walls. Max and the *Führer* fight for their
lives, each rebounding off the stairway.
There's blood in the *Führer*'s mustache, as
well as in his part line, on the right side
of his head. "Come on, *Führer*," says the
Jew. He waves him forward. "Come on, *Führer*."

When the visions dissipated and she finished her first page, Papa winked at her. Mama castigated her for hogging the paint. Max examined each and every page, perhaps watching what he planned to produce on them. Many months later, he would also paint over the cover of that book and give it a new title, after one of the stories he would write and illustrate inside it.

That afternoon, in the secret ground below 33 Himmel Street, the Hubermanns, Liesel Meminger, and Max Vandenburg prepared the pages of *The Word Shaker*.

It felt good to be a painter.

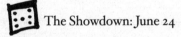 The Showdown: June 24

Then came the seventh side of the die. Two days after Germany invaded Russia. Three days before Britain and the Soviets joined forces.

Seven.

You roll and watch it coming, realizing completely that this is no regular die. You claim it to be bad luck, but you've known all along that it had to come. You brought it into the room. The table could smell it on your breath. The Jew was sticking out of your pocket from the outset. He's smeared to your lapel, and the moment you roll, you know it's a seven—the one thing that somehow finds a way to hurt you. It lands. It stares you in each eye, miraculous and loathsome, and you turn away with it feeding on your chest.

Just bad luck.

That's what you say.

Of no consequence.

That's what you make yourself believe—because deep down, you know that this small piece of changing fortune is a signal of things to come. You hide a Jew. You pay. Somehow or other, you must.

In hindsight, Liesel told herself that it was not such a big deal. Perhaps it was because so much more had happened by the time she wrote her story in the basement. In the great scheme of things, she reasoned that Rosa being fired by the mayor and his wife was not bad luck at all. It had nothing whatsoever to do with hiding Jews. It had everything to do with the greater context of the war. At the time, though, there was most definitely a feeling of punishment.

The beginning was actually a week or so earlier than June 24. Liesel scavenged a newspaper for Max Vandenburg as she always did. She reached into a garbage can just off Munich Street and tucked it under her arm. Once she delivered it to Max and he'd commenced his first reading, he glanced across at her and pointed to a picture on the front page. "Isn't this whose washing and ironing you deliver?"

Liesel came over from the wall. She'd been writing the word *argument* six times, next to Max's picture of the ropy cloud and the dripping sun. Max handed her the paper and she confirmed it. "That's him."

When she went on to read the article, Heinz Hermann, the mayor, was quoted as saying that although the war was progressing splendidly, the people of Molching, like all responsible Germans, should take adequate measures and prepare for the possibility of harder times. "You never know," he stated, "what our enemies are thinking, or how they will try to debilitate us."

A week later, the mayor's words came to nasty fruition. Liesel, as she always did, showed up at Grande Strasse and read from *The Whistler* on the floor of the mayor's library. The mayor's wife showed no signs of abnormality (or, let's be frank, no *additional* signs) until it was time to leave.

This time, when she offered Liesel *The Whistler,* she insisted on the girl taking it. "Please." She almost begged. The book was held out in a tight, measured fist. "Take it. Please, take it."

Liesel, touched by the strangeness of this woman, couldn't bear to disappoint her again. The gray-covered book with its yellowing pages found its way into her hand and she began to walk the corridor. As she was about to ask for the washing, the mayor's wife gave her a final look of bathrobed sorrow. She reached into the chest of drawers and withdrew an envelope. Her voice, lumpy from lack of use, coughed out the words. "I'm sorry. It's for your mama."

Liesel stopped breathing.

She was suddenly aware of how empty her feet felt inside her shoes. Something ridiculed her throat. She trembled. When finally she reached out and took possession of the letter, she noticed the sound of the clock in the library. Grimly, she realized that clocks don't make a sound that even remotely resembles ticking, tocking. It was more the sound of a hammer, upside down, hacking methodically at the earth. It was the sound of a grave. If only mine was ready now, she thought—because Liesel Meminger, at that moment, wanted to die. When the others had canceled, it hadn't hurt so much. There was always the mayor, his library, and her connection with his wife. Also, this was the last one, the last hope, gone. This time, it felt like the greatest betrayal.

How could she face her mama?

For Rosa, the few scraps of money had still helped in various alleyways. An extra handful of flour. A piece of fat.

Ilsa Hermann was dying now herself—to get rid of her. Liesel could see it somewhere in the way she hugged the robe a little tighter. The clumsiness of sorrow still kept her at close proximity, but clearly, she wanted this to be over. "Tell your mama," she spoke again. Her voice was adjusting now, as one sentence turned into two. "That we're sorry." She started shepherding the girl toward the door.

Liesel felt it now in the shoulders. The pain, the impact of final rejection.

That's it? she asked internally. You just boot me out?

Slowly, she picked up her empty bag and edged toward the door. Once outside, she turned and faced the mayor's wife for the second to last time that day. She looked her in the eyes with an almost savage brand of pride. *"Danke schön,"* she said, and Ilsa Hermann smiled in a rather useless, beaten way.

"If you ever want to come just to read," the woman lied (or at least the girl, in her shocked, saddened state, perceived it as a lie), "you're very welcome."

At that moment, Liesel was amazed by the width of the doorway. There was so much space. Why did people need so much space to get through the door? Had Rudy been there, he'd have called her an idiot—it was to get all their stuff inside.

"Goodbye," the girl said, and slowly, with great morosity, the door was closed.

Liesel did not leave.

For a long time, she sat on the steps and watched Molching. It was neither warm nor cool and the town was clear and still. Molching was in a jar.

She opened the letter. In it, Mayor Heinz Hermann diplomatically outlined exactly why he had to terminate the services of Rosa Hubermann. For the most part, he explained that he would be a hypocrite if he maintained his own small luxuries while advising others to *prepare for harder times.*

When she eventually stood and walked home, her moment of reaction came once again when she saw the STEINER-SCHNEIDER-MEISTER sign on Munich Street. Her sadness left her and she was overwhelmed with anger. "That bastard mayor," she whispered. "That *pathetic* woman." The fact that harder times were coming was surely the best reason for keeping Rosa employed, but no, they fired her. At any rate, she decided, they could do their own blasted washing and ironing, like normal people. Like poor people.

In her hand, *The Whistler* tightened.

"So you give me the book," the girl said, "for pity—to make yourself feel better. . . ." The fact that she'd also been offered the book prior to that day mattered little.

She turned as she had once before and marched back to 8 Grande Strasse. The temptation to run was immense, but she refrained so that she'd have enough in reserve for the words.

When she arrived, she was disappointed that the mayor himself was not there. No car was slotted nicely on the side of the road, which was perhaps a good thing. Had it been there, there was no telling what she might have done to it in this moment of rich versus poor.

Two steps at a time, she reached the door and banged it hard enough to hurt. She enjoyed the small fragments of pain.

Evidently, the mayor's wife was shocked when she saw her again. Her fluffy hair was slightly wet and her wrinkles widened when she noticed the obvious fury on Liesel's usually pallid face. She opened her mouth, but nothing came out, which was handy, really, for it was Liesel who possessed the talking.

"You think," she said, "you can buy me off with this book?" Her voice, though shaken, hooked at the woman's throat. The glittering anger was thick and unnerving, but she toiled through it. She worked herself up even further, to the point where she needed to wipe the tears from her eyes. "You give me this *Saumensch* of a book and think it'll make everything good when I go and tell my mama that we've just lost our last one? While you sit here in your mansion?"

The mayor's wife's arms.

They hung.

Her face slipped.

Liesel, however, did not buckle. She sprayed her words directly into the woman's eyes.

"You and your husband. Sitting up here." Now she became spiteful. More spiteful and evil than she thought herself capable.

The injury of words.

Yes, the brutality of words.

She summoned them from someplace she only now recognized and hurled them at Ilsa Hermann. "It's about time," she informed her, "that you do your own stinking washing anyway. It's about time you faced the fact that your son is dead. He got killed! He got strangled and cut up more than twenty years ago! Or did he freeze to death? Either way, he's dead! He's dead and it's pathetic that you sit here shivering in your own house to suffer for it. You think you're the only one?"

Immediately.

Her brother was next to her.

He whispered for her to stop, but he, too, was dead, and not worth listening to.

He died in a train.

They buried him in the snow.

Liesel glanced at him, but she could not make herself stop. Not yet.

"This book," she went on. She shoved the boy down the steps, making him fall. "I don't want it." The words were quieter now, but still just as hot. She threw *The Whistler* at the woman's slippered feet, hearing the clack of it as it landed on the cement. "I don't want your miserable book. . . ."

Now she managed it. She fell silent.

Her throat was barren now. No words for miles.

Her brother, holding his knee, disappeared.

After a miscarriaged pause, the mayor's wife edged forward and picked up the book. She was battered and beaten up, and not from smiling this time. Liesel could see it on her face. Blood leaked from her nose and licked at her lips. Her eyes had blackened. Cuts had opened up and a series of wounds were rising to the surface of her skin. All from the words. From Liesel's words.

Book in hand, and straightening from a crouch to a standing hunch, Ilsa Hermann began the process again of saying sorry, but the sentence did not make it out.

Slap me, Liesel thought. Come on, slap me.

Ilsa Hermann didn't slap her. She merely retreated backward, into the ugly air of her beautiful house, and Liesel, once again, was left alone, clutching at the steps. She was afraid to turn around because she knew that when she did, the glass casing of Molching had now been shattered, and she'd be glad of it.

As her last orders of business, she read the letter one more time, and when she was close to the gate, she screwed it up as tightly as

263

she could and threw it at the door, as if it were a rock. I have no idea what the book thief expected, but the ball of paper hit the mighty sheet of wood and twittered back down the steps. It landed at her feet.

"Typical," she stated, kicking it onto the grass. "Useless."

On the way home this time, she imagined the fate of that paper the next time it rained, when the mended glass house of Molching was turned upside down. She could already see the words dissolving letter by letter, till there was nothing left. Just paper. Just earth.

At home, as luck would have it, when Liesel walked through the door, Rosa was in the kitchen. "And?" she asked. "Where's the washing?"

"No washing today," Liesel told her.

Rosa came and sat down at the kitchen table. She knew. Suddenly, she appeared much older. Liesel imagined what she'd look like if she untied her bun, to let it fall out onto her shoulders. A gray towel of elastic hair.

"What did you do there, you little *Saumensch?*" The sentence was numb. She could not muster her usual venom.

"It was my fault," Liesel answered. "Completely. I insulted the mayor's wife and told her to stop crying over her dead son. I called her pathetic. That was when they fired you. Here." She walked to the wooden spoons, grabbed a handful, and placed them in front of her. "Take your pick."

Rosa touched one and picked it up, but she did not wield it. "I don't believe you."

Liesel was torn between distress and total mystification. The one time she desperately wanted a *Watschen* and she couldn't get one! "It's my fault."

"It's not your fault," Mama said, and she even stood and stroked Liesel's waxy, unwashed hair. "I know you wouldn't say those things."

"I said them!"

"All right, you said them."

As Liesel left the room, she could hear the wooden spoons clicking back into position in the metal jar that held them. By the time she reached her bedroom, the whole lot of them, the jar included, were thrown to the floor.

Later, she walked down to the basement, where Max was standing in the dark, most likely boxing with the *Führer*.

"Max?" The light dimmed on—a red coin, floating in the corner. "Can you teach me how to do the push-ups?"

Max showed her and occasionally lifted her torso to help, but despite her bony appearance, Liesel was strong and could hold her body weight nicely. She didn't count how many she could do, but that night, in the glow of the basement, the book thief completed enough push-ups to make her hurt for several days. Even when Max advised her that she'd already done too many, she continued.

In bed, she read with Papa, who could tell something was wrong. It was the first time in a month that he'd come in and sat with her, and she was comforted, if only slightly. Somehow, Hans Hubermann always knew what to say, when to stay, and when to leave her be. Perhaps Liesel was the one thing he was a true expert at.

"Is it the washing?" he asked.

Liesel shook her head.

Papa hadn't shaved for a few days and he rubbed the scratchy whiskers every two or three minutes. His silver eyes were flat and calm, slightly warm, as they always were when it came to Liesel.

When the reading petered out, Papa fell asleep. It was then that Liesel spoke what she'd wanted to say all along.

"Papa," she whispered, "I think I'm going to hell."

Her legs were warm. Her knees were cold.

She remembered the nights when she'd wet the bed and Papa had washed the sheets and taught her the letters of the alphabet. Now his breathing blew across the blanket and she kissed his scratchy cheek.

"You need a shave," she said.

"You're not going to hell," Papa replied.

For a few moments, she watched his face. Then she lay back down, leaned on him, and together, they slept, very much in Munich, but somewhere on the seventh side of Germany's die.

RUDY'S YOUTH

In the end, she had to give it to him.
He knew how to perform.

*** A PORTRAIT OF RUDY STEINER: ***
JULY 1941
Strings of mud clench his face. His tie
is a pendulum, long dead in its clock.
His lemon, lamp-lit hair is disheveled
and he wears a sad, absurd smile.

He stood a few meters from the step and spoke with great conviction, great joy.
"*Alles ist Scheisse,*" he announced.
All is shit.

In the first half of 1941, while Liesel went about the business of concealing Max Vandenburg, stealing newspapers, and telling off mayors' wives, Rudy was enduring a new life of his own, at the Hitler Youth. Since early February, he'd been returning from the meetings in a considerably worse state than he'd left in. On many of those return trips, Tommy Müller was by his side, in the same condition. The trouble had three elements to it.

* * * A TRIPLE-TIERED PROBLEM * * *
1. Tommy Müller's ears.
2. Franz Deutscher — the irate Hitler Youth leader.
3. Rudy's inability to stay out of things.

If only Tommy Müller hadn't disappeared for seven hours on one of the coldest days in Munich's history, six years earlier. His ear infections and nerve damage were still contorting the marching pattern at the Hitler Youth, which, I can assure you, was not a positive thing.

To begin with, the downward slide of momentum was gradual, but as the months progressed, Tommy was consistently gathering the ire of the Hitler Youth leaders, especially when it came to the marching. Remember Hitler's birthday the previous year? For some time, the ear infections were getting worse. They had reached the point where Tommy had genuine problems hearing. He could not make out the commands that were shouted at the group as they marched in line. It didn't matter if it was in the hall or outside, in the snow or the mud or the slits of rain.

The goal was always to have everyone stop at the same time.

"One click!" they were told. "That's all the *Führer* wants to hear. Everyone united. Everyone together as one!"

Then Tommy.

It was his left ear, I think. That was the most troublesome of the two, and when the bitter cry of "Halt!" wet the ears of everybody else,

Tommy marched comically and obliviously on. He could transform a marching line into a dog's breakfast in the blink of an eye.

On one particular Saturday, at the beginning of July, just after three-thirty and a litany of Tommy-inspired failed marching attempts, Franz Deutscher (the ultimate name for the ultimate teenage Nazi) was completely fed up.

"Müller, *du Affe!*" His thick blond hair massaged his head and his words manipulated Tommy's face. "You ape—what's wrong with you?"

Tommy slouched fearfully back, but his left cheek still managed to twitch in a manic, cheerful contortion. He appeared not only to be laughing with a triumphant smirk, but accepting the bucketing with glee. And Franz Deutscher wasn't having any of it. His pale eyes cooked him.

"Well?" he asked. "What can you say for yourself?"

Tommy's twitch only increased, in both speed and depth.

"Are you mocking me?"

"*Heil,*" twitched Tommy, in a desperate attempt to buy some approval, but he did not make it to the "Hitler" part.

That was when Rudy stepped forward. He faced Franz Deutscher, looking up at him. "He's got a problem, sir—"

"I can see that!"

"With his ears," Rudy finished. "He can't—"

"Right, that's it." Deutscher rubbed his hands together. "Both of you—six laps of the grounds." They obeyed, but not fast enough. "*Schnell!*" His voice chased them.

When the six laps were completed, they were given some drills of the run–drop down–get up–get down again variety, and after fifteen very long minutes, they were ordered to the ground for what should have been the last time.

Rudy looked down.

A warped circle of mud grinned up at him.

What might you be looking at? it seemed to ask.

"Down!" Franz ordered.

Rudy naturally jumped over it and dropped to his stomach.

"Up!" Franz smiled. "One step back." They did it. "Down!"

The message was clear and now, Rudy accepted it. He dived at the mud and held his breath, and at that moment, lying ear to sodden earth, the drill ended.

"Vielen Dank, meine Herren," Franz Deutscher politely said. "Many thanks, my gentlemen."

Rudy climbed to his knees, did some gardening in his ear, and looked across at Tommy.

Tommy closed his eyes, and he twitched.

When they returned to Himmel Street that day, Liesel was playing hopscotch with some of the younger kids, still in her BDM uniform. From the corner of her eye, she saw the two melancholic figures walking toward her. One of them called out.

They met on the front step of the Steiners' concrete shoe box of a house, and Rudy told her all about the day's episode.

After ten minutes, Liesel sat down.

After eleven minutes, Tommy, who was sitting next to her, said, "It's all my fault," but Rudy waved him away, somewhere between sentence and smile, chopping a mud streak in half with his finger. "It's my—" Tommy tried again, but Rudy broke the sentence completely and pointed at him.

"Tommy, please." There was a peculiar look of contentment on Rudy's face. Liesel had never seen someone so miserable yet so wholeheartedly alive. "Just sit there and—twitch—or something," and he continued with the story.

He paced.

He wrestled his tie.

The words were flung at her, landing somewhere on the concrete step.

"That Deutscher," he summed up buoyantly. "He got us, huh, Tommy?"

Tommy nodded, twitched, and spoke, not necessarily in that order. "It was because of me."

"Tommy, what did I say?"

"When?"

"Now! Just keep quiet."

"Sure, Rudy."

When Tommy walked forlornly home a short while later, Rudy tried what appeared to be a masterful new tactic.

Pity.

On the step, he perused the mud that had dried as a crusty sheet on his uniform, then looked Liesel hopelessly in the face. "What about it, *Saumensch?*"

"What about what?"

"You know. . . ."

Liesel responded in the usual fashion.

"Saukerl," she laughed, and she walked the short distance home. A disconcerting mixture of mud and pity was one thing, but kissing Rudy Steiner was something entirely different.

Smiling sadly on the step, he called out, rummaging a hand through his hair. "One day," he warned her. "One day, Liesel!"

In the basement, just over two years later, Liesel ached sometimes to go next door and see him, even if she was writing in the early hours of morning. She also realized it was most likely those sodden days at the Hitler Youth that had fed his, and subsequently her own, desire for crime.

After all, despite the usual bouts of rain, summer was beginning to arrive properly. The *Klar* apples should have been ripening. There was more stealing to be done.

THE LOSERS

When it came to stealing, Liesel and Rudy first stuck with the idea that there was safety in numbers. Andy Schmeikl invited them to the river for a meeting. Among other things, a game plan for fruit stealing would be on the agenda.

"So are you the leader now?" Rudy had asked, but Andy shook his head, heavy with disappointment. He clearly wished that he had what it took.

"No." His cool voice was unusually warm. Half-baked. "There's someone else."

✳ ✳ ✳ THE NEW ARTHUR BERG ✳ ✳ ✳
He had windy hair and cloudy eyes,
and he was the kind of delinquent
who had no other reason to
steal except that he enjoyed it.
His name was Viktor Chemmel.

Unlike most people engaged in the various arts of thievery, Viktor Chemmel had it all. He lived in the best part of Molching, high up in a villa that had been fumigated when the Jews were driven out. He had money. He had cigarettes. What he wanted, however, was more.

"No crime in wanting a little more," he claimed, lying back in the grass with a collection of boys assembled around him. "Wanting more is our fundamental right as Germans. What does our *Führer* say?" He answered his own rhetoric. "We must take what is rightfully ours!"

At face value, Viktor Chemmel was clearly your typical teenage bullshit artist. Unfortunately, when he felt like revealing it, he also possessed a certain charisma, a kind of *follow me*.

When Liesel and Rudy approached the group by the river, she heard him ask another question. "So where are these two deviants you've been bragging about? It's ten past four already."

"Not by my watch," said Rudy.

Viktor Chemmel propped himself up on an elbow. "You're not wearing a watch."

"Would I be here if I was rich enough to own a watch?"

The new leader sat up fully and smiled, with straight white teeth. He then turned his casual focus onto the girl. "Who's the little whore?" Liesel, well accustomed to verbal abuse, simply watched the fog-ridden texture of his eyes.

"Last year," she listed, "I stole at least three hundred apples and dozens of potatoes. I have little trouble with barbed wire fences and I can keep up with anyone here."

"Is that right?"

"Yes." She did not shrink or step away. "All I ask is a small part of anything we take. A dozen apples here or there. A few leftovers for me and my friend."

"Well, I suppose that can be arranged." Viktor lit a cigarette and raised it to his mouth. He made a concerted effort to blow his next mouthful in Liesel's face.

Liesel did not cough.

It was the same group as the previous year, the only exception being the leader. Liesel wondered why none of the other boys had assumed the helm, but looking from face to face, she realized that none of them had it. They had no qualms about stealing, but they needed to be told. They *liked* to be told, and Viktor Chemmel liked to be the teller. It was a nice microcosm.

For a moment, Liesel longed for the reappearance of Arthur Berg. Or would he, too, have fallen under the leadership of Chemmel? It didn't matter. Liesel only knew that Arthur Berg did not have a tyrannical bone in his body, whereas the new leader had hundreds of them. Last year, she knew that if she was stuck in a tree, Arthur would come back for her, despite claiming otherwise. This year, by comparison, she was instantly aware that Viktor Chemmel wouldn't even bother to look back.

He stood, regarding the lanky boy and the malnourished-looking girl. "So you want to steal with me?"

What did they have to lose? They nodded.

He stepped closer and grabbed Rudy's hair. "I want to hear it."

"Definitely," Rudy said, before being shoved back, fringe first.

"And you?"

"Of course." Liesel was quick enough to avoid the same treatment.

Viktor smiled. He squashed his cigarette, breathed deeply in, and scratched his chest. "My gentlemen, my whore, it looks like it's time to go shopping."

As the group walked off, Liesel and Rudy were at the back, as they'd always been in the past.

"Do you like him?" Rudy whispered.

"Do you?"

Rudy paused a moment. "I think he's a complete bastard."

"Me too."

The group was getting away from them.

"Come on," Rudy said, "we've fallen behind."

After a few miles, they reached the first farm. What greeted them was a shock. The trees they'd imagined to be swollen with fruit were frail and injured-looking, with only a small array of apples hanging miserly from each branch. The next farm was the same. Maybe it was a bad season, or their timing wasn't quite right.

By the end of the afternoon, when the spoils were handed out, Liesel and Rudy were given one diminutive apple between them. In fairness, the takings were incredibly poor, but Viktor Chemmel also ran a tighter ship.

"What do you call this?" Rudy asked, the apple resting in his palm.

Viktor didn't even turn around. "What does it look like?" The words were dropped over his shoulder.

"One lousy apple?"

"Here." A half-eaten one was also tossed their way, landing chewed-side-down in the dirt. "You can have that one, too."

Rudy was incensed. "To hell with this. We didn't walk ten miles for one and a half scrawny apples, did we, Liesel?"

Liesel did not answer.

She did not have time, for Viktor Chemmel was on top of Rudy before she could utter a word. His knees had pinned Rudy's arms and his hands were around his throat. The apples were scooped up by none other than Andy Schmeikl, at Viktor's request.

"You're hurting him," Liesel said.

"Am I?" Viktor was smiling again. She hated that smile.

"He's *not* hurting me." Rudy's words were rushed together and his face was red with strain. His nose began to bleed.

After an extended moment or two of increased pressure, Viktor let Rudy go and climbed off him, taking a few careless steps. He said, "Get up, boy," and Rudy, choosing wisely, did as he was told.

Viktor came casually closer again and faced him. He gave him a gentle rub on the arm. A whisper. "Unless you want me to turn that blood into a fountain, I suggest you go away, little boy." He looked at Liesel. "And take the little slut with you."

No one moved.

"Well, what are you waiting for?"

Liesel took Rudy's hand and they left, but not before Rudy turned one last time and spat some blood and saliva at Viktor Chemmel's feet. It evoked one final remark.

* * * A SMALL THREAT FROM * * *
VIKTOR CHEMMEL TO RUDY STEINER
"You'll pay for that at a later date, my friend."

Say what you will about Viktor Chemmel, but he certainly had patience and a good memory. It took him approximately five months to turn his statement into a true one.

SKETCHES

If the summer of 1941 was walling up around the likes of Rudy and Liesel, it was writing and painting itself into the life of Max Vandenburg. In his loneliest moments in the basement, the words started piling up around him. The visions began to pour and fall and occasionally limp from out of his hands.

He had what he called just a small ration of tools:

A painted book.

A handful of pencils.

A mindful of thoughts.

Like a simple puzzle, he put them together.

Originally, Max had intended to write his own story.

The idea was to write about everything that had happened to him—all that had led him to a Himmel Street basement—but it was not what came out. Max's exile produced something else entirely. It was a collection of random thoughts and he chose to embrace them. They felt *true*. They were more real than the letters he wrote to his family and to his friend Walter Kugler, knowing very well that he could never send them. The desecrated pages of *Mein Kampf* were becoming a series of sketches, page after page, which to him summed up the events that had swapped his former life for another. Some took minutes. Others hours. He resolved that when the book was finished, he'd give it to Liesel, when she was old enough, and hopefully, when all this nonsense was over.

From the moment he tested the pencils on the first painted page, he kept the book close at all times. Often, it was next to him or still in his fingers as he slept.

One afternoon, after his push-ups and sit-ups, he fell asleep against the basement wall. When Liesel came down, she found the book sitting next to him, slanted against his thigh, and curiosity got the better of her. She leaned over and picked it up, waiting for him to stir. He didn't. Max was sitting with his head and shoulder blades against the wall. She could barely make out the sound of his breath, coasting in and out of him, as she opened the book and glimpsed a few random pages. . . .

Not the Führer— the conductor!

• • •

Frightened by what she saw, Liesel placed the book back down, exactly as she found it, against Max's leg.

A voice startled her.

"Danke schön," it said, and when she looked across, following the trail of sound to its owner, a small sign of satisfaction was present on his Jewish lips.

"Holy Christ," Liesel gasped. "You scared me, Max."

He returned to his sleep, and behind her, the girl dragged the same thought up the steps.

You scared me, Max.

THE WHISTLER AND THE SHOES

The same pattern continued through the end of summer and well into autumn. Rudy did his best to survive the Hitler Youth. Max did his push-ups and made his sketches. Liesel found newspapers and wrote her words on the basement wall.

It's also worthy of mention that every pattern has at least one small bias, and one day it will tip itself over, or fall from one page to another. In this case, the dominant factor was Rudy. Or at least, Rudy and a freshly fertilized sports field.

Late in October, all appeared to be usual. A filthy boy was walking down Himmel Street. Within a few minutes, his family would expect his arrival, and he would lie that everyone in his Hitler Youth division was given extra drills in the field. His parents would even expect some laughter. They didn't get it.

Today Rudy was all out of laughter and lies.

On this particular Wednesday, when Liesel looked more closely, she could see that Rudy Steiner was shirtless. And he was furious.

"What happened?" she asked as he trudged past.

He reversed back and held out the shirt. "Smell it," he said.

"What?"

"Are you deaf? I said smell it."

Reluctantly, Liesel leaned in and caught a ghastly whiff of the brown garment. "Jesus, Mary, and Joseph! Is that—?"

The boy nodded. "It's on my chin, too. My chin! I'm lucky I didn't swallow it!"

"Jesus, Mary, and Joseph."

"The field at Hitler Youth just got fertilized." He gave his shirt another halfhearted, disgusted appraisal. "It's cow manure, I think."

"Did what's-his-name—Deutscher—know it was there?"

"He says he didn't. But he was grinning."

"Jesus, Mary, and—"

"Could you stop saying that?!"

What Rudy needed at this point in time was a victory. He had lost in his dealings with Viktor Chemmel. He'd endured problem after problem at the Hitler Youth. All he wanted was a small scrap of triumph, and he was determined to get it.

He continued home, but when he reached the concrete step, he changed his mind and came slowly, purposefully back to the girl.

Careful and quiet, he spoke. "You know what would cheer me up?"

Liesel cringed. "If you think I'm going to—in that state . . ."

He seemed disappointed in her. "No, not that." He sighed and stepped closer. "Something else." After a moment's thought, he raised his head, just a touch. "Look at me. I'm filthy. I stink like cow shit, or dog shit, whatever your opinion, and as usual, I'm absolutely starving." He paused. "I need a win, Liesel. Honestly."

Liesel knew.

She'd have gone closer but for the smell of him.

Stealing.

They had to steal something.

No.

They had to steal something *back*. It didn't matter what. It needed only to be soon.

"Just you and me this time," Rudy suggested. "No Chemmels, no Schmeikls. Just you and me."

The girl couldn't help it.

Her hands itched, her pulse split, and her mouth smiled all at the same time. "Sounds good."

"It's agreed, then," and although he tried not to, Rudy could not hide the fertilized grin that grew on his face. "Tomorrow?"

Liesel nodded. "Tomorrow."

Their plan was perfect but for one thing:

They had no idea where to start.

Fruit was out. Rudy snubbed his nose at onions and potatoes, and they drew the line at another attempt on Otto Sturm and his bikeful of farm produce. Once was immoral. Twice was complete bastardry.

"So where the hell do we go?" Rudy asked.

"How should I know? This was your idea, wasn't it?"

"That doesn't mean you shouldn't think a little, too. I can't think of everything."

"You can barely think of *anything*. . . ."

They argued on as they walked through town. On the outskirts, they witnessed the first of the farms and the trees standing like emaciated statues. The branches were gray and when they looked up at them, there was nothing but ragged limbs and empty sky.

Rudy spat.

They walked back through Molching, making suggestions.

"What about Frau Diller?"

"What about her?"

"Maybe if we say 'heil Hitler' and then steal something, we'll be all right."

After roaming Munich Street for an hour or so, the daylight was drawing to a close and they were on the verge of giving up. "It's pointless," Rudy said, "and I'm even hungrier now than I've ever been. I'm starving, for Christ's sake." He walked another dozen steps before he stopped and looked back. "What's with you?" because now Liesel was standing completely still, and a moment of realization was strapped to her face.

Why hadn't she thought of it before?

"What is it?" Rudy was becoming impatient. "*Saumensch,* what's going on?"

At that very moment, Liesel was presented with a decision. Could she truly carry out what she was thinking? Could she really seek revenge on a person like this? Could she despise someone *this* much?

She began walking in the opposite direction. When Rudy caught up, she slowed a little in the vain hope of achieving a little more clarity. After all, the guilt was already there. It was moist. The seed was already bursting into a dark-leafed flower. She weighed up whether she could really go through with this. At a crossroad, she stopped.

"I know a place."

They went over the river and made their way up the hill.

On Grande Strasse, they took in the splendor of the houses. The front doors glowed with polish, and the roof tiles sat like toupees, combed to perfection. The walls and windows were manicured and the chimneys almost breathed out smoke rings.

Rudy planted his feet. "The mayor's house?"

Liesel nodded, seriously. A pause. "They fired my mama."

When they angled toward it, Rudy asked just how in God's

name they were going to get inside, but Liesel knew. "Local knowledge," she answered. "Local—" But when they were able to see the window to the library at the far end of the house, she was greeted with a shock. The window was closed.

"Well?" Rudy asked.

Liesel swiveled slowly and hurried off. "Not today," she said. Rudy laughed.

"I knew it." He caught up. "I knew it, you filthy *Saumensch*. You couldn't get in there even if you had the key."

"Do you mind?" She quickened even more and brushed aside Rudy's commentary. "We just have to wait for the right opportunity." Internally, she shrugged away from a kind of gladness that the window was closed. She berated herself. Why, Liesel? she asked. Why did you have to explode when they fired Mama? Why couldn't you just keep your big mouth shut? For all you know, the mayor's wife is now completely reformed after you yelled and screamed at her. Maybe she's straightened herself out, picked herself up. Maybe she'll never let herself shiver in that house again and the window will be shut forever. . . . You stupid *Saumensch*!

A week later, however, on their fifth visit to the upper part of Molching, it was there.

The open window breathed a slice of air in.

That was all it would take.

It was Rudy who stopped first. He tapped Liesel in the ribs, with the back of his hand. "Is that window," he whispered, "open?" The eagerness in his voice leaned from his mouth, like a forearm onto Liesel's shoulder.

"*Jawohl*," she answered. "It sure is."

And how her heart began to heat.

• • •

On each previous occasion, when they found the window clamped firmly shut, Liesel's outer disappointment had masked a ferocious relief. Would she have had the neck to go in? And who and what, in fact, was she going in for? For Rudy? To locate some food?

No, the repugnant truth was this:

She didn't care about the food. Rudy, no matter how hard she tried to resist the idea, was secondary to her plan. It was the book she wanted. *The Whistler*. She wouldn't tolerate having it given to her by a lonely, pathetic old woman. Stealing it, on the other hand, seemed a little more acceptable. Stealing it, in a sick kind of sense, was like earning it.

The light was changing in blocks of shade.

The pair of them gravitated toward the immaculate, bulky house. They rustled their thoughts.

"You hungry?" Rudy asked.

Liesel replied. "Starving." For a book.

"Look—a light just came on upstairs."

"I see it."

"Still hungry, *Saumensch*?"

They laughed nervously for a moment before going through the motions of who should go in and who should stand watch. As the male in the operation, Rudy clearly felt that he should be the aggressor, but it was obvious that Liesel knew this place. It was she who was going in. She knew what was on the other side of the window.

She said it. "It has to be me."

Liesel closed her eyes. Tightly.

She compelled herself to remember, to see visions of the mayor and his wife. She watched her gathered friendship with Ilsa Hermann and made sure to see it kicked in the shins and left by the wayside. It worked. She detested them.

They scouted the street and crossed the yard silently.

Now they were crouched beneath the slit in the window on the ground floor. The sound of their breathing amplified.

"Here," Rudy said, "give me your shoes. You'll be quieter."

Without complaint, Liesel undid the worn black laces and left the shoes on the ground. She rose up and Rudy gently opened the window just wide enough for Liesel to climb through. The noise of it passed overhead, like a low-flying plane.

Liesel heaved herself onto the ledge and tussled her way inside. Taking off her shoes, she realized, was a brilliant idea, as she landed much heavier on the wooden floor than she'd anticipated. The soles of her feet expanded in that painful way, rising to the inside edges of her socks.

The room itself was as it always was.

Liesel, in the dusty dimness, shrugged off her feelings of nostalgia. She crept forward and allowed her eyes to adjust.

"What's going on?" Rudy whispered sharply from outside, but she waved him a backhander that meant *Halt's Maul*. Keep quiet.

"The food," he reminded her. "Find the *food*. And cigarettes, if you can."

Both items, however, were the last things on her mind. She was home, among the mayor's books of every color and description, with their silver and gold lettering. She could smell the pages. She could almost taste the words as they stacked up around her. Her feet took her to the right-hand wall. She knew the one she wanted—the exact position—but when she made it to *The Whistler*'s usual place on the shelf, it was not there. A slight gap was in its place.

From above, she heard footsteps.

"The light!" Rudy whispered. The words were shoved through the open window. "It's out!"

"*Scheisse.*"

"They're coming downstairs."

There was a giant length of a moment then, the eternity of split-second decision. Her eyes scanned the room and she could see *The Whistler,* sitting patiently on the mayor's desk.

"Hurry up," Rudy warned her. But very calmly and cleanly, Liesel walked over, picked up the book, and made her way cautiously out. Headfirst, she climbed from the window, managing to land on her feet again, feeling the pang of pain once more, this time in her ankles.

"Come on," Rudy implored her. "Run, run. *Schnell!*"

Once around the corner, on the road back down to the river and Munich Street, she stopped to bend over and recover. Her body was folded in the middle, the air half frozen in her mouth, her heart tolling in her ears.

Rudy was the same.

When he looked over, he saw the book under her arm. He struggled to speak. "What's"—he grappled with the words—"with the book?"

The darkness was filling up truly now. Liesel panted, the air in her throat defrosting. "It was all I could find."

Unfortunately, Rudy could smell it. The lie. He cocked his head and told her what he felt was a fact. "You didn't go in for food, did you? You got what you wanted. . . ."

Liesel straightened then and was overcome with the sickness of another realization.

The shoes.

She looked at Rudy's feet, then at his hands, and at the ground all around him.

"What?" he asked. "What is it?"

"*Saukerl,*" she accused him. "Where are my shoes?" Rudy's face whitened, which left her in no doubt. "They're back at the house," she suggested, "aren't they?"

Rudy searched desperately around himself, begging against all reality that he might have brought them with him. He imagined himself picking them up, wishing it true—but the shoes were not there. They sat uselessly, or actually, much worse, incriminatingly, by the wall at 8 Grande Strasse.

"*Dummkopf!*" he admonished himself, smacking his ear. He looked down shamefully at the sullen sight of Liesel's socks. "Idiot!" It didn't take him long to decide on making it right. Earnestly, he said, "Just wait," and he hurried back around the corner.

"Don't get caught," Liesel called after him, but he didn't hear.

The minutes were heavy while he was gone.

Darkness was now complete and Liesel was quite certain that a *Watschen* was most likely in the cards when she returned home. "Hurry," she murmured, but still Rudy didn't appear. She imagined the sound of a police siren throwing itself forward and reeling itself in. Collecting itself.

Still, nothing.

Only when she walked back to the intersection of the two streets in her damp, dirty socks did she see him. Rudy's triumphant face was held nicely up as he trotted steadily toward her. His teeth were gnashed into a grin, and the shoes dangled from his hand. "They nearly killed me," he said, "but I made it." Once they'd crossed the river, he handed Liesel the shoes, and she threw them down.

Sitting on the ground, she looked up at her best friend. "*Danke,*" she said. "Thank you."

Rudy bowed. "My pleasure." He tried for a little more. "No point asking if I get a kiss for that, I guess?"

"For bringing my shoes, which *you* left behind?"

"Fair enough." He held up his hands and continued speaking as they walked on, and Liesel made a concerted effort to ignore him. She only heard the last part. "Probably wouldn't want to kiss you anyway—not if your breath's anything like your shoes."

"You disgust me," she informed him, and she hoped he couldn't see the escaped beginnings of a smile that had fallen from her mouth.

On Himmel Street, Rudy captured the book. Under a lamppost, he read out the title and wondered what it was about.

Dreamily, Liesel answered. "Just a murderer."

"Is that all?"

"There's also a policeman trying to catch him."

Rudy handed it back. "Speaking of which, I think we're both slightly in for it when we get home. You especially."

"Why me?"

"You know—your mama."

"What about her?" Liesel was exercising the blatant right of every person who's ever belonged to a family. It's all very well for such a person to whine and moan and criticize other family members, but they won't let *anyone else* do it. That's when you get your back up and show loyalty. "Is there something wrong with her?"

Rudy backed away. "Sorry, *Saumensch*. I didn't mean to offend you."

Even in the night, Liesel could see that Rudy was growing. His face was lengthening. The blond shock of hair was darkening ever so slightly and his features seemed to be changing shape. But there was one thing that would never change. It was impossible to be angry at him for long.

"Anything good to eat at your place tonight?" he asked.

"I doubt it."

"Me neither. It's a shame you can't eat books. Arthur Berg said something like that once. Remember?"

They recounted the good old days for the remainder of the walk,

Liesel often glancing down at *The Whistler,* at the gray cover and the black imprinted title.

Before they went into their respective homes, Rudy stopped a moment and said, "Goodbye, *Saumensch.*" He laughed. "Good night, book thief."

It was the first time Liesel had been branded with her title, and she couldn't hide the fact that she liked it very much. As we're both aware, she'd stolen books previously, but in late October 1941, it became official. That night, Liesel Meminger truly became the book thief.

THREE ACTS OF STUPIDITY
BY RUDY STEINER

* * * RUDY STEINER, PURE GENIUS * * *
1. He stole the biggest potato
from Mamer's, the local grocer.
2. Taking on Franz Deutscher
on Munich Street.
3. Skipping the Hitler Youth
meetings altogether.

The problem with Rudy's first act was greed. It was a typically dreary afternoon in mid-November 1941.

Earlier, he'd woven through the women with their coupons quite brilliantly, almost, dare I say it, with a touch of criminal genius. He nearly went completely unnoticed.

Inconspicuous as he was, however, he managed to take hold of the biggest potato of the lot—the very same one that several people in the line had been watching. They all looked on as a thirteen-year-old fist rose up and grabbed it. A choir of heavyset Helgas pointed him out, and Thomas Mamer came storming toward the dirty fruit.

"Meine Erdäpfel," he said. "My earth apples."

The potato was still in Rudy's hands (he couldn't hold it in just the one), and the women gathered around him like a troop of wrestlers. Some fast talking was required.

"My family," Rudy explained. A convenient stream of clear fluid began to trickle from his nose. He made a point of not wiping it away. "We're all starving. My sister needed a new coat. The last one was stolen."

Mamer was no fool. Still holding Rudy by the collar, he said, "And you plan to dress her with a potato?"

"No, sir." He looked diagonally into the one eye he could see of his captor. Mamer was a barrel of a man, with two small bullet holes to look out of. His teeth were like a soccer crowd, crammed in. "We traded all our points for the coat three weeks ago and now we have nothing to eat."

The grocer held Rudy in one hand and the potato in the other. He called out the dreaded word to his wife. *"Polizei."*

"No," Rudy begged, "please." He would tell Liesel later on that he was not the slightest bit afraid, but his heart was certainly bursting at that moment, I'm sure. "Not the police. Please, not the police."

"Polizei." Mamer remained unmoved as the boy wriggled and fought with the air.

Also in the line that afternoon was a teacher, Herr Link. He was in the percentage of teachers at school who were not priests or nuns. Rudy found him and accosted him in the eyes.

"Herr Link." This was his last chance. "Herr Link, tell him, please. Tell him how poor I am."

The grocer looked at the teacher with inquiring eyes.

Herr Link stepped forward and said, "Yes, Herr Mamer. This boy is poor. He's from Himmel Street." The crowd of predominantly women conferred at that point, knowing that Himmel Street was not exactly the epitome of idyllic Molching living. It was well known as a relatively poor neighborhood. "He has eight brothers and sisters."

Eight!

Rudy had to hold back a smile, though he wasn't in the clear yet. At least he had the teacher lying now. He'd somehow managed to add three more children to the Steiner family.

"Often, he comes to school without breakfast," and the crowd of women was conferring again. It was like a coat of paint on the situation, adding a little extra potency and atmosphere.

"So that means he should be allowed to steal my potatoes?"

"The biggest one!" one of the women ejaculated.

"Keep quiet, Frau Metzing," Mamer warned her, and she quickly settled down.

At first, all attention was on Rudy and the scruff of his neck. It then moved back and forth, from the boy to the potato to Mamer—from best-looking to worst—and exactly what made the grocer decide in Rudy's favor would forever be unanswered.

Was it the pathetic nature of the boy?

The dignity of Herr Link?

The annoyance of Frau Metzing?

Whatever it was, Mamer dropped the potato back on the pile and dragged Rudy from his premises. He gave him a good push with his right boot and said, "Don't come back."

From outside, Rudy looked on as Mamer reached the counter to serve his next customer with food and sarcasm. "I wonder which potato *you're* going to ask for," he said, keeping one eye open for the boy.

For Rudy, it was yet another failure.

The second act of stupidity was equally dangerous, but for different reasons.

Rudy would finish this particular altercation with a black eye, cracked ribs, and a haircut.

Again, at the Hitler Youth meetings, Tommy Müller was having his problems, and Franz Deutscher was just waiting for Rudy to step in. It didn't take long.

Rudy and Tommy were given another comprehensive drill session while the others went inside to learn tactics. As they ran in the cold, they could see the warm heads and shoulders through the windows. Even when they joined the rest of the group, the drills weren't quite finished. As Rudy slumped into the corner and flicked mud from his sleeve at the window, Franz fired the Hitler Youth's favorite question at him.

"When was our *Führer,* Adolf Hitler, born?"

Rudy looked up. "Sorry?"

The question was repeated, and the very stupid Rudy Steiner, who knew all too well that it was April 20, 1889, answered with the birth of Christ. He even threw in Bethlehem as an added piece of information.

Franz smeared his hands together.

A very bad sign.

He walked over to Rudy and ordered him back outside for some more laps of the field.

Rudy ran them alone, and after every lap, he was asked again the date of the *Führer*'s birthday. He did seven laps before he got it right.

The major trouble occurred a few days after the meeting.

On Munich Street, Rudy noticed Deutscher walking along the footpath with some friends and felt the need to throw a rock at him.

You might well ask just what the hell he was thinking. The answer is, probably nothing at all. He'd probably say that he was exercising his God-given right to stupidity. Either that, or the very sight of Franz Deutscher gave him the urge to destroy himself.

The rock hit its mark on the spine, though not as hard as Rudy might have hoped. Franz Deutscher spun around and looked happy to find him standing there, with Liesel, Tommy, and Tommy's little sister, Kristina.

"Let's run," Liesel urged him, but Rudy didn't move.

"We're not at Hitler Youth now," he informed her. The older boys had already arrived. Liesel remained next to her friend, as did the twitching Tommy and the delicate Kristina.

"Mr. Steiner," Franz declared, before picking him up and throwing him to the pavement.

When Rudy stood up, it served only to infuriate Deutscher even more. He brought him to the ground for a second time, following him down with a knee to the rib cage.

Again, Rudy stood up, and the group of older boys laughed now at their friend. This was not the best news for Rudy. "Can't you make him feel it?" the tallest of them said. His eyes were as blue and cold as the sky, and the words were all the incentive Franz needed. He was determined that Rudy would hit the ground and stay there.

A larger crowd made its way around them as Rudy swung at Franz Deutscher's stomach, missing him completely. Simultaneously, he felt the burning sensation of a fist on his left eye socket. It arrived with sparks, and he was on the ground before he even realized. He was punched again, in the same place, and he could feel the bruise turn yellow and blue and black all at once. Three layers of exhilarating pain.

The developing crowd gathered and leered to see if Rudy might get up again. He didn't. This time, he remained on the cold, wet ground, feeling it rise through his clothes and spread itself out.

The sparks were still in his eyes, and he didn't notice until it was too late that Franz now stood above him with a brand-new pocket-knife, about to crouch down and cut him.

"No!" Liesel protested, but the tall one held her back. In her ear, his words were deep and old.

"Don't worry," he assured her. "He won't do it. He doesn't have the guts."

He was wrong.

Franz merged into a kneeling position as he leaned closer to Rudy and whispered:

"When was our *Führer* born?" Each word was carefully created and fed into his ear. "Come on, Rudy, when was he born? You can tell me, everything's fine, don't be afraid."

And Rudy?

How did he reply?

Did he respond prudently, or did he allow his stupidity to sink himself deeper into the mire?

He looked happily into the pale blue eyes of Franz Deutscher and whispered, "Easter Monday."

Within a few seconds, the knife was applied to his hair. It was haircut number two in this section of Liesel's life. The hair of a Jew was cut with rusty scissors. Her best friend was taken to with a gleaming knife. She knew nobody who actually paid for a haircut.

As for Rudy, so far this year he'd swallowed mud, bathed himself in fertilizer, been half-strangled by a developing criminal, and was now receiving something at least nearing the icing on the cake—public humiliation on Munich Street.

For the most part, his fringe was sliced away freely, but with each stroke, there were always a few hairs that held on for dear life and were pulled out completely. As each one was plucked, Rudy winced, his black eye throbbing in the process and his ribs flashing in pain.

"April twentieth, eighteen eighty-nine!" Franz lectured him, and when he led his cohorts away, the audience dispersed, leaving only Liesel, Tommy, and Kristina with their friend.

Rudy lay quietly on the ground, in the rising damp.

Which leaves us only with stupid act number three—skipping the Hitler Youth meetings.

He didn't stop going right away, purely to show Deutscher that he wasn't afraid of him, but after another few weeks, Rudy ceased his involvement altogether.

Dressed proudly in his uniform, he exited Himmel Street and kept walking, his loyal subject, Tommy, by his side.

Instead of attending the Hitler Youth, they walked out of town and along the Amper, skipping stones, heaving enormous rocks into the water, and generally getting up to no good. He made sure to get the uniform dirty enough to fool his mother, at least until the first letter arrived. That was when he heard the dreaded call from the kitchen.

First, his parents threatened him. He didn't attend.

They begged him to go. He refused.

Eventually, it was the opportunity to join a different division that swayed Rudy in the right direction. This was fortunate, because if he didn't show his face soon, the Steiners would be fined for his non-attendance. His older brother, Kurt, inquired as to whether Rudy might join the Flieger Division, which specialized in the teaching of aircraft and flying. Mostly, they built model airplanes, and there was no Franz Deutscher. Rudy accepted, and Tommy also joined. It was the one time in his life that his idiotic behavior delivered beneficial results.

In his new division, whenever he was asked the famous *Führer* question, Rudy would smile and answer, "April 20, 1889," and then to Tommy, he'd whisper a different date, like Beethoven's birthday, or Mozart's, or Strauss's. They'd been learning about composers in school, where despite his obvious stupidity, Rudy excelled.

THE FLOATING BOOK (Part II)

At the beginning of December, victory finally came to Rudy Steiner, though not in a typical fashion.

It was a cold day, but very still. It had come close to snowing.

After school, Rudy and Liesel stopped in at Alex Steiner's shop, and as they walked home, they saw Rudy's old friend Franz Deutscher coming around the corner. Liesel, as was her habit these days, was carrying *The Whistler*. She liked to feel it in her hand. Either the smooth spine or the rough edges of paper. It was she who saw him first.

"Look." She pointed. Deutscher was loping toward them with another Hitler Youth leader.

Rudy shrank into himself. He felt at his mending eye. "Not this time." He searched the streets. "If we go past the church, we can follow the river and cut back that way."

With no further words, Liesel followed him, and they successfully avoided Rudy's tormentor—straight into the path of another.

At first, they thought nothing of it.

The group crossing the bridge and smoking cigarettes could have been anybody, and it was too late to turn around when the two parties recognized each other.

"Oh, no, they've seen us."

Viktor Chemmel smiled.

He spoke very amiably. This could only mean that he was at his most dangerous. "Well, well, if it isn't Rudy Steiner and his little whore." Very smoothly, he met them and snatched *The Whistler* from Liesel's grip. "What are we reading?"

"This is between us." Rudy tried to reason with him. "It has nothing to do with her. Come on, give it back."

"*The Whistler.*" He addressed Liesel now. "Any good?"

She cleared her throat. "Not bad." Unfortunately, she gave herself away. In the eyes. They were agitated. She knew the exact moment when Viktor Chemmel established that the book was a prize possession.

"I'll tell you what," he said. "For fifty marks, you can have it back."

"Fifty marks!" That was Andy Schmeikl. "Come on, Viktor, you could buy a thousand books for that."

"Did I ask you to speak?"

Andy kept quiet. His mouth seemed to swing shut.

Liesel tried a poker face. "You can keep it, then. I've already read it."

"What happens at the end?"

Damn it!

She hadn't gotten that far yet.

She hesitated, and Viktor Chemmel deciphered it instantly.

Rudy rushed at him now. "Come on, Viktor, don't do this to her. It's me you're after. I'll do anything you want."

The older boy only swatted him away, the book held aloft. And he corrected him.

"No," he said. "*I'll* do anything *I* want," and he proceeded to the river. Everyone followed, at catch-up speed. Half walk, half run. Some protested. Some urged him on.

It was so quick, and relaxed. There was a question, and a mocking, friendly voice.

"Tell me," Viktor said. "Who was the last Olympic discus champion, in Berlin?" He turned to face them. He warmed up his arm. "Who *was* it? Goddamn it, it's on the tip of my tongue. It was that American, wasn't it? Carpenter or something . . ."

"Please!"—Rudy.

The water toppled.

Viktor Chemmel did *the spin*.

The book was released gloriously from his hand. It opened and flapped, the pages rattling as it covered ground in the air. More abruptly than expected, it stopped and appeared to be sucked toward the water. It clapped when it hit the surface and began to float downstream.

Viktor shook his head. "Not enough height. A poor throw." He smiled again. "But still good enough to win, huh?"

Liesel and Rudy didn't stick around to hear the laughter.

Rudy in particular had taken off down the riverbank, attempting to locate the book.

"Can you see it?" Liesel called out.

Rudy ran.

He continued down the water's edge, showing her the book's location. "Over there!" He stopped and pointed and ran farther down to overtake it. Soon, he peeled off his coat and jumped in, wading to the middle of the river.

Liesel, slowing to a walk, could see the ache of each step. The painful cold.

When she was close enough, she saw it move past him, but he soon caught up. His hand reached in and collared what was now a soggy block of cardboard and paper. *"The Whistler!"* the boy called out. It was the only book floating down the Amper River that day, but he still felt the need to announce it.

Another note of interest is that Rudy did not attempt to leave the devastatingly cold water as soon as he held the book in his hand. For a good minute or so, he stayed. He never did explain it to Liesel, but I think she knew very well that the reasons were twofold.

* * * THE FROZEN MOTIVES * * *
OF RUDY STEINER
1. After months of failure, this moment was
his only chance to revel in some victory.
2. Such a position of selflessness was a good
place to ask Liesel for the usual favor.
How could she possibly turn him down?

"How about a kiss, *Saumensch?*"

He stood waist-deep in the water for a few moments longer before climbing out and handing her the book. His pants clung to him, and he did not stop walking. In truth, I think he was afraid. Rudy Steiner was scared of the book thief's kiss. He must have longed for it so much. He must have loved her so incredibly hard. So hard that he would never ask for her lips again and would go to his grave without them.

PART SIX

the dream carrier

featuring:

death's diary—the snowman—thirteen
presents—the next book—the nightmare of
a jewish corpse—a newspaper sky—a visitor—
a *schmunzeler*—and a final kiss on poisoned cheeks

DEATH'S DIARY: 1942

It was a year for the ages, like 79, like 1346, to name just a few. Forget the scythe, Goddamn it, I needed a broom or a mop. And I needed a vacation.

* * * A SMALL PIECE OF TRUTH * * *
I do not carry a sickle or scythe.
I only wear a hooded black robe when it's cold.
And I don't have those skull-like
facial features you seem to enjoy
pinning on me from a distance. You
want to know what I truly look like?
I'll help you out. Find yourself
a mirror while I continue.

I actually feel quite self-indulgent at the moment, telling you all about me, me, me. My travels, what *I* saw in '42. On the other hand, you're a human—you should understand self-obsession. The point is, there's a reason for me explaining what I saw in that time. Much of it would have repercussions for Liesel Meminger. It brought the war closer to Himmel Street, and it dragged *me* along for the ride.

There were certainly some rounds to be made that year, from Poland to Russia to Africa and back again. You might argue that I make the rounds no matter what year it is, but sometimes the human race likes to crank things up a little. They increase the production of bodies and their escaping souls. A few bombs usually do the trick. Or some gas chambers, or the chitchat of faraway guns. If none of that finishes proceedings, it at least strips people of their living arrangements, and I witness the homeless everywhere. They often come after me as I wander through the streets of molested cities. They beg me to take them with me, not realizing I'm too busy as it is. "Your time will come," I convince them, and I try not to look back. At times, I wish I could say something like, "Don't you see I've already got enough on my plate?" but I never do. I complain internally as I go about my work, and some years, the souls and bodies don't add up; they multiply.

* * * AN ABRIDGED ROLL CALL FOR 1942 * * *
1. The desperate Jews — their spirits
in my lap as we sat on the roof,
next to the steaming chimneys.
2. The Russian soldiers — taking only
small amounts of ammunition, relying
on the fallen for the rest of it.
3. The soaked bodies of a French coast —
beached on the shingle and sand.

• • •

I could go on, but I've decided for now that three examples will suffice. Three examples, if nothing else, will give you the ashen taste in your mouth that defined my existence during that year.

So many humans.
So many colors.

They keep triggering inside me. They harass my memory. I see them tall in their heaps, all mounted on top of each other. There is air like plastic, a horizon like setting glue. There are skies manufactured by people, punctured and leaking, and there are soft, coal-colored clouds, beating like black hearts.
And then.
There is death.
Making his way through all of it.
On the surface: unflappable, unwavering.
Below: unnerved, untied, and undone.

In all honesty (and I know I'm complaining excessively now), I was still getting over Stalin, in Russia. The so-called *second revolution*—the murder of his own people.
Then came Hitler.
They say that war is death's best friend, but I must offer you a different point of view on that one. To me, war is like the new boss who expects the impossible. He stands over your shoulder repeating one thing, incessantly: "Get it done, get it done." So you work harder. You get the job done. The boss, however, does not thank you. He asks for more.

Often, I try to remember the strewn pieces of beauty I saw in that time as well. I plow through my library of stories.
In fact, I reach for one now.

I believe you know half of it already, and if you come with me, I'll show you the rest. I'll show you the second half of a book thief.

Unknowingly, she awaits a great many things that I alluded to just a minute ago, but she also waits for you.

She's carrying some snow down to a basement, of all places.

Handfuls of frosty water can make almost anyone smile, but it cannot make them forget.

Here she comes.

THE SNOWMAN

For Liesel Meminger, the early stages of 1942 could be summed up like this:

She became thirteen years of age. Her chest was still flat. She had not yet bled. The young man from her basement was now in her bed.

*** Q&A ***
**How did Max
Vandenburg end up
in Liesel's bed?
He fell.**

Opinions varied, but Rosa Hubermann claimed that the seeds were sown at Christmas the previous year.

December 24 had been hungry and cold, but there was a major bonus—no lengthy visitations. Hans Junior was simultaneously shooting at Russians and maintaining his strike on family interaction. Trudy could only stop by on the weekend before Christmas, for a few hours.

311

She was going away with her family of employment. A holiday for a very different class of Germany.

On Christmas Eve, Liesel brought down a double handful of snow as a present for Max. "Close your eyes," she'd said. "Hold out your hands." As soon as the snow was transferred, Max shivered and laughed, but he still didn't open his eyes. He only gave the snow a quick taste, allowing it to sink into his lips.

"Is this today's weather report?"

Liesel stood next to him.

Gently, she touched his arm.

He raised it again to his mouth. "Thanks, Liesel."

It was the beginning of the greatest Christmas ever. Little food. No presents. But there was a snowman in their basement.

After delivering the first handfuls of snow, Liesel checked that no one else was outside, then proceeded to take as many buckets and pots out as she could. She filled them with the mounds of snow and ice that blanketed the small strip of world that was Himmel Street. Once they were full, she brought them in and carried them down to the basement.

All things being fair, she first threw a snowball at Max and collected a reply in the stomach. Max even threw one at Hans Hubermann as he made his way down the basement steps.

"Arschloch!" Papa yelped. "Liesel, give me some of that snow. A whole bucket!" For a few minutes, they all forgot. There was no more yelling or calling out, but they could not contain the small snatches of laughter. They were only humans, playing in the snow, in a house.

Papa looked at the snow-filled pots. "What do we do with the rest of it?"

"A snowman," Liesel replied. "We have to make a snowman."

Papa called out to Rosa.

The usual distant voice was hurled back. "What is it now, *Saukerl?*"

"Come down here, will you!"

When his wife appeared, Hans Hubermann risked his life by throwing a most excellent snowball at her. Just missing, it disintegrated when it hit the wall, and Mama had an excuse to swear for a long time without taking a breath. Once she recovered, she came down and helped them. She even brought the buttons for the eyes and nose and some string for a snowman smile. Even a scarf and hat were provided for what was really only a two-foot man of snow.

"A midget," Max had said.

"What do we do when it melts?" Liesel asked.

Rosa had the answer. "You mop it up, *Saumensch,* in a hurry."

Papa disagreed. "It won't melt." He rubbed his hands and blew into them. "It's freezing down here."

Melt it did, though, but somewhere in each of them, that snowman was still upright. It must have been the last thing they saw that Christmas Eve when they finally fell asleep. There was an accordion in their ears, a snowman in their eyes, and for Liesel, there was the thought of Max's last words before she left him by the fire.

* * * CHRISTMAS GREETINGS FROM * * *
MAX VANDENBURG
**"Often I wish this would all
be over, Liesel, but then somehow you
do something like walk down the basement
steps with a snowman in your hands."**

Unfortunately, that night signaled a severe downslide in Max's health. The early signs were innocent enough, and typical. Constant coldness. Swimming hands. Increased visions of boxing with the *Führer.* It was only when he couldn't warm up after his push-ups and sit-ups that it truly began to worry him. As close to the fire as he sat, he could not raise himself to any degree of approximate health. Day by day, his weight began to stumble off him. His exercise regimen faltered and fell apart, with his cheek against the surly basement floor.

All through January, he managed to hold himself together, but by early February, Max was in worrisome shape. He would struggle to wake up next to the fire, sleeping well into the morning instead, his mouth distorted and his cheekbones starting to swell. When asked, he said he was fine.

In mid-February, a few days before Liesel was thirteen, he came to the fireplace on the verge of collapse. He nearly fell into the fire.

"Hans," he whispered, and his face seemed to cramp. His legs gave way and his head hit the accordion case.

At once, a wooden spoon fell into some soup and Rosa Hubermann was at his side. She held Max's head and barked across the room at Liesel, "Don't just stand there, get the extra blankets. Take them to your bed. And you!" Papa was next. "Help me pick him up and carry him to Liesel's room. *Schnell!*"

Papa's face was stretched with concern. His gray eyes clanged and he picked him up on his own. Max was light as a child. "Can't we put him here, in our bed?"

Rosa had already considered that. "No. We have to keep these curtains open in the day or else it looks suspicious."

"Good point." Hans carried him out.

Blankets in hand, Liesel watched.

Limp feet and hanging hair in the hallway. One shoe had fallen off him.

"Move."

Mama marched in behind them, in her waddlesome way.

Once Max was in the bed, blankets were heaped on top and fastened around his body.

"Mama?"

Liesel couldn't bring herself to say anything else.

314

"What?" The bun of Rosa Hubermann's hair was wound tight enough to frighten from behind. It seemed to tighten further when she repeated the question. "What, Liesel?"

She stepped closer, afraid of the answer. "Is he alive?"

The bun nodded.

Rosa turned then and said something with great assurance. "Now listen to me, Liesel. I didn't take this man into my house to watch him die. Understand?"

Liesel nodded.

"Now go."

In the hall, Papa hugged her.

She desperately needed it.

Later on, she heard Hans and Rosa speaking in the night. Rosa made her sleep in their room, and she lay next to their bed, on the floor, on the mattress they'd dragged up from the basement. (There was concern as to whether it was infected, but they came to the conclusion that such thoughts were unfounded. This was no virus Max was suffering from, so they carried it up and replaced the sheet.)

Imagining the girl to be asleep, Mama voiced her opinion.

"That damn snowman," she whispered. "I bet it started with the snowman—fooling around with ice and snow in the cold down there."

Papa was more philosophical. "Rosa, it started with Adolf." He lifted himself. "We should check on him."

In the course of the night, Max was visited seven times.

* * * MAX VANDENBURG'S VISITOR * * *
SCORE SHEET
Hans Hubermann: 2
Rosa Hubermann: 2
Liesel Meminger: 3

In the morning, Liesel brought him his sketchbook from the basement and placed it on the bedside table. She felt awful for having looked at it the previous year, and this time, she kept it firmly closed, out of respect.

When Papa came in, she did not turn to face him but talked across Max Vandenburg, at the wall. "Why did I have to bring all that snow down?" she asked. "It started all of this, didn't it, Papa?" She clenched her hands, as if to pray. "Why did I have to build that snowman?"

Papa, to his enduring credit, was adamant. "Liesel," he said, "you had to."

For hours, she sat with him as he shivered and slept.

"Don't die," she whispered. "Please, Max, just don't die."

He was the second snowman to be melting away before her eyes, only this one was different. It was a paradox.

The colder he became, the more he melted.

THIRTEEN PRESENTS

It was Max's arrival, revisited.

Feathers turned to twigs again. Smooth face turned to rough. The proof she needed was there. He was alive.

The first few days, she sat and talked to him. On her birthday, she told him there was an enormous cake waiting in the kitchen, if only he'd wake up.

There was no waking.

There was no cake.

* * * A LATE-NIGHT EXCERPT * * *
I realized much later that I actually visited
33 Himmel Street in that period of time.
It must have been one of the few moments when the
girl was not there with him, for all I saw was a
man in bed. I knelt. I readied myself to insert
my hands through the blankets. Then there was a

resurgence — an immense struggle against my weight.
I withdrew, and with so much work ahead of me,
it was nice to be fought off in that dark little room.
I even managed a short, closed-eyed pause of
serenity before I made my way out.

On the fifth day, there was much excitement when Max opened his eyes, if only for a few moments. What he predominantly saw (and what a frightening version it must have been close-up) was Rosa Hubermann, practically slinging an armful of soup into his mouth. "Swallow," she advised him. "Don't think. Just swallow." As soon as Mama handed back the bowl, Liesel tried to see his face again, but there was a soup-feeder's backside in the way.

"Is he still awake?"

When she turned, Rosa did not have to answer.

After close to a week, Max woke up a second time, on this occasion with Liesel and Papa in the room. They were both watching the body in the bed when there was a small groan. If it's possible, Papa fell up- ward, out of the chair.

"Look," Liesel gasped. "Stay awake, Max, stay awake."

He looked at her briefly, but there was no recognition. The eyes studied her as if she were a riddle. Then gone again.

"Papa, what happened?"

Hans dropped, back to the chair.

Later, he suggested that perhaps she should read to him. "Come on, Liesel, you're such a good reader these days — even if it's a mystery to all of us where that book came from."

"I told you, Papa. One of the nuns at school gave it to me."

Papa held his hands up in mock-protest. "I know, I know." He sighed, from a height. "Just . . ." He chose his words gradually. "Don't get caught." This from a man who'd stolen a Jew.

From that day on, Liesel read *The Whistler* aloud to Max as he occupied her bed. The one frustration was that she kept having to skip whole chapters on account of many of the pages being stuck together. It had not dried well. Still, she struggled on, to the point where she was nearly three-quarters of the way through it. The book was 396 pages.

In the outside world, Liesel rushed from school each day in the hope that Max was feeling better. "Has he woken up? Has he eaten?"

"Go back out," Mama begged her. "You're chewing a hole in my stomach with all this talking. Go on. Get out there and play soccer, for God's sake."

"Yes, Mama." She was about to open the door. "But you'll come and get me if he wakes up, won't you? Just make something up. Scream out like I've done something wrong. Start swearing at me. Everyone will believe it, don't worry."

Even Rosa had to smile at that. She placed her knuckles on her hips and explained that Liesel wasn't too old yet to avoid a *Watschen* for talking in such a way. "And score a goal," she threatened, "or don't come home at all."

"Sure, Mama."

"Make that *two* goals, *Saumensch!*"

"Yes, Mama."

"And stop answering back!"

Liesel considered, but she ran onto the street, to oppose Rudy on the mud-slippery road.

"About time, ass scratcher." He welcomed her in the customary way as they fought for the ball. "Where have you been?"

Half an hour later, when the ball was squashed by the rare passage of a car on Himmel Street, Liesel had found her first present for Max Vandenburg. After judging it irreparable, all of the kids walked home in disgust, leaving the ball twitching on the cold, blistered road. Liesel and Rudy remained stooped over the carcass. There was a gaping hole on its side like a mouth.

"You want it?" Liesel asked.

Rudy shrugged. "What do I want with this squashed shit heap of a ball? There's no chance of getting air into it now, is there?"

"Do you want it or not?"

"No thanks." Rudy prodded it cautiously with his foot, as if it were a dead animal. Or an animal that *might* be dead.

As he walked home, Liesel picked the ball up and placed it under her arm. She could hear him call out, "Hey, *Saumensch*." She waited. *"Saumensch!"*

She relented. "What?"

"I've got a bike without wheels here, too, if you want it."

"Stick your bike."

From her position on the street, the last thing she heard was the laughter of that *Saukerl,* Rudy Steiner.

Inside, she made her way to the bedroom. She took the ball in to Max and placed it at the end of the bed.

"I'm sorry," she said, "it's not much. But when you wake up, I'll tell you all about it. I'll tell you it was the grayest afternoon you can imagine, and this car without its lights on ran straight over the ball. Then the man got out and yelled at us. And *then* he asked for directions. The nerve of him . . ."

Wake up! she wanted to scream.

Or shake him.

She didn't.

All Liesel could do was watch the ball and its trampled, flaking skin. It was the first gift of many.

∗ ∗ ∗ PRESENTS #2–#5 ∗ ∗ ∗
One ribbon, one pinecone.
One button, one stone.

The soccer ball had given her an idea.

Whenever she walked to and from school now, Liesel was on the lookout for discarded items that might be valuable to a dying man. She wondered at first why it mattered so much. How could something so seemingly insignificant give comfort to someone? A ribbon in a gutter. A pinecone on the street. A button leaning casually against a classroom wall. A flat round stone from the river. If nothing else, it showed that she cared, and it might give them something to talk about when Max woke up.

When she was alone, she would conduct those conversations.

"So what's all this?" Max would say. "What's all this junk?"

"Junk?" In her mind, she was sitting on the side of the bed. "This isn't junk, Max. These are what made you wake up."

∗ ∗ ∗ PRESENTS #6–#9 ∗ ∗ ∗
One feather, two newspapers.
A candy wrapper. A cloud.

The feather was lovely and trapped, in the door hinges of the church on Munich Street. It poked itself crookedly out and Liesel hurried over to rescue it. The fibers were combed flat on the left, but the right side was

321

made of delicate edges and sections of jagged triangles. There was no other way of describing it.

The newspapers came from the cold depths of a garbage can (enough said), and the candy wrapper was flat and faded. She found it near the school and held it up to the light. It contained a collage of shoe prints.

Then the cloud.

How do you give someone a piece of sky?

Late in February, she stood on Munich Street and watched a single giant cloud come over the hills like a white monster. It climbed the mountains. The sun was eclipsed, and in its place, a white beast with a gray heart watched the town.

"Would you look at that?" she said to Papa.

Hans cocked his head and stated what he felt was the obvious. "You should give it to Max, Liesel. See if you can leave it on the bedside table, like all the other things."

Liesel watched him as if he'd gone insane. "How, though?"

Lightly, he tapped her skull with his knuckles. "Memorize it. Then write it down for him."

". . . It was like a great white beast," she said at her next bedside vigil, "and it came from over the mountains."

When the sentence was completed with several different adjustments and additions, Liesel felt like she'd done it. She imagined the vision of it passing from her hand to his, through the blankets, and she wrote it down on a scrap of paper, placing the stone on top of it.

* * * PRESENTS #10–#13 * * *
One toy soldier.
One miraculous leaf.
A finished whistler.
A slab of grief.

The soldier was buried in the dirt, not far from Tommy Müller's place. It was scratched and trodden, which, to Liesel, was the whole point. Even with injury, it could still stand up.

The leaf was a maple and she found it in the school broom closet, among the buckets and feather dusters. The door was slightly ajar. The leaf was dry and hard, like toasted bread, and there were hills and valleys all over its skin. Somehow, the leaf had made its way into the school hallway and into that closet. Like half a star with a stem. Liesel reached in and twirled it in her fingers.

Unlike the other items, she did not place the leaf on the bedside table. She pinned it to the closed curtain, just before reading the final thirty-four pages of *The Whistler*.

She did not have dinner that afternoon or go to the toilet. She didn't drink. All day at school, she had promised herself that she would finish reading the book today, and Max Vandenburg was going to listen. He was going to wake up.

Papa sat on the floor, in the corner, workless as usual. Luckily, he would soon be leaving for the Knoller with his accordion. His chin resting on his knees, he listened to the girl he'd struggled to teach the alphabet. Reading proudly, she unloaded the final frightening words of the book to Max Vandenburg.

* * * THE LAST REMNANTS OF * * *
THE WHISTLER
*The Viennese air was fogging up the windows of the train
that morning, and as the people traveled obliviously to work,
a murderer whistled his happy tune. He bought his ticket.
There were polite greetings with fellow passengers and the
conductor. He even gave up his seat for an elderly lady and*

made polite conversation with a gambler who spoke of American horses. After all, the whistler loved talking. He talked to people and fooled them into liking him, trusting him. He talked to them while he was killing them, torturing and turning the knife. It was only when there was no one to talk to that he whistled, which was why he did so after a murder. . . .

"So you think the track will suit number seven, do you?"

"Of course." The gambler grinned. Trust was already there. "He'll come from behind and kill the whole lot of them!" He shouted it above the noise of the train.

"If you insist." The whistler smirked, and he wondered at length when they would find the inspector's body in that brand-new BMW.

"Jesus, Mary, and Joseph." Hans couldn't resist an incredulous tone. "A nun gave you *that?*" He stood up and made his way over, kissing her forehead. "Bye, Liesel, the Knoller awaits."

"Bye, Papa."

"Liesel!"

She ignored it.

"Come and eat something!"

She answered now. "I'm coming, Mama." She actually spoke those words to Max as she came closer and placed the finished book on the bedside table, with everything else. As she hovered above him, she couldn't help herself. "Come on, Max," she whispered, and even the sound of Mama's arrival at her back did not stop her from silently crying. It didn't stop her from pulling a lump of salt water from her eye and feeding it onto Max Vandenburg's face.

Mama took her.

Her arms swallowed her.

"I know," she said.

She knew.

FRESH AIR, AN OLD NIGHTMARE, AND WHAT TO DO WITH A JEWISH CORPSE

They were by the Amper River and Liesel had just told Rudy that she was interested in attaining another book from the mayor's house. In place of *The Whistler,* she'd read *The Standover Man* several times at Max's bedside. That was only a few minutes per reading. She'd also tried *The Shoulder Shrug,* even *The Grave Digger's Handbook,* but none of it seemed quite right. I want something new, she thought.

"Did you even read the last one?"

"Of course I did."

Rudy threw a stone into the water. "Was it any good?"

"Of course it was."

"Of course I did, of course it was." He tried to dig another rock out of the ground but cut his finger.

"That'll teach you."

"Saumensch."

When a person's last response was *Saumensch* or *Saukerl* or *Arschloch,* you knew you had them beaten.

• • •

In terms of stealing, conditions were perfect. It was a gloomy afternoon early in March and only a few degrees above freezing—always more uncomfortable than ten degrees below. Very few people were out on the streets. Rain like gray pencil shavings.

"Are we going?"

"Bikes," said Rudy. "You can use one of ours."

On this occasion, Rudy was considerably more enthusiastic about being the *enterer*. "Today it's my turn," he said as their fingers froze to the bike handles.

Liesel thought fast. "Maybe you shouldn't, Rudy. There's stuff all over the place in there. And it's dark. An idiot like you is bound to trip over or run into something."

"Thanks very much." In this mood, Rudy was hard to contain.

"There's the drop, too. It's deeper than you think."

"Are you saying you don't think I can do it?"

Liesel stood up on the pedals. "Not at all."

They crossed the bridge and serpentined up the hill to Grande Strasse. The window was open.

Like last time, they surveyed the house. Vaguely, they could see inside, to where a light was on downstairs, in what was probably the kitchen. A shadow moved back and forth.

"We'll just ride around the block a few times," Rudy said. "Lucky we brought the bikes, huh?"

"Just make sure you remember to take yours home."

"Very funny, *Saumensch*. It's a bit bigger than your filthy shoes."

They rode for perhaps fifteen minutes, and still, the mayor's wife was downstairs, a little too close for comfort. How dare she occupy the kitchen with such vigilance! For Rudy, the kitchen was undoubtedly the actual goal. He'd have gone in, robbed as much food as was physically possible, then if (and only if) he had a last moment to spare, he would stuff a book down his pants on the way out. Any book would do.

Rudy's weakness, however, was impatience. "It's getting late," he said, and began to ride off. "You coming?"

Liesel didn't come.

There was no decision to be made. She'd lugged that rusty bike all the way up there and she wasn't leaving without a book. She placed the handlebars in the gutter, looked out for any neighbors, and walked to the window. There was good speed but no hurry. She took her shoes off using her feet, treading on the heels with her toes.

Her fingers tightened on the wood and she made her way inside.

This time, if only slightly, she felt more at ease. In a few precious moments, she circled the room, looking for a title that grabbed her. On three or four occasions, she nearly reached out. She even considered taking more than one, but again, she didn't want to abuse what was a kind of system. For now, only one book was necessary. She studied the shelves and waited.

An extra darkness climbed through the window behind her. The smell of dust and theft loitered in the background, and she saw it.

The book was red, with black writing on the spine. *Der Traumträger. The Dream Carrier.* She thought of Max Vandenburg and his dreams. Of guilt. Surviving. Leaving his family. Fighting the *Führer*. She also thought of her own dream—her brother, dead on the train, and his appearance on the steps just around the corner from this very room. The book thief watched his bloodied knee from the shove of her own hand.

She slid the book from the shelf, tucked it under her arm, climbed to the window ledge, and jumped out, all in one motion.

Rudy had her shoes. He had her bike ready. Once the shoes were on, they rode.

"Jesus, Mary, and Joseph, Meminger." He'd never called her Meminger before. "You're an absolute lunatic. Do you know that?"

Liesel agreed as she pedaled like hell. "I know it."

At the bridge, Rudy summed up the afternoon's proceedings. "Those people are either completely crazy," he said, "or they just like their fresh air."

* * * A SMALL SUGGESTION * * *
Or maybe there was a woman on
Grande Strasse who now kept her
library window open for another
reason—but that's just me being
cynical, or hopeful. Or both.

Liesel placed *The Dream Carrier* beneath her jacket and began reading it the minute she returned home. In the wooden chair next to her bed, she opened the book and whispered, "It's a new one, Max. Just for you." She started reading. "'Chapter one: It was quite fitting that the entire town was sleeping when the dream carrier was born....'"

Every day, Liesel read two chapters of the book. One in the morning before school and one as soon as she came home. On certain nights, when she was not able to sleep, she read half of a third chapter as well. Sometimes she would fall asleep slumped forward onto the side of the bed.

It became her mission.

She gave *The Dream Carrier* to Max as if the words alone could nourish him. On a Tuesday, she thought there was movement. She could have sworn his eyes had opened. If they had, it was only momentarily, and it was more likely just her imagination and wishful thinking.

By mid-March, the cracks began to appear.

Rosa Hubermann—the good woman for a crisis—was at breaking point one afternoon in the kitchen. She raised her voice, then brought it quickly down. Liesel stopped reading and made her way quietly to the hall. As close as she stood, she could still barely make out her mama's words. When she was able to hear them, she wished she hadn't, for what she heard was horrific. It was reality.

* * * THE CONTENTS OF MAMA'S VOICE * * *
"What if he doesn't wake up?
What if he dies here, Hansi?
Tell me. What in God's name will
we do with the body? We can't
leave him here, the smell will
kill us . . . and we can't carry
him out the door and drag him up
the street, either. We can't just
say, 'You'll never guess what we
found in our basement this morning. . . .'
They'll put us away for good."

She was absolutely right.

A Jewish corpse was a major problem. The Hubermanns needed to revive Max Vandenburg not only for his sake, but for their own. Even Papa, who was always the ultimate calming influence, was feeling the pressure.

"Look." His voice was quiet but heavy. "If it happens—if he dies—we'll simply need to find a way." Liesel could have sworn she heard him swallow. A gulp like a blow to the windpipe. "My paint cart, some drop sheets . . ."

Liesel entered the kitchen.

"Not now, Liesel." It was Papa who spoke, though he did not look at her. He was watching his warped face in a turned-over spoon. His elbows were buried into the table.

The book thief did not retreat. She took a few extra steps and sat down. Her cold hands felt for her sleeves and a sentence dropped from her mouth. "He's not dead yet." The words landed on the table and positioned themselves in the middle. All three people looked at them. Half hopes didn't dare rise any higher. He isn't dead yet. He isn't dead yet. It was Rosa who spoke next.

"Who's hungry?"

Possibly the only time that Max's illness didn't hurt was at dinner. There was no denying it as the three of them sat at the kitchen table with their extra bread and extra soup or potatoes. They all thought it, but no one spoke.

In the night, just a few hours later, Liesel awoke and wondered at the height of her heart. (She had learned that expression from *The Dream Carrier,* which was essentially the complete antithesis of *The Whistler*— a book about an abandoned child who wanted to be a priest.) She sat up and sucked deeply at the nighttime air.

"Liesel?" Papa rolled over. "What is it?"

"Nothing, Papa, everything's good." But the very moment she'd finished the sentence, she saw exactly what had happened in her dream.

* * * ONE SMALL IMAGE * * *
For the most part, all is identical.
The train moves at the same speed.
Copiously, her brother coughs. This

time, however, Liesel cannot see his
face watching the floor. Slowly,
she leans over. Her hand lifts him
gently, from his chin, and there
in front of her is the wide-eyed face
of Max Vandenburg. He stares at her.
A feather drops to the floor. The
body is bigger now, matching the
size of the face. The train screams.

"Liesel?"

"I said everything's good."

Shivering, she climbed from the mattress. Stupid with fear, she walked through the hallway to Max. After many minutes at his side, when everything slowed, she attempted to interpret the dream. Was it a premonition of Max's death? Or was it merely a reaction to the afternoon conversation in the kitchen? Had Max now replaced her brother? And if so, how could she discard her own flesh and blood in such a way? Perhaps it was even a deep-seated wish for Max to die. After all, if it was good enough for Werner, her brother, it was good enough for this Jew.

"Is that what you think?" she whispered, standing above the bed. "No." She could not believe it. Her answer was sustained as the numbness of the dark waned and outlined the various shapes, big and small, on the bedside table. The presents.

"Wake up," she said.

Max did not wake up.

For eight more days.

At school, there was a rapping of knuckles on the door.

"Come in," called Frau Olendrich.

The door opened and the entire classroom of children looked on in surprise as Rosa Hubermann stood in the doorway. One or two gasped at the sight—a small wardrobe of a woman with a lipstick sneer and chlorine eyes. This. Was the legend. She was wearing her best clothes, but her hair was a mess, and it *was* a towel of elastic gray strands.

The teacher was obviously afraid. "Frau *Hu*bermann . . ." Her movements were cluttered. She searched through the class. "Liesel?"

Liesel looked at Rudy, stood, and walked quickly toward the door to end the embarrassment as fast as possible. It shut behind her, and now she was alone, in the corridor, with Rosa.

Rosa faced the other way.

"What, Mama?"

She turned. "Don't you 'what Mama' me, you little *Saumensch!*" Liesel was gored by the speed of it. "My hairbrush!" A trickle of laughter rolled from under the door, but it was drawn instantly back.

"Mama?"

Her face was severe, but it was smiling. "What the hell did you do with my hairbrush, you stupid *Saumensch,* you little thief? I've told you a hundred times to leave that thing alone, but do you listen? Of course not!"

The tirade went on for perhaps another minute, with Liesel making a desperate suggestion or two about the possible location of the said brush. It ended abruptly, with Rosa pulling Liesel close, just for a few seconds. Her whisper was almost impossible to hear, even at such close proximity. "You told me to yell at you. You said they'd all believe it." She looked left and right, her voice like needle and thread. "He woke up, Liesel. He's awake." From her pocket, she pulled out the toy soldier with the scratched exterior. "He said to give you this. It was his favorite." She handed it over, held her arms tightly, and smiled. Before Liesel had a chance to answer, she finished it off. "Well? Answer me! Do you have any other idea where you might have left it?"

He's alive, Liesel thought. ". . . No, Mama. I'm sorry, Mama, I—"

"Well, what good are you, then?" She let go, nodded, and walked away.

For a few moments, Liesel stood. The corridor was huge. She examined the soldier in her palm. Instinct told her to run home immediately, but common sense did not allow it. Instead, she placed the ragged soldier in her pocket and returned to the classroom.

Everyone waited.

"Stupid cow," she whispered under her breath.

Again, kids laughed. Frau Olendrich did not.

"What was that?"

Liesel was on such a high that she felt indestructible. "I said," she beamed, "stupid cow," and she didn't have to wait a single moment for the teacher's hand to slap her.

"Don't speak about your mother like that," she said, but it had little effect. The girl merely stood there and attempted to hold off the grin. After all, she could take a *Watschen* with the best of them. "Now get to your seat."

"Yes, Frau Olendrich."

Next to her, Rudy dared to speak.

"Jesus, Mary, and Joseph," he whispered, "I can see her hand on your face. A big red hand. Five fingers!"

"Good," said Liesel, because Max was alive.

When she made it home that afternoon, he was sitting up in bed with the deflated soccer ball on his lap. His beard itched him and his swampy eyes fought to stay open. An empty bowl of soup was next to the gifts.

They did not say hello.

It was more like edges.

The door creaked, the girl came in, and she stood before him, looking at the bowl. "Is Mama forcing it down your throat?"

He nodded, content, fatigued. "It was very good, though."

"Mama's soup? Really?"

It was not a smile he gave her. "Thank you for the presents." More just a slight tear of the mouth. "Thank you for the cloud. Your papa explained that one a little further."

After an hour, Liesel also made an attempt on the truth. "We didn't know what we'd do if you'd died, Max. We—"

It didn't take him long. "You mean, how to get rid of me?"

"I'm sorry."

"No." He was not offended. "You were right." He played weakly with the ball. "You were right to think that way. In your situation, a dead Jew is just as dangerous as a live one, if not worse."

"I also dreamed." In detail, she explained it, with the soldier in her grip. She was on the verge of apologizing again when Max intervened.

"Liesel." He made her look at him. "Don't ever apologize to me. It should be me who apologizes to you." He looked at everything she'd brought him. "Look at all this. These gifts." He held the button in his hand. "And Rosa said you read to me twice every day, sometimes three times." Now he looked at the curtains as if he could see out of them. He sat up a little higher and paused for a dozen silent sentences. Trepidation found its way onto his face and he made a confession to the girl. "Liesel?" He moved slightly to the right. "I'm afraid," he said, "of falling asleep again."

Liesel was resolute. "Then I'll read to you. And I'll slap your face if you start dozing off. I'll close the book and shake you till you wake up."

That afternoon, and well into the night, Liesel read to Max Vandenburg. He sat in bed and absorbed the words, awake this time, until just after ten o'clock. When Liesel took a quick rest from *The Dream Carrier,* she looked over the book and Max was asleep. Nervously, she nudged him with it. He awoke.

Another three times, he fell asleep. Twice more, she woke him.

For the next four days, he woke up every morning in Liesel's bed, then next to the fireplace, and eventually, by mid-April, in the basement. His health had improved, the beard was gone, and small scraps of weight had returned.

In Liesel's inside world, there was great relief in that time. Outside, things were starting to look shaky. Late in March, a place called Lübeck was hailed with bombs. Next in line would be Cologne, and soon enough, many more German cities, including Munich.

Yes, the boss was at my shoulder.

"Get it done, get it done."

The bombs were coming—and so was I.

DEATH'S DIARY: COLOGNE

The fallen hours of May 30.

I'm sure Liesel Meminger was fast asleep when more than a thousand bomber planes flew toward a place known as Köln. For me, the result was five hundred people or thereabouts. Fifty thousand others ambled homelessly around the ghostly piles of rubble, trying to work out which way was which, and which slabs of broken home belonged to whom.

Five hundred souls.

I carried them in my fingers, like suitcases. Or I'd throw them over my shoulder. It was only the children I carried in my arms.

By the time I was finished, the sky was yellow, like burning newspaper. If I looked closely, I could see the words, reporting headlines, commentating on the progress of the war and so forth. How I'd have loved to pull it all down, to screw up the newspaper sky and toss it away. My arms ached and I couldn't afford to burn my fingers. There was still so much work to be done.

As you might expect, many people died instantly. Others took a while longer. There were several more places to go, skies to meet and souls to collect, and when I came back to Cologne later on, not long after the final planes, I managed to notice a most unique thing.

I was carrying the charred soul of a teenager when I looked gravely up at what was now a sulfuric sky. A group of ten-year-old girls was close by. One of them called out.

"What's that?"

Her arm extended and her finger pointed out the black, slow object, falling from above. It began as a black feather, lilting, floating. Or a piece of ash. Then it grew larger. The same girl—a redhead with period freckles—spoke once again, this time more emphatically. "What *is* that?"

"It's a body," another girl suggested. Black hair, pigtails, and a crooked part down the center.

"It's another bomb!"

It was too slow to be a bomb.

With the adolescent spirit still burning lightly in my arms, I walked a few hundred meters with the rest of them. Like the girls, I remained focused on the sky. The last thing I wanted was to look down at the stranded face of my teenager. A pretty girl. Her whole death was now ahead of her.

Like the rest of them, I was taken aback when a voice lunged out. It was a disgruntled father, ordering his kids inside. The redhead reacted. Her freckles lengthened into commas. "But, Papa, look."

The man took several small steps and soon figured out what it was. "It's the fuel," he said.

"What do you mean?"

"The fuel," he repeated. "The tank." He was a bald man in disrupted bedclothes. "They used up all their fuel in that one and got rid of the empty container. Look, there's another one over there."

"And there!"

Kids being kids, they all searched frantically at that point, trying to find an empty fuel container floating to the ground.

The first one landed with a hollow thud.

"Can we keep it, Papa?"

"No." He was bombed and shocked, this papa, and clearly not in the mood. "We cannot keep it."

"Why not?"

"I'm going to ask my papa if *I* can have it," said another of the girls.

"Me too."

Just past the rubble of Cologne, a group of kids collected empty fuel containers, dropped by their enemies. As usual, I collected humans. I was tired. And the year wasn't even halfway over yet.

THE VISITOR

A new ball had been found for Himmel Street soccer. That was the good news. The somewhat unsettling news was that a division of the NSDAP was heading toward them.

They'd progressed all the way through Molching, street by street, house by house, and now they stood at Frau Diller's shop, having a quick smoke before they continued with their business.

There was already a smattering of air-raid shelters in Molching, but it was decided soon after the bombing of Cologne that a few more certainly wouldn't hurt. The NSDAP was inspecting each and every house in order to see if its basement was a good enough candidate.

From afar, the children watched.

They could see the smoke rising out of the pack.

Liesel had only just come out and she'd walked over to Rudy and Tommy. Harald Mollenhauer was retrieving the ball. "What's going on up there?"

Rudy put his hands in his pockets. "The party." He inspected his friend's progress with the ball in Frau Holtzapfel's front hedge. "They're checking all the houses and apartment blocks."

Instant dryness seized the interior of Liesel's mouth. "For what?"

"Don't you know anything? Tell her, Tommy."

Tommy was perplexed. "Well, *I* don't know."

"You're hopeless, the pair of you. They need more air-raid shelters."

"What—basements?"

"No, attics. Of course basements. Jesus, Liesel, you really are thick, aren't you?"

The ball was back.

"Rudy!"

He played onto it and Liesel was still standing. How could she get back inside without looking too suspicious? The smoke up at Frau Diller's was disappearing and the small crowd of men was starting to disperse. Panic generated in that awful way. Throat and mouth. Air became sand. Think, she thought. Come on, Liesel, think, think.

Rudy scored.

Faraway voices congratulated him.

Think, Liesel—

She had it.

That's it, she decided, but I have to make it real.

As the Nazis progressed down the street, painting the letters LSR on some of the doors, the ball was passed through the air to one of the bigger kids, Klaus Behrig.

* * * LSR * * *
Luft Schutz Raum:
Air-Raid Shelter

The boy turned with the ball just as Liesel arrived, and they collided with such force that the game stopped automatically. As the ball rolled off, players ran in. Liesel held her grazed knee with one hand

and her head with the other. Klaus Behrig only held his right shin, grimacing and cursing. "Where is she?" he spat. "I'm going to kill her!"

There would be no killing.

It was worse.

A kindly party member had seen the incident and jogged dutifully down to the group. "What happened here?" he asked.

"Well, *she's* a maniac." Klaus pointed at Liesel, prompting the man to help her up. His tobacco breath formed a smoky sandhill in front of her face.

"I don't think you're in any state to keep playing, my girl," he said. "Where do you live?"

"I'm fine," she answered, "really. I can make it myself." Just get off me, get off me!

That was when Rudy stepped in, the eternal stepper-inner. "I'll help you home," he said. Why couldn't he just mind his own business for a change?

"Really," Liesel said. "Just keep playing, Rudy. I can make it."

"No, no." He wouldn't be shifted. The stubbornness of him! "It'll only take a minute or two."

Again, she had to think, and again, she was able. With Rudy holding her up, she made herself drop once more to the ground, on her back. "My papa," she said. The sky, she noticed, was utterly blue. Not even the suggestion of a cloud. "Could you get him, Rudy?"

"Stay there." To his right, he called out, "Tommy, watch her, will you? Don't let her move."

Tommy snapped into action. "I'll watch her, Rudy." He stood above her, twitching and trying not to smile, as Liesel kept an eye on the party man.

A minute later, Hans Hubermann was standing calmly above her. "Hey, Papa."

A disappointed smile mingled with his lips. "I was wondering when this would happen."

He picked her up and helped her home. The game went on, and the Nazi was already at the door of a lodging a few doors up. No one answered. Rudy was calling out again.

"Do you need help, Herr Hubermann?"

"No, no, you keep playing, Herr Steiner." Herr Steiner. You had to love Liesel's papa.

Once inside, Liesel gave him the information. She attempted to find the middle ground between silence and despair. "Papa."

"Don't talk."

"The party," she whispered. Papa stopped. He fought off the urge to open the door and look up the street. "They're checking basements to make shelters."

He set her down. "Smart girl," he said, then called for Rosa.

They had a minute to come up with a plan. A shemozzle of thoughts.

"We'll just put him in Liesel's room," was Mama's suggestion. "Under the bed."

"That's *it*? What if they decide to search our rooms as well?"

"Do you have a better plan?"

Correction: they did not have a minute.

A seven-punch knock was hammered into the door of 33 Himmel Street, and it was too late to move anyone anywhere.

The voice.

"Open up!"

Their heartbeats fought each other, a mess of rhythm. Liesel tried to eat hers down. The taste of heart was not too cheerful.

Rosa whispered, "Jesus, Mary—"

On this day, it was Papa who rose to the occasion. He rushed to the basement door and threw a warning down the steps. When he returned, he spoke fast and fluent. "Look, there is no time for tricks.

We could distract him a hundred different ways, but there is only one solution." He eyed the door and summed up. "Nothing."

That was not the answer Rosa wanted. Her eyes widened. "Nothing? Are you *crazy?*"

The knocking resumed.

Papa was strict. "Nothing. We don't even go down there—not a care in the world."

Everything slowed.

Rosa accepted it.

Clenched with distress, she shook her head and proceeded to answer the door.

"Liesel." Papa's voice sliced her up. "Just stay calm, *verstehst?*"

"Yes, Papa."

She tried to concentrate on her bleeding leg.

"Aha!"

At the door, Rosa was still asking the meaning of this interruption when the kindly party man noticed Liesel.

"The maniacal soccer player!" He grinned. "How's the knee?" You don't usually imagine the Nazis being too chirpy, but this man certainly was. He came in and made as if to crouch and view the injury.

Does he know? Liesel thought. Can he smell we're hiding a Jew?

Papa came from the sink with a wet cloth and soaked it onto Liesel's knee. "Does it sting?" His silver eyes were caring and calm. The scare in them could easily be mistaken as concern for the injury.

Rosa called across the kitchen, "It can't sting enough. Maybe it will teach her a lesson."

The party man stood and laughed. "I don't think this girl is learning any lessons out there, Frau . . . ?"

"Hubermann." The cardboard contorted.

". . . Frau Hubermann—I think she *teaches* lessons." He handed Liesel a smile. "To all those boys. Am I right, young girl?"

Papa shoved the cloth into the graze and Liesel winced rather than answered. It was Hans who spoke. A quiet "sorry," to the girl.

There was the discomfort of silence then, and the party man remembered his purpose. "If you don't mind," he explained, "I need to inspect your basement, just for a minute or two, to see if it's suitable for a shelter."

Papa gave Liesel's knee a final dab. "You'll have a nice bruise there, too, Liesel." Casually, he acknowledged the man above them. "Certainly. First door on the right. Please excuse the mess."

"I wouldn't worry—it can't be worse than some of the others I've seen today. . . . This one?"

"That's it."

* * * THE LONGEST THREE MINUTES * * *
IN HUBERMANN HISTORY
Papa sat at the table. Rosa prayed in the corner,
mouthing the words. Liesel was cooked: her knee,
her chest, the muscles in her arms. I doubt any
of them had the audacity to consider what they'd
do if the basement was appointed as a shelter.
They had to survive the inspection first.

They listened to Nazi footsteps in the basement. There was the sound of measuring tape. Liesel could not ward off the thought of Max sitting beneath the steps, huddled around his sketchbook, hugging it to his chest.

Papa stood. Another idea.

He walked to the hall and called out, "Everything good down there?"

The answer ascended the steps, on top of Max Vandenburg. "Another minute, perhaps!"

"Would you like some coffee, some tea?"

"No thank you!"

When Papa returned, he ordered Liesel to fetch a book and for Rosa to start cooking. He decided the last thing they should do was sit around looking worried. "Well, come on," he said loudly, "move it, Liesel. I don't care if your knee hurts. You have to finish that book, like you said."

Liesel tried not to break. "Yes, Papa."

"What are you waiting for?" It took great effort to wink at her, she could tell.

In the corridor, she nearly collided with the party man.

"In trouble with your papa, huh? Never mind. I'm the same with my own children."

They walked their separate ways, and when Liesel made it to her room, she closed the door and fell to her knees, despite the added pain. She listened first to the judgment that the basement was too shallow, then the goodbyes, one of which was sent down the corridor. "Goodbye, maniacal soccer player!"

She remembered herself. "*Auf Wiedersehen!* Goodbye!"

The Dream Carrier simmered in her hands.

According to Papa, Rosa melted next to the stove the moment the party man was gone. They collected Liesel and made their way to the basement, removing the well-placed drop sheets and paint cans. Max Vandenburg sat beneath the steps, holding his rusty scissors like a knife. His armpits were soggy and the words fell like injuries from his mouth.

345

"I wouldn't have used them," he quietly said. "I'm . . ." He held the rusty arms flat against his forehead. "I'm so sorry I put you through that."

Papa lit a cigarette. Rosa took the scissors.

"You're alive," she said. "We all are."

It was too late now for apologies.

THE SCHMUNZELER

Minutes later, a second knocker was at the door.

"Good Lord, another one!"

Worry resumed immediately.

Max was covered up.

Rosa trudged up the basement steps, but when she opened the door this time, it was not the Nazis. It was none other than Rudy Steiner. He stood there, yellow-haired and good-intentioned. "I just came to see how Liesel is."

When she heard his voice, Liesel started making her way up the steps. "I can deal with this one."

"Her boyfriend," Papa mentioned to the paint cans. He blew another mouthful of smoke.

"He is *not* my boyfriend," Liesel countered, but she was not irritated. It was impossible after such a close call. "I'm only going up because Mama will be yelling out any second."

"Liesel!"

She was on the fifth step. "See?"

• • •

347

When she reached the door, Rudy moved from foot to foot. "I just came to see—" He stopped. "What's that smell?" He sniffed. "Have you been smoking in there?"

"Oh. I was sitting with Papa."

"Do you have any cigarettes? Maybe we can sell some."

Liesel wasn't in the mood for this. She spoke quietly enough so that Mama wouldn't hear. "I don't steal from my papa."

"But you steal from certain other places."

"Talk a bit louder, why don't you."

Rudy *schmunzel*ed. "See what stealing does? You're all worried."

"Like you've never stolen anything."

"Yes, but you reek of it." Rudy was really warming up now. "Maybe that's not cigarette smoke after all." He leaned closer and smiled. "It's a criminal I can smell. You should have a bath." He shouted back to Tommy Müller. "Hey, Tommy, you should come and have a smell of this!"

"What did you say?" Trust Tommy. "I can't hear you!"

Rudy shook his head in Liesel's direction. "Useless."

She started shutting the door. "Get lost, *Saukerl,* you're the last thing I need right now."

Very pleased with himself, Rudy made his way back to the street. At the mailbox, he seemed to remember what he'd wanted to verify all along. He came back a few steps. "*Alles gut, Saumensch?* The injury, I mean."

It was June. It was Germany.

Things were on the verge of decay.

Liesel was unaware of this. For her, the Jew in her basement had not been revealed. Her foster parents were not taken away, and she herself had contributed greatly to both of these accomplishments.

"Everything's good," she said, and she was not talking about a soccer injury of any description.

She was fine.

DEATH'S DIARY: THE PARISIANS

Summer came.

For the book thief, everything was going nicely.

For me, the sky was the color of Jews.

When their bodies had finished scouring for gaps in the door, their souls rose up. When their fingernails had scratched at the wood and in some cases were nailed into it by the sheer force of desperation, their spirits came toward me, into my arms, and we climbed out of those shower facilities, onto the roof and up, into eternity's certain breadth. They just kept feeding me. Minute after minute. Shower after shower.

I'll never forget the first day in Auschwitz, the first time in Mauthausen. At that second place, as time wore on, I also picked them up from the bottom of the great cliff, when their escapes fell awfully awry. There were broken bodies and dead, sweet hearts. Still, it was better than the gas. Some of them I caught when they were only halfway down. Saved you, I'd think, holding their souls in midair as the rest of their being—their physical shells—plummeted to the earth. All of them were light, like the cases of empty walnuts. Smoky sky in those places. The smell like a stove, but still so cold.

I shiver when I remember—as I try to de-realize it.

I blow warm air into my hands, to heat them up.

But it's hard to keep them warm when the souls still shiver.

God.

I always say that name when I think of it.

God.

Twice, I speak it.

I say His name in a futile attempt to understand. "But it's not your job to understand." That's me who answers. God never says anything. You think you're the only one he never answers? "Your job is to . . ." And I stop listening to me, because to put it bluntly, I tire me. When I start thinking like that, I become so exhausted, and I don't have the luxury of indulging fatigue. I'm compelled to continue on, because although it's not true for every person on earth, it's true for the vast majority—that death waits for no man—and if he does, he doesn't usually wait very long.

On June 23, 1942, there was a group of French Jews in a German prison, on Polish soil. The first person I took was close to the door, his mind racing, then reduced to pacing, then slowing down, slowing down. . . .

Please believe me when I tell you that I picked up each soul that day as if it were newly born. I even kissed a few weary, poisoned cheeks. I listened to their last, gasping cries. Their vanishing words. I watched their love visions and freed them from their fear.

I took them all away, and if ever there was a time I needed distraction, this was it. In complete desolation, I looked at the world above. I watched the sky as it turned from silver to gray to the color of rain. Even the clouds were trying to get away.

Sometimes I imagined how everything looked above those clouds, knowing without question that the sun was blond, and the endless atmosphere was a giant blue eye.

They were French, they were Jews, and they were you.

PART SEVEN

the complete duden dictionary
and thesaurus

featuring:

champagne and accordions—

a trilogy—some sirens—a sky

stealer—an offer—the long

walk to dachau—peace—

an idiot and some coat men

CHAMPAGNE AND ACCORDIONS

In the summer of 1942, the town of Molching was preparing for the inevitable. There were still people who refused to believe that this small town on Munich's outskirts could be a target, but the majority of the population was well aware that it was not a question of if, but when. Shelters were more clearly marked, windows were in the process of being blackened for the nights, and everyone knew where the closest basement or cellar was.

For Hans Hubermann, this uneasy development was actually a slight reprieve. At an unfortunate time, good luck had somehow found its way into his painting business. People with blinds were desperate enough to enlist his services to paint them. His problem was that black paint was normally used more as a mixer, to darken other colors, and it was soon depleted and hard to find. What he did have was the knack of being a good tradesman, and a good tradesman has many tricks. He took coal dust and stirred it through, and he worked cheap. There were many houses in all parts of Molching in which he confiscated the window light from enemy eyes.

On some of his workdays, Liesel went with him.

They carted his paint through town, smelling the hunger on some of the streets and shaking their heads at the wealth on others. Many times, on the way home, women with nothing but kids and poverty would come running out and plead with him to paint their blinds.

"Frau Hallah, I'm sorry, I have no black paint left," he would say, but a little farther down the road, he would always break. There was tall man and long street. "Tomorrow," he'd promise, "first thing," and when the next morning dawned, there he was, painting those blinds for nothing, or for a cookie or a warm cup of tea. The previous evening, he'd have found another way to turn blue or green or beige to black. Never did he tell them to cover their windows with spare blankets, for he knew they'd need them when winter came. He was even known to paint people's blinds for half a cigarette, sitting on the front step of a house, sharing a smoke with the occupant. Laughter and smoke rose out of the conversation before they moved on to the next job.

When the time came to write, I remember clearly what Liesel Meminger had to say about that summer. A lot of the words have faded over the decades. The paper has suffered from the friction of movement in my pocket, but still, many of her sentences have been impossible to forget.

* * * A SMALL SAMPLE OF SOME * * * GIRL-WRITTEN WORDS

That summer was a new beginning, a new end.
When I look back, I remember my slippery
hands of paint and the sound of Papa's feet
on Munich Street, and I know that a small
piece of the summer of 1942 belonged to only
one man. Who else would do some painting for

the price of half a cigarette? That was Papa,
that was typical, and I loved him.

Every day when they worked together, he would tell Liesel his stories. There was the Great War and how his miserable handwriting helped save his life, and the day he met Mama. He said that she was beautiful once, and actually very quiet-spoken. "Hard to believe, I know, but absolutely true." Each day, there was a story, and Liesel forgave him if he told the same one more than once.

On other occasions, when she was daydreaming, Papa would dab her lightly with his brush, right between the eyes. If he misjudged and there was too much on it, a small path of paint would dribble down the side of her nose. She would laugh and try to return the favor, but Hans Hubermann was a hard man to catch out at work. It was there that he was most alive.

Whenever they had a break, to eat or drink, he would play the accordion, and it was this that Liesel remembered best. Each morning, while Papa pushed or dragged the paint cart, Liesel carried the instrument. "Better that we leave the paint behind," Hans told her, "than ever forget the music." When they paused to eat, he would cut up the bread, smearing it with what little jam remained from the last ration card. Or he'd lay a small slice of meat on top of it. They would eat together, sitting on their cans of paint, and with the last mouthfuls still in the chewing stages, Papa would be wiping his fingers, unbuckling the accordion case.

Traces of bread crumbs were in the creases of his overalls. Paint-specked hands made their way across the buttons and raked over the keys, or held on to a note for a while. His arms worked the bellows, giving the instrument the air it needed to breathe.

Liesel would sit each day with her hands between her knees, in the long legs of daylight. She wanted none of those days to end, and it was always with disappointment that she watched the darkness stride forward.

As far as the painting itself was concerned, probably the most interesting aspect for Liesel was the mixing. Like most people, she assumed her papa simply took his cart to the paint shop or hardware store and asked for the right color and away he went. She didn't realize that most of the paint was in lumps, in the shape of a brick. It was then rolled out with an empty champagne bottle. (Champagne bottles, Hans explained, were ideal for the job, as their glass was slightly thicker than that of an ordinary bottle of wine.) Once that was completed, there was the addition of water, whiting, and glue, not to mention the complexities of matching the right color.

The science of Papa's trade brought him an even greater level of respect. It was well and good to share bread and music, but it was nice for Liesel to know that he was also more than capable in his occupation. Competence was attractive.

One afternoon, a few days after Papa's explanation of the mixing, they were working at one of the wealthier houses just east of Munich Street. Papa called Liesel inside in the early afternoon. They were just about to move on to another job when she heard the unusual volume in his voice.

Once inside, she was taken to the kitchen, where two older women and a man sat on delicate, highly civilized chairs. The women were well dressed. The man had white hair and sideburns like hedges. Tall glasses stood on the table. They were filled with crackling liquid.

"Well," said the man, "here we go."

He took up his glass and urged the others to do the same.

The afternoon had been warm. Liesel was slightly put off by the coolness of her glass. She looked at Papa for approval. He grinned and said, "*Prost, Mädel*—cheers, girl." Their glasses chimed together and the moment Liesel raised it to her mouth, she was bitten by the fizzy, sickly sweet taste of champagne. Her reflexes forced her to spit straight onto her papa's overalls, watching it foam and dribble. A shot of laughter followed from all of them, and Hans encouraged her to give it another try. On the second attempt she was able to swallow it, and enjoy the taste of a glorious broken rule. It felt great. The bubbles ate her tongue. They prickled her stomach. Even as they walked to the next job, she could feel the warmth of pins and needles inside her.

Dragging the cart, Papa told her that those people claimed to have no money.

"So you asked for champagne?"

"Why not?" He looked across, and never had his eyes been so silver. "I didn't want you thinking that champagne bottles are only used for rolling paint." He warned her, "Just don't tell Mama. Agreed?"

"Can I tell Max?"

"Sure, you can tell Max."

In the basement, when she wrote about her life, Liesel vowed that she would never drink champagne again, for it would never taste as good as it did on that warm afternoon in July.

It was the same with accordions.

Many times, she wanted to ask her papa if he might teach her to play, but somehow, something always stopped her. Perhaps an unknown intuition told her that she would never be able to play it like Hans Hubermann. Surely, not even the world's greatest accordionists could compare. They could never be equal to the casual concentration on Papa's face. Or there wouldn't be a paintwork-traded cigarette slouched on the player's lips. And they could never make a small mistake with a three-note laugh of hindsight. Not the way he could.

At times, in that basement, she woke up tasting the sound of the accordion in her ears. She could feel the sweet burn of champagne on her tongue.

Sometimes she sat against the wall, longing for the warm finger of paint to wander just once more down the side of her nose, or to watch the sandpaper texture of her papa's hands.

If only she could be so oblivious again, to feel such love without knowing it, mistaking it for laughter and bread with only the scent of jam spread out on top of it.

It was the best time of her life.

But it was bombing carpet.

Make no mistake.

Bold and bright, a trilogy of happiness would continue for summer's duration and into autumn. It would then be brought abruptly to an end, for the brightness had shown suffering the way.

Hard times were coming.

Like a parade.

* * * DUDEN DICTIONARY MEANING #1 * * *
Zufriedenheit — Happiness:
Coming from *happy* — enjoying
pleasure and contentment.
Related words: *joy, gladness,*
feeling fortunate or prosperous.

THE TRILOGY

While Liesel worked, Rudy ran.

He did laps of Hubert Oval, ran around the block, and raced almost everyone from the bottom of Himmel Street to Frau Diller's, giving varied head starts.

On a few occasions, when Liesel was helping Mama in the kitchen, Rosa would look out the window and say, "What's that little *Saukerl* up to *this* time? All that running out there."

Liesel would move to the window. "At least he hasn't painted himself black again."

"Well, that's something, isn't it?"

* * * RUDY'S REASONS * * *
In the middle of August, a Hitler Youth
carnival was being held, and Rudy was
intent on winning four events: the 1500,
400, 200, and of course, the 100. He liked
his new Hitler Youth leaders and wanted to
please them, and he wanted to show his old
friend Franz Deutscher a thing or two.

. . .

"Four gold medals," he said to Liesel one afternoon when she did laps with him at Hubert Oval. "Like Jesse Owens back in '36."

"You're not still obsessed with him, are you?"

Rudy's feet rhymed with his breathing. "Not really, but it would be nice, wouldn't it? It would show all those bastards who said I was crazy. They'd see that I wasn't so stupid after all."

"But can you really win all four events?"

They slowed to a stop at the end of the track, and Rudy placed his hands on his hips. "I have to."

For six weeks, he trained, and when the day of the carnival arrived in mid-August, the sky was hot-sunned and cloudless. The grass was overrun with Hitler Youths, parents, and a glut of brown-shirted leaders. Rudy Steiner was in peak condition.

"Look," he pointed out. "There's Deutscher."

Through the clusters of crowd, the blond epitome of Hitler Youth standards was giving instructions to two members of his division. They were nodding and occasionally stretching. One of them shielded his eyes from the sun like a salute.

"You want to say hello?" Liesel asked.

"No thanks. I'll do that later."

When I've won.

The words were not spoken, but they were definitely there, somewhere between Rudy's blue eyes and Deutscher's advisory hands.

There was the obligatory march around the grounds.

The anthem.

Heil Hitler.

Only then could they begin.

• • •

When Rudy's age group was called for the 1500, Liesel wished him luck in a typically German manner.

"Hals und Beinbruch, Saukerl."

She'd told him to break his neck and leg.

Boys collected themselves on the far side of the circular field. Some stretched, some focused, and the rest were there because they had to be.

Next to Liesel, Rudy's mother, Barbara, sat with her youngest children. A thin blanket was brimming with kids and loosened grass. "Can you see Rudy?" she asked them. "He's the one on the far left." Barbara Steiner was a kind woman whose hair always looked recently combed.

"Where?" said one of the girls. Probably Bettina, the youngest. "I can't see him at all."

"That last one. No, not there. *There.*"

They were still in the identification process when the starter's gun gave off its smoke and sound. The small Steiners rushed to the fence.

For the first lap, a group of seven boys led the field. On the second, it dropped to five, and on the next lap, four. Rudy was the fourth runner on every lap until the last. A man on the right was saying that the boy coming second looked the best. He was the tallest. "You wait," he told his nonplussed wife. "With two hundred left, he'll break away." The man was wrong.

A gargantuan brown-shirted official informed the group that there was one lap to go. He certainly wasn't suffering under the ration system. He called out as the lead pack crossed the line, and it was not the second boy who accelerated, but the fourth. And he was two hundred meters early.

Rudy ran.

He did not look back at any stage.

Like an elastic rope, he lengthened his lead until any thought of someone else winning snapped altogether. He took himself around the

361

track as the three runners behind him fought each other for the scraps. In the homestretch, there was nothing but blond hair and space, and when he crossed the line, he didn't stop. He didn't raise his arm. There wasn't even a bent-over relief. He simply walked another twenty meters and eventually looked over his shoulder to watch the others cross the line.

On the way back to his family, he met first with his leaders and then with Franz Deutscher. They both nodded.

"Steiner."

"Deutscher."

"Looks like all those laps I gave you paid off, huh?"

"Looks like it."

He would not smile until he'd won all four.

❊ ❊ ❊ A POINT FOR LATER REFERENCE ❊ ❊ ❊
Not only was Rudy recognized now as a good
school student. He was a gifted athlete, too.

For Liesel, there was the 400. She finished seventh, then fourth in her heat of the 200. All she could see up ahead were the hamstrings and bobbing ponytails of the girls in front. In the long jump, she enjoyed the sand packed around her feet more than any distance, and the shot put wasn't her greatest moment, either. This day, she realized, was Rudy's.

In the 400 final, he led from the backstretch to the end, and he won the 200 only narrowly.

"You getting tired?" Liesel asked him. It was early afternoon by then.

"Of course not." He was breathing heavily and stretching his calves. "What are you talking about, *Saumensch*? What the hell would you know?"

When the heats of the 100 were called, he rose slowly to his feet and followed the trail of adolescents toward the track. Liesel went after him. "Hey, Rudy." She pulled at his shirtsleeve. "Good luck."

"I'm not tired," he said.

"I know."

He winked at her.

He was tired.

In his heat, Rudy slowed to finish second, and after ten minutes of other races, the final was called. Two other boys had looked formidable, and Liesel had a feeling in her stomach that Rudy could not win this one. Tommy Müller, who'd finished second to last in his heat, stood with her at the fence. "He'll win it," he informed her.

"I know."

No, he won't.

When the finalists reached the starting line, Rudy dropped to his knees and began digging starting holes with his hands. A balding brownshirt wasted no time in walking over and telling him to cut it out. Liesel watched the adult finger, pointing, and she could see the dirt falling to the ground as Rudy brushed his hands together.

When they were called forward, Liesel tightened her grip on the fence. One of the boys false-started; the gun was shot twice. It was Rudy. Again, the official had words with him and the boy nodded. Once more and he was out.

Set for the second time, Liesel watched with concentration, and for the first few seconds, she could not believe what she was seeing. Another false start was recorded and it was the same athlete who had done it. In front of her, she created a perfect race, in which Rudy trailed but came home to win in the last ten meters. What she actually saw, however, was Rudy's disqualification. He was escorted to the side of the track and was made to stand there, alone, as the remainder of boys stepped forward.

They lined up and raced.

A boy with rusty brown hair and a big stride won by at least five meters.

Rudy remained.

Later, when the day was complete and the sun was taken from Himmel Street, Liesel sat with her friend on the footpath.

They talked about everything else, from Franz Deutscher's face after the 1500 to one of the eleven-year-old girls having a tantrum after losing the discus.

Before they proceeded to their respective homes, Rudy's voice reached over and handed Liesel the truth. For a while, it sat on her shoulder, but a few thoughts later, it made its way to her ear.

✳ ✳ ✳ RUDY'S VOICE ✳ ✳ ✳
"I did it on purpose."

When the confession registered, Liesel asked the only question available. "But why, Rudy? Why did you do it?"

He was standing with a hand on his hip, and he did not answer. There was nothing but a knowing smile and a slow walk that lolled him home. They never talked about it again.

For Liesel's part, she often wondered what Rudy's answer might have been had she pushed him. Perhaps three medals had shown what he'd wanted to show, or he was afraid to lose that final race. In the end, the only explanation she allowed herself to hear was an inner teenage voice.

"Because he isn't Jesse Owens."

Only when she got up to leave did she notice the three imitation-gold medals sitting next to her. She knocked on the Steiners' door and held them out to him. "You forgot these."

"No, I didn't." He closed the door and Liesel took the medals home. She walked with them down to the basement and told Max about her friend Rudy Steiner.

"He truly is stupid," she concluded.

"Clearly," Max agreed, but I doubt he was fooled.

They both started work then, Max on his sketchbook, Liesel on *The Dream Carrier*. She was in the latter stages of the novel, where the young priest was doubting his faith after meeting a strange and elegant woman.

When she placed it facedown on her lap, Max asked when she thought she'd finish it.

"A few days at the most."

"Then a new one?"

The book thief looked at the basement ceiling. "Maybe, Max." She closed the book and leaned back. "If I'm lucky."

✳ ✳ ✳ THE NEXT BOOK ✳ ✳ ✳
It's not the *Duden Dictionary and*
***Thesaurus,* as you might be expecting.**

No, the dictionary comes at the end of this small trilogy, and this is only the second installment. This is the part where Liesel finishes *The Dream Carrier* and steals a story called *A Song in the Dark*. As always, it was taken from the mayor's house. The only difference was that she made her way to the upper part of town alone. There was no Rudy that day.

It was a morning rich with both sun and frothy clouds.

Liesel stood in the mayor's library with greed in her fingers and book titles at her lips. She was comfortable enough on this occasion to run her fingers along the shelves—a short replay of her original visit to the room—and she whispered many of the titles as she made her way along.

Under the Cherry Tree.

The Tenth Lieutenant.

Typically, many of the titles tempted her, but after a good minute or two in the room, she settled for *A Song in the Dark,* most likely because the book was green, and she did not yet own a book of that color. The engraved writing on the cover was white, and there was a small insignia of a flute between the title and the name of the author. She climbed with it from the window, saying thanks on her way out.

Without Rudy, she felt a good degree of absence, but on that particular morning, for some reason, the book thief was happiest alone. She went about her work and read the book next to the Amper River, far enough away from the occasional headquarters of Viktor Chemmel and the previous gang of Arthur Berg. No one came, no one interrupted, and Liesel read four of the very short chapters of *A Song in the Dark,* and she was happy.

It was the pleasure and satisfaction.

Of good stealing.

A week later, the trilogy of happiness was completed.

In the last days of August, a gift arrived, or in fact, was noticed.

It was late afternoon. Liesel was watching Kristina Müller jumping rope on Himmel Street. Rudy Steiner skidded to a stop in front of her on his brother's bike. "Do you have some time?" he asked.

She shrugged. "For what?"

"I think you'd better come." He dumped the bike and went to collect the other one from home. In front of her, Liesel watched the pedal spin.

They rode up to Grande Strasse, where Rudy stopped and waited.

"Well," Liesel asked, "what is it?"

Rudy pointed. "Look closer."

Gradually, they rode to a better position, behind a blue spruce tree. Through the prickly branches, Liesel noticed the closed window, and then the object leaning on the glass.

"Is that . . . ?"

Rudy nodded.

They debated the issue for many minutes before they agreed it needed to be done. It had obviously been placed there intentionally, and if it was a trap, it was worth it.

Among the powdery blue branches, Liesel said, "A book thief would do it."

She dropped the bike, observed the street, and crossed the yard. The shadows of clouds were buried among the dusky grass. Were they holes for falling into, or patches of extra darkness for hiding in? Her imagination sent her sliding down one of those holes into the evil clutches of the mayor himself. If nothing else, those thoughts distracted her and she was at the window even quicker than she'd hoped.

It was like *The Whistler* all over again.

Her nerves licked her palms.

Small streams of sweat rippled under her arms.

When she raised her head, she could read the title. *The Complete Duden Dictionary and Thesaurus*. Briefly, she turned to Rudy and mouthed the words, *It's a dictionary*. He shrugged and held out his arms.

She worked methodically, sliding the window upward, wondering how all of this would look from inside the house. She envisioned the sight of her thieving hand reaching up, making the window rise until the book was felled. It seemed to surrender slowly, like a falling tree.

Got it.

There was barely a disturbance or sound.

The book simply tilted toward her and she took it with her free hand. She even closed the window, nice and smooth, then turned and walked back across the potholes of clouds.

"Nice," Rudy said as he gave her the bike.

"Thank you."

They rode toward the corner, where the day's importance reached them. Liesel knew. It was that feeling again, of being watched. A voice pedaled inside her. Two laps.

Look at the window. Look at the window.

She was compelled.

Like an itch that demands a fingernail, she felt an intense desire to stop.

She placed her feet on the ground and turned to face the mayor's house and the library window, and she saw. Certainly, she should have known this might happen, but she could not hide the shock that loitered inside when she witnessed the mayor's wife, standing behind the glass. She was transparent, but she was there. Her fluffy hair was as it always was, and her wounded eyes and mouth and expression held themselves up, for viewing.

Very slowly, she lifted her hand to the book thief on the street. A motionless wave.

In her state of shock, Liesel said nothing, to Rudy or herself. She only steadied herself and raised her hand to acknowledge the mayor's wife, in the window.

* * * *DUDEN DICTIONARY* MEANING #2 * * *
Verzeihung —Forgiveness:
To stop feeling anger,
animosity, or resentment.
Related words: *absolution,*
acquittal, mercy.

On the way home, they stopped at the bridge and inspected the heavy black book. As Rudy flipped through the pages, he arrived at a letter. He picked it up and looked slowly toward the book thief. "It's got your name on it."

The river ran.

Liesel took hold of the paper.

* * * THE LETTER * * *

Dear Liesel,

I know you find me pathetic and loathsome (look that word up if you don't know it), but I must tell you that I am not so stupid as to not see your footprints in the library. When I noticed the first book missing, I thought I had simply misplaced it, but then I saw the outlines of some feet on the floor in certain patches of the light.

It made me smile.

I was glad that you took what was rightfully yours. I then made the mistake of thinking that would be the end of it.

When you came back, I should have been angry, but I wasn't. I could hear you the last time, but I decided to leave you alone. You only ever take one book, and it will take a thousand visits till all of them are gone. My only hope is that one day you will knock on the front door and enter the library in the more civilized manner.

Again, I am sorry we could no longer keep your foster mother employed.

Lastly, I hope you find this dictionary and thesaurus useful as you read your stolen books.

Yours sincerely,

Ilsa Hermann

"We'd better head home," Rudy suggested, but Liesel did not go.

"Can you wait here for ten minutes?"

"Of course."

369

Liesel struggled back up to 8 Grande Strasse and sat on the familiar territory of the front entrance. The book was with Rudy, but she held the letter and rubbed her fingers on the folded paper as the steps grew heavier around her. She tried four times to knock on the daunting flesh of the door, but she could not bring herself to do it. The most she could accomplish was to place her knuckles gently on the warmness of the wood.

Again, her brother found her.

From the bottom of the steps, his knee healing nicely, he said, "Come on, Liesel, knock."

As she made her second getaway, she could soon see the distant figure of Rudy at the bridge. The wind showered through her hair. Her feet swam with the pedals.

Liesel Meminger was a criminal.

But not because she'd stolen a handful of books through an open window.

You should have knocked, she thought, and although there was a good portion of guilt, there was also the juvenile trace of laughter.

As she rode, she tried to tell herself something.

You don't deserve to be this happy, Liesel. You really don't.

Can a person steal happiness? Or is it just another internal, infernal human trick?

Liesel shrugged away from her thoughts. She crossed the bridge and told Rudy to hurry up and not to forget the book.

They rode home on rusty bikes.

They rode home a couple of miles, from summer to autumn, and from a quiet night to the noisy breath of the bombing of Munich.

THE SOUND OF SIRENS

With the small collection of money Hans had earned in the summer, he brought home a secondhand radio. "This way," he said, "we can hear when the raids are coming even before the sirens start. They make a *cuckoo* sound and then announce the regions at risk."

He placed it on the kitchen table and switched it on. They also tried to make it work in the basement, for Max, but there was nothing but static and severed voices in the speakers.

In September, they did not hear it as they slept.

Either the radio was already half broken, or it was swallowed immediately by the crying sound of sirens.

A hand was shoved gently at Liesel's shoulder as she slept.

Papa's voice followed it in, afraid.

"Liesel, wake up. We have to go."

There was the disorientation of interrupted sleep, and Liesel could barely decipher the outline of Papa's face. The only thing truly visible was his voice.

● ● ●

In the hallway, they stopped.

"Wait," said Rosa.

Through the dark, they rushed to the basement.

The lamp was lit.

Max edged out from behind the paint cans and drop sheets. His face was tired and he hitched his thumbs nervously into his pants. "Time to go, huh?"

Hans walked to him. "Yes, time to go." He shook his hand and slapped his arm. "We'll see you when we get back, right?"

"Of course."

Rosa hugged him, as did Liesel.

"Goodbye, Max."

Weeks earlier, they'd discussed whether they should all stay together in their own basement or if the three of them should go down the road, to a family by the name of Fiedler. It was Max who convinced them. "They said it's not deep enough here. I've already put you in enough danger."

Hans had nodded. "It's a shame we can't take you with us. It's a disgrace."

"It's how it is."

Outside, the sirens howled at the houses, and the people came running, hobbling, and recoiling as they exited their homes. Night watched. Some people watched it back, trying to find the tin-can planes as they drove across the sky.

Himmel Street was a procession of tangled people, all wrestling with their most precious possessions. In some cases, it was a baby. In others, a stack of photo albums or a wooden box. Liesel carried her books, between her arm and her ribs. Frau Holtzapfel was heaving a suitcase, laboring on the footpath with bulbous eyes and small-stepped feet.

Papa, who'd forgotten everything—even his accordion—rushed back to her and rescued the suitcase from her grip. "Jesus, Mary, and Joseph, what have you got in here?" he asked. "An anvil?"

Frau Holtzapfel advanced alongside him. "The necessities."

The Fiedlers lived six houses down. They were a family of four, all with wheat-colored hair and good German eyes. More important, they had a nice, deep basement. Twenty-two people crammed themselves into it, including the Steiner family, Frau Holtzapfel, Pfiffikus, a young man, and a family named Jenson. In the interest of a civil environment, Rosa Hubermann and Frau Holtzapfel were kept separated, though some things were above petty arguments.

One light globe dangled from the ceiling and the room was dank and cold. Jagged walls jutted out and poked people in the back as they stood and spoke. The muffled sound of sirens leaked in from somewhere. They could hear a distorted version of them that somehow found a way inside. Although creating considerable apprehension about the quality of the shelter, at least they could hear the three sirens that would signal the end of the raid and safety. They didn't need a *Luftschutzwart*—an air-raid supervisor.

It wasn't long before Rudy found Liesel and was standing next to her. His hair was pointing at something on the ceiling. "Isn't this great?"

She couldn't resist some sarcasm. "It's lovely."

"Ah, come on, Liesel, don't be like that. What's the worst that can happen, apart from all of us being flattened or fried or whatever bombs do?"

Liesel looked around, gauging the faces. She started compiling a list of who was most afraid.

★ ★ ★ THE HIT LIST ★ ★ ★
1. Frau Holtzapfel
2. Mr. Fiedler
3. The young man
4. Rosa Hubermann

Frau Holtzapfel's eyes were trapped open. Her wiry frame was stooped forward, and her mouth was a circle. Herr Fiedler busied himself by asking people, sometimes repeatedly, how they were feeling. The young man, Rolf Schultz, kept to himself in the corner, speaking silently at the air around him, castigating it. His hands were cemented into his pockets. Rosa rocked back and forth, ever so gently. "Liesel," she whispered, "come here." She held the girl from behind, tightening her grip. She sang a song, but it was so quiet that Liesel could not make it out. The notes were born on her breath, and they died at her lips. Next to them, Papa remained quiet and motionless. At one point, he placed his warm hand on Liesel's cool skull. *You'll live, it said, and it was right.*

To their left, Alex and Barbara Steiner stood with the younger of their children, Emma and Bettina. The two girls were attached to their mother's right leg. The oldest boy, Kurt, stared ahead in a perfect Hitler Youth stance, holding the hand of Karin, who was tiny, even for her seven years. The ten-year-old, Anna-Marie, played with the pulpy surface of the cement wall.

On the other side of the Steiners were Pfiffikus and the Jenson family.

Pfiffikus kept himself from whistling.

The bearded Mr. Jenson held his wife tightly, and their two kids drifted in and out of silence. Occasionally they pestered each other, but they held back when it came to the beginning of true argument.

After ten minutes or so, what was most prominent in the cellar

374

was a kind of nonmovement. Their bodies were welded together and only their feet changed position or pressure. Stillness was shackled to their faces. They watched each other and waited.

* * * *DUDEN DICTIONARY* MEANING #3 * * *
Angst — Fear:
An unpleasant, often strong
emotion caused by anticipation
or awareness of danger.
Related words: *terror, horror,*
panic, fright, alarm.

From other shelters, there were stories of singing *"Deutschland über Alles"* or of people arguing amid the staleness of their own breath. No such things happened in the Fiedler shelter. In that place, there was only fear and apprehension, and the dead song at Rosa Hubermann's cardboard lips.

Not long before the sirens signaled the end, Alex Steiner—the man with the immovable, wooden face—coaxed the kids from his wife's legs. He was able to reach out and grapple for his son's free hand. Kurt, still stoic and full of stare, took it up and tightened his grip gently on the hand of his sister. Soon, everyone in the cellar was holding the hand of another, and the group of Germans stood in a lumpy circle. The cold hands melted into the warm ones, and in some cases, the feeling of another human pulse was transported. It came through the layers of pale, stiffened skin. Some of them closed their eyes, waiting for their final demise, or hoping for a sign that the raid was finally over.

Did they deserve any better, these people?

How many had actively persecuted others, high on the scent of

Hitler's gaze, repeating his sentences, his paragraphs, his opus? Was Rosa Hubermann responsible? The hider of a Jew? Or Hans? Did they all deserve to die? The children?

The answer to each of these questions interests me very much, though I cannot allow them to seduce me. I only know that all of those people would have sensed me that night, excluding the youngest of the children. I was the suggestion. I was the advice, my imagined feet walking into the kitchen and down the corridor.

As is often the case with humans, when I read about them in the book thief's words, I pitied them, though not as much as I felt for the ones I scooped up from various camps in that time. The Germans in basements were pitiable, surely, but at least they had a chance. That basement was not a washroom. They were not sent there for a shower. For those people, life was still achievable.

In the uneven circle, the minutes soaked by.

Liesel held Rudy's hand, and her mama's.

Only one thought saddened her.

Max.

How would Max survive if the bombs arrived on Himmel Street?

Around her, she examined the Fiedlers' basement. It was much sturdier and considerably deeper than the one at 33 Himmel Street.

Silently, she asked her papa.

Are you thinking about him, too?

Whether the silent question registered or not, he gave the girl a quick nod. It was followed a few minutes later by the three sirens of temporary peace.

The people at 45 Himmel Street sank with relief.

Some clenched their eyes and opened them again.

A cigarette was passed around.

Just as it made its way to Rudy Steiner's lips, it was snatched away by his father. "Not you, Jesse Owens."

The children hugged their parents, and it took many minutes for all of them to fully realize that they were alive, and that they were *going* to be alive. Only then did their feet climb the stairs, to Herbert Fiedler's kitchen.

Outside, a procession of people made its way silently along the street. Many of them looked up and thanked God for their lives.

When the Hubermanns made it home, they headed directly to the basement, but it seemed that Max was not there. The lamp was small and orange and they could not see him or hear an answer.

"Max?"

"He's disappeared."

"Max, are you there?"

"I'm here."

They originally thought the words had come from behind the drop sheets and paint cans, but Liesel was first to see him, in front of them. His jaded face was camouflaged among the painting materials and fabric. He was sitting there with stunned eyes and lips.

When they walked across, he spoke again.

"I couldn't help it," he said.

It was Rosa who replied. She crouched down to face him. "What are you talking about, Max?"

"I . . ." He struggled to answer. "When everything was quiet, I went up to the corridor and the curtain in the living room was open just a crack. . . . I could see outside. I watched, only for a few seconds." He had not seen the outside world for twenty-two months.

There was no anger or reproach.

It was Papa who spoke.

"How did it look?"

Max lifted his head, with great sorrow and great astonishment. "There were stars," he said. "They burned my eyes."

Four of them.

Two people on their feet. The other two remained seated.

All had seen a thing or two that night.

This place was the real basement. This was the real fear. Max gathered himself and stood to move back behind the sheets. He wished them good night, but he didn't make it beneath the stairs. With Mama's permission, Liesel stayed with him till morning, reading *A Song in the Dark* as he sketched and wrote in his book.

From a Himmel Street window, he wrote, *the stars set fire to my eyes.*

THE SKY STEALER

The first raid, as it turned out, was not a raid at all. Had people waited to see the planes, they would have stood there all night. That accounted for the fact that no cuckoo had called from the radio. The *Molching Express* reported that a certain flak tower operator had become a little overexcited. He'd sworn that he could hear the rattle of planes and see them on the horizon. He sent the word.

"He might have done it on purpose," Hans Hubermann pointed out. "Would you want to sit in a flak tower, shooting up at planes carrying bombs?"

Sure enough, as Max continued reading the article in the basement, it was reported that the man with the outlandish imagination had been stood down from his original duty. His fate was most likely some sort of service elsewhere.

"Good luck to him," Max said. He seemed to understand as he moved on to the crossword.

The next raid was real.

On the night of September 19, the cuckoo called from the radio, and it was followed by a deep, informative voice. It listed Molching as a possible target.

Again, Himmel Street was a trail of people, and again, Papa left his accordion. Rosa reminded him to take it, but he refused. "I didn't take it last time," he explained, "and we lived." War clearly blurred the distinction between logic and superstition.

Eerie air followed them down to the Fiedlers' basement. "I think it's real tonight," said Mr. Fiedler, and the children quickly realized that their parents were even more afraid this time around. Reacting the only way they knew, the youngest of them began to wail and cry as the room seemed to swing.

Even from the cellar, they could vaguely hear the tune of bombs. Air pressure shoved itself down like a ceiling, as if to mash the earth. A bite was taken of Molching's empty streets.

Rosa held furiously on to Liesel's hand.

The sound of crying children kicked and punched.

Even Rudy stood completely erect, feigning nonchalance, tensing himself against the tension. Arms and elbows fought for room. Some of the adults tried to calm the infants. Others were unsuccessful in calming themselves.

"Shut that kid up!" Frau Holtzapfel clamored, but her sentence was just another hapless voice in the warm chaos of the shelter. Grimy tears were loosened from children's eyes, and the smell of night breath, underarm sweat, and overworn clothes was stirred and stewed in what was now a cauldron swimming with humans.

Although they were right next to each other, Liesel was forced to call out, "Mama?" Again, "Mama, you're squashing my hand!"

"What?"

"My hand!"

Rosa released her, and for comfort, to shut out the din of the basement, Liesel opened one of her books and began to read. The book on top of the pile was *The Whistler* and she spoke it aloud to help her concentrate. The opening paragraph was numb in her ears.

"What did you say?" Mama roared, but Liesel ignored her. She remained focused on the first page.

When she turned to page two, it was Rudy who noticed. He paid direct attention to what Liesel was reading, and he tapped his brother and his sisters, telling them to do the same. Hans Hubermann came closer and called out, and soon, a quietness started bleeding through the crowded basement. By page three, everyone was silent but Liesel.

She didn't dare to look up, but she could feel their frightened eyes hanging on to her as she hauled the words in and breathed them out. A voice played the notes inside her. This, it said, is your accordion.

The sound of the turning page carved them in half.

Liesel read on.

For at least twenty minutes, she handed out the story. The youngest kids were soothed by her voice, and everyone else saw visions of the whistler running from the crime scene. Liesel did not. The book thief saw only the mechanics of the words—their bodies stranded on the paper, beaten down for her to walk on. Somewhere, too, in the gaps between a period and the next capital letter, there was also Max. She remembered reading to him when he was sick. Is he in the basement? she wondered. Or is he stealing a glimpse of the sky again?

* * * A NICE THOUGHT * * *
One was a book thief.
The other stole the sky.

381

• • •

Everyone waited for the ground to shake.

That was still an immutable fact, but at least they were distracted now, by the girl with the book. One of the younger boys contemplated crying again, but Liesel stopped at that moment and imitated her papa, or even Rudy for that matter. She winked at him and resumed.

Only when the sirens leaked into the cellar again did someone interrupt her. "We're safe," said Mr. Jenson.

"Shhh!" said Frau Holtzapfel.

Liesel looked up. "There are only two paragraphs till the end of the chapter," she said, and she continued reading with no fanfare or added speed. Just the words.

✴ ✴ ✴ DUDEN DICTIONARY MEANING #4 ✴ ✴ ✴
Wort — Word:
A meaningful unit of
language / a promise / a
short remark, statement,
or conversation.
Related words: *term,*
name, expression.

Out of respect, the adults kept everyone quiet, and Liesel finished chapter one of *The Whistler*.

On their way up the stairs, the children rushed by her, but many of the older people—even Frau Holtzapfel, even Pfiffikus (how appropriate, considering the title she read from)—thanked the girl for the distraction. They did so as they made their way past and hurried from the house to see if Himmel Street had sustained any damage.

Himmel Street was untouched.

The only sign of war was a cloud of dust migrating from east to west. It looked through the windows, trying to find a way inside, and as it simultaneously thickened and spread, it turned the trail of humans into apparitions.

There were no people on the street anymore.

They were rumors carrying bags.

At home, Papa told Max all about it. "There's fog and ash—I think they let us out too early." He looked to Rosa. "Should I go out? To see if they need help where the bombs dropped?"

Rosa was not impressed. "Don't be so idiotic," she said. "You'll choke on the dust. No, no, *Saukerl,* you're staying here." A thought came to her. She looked at Hans very seriously now. In fact, her face was crayoned with pride. "Stay here and tell him about the girl." Her voice loudened, just slightly. "About the book."

Max gave her some added attention.

"The Whistler," Rosa informed him. "Chapter one." She explained exactly what had happened in the shelter.

As Liesel stood in a corner of the basement, Max watched her and rubbed a hand along his jaw. Personally, I think that was the moment he conceived the next body of work for his sketchbook.

The Word Shaker.

He imagined the girl reading in the shelter. He must have watched her literally handing out the words. However, as always, he must also have seen the shadow of Hitler. He could probably already hear his footsteps coming toward Himmel Street and the basement, for later.

After a lengthy pause, he looked ready to speak, but Liesel beat him to it.

"Did you see the sky tonight?"

"No." Max looked at the wall and pointed. On it, they all watched the words and the picture he'd painted more than a year earlier—the rope and the dripping sun. "Only that one tonight," and from there, no more was spoken. Nothing but thoughts.

Max, Hans, and Rosa I cannot account for, but I know that Liesel Meminger was thinking that if the bombs ever landed on Himmel Street, not only did Max have less chance of survival than everyone else, but he would die completely alone.

FRAU HOLTZAPFEL'S OFFER

In the morning, the damage was inspected. No one died, but two apartment blocks were reduced to pyramids of rubble, and Rudy's favorite Hitler Youth field had an enormous bowl spooned out of it. Half the town stood around its circumference. People estimated its depth, to compare it with their shelters. Several boys and girls spat into it.

Rudy was standing next to Liesel. "Looks like they need to fertilize again."

When the next few weeks were raid-free, life almost returned to normal. Two telling moments, however, were on their way.

* * * THE DUAL EVENTS * * *
OF OCTOBER
The hands of Frau Holtzapfel.
The parade of Jews.

Her wrinkles were like slander. Her voice was akin to a beating with a stick.

It was actually quite fortunate that they saw Frau Holtzapfel coming from the living room window, for her knuckles on the door were hard and decisive. They meant business.

Liesel heard the words she dreaded.

"You go and answer it," Mama said, and the girl, knowing only too well what was good for her, did as she was told.

"Is your mama home?" Frau Holtzapfel inquired. Constructed of fifty-year-old wire, she stood on the front step, looking back every so often to view the street. "Is that swine of a mother of yours here today?"

Liesel turned and called out.

* * * *DUDEN DICTIONARY* MEANING #5 * * *
Gelegenheit — Opportunity:
A chance for advancement or progress.
Related words:
prospect, opening, break.

Soon, Rosa was behind her. "What do *you* want here? You want to spit on my kitchen floor now, too?"

Frau Holtzapfel was not deterred in the slightest. "Is that how you greet *everyone* who shows up at your front door? What a *G'sindel.*"

Liesel watched. She was unfortunate enough to be sandwiched between them. Rosa pulled her out of the way. "Well, are you going to tell me why you're here or not?"

Frau Holtzapfel looked once more at the street and back. "I have an offer for you."

Mama shifted her weight. "Is that right?"

"No, not you." She dismissed Rosa with a shrug of the voice and focused now on Liesel. "You."

386

"Why did you ask for me, then?"

"Well, I at least need your *permission*."

Oh, Maria, Liesel thought, this is all I need. What the hell can Holtzapfel want with me?

"I liked that book you read in the shelter."

No. You're not getting it. Liesel was convinced of that. "Yes?"

"I was hoping to hear the rest of it in the shelter, but it looks like we're safe for now." She rolled her shoulders and straightened the wire in her back. "So I want you to come to my place and read it to me."

"You've got some nerve, Holtzapfel." Rosa was deciding whether to be furious or not. "If you think—"

"I'll stop spitting on your door," she interrupted. "And I'll give you my coffee ration."

Rosa decided against being furious. "And some flour?"

"What, are you a Jew? Just the coffee. You can swap the coffee with someone else for the flour."

It was decided.

By everyone but the girl.

"Good, then, it's done."

"Mama?"

"Quiet, *Saumensch*. Go and get the book." Mama faced Frau Holtzapfel again. "What days suit you?"

"Monday and Friday, four o'clock. And today, right now."

Liesel followed the regimented footsteps to Frau Holtzapfel's lodging next door, which was a mirror image of the Hubermanns'. If anything, it was slightly larger.

When she sat down at the kitchen table, Frau Holtzapfel sat directly in front of her but faced the window. "Read," she said.

"Chapter two?"

"No, chapter eight. Of course chapter two! Now get reading before I throw you out."

"Yes, Frau Holtzapfel."

"Never mind the 'yes, Frau Holtzapfels.' Just open the book. We don't have all day."

Good God, Liesel thought. This is my punishment for all that stealing. It's finally caught up with me.

She read for forty-five minutes, and when the chapter was finished, a bag of coffee was deposited on the table.

"Thank you," the woman said. "It's a good story." She turned toward the stove and started on some potatoes. Without looking back, she said, "Are you still here, are you?"

Liesel took that as her cue to leave. "*Danke schön*, Frau Holtzapfel." By the door, when she saw the framed photos of two young men in military uniform, she also threw in a "*heil* Hitler," her arm raised in the kitchen.

"Yes." Frau Holtzapfel was proud and afraid. Two sons in Russia. "*Heil* Hitler." She put her water down to boil and even found the manners to walk the few steps with Liesel to the front door. "*Bis morgen?*"

The next day was Friday. "Yes, Frau Holtzapfel. Until tomorrow."

Liesel calculated that there were four more reading sessions like that with Frau Holtzapfel before the Jews were marched through Molching.

They were going to Dachau, to concentrate.

That makes two weeks, she would later write in the basement. *Two weeks to change the world, and fourteen days to ruin it.*

THE LONG WALK TO DACHAU

Some people said that the truck had broken down, but I can personally testify that this was not the case. I was there.

What had happened was an ocean sky, with whitecap clouds.

Also, there was more than just the one vehicle. Three trucks don't all break down at once.

When the soldiers pulled over to share some food and cigarettes and to poke at the package of Jews, one of the prisoners collapsed from starvation and sickness. I have no idea where the convoy had traveled from, but it was perhaps four miles from Molching, and many steps more to the concentration camp at Dachau.

I climbed through the windshield of the truck, found the diseased man, and jumped out the back. His soul was skinny. His beard was a ball and chain. My feet landed loudly in the gravel, though not a sound was heard by a soldier or prisoner. But they could all smell me.

Recollection tells me that there were many wishes in the back of that truck. Inner voices called out to me.

Why him and not me?

Thank God it *isn't* me.

The soldiers, on the other hand, were occupied with a different discussion. The leader squashed his cigarette and asked the others a smoggy question. "When was the last time we took these rats for some fresh air?"

His first lieutenant choked back a cough. "They could sure use it, couldn't they?"

"Well, how about it, then? We've got time, don't we?"

"We've always got time, sir."

"And it's perfect weather for a parade, don't you think?"

"It is, sir."

"So what are you waiting for?"

On Himmel Street, Liesel was playing soccer when the noise arrived. Two boys were fighting for the ball in the midfield when everything stopped. Even Tommy Müller could hear it. "What *is* that?" he asked from his position in goal.

Everyone turned toward the sound of shuffling feet and regimented voices as they made their way closer.

"Is that a herd of cows?" Rudy asked. "It can't be. It never sounds quite like that, does it?"

Slowly at first, the street of children walked toward the magnetic sound, up toward Frau Diller's. Once in a while there was added emphasis in the shouting.

In a tall apartment just around the corner on Munich Street, an old lady with a foreboding voice deciphered for everyone the exact source of the commotion. Up high, in the window, her face appeared like a white flag with moist eyes and an open mouth. Her voice was like suicide, landing with a clunk at Liesel's feet.

She had gray hair.

The eyes were dark, dark blue.

"Die Juden," she said. "The Jews."

Elend — Misery:
**Great suffering,
unhappiness, and distress.
Related words:**
*anguish, torment, despair,
wretchedness, desolation.*

More people appeared on the street, where a collection of Jews and other criminals had already been shoved past. Perhaps the death camps were kept secret, but at times, people were shown the glory of a labor camp like Dachau.

Far up, on the other side, Liesel spotted the man with his paint cart. He was running his hand uncomfortably through his hair.

"Up there," she pointed out to Rudy. "My papa."

They both crossed and made their way up, and Hans Hubermann attempted at first to take them away. "Liesel," he said. "Maybe . . ."

He realized, however, that the girl was determined to stay, and perhaps it was something she should see. In the breezy autumn air, he stood with her. He did not speak.

On Munich Street, they watched.

Others moved in around and in front of them.

They watched the Jews come down the road like a catalog of colors. That wasn't how the book thief described them, but I can tell you that that's exactly what they were, for many of them would die. They would each greet me like their last true friend, with bones like smoke and their souls trailing behind.

When they arrived in full, the noise of their feet throbbed on top of the road. Their eyes were enormous in their starving skulls. And the dirt. The dirt was molded to them. Their legs staggered as they were pushed by soldiers' hands—a few wayward steps of forced running before the slow return to a malnourished walk.

Hans watched them above the heads of the crowding audience. I'm sure his eyes were silver and strained. Liesel looked through the gaps or over shoulders.

The suffering faces of depleted men and women reached across to them, pleading not so much for help—they were beyond that—but for an explanation. Just something to subdue this confusion.

Their feet could barely rise above the ground.

Stars of David were plastered to their shirts, and misery was attached to them as if assigned. "Don't forget your misery . . ." In some cases, it grew on them like a vine.

At their side, the soldiers also made their way past, ordering them to hurry up and to stop moaning. Some of those soldiers were only boys. They had the *Führer* in their eyes.

As she watched all of this, Liesel was certain that these were the poorest souls alive. That's what she wrote about them. Their gaunt faces were stretched with torture. Hunger ate them as they continued forward, some of them watching the ground to avoid the people on the side of the road. Some looked appealingly at those who had come to observe their humiliation, this prelude to their deaths. Others pleaded for someone, anyone, to step forward and catch them in their arms.

No one did.

Whether they watched this parade with pride, temerity, or shame, nobody came forward to interrupt it. Not yet.

Once in a while a man or woman—no, they were not men and women; they were Jews—would find Liesel's face among the crowd. They would meet her with their defeat, and the book thief could do nothing but watch them back in a long, incurable moment before they were gone again. She could only hope they could read the depth of sorrow in her face, to recognize that it was true, and not fleeting.

I have one of you in my basement! she wanted to say. We built a snowman together! I gave him thirteen presents when he was sick!

Liesel said nothing at all.

What good would it be?

She understood that she was utterly worthless to these people. They could not be saved, and in a few minutes, she would see what would happen to those who might try to help them.

In a small gap in the procession, there was a man, older than the others.

He wore a beard and torn clothes.

His eyes were the color of agony, and weightless as he was, he was too heavy for his legs to carry.

Several times, he fell.

The side of his face was flattened against the road.

On each occasion, a soldier stood above him. *"Steh' auf,"* he called down. "Stand up."

The man rose to his knees and fought his way up. He walked on.

Every time he caught up sufficiently to the back of the line, he would soon lose momentum and stumble again to the ground. There were more behind him—a good truck's worth—and they threatened to overtake and trample him.

The ache in his arms was unbearable to watch as they shook, trying to lift his body. They gave way one more time before he stood and took another group of steps.

He was dead.

The man was dead.

Just give him five more minutes and he would surely fall into the German gutter and die. They would all let him, and they would all watch.

Then, one human.

Hans Hubermann.

. . .

It happened so quickly.

The hand that held firmly on to Liesel's let it drop to her side as the man came struggling by. She felt her palm slap her hip.

Papa reached into his paint cart and pulled something out. He made his way through the people, onto the road.

The Jew stood before him, expecting another handful of derision, but he watched with everyone else as Hans Hubermann held his hand out and presented a piece of bread, like magic.

When it changed hands, the Jew slid down. He fell to his knees and held Papa's shins. He buried his face between them and thanked him.

Liesel watched.

With tears in her eyes, she saw the man slide farther forward, pushing Papa back to cry into his ankles.

Other Jews walked past, all of them watching this small, futile miracle. They streamed by, like human water. That day, a few would reach the ocean. They would be handed a white cap.

Wading through, a soldier was soon at the scene of the crime. He studied the kneeling man and Papa, and he looked at the crowd. After another moment's thought, he took the whip from his belt and began.

The Jew was whipped six times. On his back, his head, and his legs. "You filth! You swine!" Blood dripped now from his ear.

Then it was Papa's turn.

A new hand held Liesel's now, and when she looked in horror next to her, Rudy Steiner swallowed as Hans Hubermann was whipped on the street. The sound sickened her and she expected cracks to appear on her papa's body. He was struck four times before he, too, hit the ground.

When the elderly Jew climbed to his feet for the last time and continued on, he looked briefly back. He took a last sad glance at the man who was kneeling now himself, whose back was burning with four lines of fire, whose knees were aching on the road. If nothing else, the old man would die like a human. Or at least with the thought that he *was* a human.

Me?

I'm not so sure if that's such a good thing.

When Liesel and Rudy made it through and helped Hans to his feet, there were so many voices. Words and sunlight. That's how she remembered it. The light sparkling on the road and the words like waves, breaking on her back. Only as they walked away did they notice the bread sitting rejected on the street.

As Rudy attempted to pick it up, a passing Jew snatched it from his hand and another two fought him for it as they continued on their way to Dachau.

Silver eyes were pelted then.

A cart was turned over and paint flowed onto the street.

They called him a Jew lover.

Others were silent, helping him back to safety.

Hans Hubermann leaned forward, arms outstretched against a house wall. He was suddenly overwhelmed by what had just happened.

There was an image, fast and hot.

33 Himmel Street—its basement.

Thoughts of panic were caught between the in-and-out struggle of his breath.

They'll come now. They'll come.

Oh, Christ, oh, crucified Christ.

He looked at the girl and closed his eyes.

"Are you hurt, Papa?"

She received questions rather than an answer.

"What was I thinking?" His eyes closed tighter and opened again. His overalls creased. There was paint and blood on his hands. And bread crumbs. How different from the bread of summer. "Oh my God, Liesel, what have I done?"

Yes.
    I must agree.

What had Papa done?

PEACE

At just after 11 p.m. that same night, Max Vandenburg walked up Himmel Street with a suitcase full of food and warm clothes. German air was in his lungs. The yellow stars were on fire. When he made it to Frau Diller's, he looked back one last time to number thirty-three. He could not see the figure in the kitchen window, but *she* could see him. She waved and he did not wave back.

Liesel could still feel his mouth on her forehead. She could smell his breath of goodbye.

"I have left something for you," he'd said, "but you will not get it until you're ready."

He left.

"Max?"

But he did not come back.

He had walked from her room and silently shut the door.

The hallway murmured.

He was gone.

When she made it to the kitchen, Mama and Papa stood with crooked bodies and preserved faces. They'd been standing like that for thirty seconds of forever.

★ ★ ★ *DUDEN DICTIONARY* MEANING #7 ★ ★ ★
Schweigen — Silence:
The absence of sound or noise.
Related words:
quiet, calmness, peace.

How perfect.
Peace.

Somewhere near Munich, a German Jew was making his way through
the darkness. An arrangement had been made to meet Hans Hubermann in four days (that is, if he wasn't taken away). It was at a place
far down the Amper, where a broken bridge leaned among the river
and trees.

He would make it there, but he would not stay longer than a few
minutes.

The only thing to be found there when Papa arrived four days
later was a note under a rock, at the base of a tree. It was addressed to
nobody and contained only one sentence.

★ ★ ★ THE LAST WORDS OF ★ ★ ★
MAX VANDENBURG
You've done enough.

Now more than ever, 33 Himmel Street was a place of silence, and it
did not go unnoticed that the *Duden Dictionary* was completely and
utterly mistaken, especially with its related words.

Silence was not quiet or calm, and it was not peace.

THE IDIOT AND THE COAT MEN

On the night of the parade, the idiot sat in the kitchen, drinking bitter gulps of Holtzapfel's coffee and hankering for a cigarette. He waited for the Gestapo, the soldiers, the police—for anyone—to take him away, as he felt he deserved. Rosa ordered him to come to bed. The girl loitered in the doorway. He sent them both away and spent the hours till morning with his head in his hands, waiting.

Nothing came.

Every unit of time carried with it the expected noise of knocking and threatening words.

They did not come.

The only sound was of himself.

"What have I done?" he whispered again.

"God, I'd love a cigarette," he answered. He was all out.

Liesel heard the repeated sentences several times, and it took a lot to stay by the door. She'd have loved to comfort him, but she had never seen a man so devastated. There were no consolations that night. Max was gone, and Hans Hubermann was to blame.

The kitchen cupboards were the shape of guilt, and his palms were oily with the memory of what he'd done. They *must* be sweaty, Liesel thought, for her own hands were soaked to the wrists.

In her room, she prayed.
Hands and knees, forearms against the mattress.
"Please, God, please let Max survive. Please, God, please . . ."
Her suffering knees.
Her painful feet.

When first light appeared, she awoke and made her way back to the kitchen. Papa was asleep with his head parallel to the tabletop, and there was some saliva at the corner of his mouth. The smell of coffee was overpowering, and the image of Hans Hubermann's stupid kindness was still in the air. It was like a number or an address. Repeat it enough times and it sticks.

Her first attempt to wake him was unfelt, but her second nudge of the shoulder brought his head from the table in an upward shock.

"Are they here?"

"No, Papa, it's me."

He finished the stale pool of coffee in his mug. His Adam's apple lifted and sank. "They should have come by now. Why haven't they come, Liesel?"

It was an insult.

They should have come by now and swept through the house, looking for any evidence of Jew loving or treason, but it appeared that Max had left for no reason at all. He could have been asleep in the basement or sketching in his book.

"You can't have known that they wouldn't come, Papa."

"I should have *known* not to give the man some bread. I just didn't think."

"Papa, you did nothing wrong."

"I don't believe you."

He stood and walked out the kitchen door, leaving it ajar. Lending even more insult to injury, it was going to be a lovely morning.

When four days had elapsed, Papa walked a long length of the Amper River. He brought back a small note and placed it on the kitchen table.

Another week passed, and still, Hans Hubermann waited for his punishment. The welts on his back were turning to scars, and he spent the majority of his time walking around Molching. Frau Diller spat at his feet. Frau Holtzapfel, true to her word, had ceased spitting at the Hubermanns' door, but here was a handy replacement. "I knew it," the shopkeeper damned him. "You dirty Jew lover."

He walked obliviously on, and Liesel would often catch him at the Amper River, on the bridge. His arms rested on the rail and he leaned his upper body over the edge. Kids on bikes rushed past him, or they ran with loud voices and the slaps of feet on wood. None of it moved him in the slightest.

* * * *DUDEN DICTIONARY* MEANING #8 * * *
Nachtrauern — Regret:
Sorrow filled with longing,
disappointment, or loss.
Related words: *rue, repent,*
mourn, grieve.

"Do you see him?" he asked her one afternoon, when she leaned with him. "In the water there?"

The river was not running very fast. In the slow ripples, Liesel could see the outline of Max Vandenburg's face. She could see his feathery hair and the rest of him. "He used to fight the *Führer* in our basement."

"Jesus, Mary, and Joseph." Papa's hands tightened on the splintery wood. "I'm an idiot."

No, Papa.

You're just a man.

The words came to her more than a year later, when she wrote in the basement. She wished she'd thought of them at the time.

"I am stupid," Hans Hubermann told his foster daughter. "And kind. Which makes the biggest idiot in the world. The thing is, I *want* them to come for me. Anything's better than this waiting."

Hans Hubermann needed vindication. He needed to know that Max Vandenburg had left his house for good reason.

Finally, after nearly three weeks of waiting, he thought his moment had come.

It was late.

Liesel was returning from Frau Holtzapfel's when she saw the two men in their long black coats, and she ran inside.

"Papa, Papa!" She nearly wiped out the kitchen table. "Papa, they're here!"

Mama came first. "What's all this shouting about, *Saumensch?* Who's here?"

"The Gestapo."

"Hansi!"

He was already there, and he walked out of the house to greet them. Liesel wanted to join him, but Rosa held her back and they watched from the window.

Papa was poised at the front gate. He fidgeted.

Mama tightened her grip on Liesel's arms.

The men walked past.

Papa looked back at the window, alarmed, then made his way out of the gate. He called after them. "Hey! I'm right here. It's me you want. I live in this one."

The coat men only stopped momentarily and checked their notebooks. "No, no," they told him. Their voices were deep and bulky. "Unfortunately, you're a little old for our purposes."

They continued walking, but they did not travel very far, stopping at number thirty-five and proceeding through the open gate.

"Frau Steiner?" they asked when the door was opened.

"Yes, that's right."

"We've come to talk to you about something."

The coat men stood like jacketed columns on the threshold of the Steiners' shoe-box house.

For some reason, they'd come for the boy.

The coat men wanted Rudy.

PART EIGHT

the word shaker

featuring:

dominoes and darkness—the thought of
rudy naked—punishment—a promise keeper's
wife—a collector—the bread eaters—
a candle in the trees—a hidden sketchbook—
and the anarchist's suit collection

DOMINOES AND DARKNESS

In the words of Rudy's youngest sisters, there were two monsters sitting in the kitchen. Their voices kneaded methodically at the door as three of the Steiner children played dominoes on the other side. The remaining three listened to the radio in the bedroom, oblivious. Rudy hoped this had nothing to do with what had happened at school the previous week. It was something he had refused to tell Liesel and did not talk about at home.

* * * A GRAY AFTERNOON, * * *
A SMALL SCHOOL OFFICE
Three boys stood in a line. Their records
and bodies were thoroughly examined.

When the fourth game of dominoes was completed, Rudy began to stand them up in lines, creating patterns that wound their way across the living room floor. As was his habit, he also left a few gaps, in case the rogue finger of a sibling interfered, which it usually did.

"Can I knock them down, Rudy?"

"No."

"What about me?"

"No. We all will."

He made three separate formations that led to the same tower of dominoes in the middle. Together, they would watch everything that was so carefully planned collapse, and they would all smile at the beauty of destruction.

The kitchen voices were becoming louder now, each heaping itself upon the other to be heard. Different sentences fought for attention until one person, previously silent, came between them.

"No," she said. It was repeated. "No." Even when the rest of them resumed their arguments, they were silenced again by the same voice, but now it gained momentum. "Please," Barbara Steiner begged them. "Not my boy."

"Can we light a candle, Rudy?"

It was something their father had often done with them. He would turn out the light and they'd watch the dominoes fall in the candlelight. It somehow made the event grander, a greater spectacle.

His legs were aching anyway. "Let me find a match."

The light switch was at the door.

Quietly, he walked toward it with the matchbox in one hand, the candle in the other.

From the other side, the three men and one woman climbed to the hinges. "The best scores in the class," said one of the monsters. Such depth and dryness. "Not to mention his athletic ability." Damn it, why did he have to win all those races at the carnival?

Deutscher.

Damn that Franz Deutscher!

But then he understood.

This was not Franz Deutscher's fault, but his own. He'd wanted to show his past tormentor what he was capable of, but he also wanted to prove himself to everyone. Now *everyone* was in the kitchen.

He lit the candle and switched off the light.

"Ready?"

"But I've heard what happens there." That was the unmistakable, oaky voice of his father.

"Come on, Rudy, hurry up."

"Yes, but understand, Herr Steiner, this is all for a greater purpose. Think of the opportunities your son can have. This is really a privilege."

"Rudy, the candle's dripping."

He waved them away, waiting again for Alex Steiner. He came.

"Privileges? Like running barefoot through the snow? Like jumping from ten-meter platforms into three feet of water?"

Rudy's ear was pressed to the door now. Candle wax melted onto his hand.

"Rumors." The arid voice, low and matter-of-fact, had an answer for everything. "Our school is one of the finest ever established. It's better than world-class. We're creating an elite group of German citizens in the name of the *Führer*...."

Rudy could listen no longer.

He scraped the candle wax from his hand and drew back from the splice of light that came through the crack in the door. When he sat down, the flame went out. Too much movement. Darkness flowed in. The only light available was a white rectangular stencil, the shape of the kitchen door.

He struck another match and reignited the candle. The sweet smell of fire and carbon.

Rudy and his sisters each tapped a different domino and they watched them fall until the tower in the middle was brought to its knees. The girls cheered.

Kurt, his older brother, arrived in the room.

"They look like dead bodies," he said.

"What?"

Rudy peered up at the dark face, but Kurt did not answer. He'd noticed the arguing from the kitchen. "What's going on in there?"

It was one of the girls who answered. The youngest, Bettina. She was five. "There are two monsters," she said. "They've come for Rudy."

Again, the human child. So much cannier.

Later, when the coat men left, the two boys, one seventeen, the other fourteen, found the courage to face the kitchen.

They stood in the doorway. The light punished their eyes.

It was Kurt who spoke. "Are they taking him?"

Their mother's forearms were flat on the table. Her palms were facing up.

Alex Steiner raised his head.

It was heavy.

His expression was sharp and definite, freshly cut.

A wooden hand wiped at the splinters of his fringe, and he made several attempts to speak.

"Papa?"

But Rudy did not walk toward his father.

He sat at the kitchen table and took hold of his mother's facing-up hand.

Alex and Barbara Steiner would not disclose what was said while the dominoes were falling like dead bodies in the living room. If only Rudy had kept listening at the door, just for another few minutes . . .

He told himself in the weeks to come—or in fact, pleaded with himself—that if he'd heard the rest of the conversation that night, he'd have entered the kitchen much earlier. "I'll go," he'd have said. "Please, take me, I'm ready now."

If he'd intervened, it might have changed everything.

* * * THREE POSSIBILITIES * * *
1. Alex Steiner wouldn't have suffered
the same punishment as Hans Hubermann.
2. Rudy would have gone away to school.
3. And just maybe, he would have lived.

The cruelty of fate, however, did not allow Rudy Steiner to enter the kitchen at the opportune moment.

He'd returned to his sisters and the dominoes.

He sat down.

Rudy Steiner wasn't going anywhere.

THE THOUGHT OF RUDY NAKED

There had been a woman.

Standing in the corner.

She had the thickest braid he'd ever seen. It roped down her back, and occasionally, when she brought it over her shoulder, it lurked at her colossal breast like an overfed pet. In fact, everything about her was magnified. Her lips, her legs. Her paved teeth. She had a large, direct voice. No time to waste. *"Komm,"* she instructed them. "Come. Stand here."

The doctor, by comparison, was like a balding rodent. He was small and nimble, pacing the school office with his manic yet business-like movements and mannerisms. And he had a cold.

Out of the three boys, it was difficult to decide which was the more reluctant to take off his clothes when ordered to do so. The first one looked from person to person, from the aging teacher to the gargantuan nurse to the pint-sized doctor. The one in the middle looked only at his feet, and the one on the far left counted his blessings that he was in the school office and not a dark alley. The nurse, Rudy decided, was a frightener.

"Who's first?" she asked.

It was the supervising teacher, Herr Heckenstaller, who answered. He was more a black suit than a man. His face was a mustache. Examining the boys, his choice came swiftly.

"Schwarz."

The unfortunate Jürgen Schwarz undid his uniform with great discomfort. He was left standing only in his shoes and underwear. A luckless plea was marooned on his German face.

"And?" Herr Heckenstaller asked. "The shoes?"

He removed both shoes, both socks.

"Und die Unterhosen," said the nurse. "And the underpants."

Both Rudy and the other boy, Olaf Spiegel, had started undressing now as well, but they were nowhere near the perilous position of Jürgen Schwarz. The boy was shaking. He was a year younger than the other two, but taller. When his underpants came down, it was with abject humiliation that he stood in the small, cool office. His self-respect was around his ankles.

The nurse watched him with intent, her arms folded across her devastating chest.

Heckenstaller ordered the other two to get moving.

The doctor scratched his scalp and coughed. His cold was killing him.

The three naked boys were each examined on the cold flooring.

They cupped their genitals in their hands and shivered like the future.

Between the doctor's coughing and wheezing, they were put through their paces.

"Breathe in." Sniffle.

"Breathe out." Second sniffle.

"Arms out now." A cough. "I said arms *out*." A horrendous hail of coughing.

As humans do, the boys looked constantly at each other for some sign of mutual sympathy. None was there. All three pried their hands from their penises and held out their arms. Rudy did not feel like he was part of a master race.

"We are gradually succeeding," the nurse was informing the teacher, "in creating a new future. It will be a new class of physically and mentally advanced Germans. An officer class."

Unfortunately, her sermon was cut short when the doctor creased in half and coughed with all his might over the abandoned clothes. Tears welled up in his eyes and Rudy couldn't help but wonder.

A new future? Like him?

Wisely, he did not speak it.

The examination was completed and he managed to perform his first nude "*heil* Hitler." In a perverse kind of way, he conceded that it didn't feel half bad.

Stripped of their dignity, the boys were allowed to dress again, and as they were shown from the office, they could already hear the discussion held in their honor behind them.

"They're a little older than usual," the doctor said, "but I'm thinking at least two of them."

The nurse agreed. "The first and the third."

Three boys stood outside.

First and third.

"First was you, Schwarz," said Rudy. He then questioned Olaf Spiegel. "Who was third?"

Spiegel made a few calculations. Did she mean third in line or third examined? It didn't matter. He knew what he wanted to believe. "That was you, I think."

"Cow shit, Spiegel, it was you."

* * * A SMALL GUARANTEE * * *
The coat men knew who was third.

The day after they'd visited Himmel Street, Rudy sat on his front step with Liesel and related the whole saga, even the smallest details. He gave up and admitted what had happened that day at school when he was taken out of class. There was even some laughter about the tremendous nurse and the look on Jürgen Schwarz's face. For the most part, though, it was a tale of anxiety, especially when it came to the voices in the kitchen and the dead-body dominoes.

For days, Liesel could not shift one thought from her head.

It was the examination of the three boys, or if she was honest, it was Rudy.

She would lie in bed, missing Max, wondering where he was, praying that he was alive, but somewhere, standing among all of it, was Rudy.

He glowed in the dark, completely naked.

There was great dread in that vision, especially the moment when he was forced to remove his hands. It was disconcerting to say the least, but for some reason, she couldn't stop thinking about it.

PUNISHMENT

On the ration cards of Nazi Germany, there was no listing for punishment, but everyone had to take their turn. For some it was death in a foreign country during the war. For others it was poverty and guilt when the war was over, when six million discoveries were made throughout Europe. Many people must have seen their punishments coming, but only a small percentage welcomed it. One such person was Hans Hubermann.

You do not help Jews on the street.

Your basement should not be hiding one.

At first, his punishment was conscience. His oblivious unearthing of Max Vandenburg plagued him. Liesel could see it sitting next to his plate as he ignored his dinner, or standing with him at the bridge over the Amper. He no longer played the accordion. His silver-eyed optimism was wounded and motionless. That was bad enough, but it was only the beginning.

One Wednesday in early November, his true punishment arrived in the mailbox. On the surface, it appeared to be good news.

✳ ✳ ✳ PAPER IN THE KITCHEN ✳ ✳ ✳
*We are delighted to inform you that
your application to join the NSDAP
has been approved.* . . .

"The Nazi Party?" Rosa asked. "I thought they didn't want you."

"They didn't."

Papa sat down and read the letter again.

He was not being put on trial for treason or for helping Jews or anything of the sort. Hans Hubermann was being *rewarded,* at least as far as some people were concerned. How could this be possible?

"There has to be more."

There was.

On Friday, a statement arrived to say that Hans Hubermann was to be drafted into the German army. A member of the party would be happy to play a role in the war effort, it concluded. If he wasn't, there would certainly be consequences.

Liesel had just returned from reading with Frau Holtzapfel. The kitchen was heavy with soup steam and the vacant faces of Hans and Rosa Hubermann. Papa was seated. Mama stood above him as the soup started to burn.

"God, please don't send me to Russia," Papa said.

"Mama, the soup's burning."

"What?"

Liesel hurried across and took it from the stove. "The soup." When she'd successfully rescued it, she turned and viewed her foster parents. Faces like ghost towns. "Papa, what's wrong?"

He handed her the letter and her hands began to shake as she made her way through it. The words had been punched forcefully into the paper.

417

* * * THE CONTENTS OF * * * LIESEL MEMINGER'S IMAGINATION
In the shell-shocked kitchen, somewhere near the
stove, there's an image of a lonely, overworked
typewriter. It sits in a distant, near-empty room. Its keys are
faded and a blank sheet waits patiently upright in the assumed
position. It wavers slightly in the breeze from the window.
Coffee break is nearly over. A pile of paper the height of a
human stands casually by the door. It could easily be smoking.

In truth, Liesel only saw the typewriter later, when she wrote. She wondered how many letters like that were sent out as punishment to Germany's Hans Hubermanns and Alex Steiners—to those who helped the helpless, and those who refused to let go of their children.

It was a sign of the German army's growing desperation.

They were losing in Russia.

Their cities were being bombed.

More people were needed, as were ways of attaining them, and in most cases, the worst possible jobs would be given to the worst possible people.

As her eyes scanned the paper, Liesel could see through the punched letter holes to the wooden table. Words like *compulsory* and *duty* were beaten into the page. Saliva was triggered. It was the urge to vomit. "What is this?"

Papa's answer was quiet. "I thought I taught you to read, my girl." He did not speak with anger or sarcasm. It was a voice of vacancy, to match his face.

Liesel looked now to Mama.

Rosa had a small rip beneath her right eye, and within the

minute, her cardboard face was broken. Not down the center, but to the right. It gnarled down her cheek in an arc, finishing at her chin.

✳ ✳ ✳ TWENTY MINUTES LATER: ✳ ✳ ✳
A GIRL ON HIMMEL STREET
She looks up. She speaks in a whisper.
"The sky is soft today, Max. The clouds
are so soft and sad, and . . ." She looks
away and crosses her arms. She thinks
of her papa going to war and grabs
her jacket at each side of her body.
"And it's cold, Max. It's so cold. . . ."

Five days later, when she continued her habit of looking at the weather, she did not get a chance to see the sky.

Next door, Barbara Steiner was sitting on the front step with her neatly combed hair. She was smoking a cigarette and shivering. On her way over, Liesel was interrupted by the sight of Kurt. He came out and sat with his mother. When he saw the girl stop, he called out.

"Come on, Liesel. Rudy will be out soon."

After a short pause, she continued walking toward the step.

Barbara smoked.

A wrinkle of ash was teetering at the end of the cigarette. Kurt took it, ashed it, inhaled, then gave it back.

When the cigarette was done, Rudy's mother looked up. She ran a hand through her tidy lines of hair.

"Our papa's going, too," Kurt said.

Quietness then.

A group of kids was kicking a ball, up near Frau Diller's.

"When they come and ask you for one of your children," Barbara Steiner explained, to no one in particular, "you're supposed to say yes."

THE PROMISE KEEPER'S WIFE

* * * THE BASEMENT, 9 A.M. * * *
Six hours till goodbye:
"I played an accordion, Liesel. Someone else's."
He closes his eyes: "It brought the house down."

Not counting the glass of champagne the previous summer, Hans Hubermann had not consumed a drop of alcohol for a decade. Then came the night before he left for training.

He made his way to the Knoller with Alex Steiner in the afternoon and stayed well into the evening. Ignoring the warnings of their wives, both men drank themselves into oblivion. It didn't help that the Knoller's owner, Dieter Westheimer, gave them free drinks.

Apparently, while he was still sober, Hans was invited to the stage to play the accordion. Appropriately, he played the infamous "Gloomy Sunday"—the anthem of suicide from Hungary—and although he aroused all the sadness for which the song was renowned, he brought the house down. Liesel imagined the scene of it, and the sound. Mouths were full. Empty beer glasses were streaked with foam. The bellows sighed and the song was over. People clapped. Their beer-filled mouths cheered him back to the bar.

When they managed to find their way home, Hans couldn't get his key to fit the door. So he knocked. Repeatedly.

"Rosa!"

It was the wrong door.

Frau Holtzapfel was not thrilled.

"*Schwein!* You're at the wrong house." She rammed the words through the keyhole. "Next door, you stupid *Saukerl*."

"Thanks, Frau Holtzapfel."

"You know what you can do with your thanks, you asshole."

"Excuse me?"

"Just go home."

"Thanks, Frau Holtzapfel."

"Didn't I just tell you what you can do with your thanks?"

"Did you?"

(It's amazing what you can piece together from a basement conversation and a reading session in a nasty old woman's kitchen.)

"Just get lost, will you!"

When at long last he came home, Papa made his way not to bed, but to Liesel's room. He stood drunkenly in the doorway and watched her sleep. She awoke and thought immediately that it was Max.

"Is it you?" she asked.

"No," he said. He knew exactly what she was thinking. "It's Papa."

He backed out of the room and she heard his footsteps making their way down to the basement.

In the living room, Rosa was snoring with enthusiasm.

Close to nine o'clock the next morning, in the kitchen, Liesel was given an order by Rosa. "Hand me that bucket there."

She filled it with cold water and walked with it down to the basement. Liesel followed, in a vain attempt to stop her. "Mama, you can't!"

"Can't I?" She faced her briefly on the steps. "Did I miss something, *Saumensch*? Do you give the orders around here now?"

Both of them were completely still.

No answer from the girl.

"I thought not."

They continued on and found him on his back, among a bed of drop sheets. He felt he didn't deserve Max's mattress.

"Now, let's see"—Rosa lifted the bucket—"if he's alive."

"Jesus, Mary, and Joseph!"

The watermark was oval-shaped, from halfway up his chest to his head. His hair was plastered to one side and even his eyelashes dripped. "What was that for?"

"You old drunk!"

"Jesus . . ."

Steam was rising weirdly from his clothes. His hangover was visible. It heaved itself to his shoulders and sat there like a bag of wet cement.

Rosa swapped the bucket from left hand to right. "It's lucky you're going to the war," she said. She held her finger in the air and wasn't afraid to wave it. "Otherwise I'd kill you myself, you know that, don't you?"

Papa wiped a stream of water from his throat. "Did you have to do that?"

"Yes. I did." She started up the steps. "If you're not up there in five minutes, you get another bucketful."

Left in the basement with Papa, Liesel busied herself by mopping up the excess water with some drop sheets.

Papa spoke. With his wet hand, he made the girl stop. He held her forearm. "Liesel?" His face clung to her. "Do you think he's alive?"

Liesel sat.

She crossed her legs.

The wet drop sheet soaked onto her knee.

"I hope so, Papa."

It felt like such a stupid thing to say, so obvious, but there seemed little alternative.

To say at least something of value, and to distract them from thoughts of Max, she made herself crouch and placed a finger in a small pool of water on the floor. *"Guten Morgen,* Papa."

In response, Hans winked at her.

But it was not the usual wink. It was heavier, clumsier. The post-Max version, the hangover version. He sat up and told her about the accordion of the previous night, and Frau Holtzapfel.

✳ ✳ ✳ THE KITCHEN: 1 P.M. ✳ ✳ ✳

Two hours till goodbye: "Don't go, Papa. Please."

Her spoon-holding hand is shaking. "First we lost Max.

I can't lose you now, too." In response, the hungover

man digs his elbow into the table and covers his right eye.

"You're half a woman now, Liesel." He wants to break down but

wards it off. He rides through it. "Look after

Mama, will you?" The girl can make only half a nod

to agree. "Yes, Papa."

He left Himmel Street wearing his hangover and a suit.

Alex Steiner was not leaving for another four days. He came over an hour before they left for the station and wished Hans all the best. The whole Steiner family had come. They all shook his hand. Barbara embraced him, kissing both cheeks. "Come back alive."

"Yes, Barbara," and the way he'd said it was full of confidence. "Of course I will." He even managed to laugh. "It's just a war, you know. I've survived one before."

When they walked up Himmel Street, the wiry woman from next door came out and stood on the pavement.

"Goodbye, Frau Holtzapfel. My apologies for last night."

"Goodbye, Hans, you drunken *Saukerl*," but she offered him a note of friendship, too. "Come home soon."

"Yes, Frau Holtzapfel. Thank you."

She even played along a little. "You know what you can do with your thanks."

At the corner, Frau Diller watched defensively from her shop window and Liesel took Papa's hand. She held it all the way along Munich Street, to the *Bahnhof*. The train was already there.

They stood on the platform.

Rosa embraced him first.

No words.

Her head was buried tightly into his chest, then gone.

Then the girl.

"Papa?"

Nothing.

Don't go, Papa. Just don't go. Let them come for you if you stay. But don't go, please don't go.

"Papa?"

* * * THE TRAIN STATION, 3 P.M. * * *
No hours, no minutes till goodbye:
He holds her. To say something, to say *anything* ,
he speaks over her shoulder. "Could you look after my
accordion, Liesel? I decided not to take it."
Now he finds something he truly means. "And if
there are more raids, keep reading in the shelter."
The girl feels the continued sign of her slightly

424

growing chest. It hurts as it touches the bottom of his ribs.
"Yes, Papa." A millimeter from her eyes, she
stares at the fabric of his suit. She speaks into
him. "Will you play us something when you come home?"

Hans Hubermann smiled at his daughter then and the train was ready
to leave. He reached out and gently held her face in his hand. "I promise," he said, and he made his way into the carriage.

They watched each other as the train pulled away.

Liesel and Rosa waved.

Hans Hubermann grew smaller and smaller, and his hand held
nothing now but empty air.

On the platform, people disappeared around them until no one
else was left. There was only the wardrobe-shaped woman and the
thirteen-year-old girl.

For the next few weeks, while Hans Hubermann and Alex Steiner were
at their various fast-tracked training camps, Himmel Street was swollen.
Rudy was not the same—he didn't talk. Mama was not the same—she
didn't berate. Liesel, too, was feeling the effects. There was no desire
to steal a book, no matter how much she tried to convince herself that
it would cheer her up.

After twelve days of Alex Steiner's absence, Rudy decided he'd
had enough. He hurried through the gate and knocked on Liesel's
door.

"Kommst?"

"Ja."

She didn't care where he was going or what he was planning, but he
would not be going without her. They walked up Himmel, along
Munich Street and out of Molching altogether. It was after

approximately an hour that Liesel asked the vital question. Up till then, she'd only glanced over at Rudy's determined face, or examined his stiff arms and the fisted hands in his pockets.

"Where are we going?"

"Isn't it obvious?"

She struggled to keep up. "Well, to tell you the truth — not really."

"I'm going to find him."

"Your papa?"

"Yes." He thought about it. "Actually, no. I think I'll find the *Führer* instead."

Faster footsteps. "Why?"

Rudy stopped. "Because I want to kill him." He even turned on the spot, to the rest of the world. "Did you hear that, you bastards?" he shouted. "I want to kill the *Führer*!"

They resumed walking and made it another few miles or so. That was when Liesel felt the urge to turn around. "It'll be dark soon, Rudy."

He walked on. "So what?"

"I'm going back."

Rudy stopped and watched her now as if she were betraying him. "That's right, book thief. Leave me now. I bet if there was a lousy book at the end of this road, you'd keep walking. Wouldn't you?"

For a while, neither of them spoke, but Liesel soon found the will. "You think you're the only one, *Saukerl*?" She turned away. "And you only lost your father. . . ."

"What does that mean?"

Liesel took a moment to count.

Her mother. Her brother. Max Vandenburg. Hans Hubermann. All of them gone. And she'd never even *had* a real father.

"It means," she said, "I'm going home."

For fifteen minutes she walked alone, and even when Rudy arrived at her side with jogging breath and sweaty cheeks, not another word was said for more than an hour. They only walked home together with aching feet and tired hearts.

There was a chapter called "Tired Hearts" in *A Song in the Dark*. A romantic girl had promised herself to a young man, but it appeared that he had run away with her best friend. Liesel was sure it was chapter thirteen. "'My heart is so tired,'" the girl had said. She was sitting in a chapel, writing in her diary.

No, thought Liesel as she walked. It's my heart that is tired. A thirteen-year-old heart shouldn't feel like this.

When they reached the perimeter of Molching, Liesel threw some words across. She could see Hubert Oval. "Remember when we raced there, Rudy?"

"Of course. I was just thinking about that myself—how we both fell."

"You said you were covered in shit."

"It was only mud." He couldn't hold his amusement now. "I was covered in shit at Hitler Youth. You're getting mixed up, *Saumensch*."

"I'm not mixed up at all. I'm only telling you what you *said*. What someone says and what happened are usually two different things, Rudy, especially when it comes to you."

This was better.

When they walked down Munich Street again, Rudy stopped and looked into the window of his father's shop. Before Alex left, he and Barbara had discussed whether she should keep it running in his absence. They decided against it, considering that work had been slow lately anyway, and there was at least a partial threat of party members making their presence felt. Business was never good for agitators. The army pay would have to do.

Suits hung from the rails and the mannequins held their ridiculous poses. "I think that one likes you," Liesel said after a while. It was her way of telling him it was time to keep going.

On Himmel Street, Rosa Hubermann and Barbara Steiner stood together on the footpath.

"Oh, Maria," Liesel said. "Do they look worried?"

"They look mad."

There were many questions when they arrived, mainly of the "Just where in the hell have you two been?" nature, but the anger quickly gave way to relief.

It was Barbara who pursued the answers. "Well, Rudy?"

Liesel answered for him. "He was killing the *Führer*," she said, and Rudy looked genuinely happy for a long enough moment to please her.

"Bye, Liesel."

Several hours later, there was a noise in the living room. It stretched toward Liesel in bed. She awoke and remained still, thinking ghosts and Papa and intruders and Max. There was the sound of opening and dragging, and then the fuzzy silence who followed. The silence was always the greatest temptation.

Don't move.

She thought that thought many times, but she didn't think it enough.

Her feet scolded the floor.

Air breathed up her pajama sleeves.

She walked through the corridor darkness in the direction of silence that had once been noisy, toward the thread of moonlight standing in the living room. She stopped, feeling the bareness of her ankles and toes. She watched.

It took longer than she expected for her eyes to adjust, and when they did, there was no denying the fact that Rosa Hubermann was sitting on the edge of the bed with her husband's accordion tied to her chest. Her fingers hovered above the keys. She did not move. She didn't even appear to be breathing.

The sight of it propelled itself to the girl in the hallway.

✸ ✸ ✸ A PAINTED IMAGE ✸ ✸ ✸
Rosa with Accordion.
Moonlight on Dark.
5'1" × Instrument × Silence.

Liesel stayed and watched.

Many minutes dripped past. The book thief's desire to hear a note was exhausting, and still, it would not come. The keys were not struck. The bellows didn't breathe. There was only the moonlight, like a long strand of hair in the curtain, and there was Rosa.

The accordion remained strapped to her chest. When she bowed her head, it sank to her lap. Liesel watched. She knew that for the next few days, Mama would be walking around with the imprint of an accordion on her body. There was also an acknowledgment that there was great beauty in what she was currently witnessing, and she chose not to disturb it.

She returned to bed and fell asleep to the vision of Mama and the silent music. Later, when she woke up from her usual dream and crept again to the hallway, Rosa was still there, as was the accordion.

Like an anchor, it pulled her forward. Her body was sinking. She appeared dead.

She can't possibly be breathing in that position, Liesel thought, but when she made her way closer, she could hear it.

Mama was snoring again.

Who needs bellows, she thought, when you've got a pair of lungs like that?

Eventually, when Liesel returned to bed, the image of Rosa Huber-mann and the accordion would not leave her. The book thief's eyes remained open. She waited for the suffocation of sleep.

THE COLLECTOR

Neither Hans Hubermann nor Alex Steiner was sent to fight. Alex was sent to Austria, to an army hospital outside Vienna. Given his expertise in tailoring, he was given a job that at least resembled his profession. Cartloads of uniforms and socks and shirts would come in every week and he would mend what needed mending, even if they could only be used as underclothes for the suffering soldiers in Russia.

Hans was sent first, quite ironically, to Stuttgart, and later, to Essen. He was given one of the most undesirable positions on the home front. The LSE.

* * * A NECESSARY EXPLANATION * * *
LSE
Luftwaffe Sondereinheit—
Air Raid Special Unit

The job of the LSE was to remain aboveground during air raids and put out fires, prop up the walls of buildings, and rescue anyone who had been trapped during the raid. As Hans soon discovered, there was also an alternative definition for the acronym. The men in the unit would explain to him on his first day that it really stood for *Leichensammler Einheit*—Dead Body Collectors.

When he arrived, Hans could only guess what those men had done to deserve such a task, and in turn, they wondered the same of him. Their leader, Sergeant Boris Schipper, asked him straight out. When Hans explained the bread, the Jews, and the whip, the round-faced sergeant gave out a short spurt of laughter. "You're lucky to be alive." His eyes were also round and he was constantly wiping them. They were either tired or itchy or full of smoke and dust. "Just remember that the enemy here is not in front of you."

Hans was about to ask the obvious question when a voice arrived from behind. Attached to it was the slender face of a young man with a smile like a sneer. Reinhold Zucker. "With us," he said, "the enemy isn't over the hill or in any specific direction. It's all around." He returned his focus to the letter he was writing. "You'll see."

In the messy space of a few months, Reinhold Zucker would be dead. He would be killed by Hans Hubermann's seat.

As the war flew into Germany with more intensity, Hans would learn that every one of his shifts started in the same fashion. The men would gather at the truck to be briefed on what had been hit during their break, what was most likely to be hit next, and who was working with whom.

Even when no raids were in operation, there would still be a great deal of work to be done. They would drive through broken towns, cleaning up. In the truck, there were twelve slouched men, all rising and falling with the various inconsistencies in the road.

From the beginning, it was clear that they all owned a seat.

Reinhold Zucker's was in the middle of the left row.

Hans Hubermann's was at the very back, where the daylight

stretched itself out. He learned quickly to be on the lookout for any rubbish that might be thrown from anywhere in the truck's interior. Hans reserved a special respect for cigarette butts, still burning as they whistled by.

✳ ✳ ✳ A COMPLETE LETTER HOME ✳ ✳ ✳
To my dear Rosa and Liesel,
Everything is fine here.
I hope you are both well.
With love, Papa

In late November, he had his first smoky taste of an actual raid. The truck was mobbed by rubble and there was much running and shouting. Fires were burning and the ruined cases of buildings were piled up in mounds. Framework leaned. The smoke bombs stood like matchsticks in the ground, filling the city's lungs.

Hans Hubermann was in a group of four. They formed a line. Sergeant Boris Schipper was at the front, his arms disappearing into the smoke. Behind him was Kessler, then Brunnenweg, then Hubermann. As the sergeant hosed the fire, the other two men hosed the sergeant, and just to make sure, Hubermann hosed all three of them.

Behind him, a building groaned and tripped.

It fell face-first, stopping a few meters from his heels. The concrete smelled brand-new, and the wall of powder rushed at them.

"*Gottverdammt*, Hubermann!" The voice struggled out of the flames. It was followed immediately by three men. Their throats were filled with particles of ash. Even when they made it around the corner, away from the center of the wreckage, the haze of the collapsed building attempted to follow. It was white and warm, and it crept behind them.

Slumped in temporary safety, there was much coughing and swearing. The sergeant repeated his earlier sentiments. "Goddamn it, Hubermann." He scraped at his lips to loosen them. "What the hell was that?"

"It just collapsed, right behind us."

"That much I know already. The question is, how big was it? It must have been ten stories high."

"No, sir, just two, I think."

"Jesus." A coughing fit. "Mary and Joseph." Now he yanked at the paste of sweat and powder in his eye sockets. "Not much you could do about that."

One of the other men wiped his face and said, "Just once I want to be there when they hit a pub, for Christ's sake. I'm dying for a beer."

Each man leaned back.

They could all taste it, putting out the fires in their throats and softening the smoke. It was a nice dream, and an impossible one. They were all aware that any beer that flowed in these streets would not be beer at all, but a kind of milk shake or porridge.

All four men were plastered with the gray-and-white conglomeration of dust. When they stood up fully, to resume work, only small cracks of their uniform could be seen.

The sergeant walked to Brunnenweg. He brushed heavily at his chest. Several smacks. "That's better. You had some dust on there, my friend." As Brunnenweg laughed, the sergeant turned to his newest recruit. "You first this time, Hubermann."

They put the fires out for several hours, and they found anything they could to convince a building to remain standing. In some cases, where the sides were damaged, the remaining edges poked out like elbows. This was Hans Hubermann's strong point. He almost came to enjoy finding a smoldering rafter or disheveled slab of concrete to prop those elbows up, to give them something to rest on.

434

His hands were packed tightly with splinters, and his teeth were caked with residue from the fallout. Both lips were set with moist dust that had hardened, and there wasn't a pocket, a thread, or a hidden crease in his uniform that wasn't covered in a film left by the loaded air.

The worst part of the job was the people.

Once in a while there was a person roaming doggedly through the fog, mostly single-worded. They always shouted a name.

Sometimes it was Wolfgang.

"Have you seen my Wolfgang?"

Their handprints would remain on his jacket.

"Stephanie!"

"Hansi!"

"Gustel! Gustel Stoboi!"

As the density subsided, the roll call of names limped through the ruptured streets, sometimes ending with an ash-filled embrace or a knelt-down howl of grief. They accumulated, hour by hour, like sweet and sour dreams, waiting to happen.

The dangers merged into one. Powder and smoke and the gusty flames. The damaged people. Like the rest of the men in the unit, Hans would need to perfect the art of forgetting.

"How are you, Hubermann?" the sergeant asked at one point. Fire was at his shoulder.

Hans nodded, uneasily, at the pair of them.

Midway through the shift, there was an old man who staggered defenselessly through the streets. As Hans finished stabilizing a building, he turned to find him at his back, waiting calmly for his turn. A bloodstain was signed across his face. It trailed off down his throat and neck. He was wearing a white shirt with a dark red collar and he held his leg as if it was next to him. "Could you prop *me* up now, young man?"

Hans picked him up and carried him out of the haze.

✱ ✱ ✱ A SMALL, SAD NOTE ✱ ✱ ✱
I visited that small city
street with the man still in
Hans Hubermann's arms.
The sky was white-horse gray.

It wasn't until he placed him down on a patch of concrete-coated grass that Hans noticed.

"What is it?" one of the other men asked.

Hans could only point.

"Oh." A hand pulled him away. "Get used to it, Hubermann."

For the rest of the shift, he threw himself into duty. He tried to ignore the distant echoes of calling people.

After perhaps two hours, he rushed from a building with the sergeant and two other men. He didn't watch the ground and tripped. Only when he returned to his haunches and saw the others looking in distress at the obstacle did he realize.

The corpse was facedown.

It lay in a blanket of powder and dust, and it was holding its ears.

It was a boy.

Perhaps eleven or twelve years old.

Not far away, as they progressed along the street, they found a woman calling the name Rudolf. She was drawn to the four men and met them in the mist. Her body was frail and bent with worry.

"Have you seen my boy?"

"How old is he?" the sergeant asked.

"Twelve."

Oh, Christ. Oh, crucified Christ.

They all thought it, but the sergeant could not bring himself to tell her or point the way.

As the woman tried to push past, Boris Schipper held her back. "We've just come from that street," he assured her. "You won't find him down there."

The bent woman still clung to hope. She called over her shoulder as she half walked, half ran. "Rudy!"

Hans Hubermann thought of another Rudy then. The Himmel Street variety. Please, he asked into a sky he couldn't see, let Rudy be safe. His thoughts naturally progressed to Liesel and Rosa and the Steiners, and Max.

When they made it to the rest of the men, he dropped down and lay on his back.

"How was it down there?" someone asked.

Papa's lungs were full of sky.

A few hours later, when he'd washed and eaten and thrown up, he attempted to write a detailed letter home. His hands were uncontrollable, forcing him to make it short. If he could bring himself, the remainder would be told verbally, when and if he made it home.

To my dear Rosa and Liesel, he began.

It took many minutes to write those six words down.

THE BREAD EATERS

It had been a long and eventful year in Molching, and it was finally drawing to a close.

Liesel spent the last few months of 1942 consumed by thoughts of what she called three desperate men. She wondered where they were and what they were doing.

One afternoon, she lifted the accordion from its case and polished it with a rag. Only once, just before she put it away, did she take the step that Mama could not. She placed her finger on one of the keys and softly pumped the bellows. Rosa had been right. It only made the room feel emptier.

Whenever she met Rudy, she asked if there had been any word from his father. Sometimes he described to her in detail one of Alex Steiner's letters. By comparison, the one letter her own papa had sent was somewhat of a disappointment.

Max, of course, was entirely up to her imagination.

It was with great optimism that she envisioned him walking alone on a deserted road. Once in a while she imagined him falling into a doorway of safety somewhere, his identity card enough to fool the right person.

The three men would turn up everywhere.

She saw her papa in the window at school. Max often sat with her by the fire. Alex Steiner arrived when she was with Rudy, staring back at them after they'd slammed the bikes down on Munich Street and looked into the shop.

"Look at those suits," Rudy would say to her, his head and hands against the glass. "All going to waste."

Strangely, one of Liesel's favorite distractions was Frau Holtzapfel. The reading sessions included Wednesday now as well, and they'd finished the water-abridged version of *The Whistler* and were on to *The Dream Carrier*. The old woman sometimes made tea or gave Liesel some soup that was infinitely better than Mama's. Less watery.

Between October and December, there had been one more parade of Jews, with one to follow. As on the previous occasion, Liesel had rushed to Munich Street, this time to see if Max Vandenburg was among them. She was torn between the obvious urge to see him— to know that he was still alive—and an absence that could mean any number of things, one of which being freedom.

In mid-December, a small collection of Jews and other miscreants was brought down Munich Street again, to Dachau. Parade number three.

Rudy walked purposefully down Himmel Street and returned from number thirty-five with a small bag and two bikes.

"You game, *Saumensch?*"

* * * THE CONTENTS OF RUDY'S BAG * * *
Six stale pieces of bread,
broken into quarters.

439

They pedaled ahead of the parade, toward Dachau, and stopped at an empty piece of road. Rudy passed Liesel the bag. "Take a handful."

"I'm not sure this is a good idea."

He slapped some bread onto her palm. "Your papa did."

How could she argue? It was worth a whipping.

"If we're fast, we won't get caught." He started distributing the bread. "So move it, *Saumensch.*"

Liesel couldn't help herself. There was the trace of a grin on her face as she and Rudy Steiner, her best friend, handed out the pieces of bread on the road. When they were finished, they took their bikes and hid among the Christmas trees.

The road was cold and straight. It wasn't long till the soldiers came with the Jews.

In the tree shadows, Liesel watched the boy. How things had changed, from fruit stealer to bread giver. His blond hair, although darkening, was like a candle. She heard his stomach growl—and he was giving people bread.

Was this Germany?

Was this Nazi Germany?

The first soldier did not see the bread—he was not hungry—but the first Jew saw it.

His ragged hand reached down and picked a piece up and shoved it deliriously to his mouth.

Is that Max? Liesel thought.

She could not see properly and moved to get a better view.

"Hey!" Rudy was livid. "Don't move. If they find us here and match us to the bread, we're history."

Liesel continued.

More Jews were bending down and taking bread from the road, and from the edge of the trees, the book thief examined each and every one of them. Max Vandenburg was not there.

Relief was short-lived.

It stirred itself around her just as one of the soldiers noticed a prisoner drop a hand to the ground. Everyone was ordered to stop. The road was closely examined. The prisoners chewed as fast and silently as they could. Collectively, they gulped.

The soldier picked up a few pieces and studied each side of the road. The prisoners also looked. .

"In there!"

One of the soldiers was striding over, to the girl by the closest trees. Next he saw the boy. Both began to run.

They chose different directions, under the rafters of branches and the tall ceiling of the trees.

"Don't stop running, Liesel!"

"What about the bikes?"

"*Scheiss drauf!* Shit on them, who cares!"

They ran, and after a hundred meters, the hunched breath of the soldier drew closer. It sidled up next to her and she waited for the accompanying hand.

She was lucky.

All she received was a boot up the ass and a fistful of words. "Keep running, little girl, you don't belong here!" She ran and she did not stop for at least another mile. Branches sliced her arms, pinecones rolled at her feet, and the taste of Christmas needles chimed inside her lungs.

A good forty-five minutes had passed by the time she made it back, and Rudy was sitting by the rusty bikes. He'd collected what was left of the bread and was chewing on a stale, stiff portion.

"I told you not to get too close," he said.

She showed him her backside. "Have I got a footprint?"

THE HIDDEN SKETCHBOOK

A few days before Christmas, there was another raid, although nothing dropped on the town of Molching. According to the radio news, most of the bombs fell in open country.

What was most important was the reaction in the Fiedlers' shelter. Once the last few patrons had arrived, everyone settled down solemnly and waited. They looked at her, expectantly.

Papa's voice arrived, loud in her ears.

"And if there are more raids, keep reading in the shelter."

Liesel waited. She needed to be sure that they wanted it.

Rudy spoke for everyone. "Read, *Saumensch*."

She opened the book, and again, the words found their way upon all those present in the shelter.

At home, once the sirens had given permission for everyone to return aboveground, Liesel sat in the kitchen with her mama. A preoccupation was at the forefront of Rosa Hubermann's expression, and it was not long until she picked up a knife and left the room. "Come with me."

She walked to the living room and took the sheet from the edge of her mattress. In the side, there was a sewn-up slit. If you didn't know beforehand that it was there, there was almost no chance of finding it. Rosa cut it carefully open and inserted her hand, reaching in the length of her entire arm. When it came back out, she was holding Max Vandenburg's sketchbook.

"He said to give this to you when you were ready," she said. "I was thinking your birthday. Then I brought it back to Christmas." Rosa Hubermann stood and there was a strange look on her face. It was not made up of pride. Perhaps it was the thickness, the heaviness of recollection. She said, "I think you've always been ready, Liesel. From the moment you arrived here, clinging to that gate, you were meant to have this."

Rosa gave her the book.

The cover looked like this:

* * * THE WORD SHAKER * * *
A Small Collection
of Thoughts
for Liesel Meminger

Liesel held it with soft hands. She stared. "Thanks, Mama."

She embraced her.

There was also a great longing to tell Rosa Hubermann that she loved her. It's a shame she didn't say it.

She wanted to read the book in the basement, for old times' sake, but Mama convinced her otherwise. "There's a reason Max got sick down there," she said, "and I can tell you one thing, girl, I'm not letting you get sick."

She read in the kitchen.

Red and yellow gaps in the stove.

The Word Shaker.

* * *

She made her way through the countless sketches and stories, and the pictures with captions. Things like Rudy on a dais with three gold medals slung around his neck. *Hair the color of lemons* was written beneath it. The snowman made an appearance, as did a list of the thirteen presents, not to mention the records of countless nights in the basement or by the fire.

Of course, there were many thoughts, sketches, and dreams relating to Stuttgart and Germany and the *Führer*. Recollections of Max's family were also there. In the end, he could not resist including them. He had to.

Then came page 117.

That was where *The Word Shaker* itself made its appearance.

It was a fable or a fairy tale. Liesel was not sure which. Even days later, when she looked up both terms in the *Duden Dictionary,* she couldn't distinguish between the two.

On the previous page, there was a small note.

* * * **PAGE 116** * * *
Liesel—I almost scribbled this story out. I thought you might
be too old for such a tale, but maybe no one is. I thought of
you and your books and words, and this strange story came
into my head. I hope you can find some good in it.

She turned the page.

THERE WAS once a strange, small man. He decided three important details about his life:
1. He would part his hair from the opposite side to everyone else.
2. He would make himself a small, strange mustache.
3. He would one day rule the world.

The young man wandered around for quite some time, thinking, planning, and figuring out exactly how to make the world his. Then one day, out of nowhere, it struck him—the perfect plan. He'd seen a mother walking with her child. At one point, she admonished the small boy, until finally, he began to cry. Within a few minutes, she spoke very softly to him, after which he was soothed and even smiled.

The young man rushed to the woman and embraced her. "Words!" He grinned.

"What?"

But there was no reply. He was already gone.

Yes, the Führer decided that he would rule the world with words. "I will never fire a gun," he devised. "I will not have to." Still, he was not rash. Let's allow him at least that much. He was not a stupid man at all. His first plan of attack was to plant the words in as many areas of his homeland as possible.

He planted them day and night, and cultivated them.

He watched them grow, until eventually, great forests of words had risen throughout Germany. . . . It was a nation of farmed thoughts.

WHILE THE words were growing, our young Führer also planted seeds to create symbols, and these, too, were well on their way to full bloom. Now the time had come. The Führer was ready.

He invited his people toward his own glorious heart, beckoning them with his finest, ugliest words, handpicked from his forests. And the people came.

They were all placed on a conveyor belt and run through a rampant machine that gave them a lifetime in ten minutes. Words were fed into them. Time disappeared and they now knew everything they needed to know. They were hypnotized.

Next, they were fitted with their symbols, and everyone was happy.

Soon, the demand for the lovely ugly words and symbols increased to such a point that as the forests grew, many people were needed to maintain them. Some were employed to climb the trees and throw the words down to those below. They were then fed directly into the remainder of the Führer's people, not to mention those who came back for more.

The people who climbed the trees were called word shakers.

THE BEST word shakers were the ones who understood the true power of words. They were the ones who could climb the highest. One such word shaker was a small, skinny girl. She was renowned as the best word shaker of her region because she knew how powerless a person could be WITHOUT words.

That's why she could climb higher than anyone else. She had desire. She was hungry for them.

One day, however, she met a man who was despised by her homeland, even though he was born in it. They became good friends, and when the man was sick, the word shaker allowed a single teardrop to fall on his face. The tear was made of friendship—a single word—and it dried and became a seed, and when next the girl was in the forest, she planted that seed among the other trees. She watered it every day.

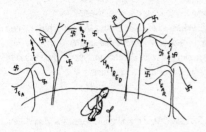

At first, there was nothing, but one afternoon, when she checked it after a day of word-shaking, a small sprout had shot up. She stared at it for a long time.

The tree grew every day, faster than everything else, till it was the tallest tree in the forest. Everyone came to look at it. They all whispered about it, and they waited . . . for the Führer.

Incensed, he immediately ordered the tree to be cut down. That was when the word shaker made her way through the crowd. She fell to her hands and knees. "Please," she cried, "you can't cut it down."

The Führer, however, was unmoved. He could not afford to make exceptions. As the word shaker was dragged away, he turned to his right-hand man and made a request. "Ax, please."

AT THAT moment, the word shaker twisted free. She ran. She boarded the tree, and even as the Führer hammered at the trunk with his ax, she climbed until she reached the highest of the branches. The voices and ax beats continued faintly on. Clouds walked by—like white monsters with gray hearts. Afraid but stubborn, the word shaker remained. She waited for the tree to fall.

But the tree would not move.

Many hours passed, and still, the Führer's ax could not take a single bite out of the trunk. In a state nearing collapse, he ordered another man to continue.

Days passed.

Weeks took over.

A hundred and ninety-six soldiers could not make any impact on the word shaker's tree.

"But how does she eat?" the people asked. "How does she sleep?"

What they didn't know was that other word shakers threw supplies across, and the girl climbed down to the lower branches to collect them.

IT SNOWED. It rained. Seasons came and went. The word shaker remained.

When the last axman gave up, he called up to her. "Word shaker! You can come down now! There is no one who can defeat this tree!"

The word shaker, who could only just make out the man's sentences, replied with a whisper. She handed it down through the branches. "No thank you," she said, for she knew that it was only herself who was holding the tree upright.

NO ONE knew how long it had taken, but one afternoon, a new axman walked into town. His bag looked too heavy for him. His eyes dragged. His feet drooped with exhaustion. "The tree," he asked the people. "Where is the tree?"

An audience followed him, and when he arrived, clouds had covered the highest regions of the branches. The word shaker could hear the people calling out that a new axman had come to put an end to her vigil.

"She will not come down," the people said, "for anyone."

They did not know who the axman was, and they did not know that he was undeterred.

He opened his bag and pulled out something much smaller than an ax.

The people laughed. They said, "You can't chop a tree down with an old hammer!"

The young man did not listen to them. He only looked through his bag for some nails. He placed three of them in his mouth and attempted to hammer a fourth one into the tree. The first branches were now extremely high and he estimated that he needed four nails to use as footholds to reach them.

"Look at this idiot," roared one of the watching men. "No one else could chop it down with an ax, and this fool thinks he can do it with—"

The man fell silent.

THE FIRST nail entered the tree and was held steady after five blows. Then the second went in, and the young man started to climb.

By the fourth nail, he was up in the arms and continued on his way. He was tempted to call out as he did so, but he decided against it.

The climb seemed to last for miles. It took many hours for him to reach the final branches, and when he did, he found the word shaker asleep in her blankets and the clouds.

He watched her for many minutes.

The warmth of the sun heated the cloudy rooftop.

He reached down, touching her arm, and the word shaker woke up.

She rubbed her eyes, and after a long study of his face, she spoke.

"Is it really you?"

Is it from your cheek, she thought, that I took the seed?

The man nodded.

His heart wobbled and he held tighter to the branches. "It is."

TOGETHER, THEY stayed in the summit of the tree. They waited for the clouds to disappear, and when they did, they could see the rest of the forest.

"It wouldn't stop growing," she explained.

"But neither would this." The young man looked at the branch that held his hand. He had a point.

When they had looked and talked enough, they made their way back down. They left the blankets and remaining food behind.

The people could not believe what they were seeing, and the moment the word shaker and the young man set foot in the world, the tree finally began to show the ax marks. Bruises appeared. Slits were made in the trunk and the earth began to shiver.

"It's going to fall!" a young woman screamed. "The tree is going to fall!" She was right. The word shaker's tree, in all its miles and miles of height, slowly began to tip. It moaned as it was sucked to the ground. The world shook, and when everything finally settled, the tree was laid out among the rest of the forest. It could never destroy all of it, but if nothing else, a different-colored path was carved through it.

The word shaker and the young man climbed up to the horizontal trunk. They navigated the branches and began to walk. When they looked back, they noticed that the majority of onlookers had started to return to their own places. In there. Out there. In the forest.

But as they walked on, they stopped several times, to listen. They thought they could hear voices and words behind them, on the word shaker's tree.

For a long time, Liesel sat at the kitchen table and wondered where Max Vandenburg was, in all that forest out there. The light lay down around her. She fell asleep. Mama made her go to bed, and she did so, with Max's sketchbook against her chest.

It was hours later, when she woke up, that the answer to her question came. "Of course," she whispered. "Of course I know where he is," and she went back to sleep.

She dreamed of the tree.

THE ANARCHIST'S SUIT
COLLECTION

* * * 35 HIMMEL STREET, * * *
DECEMBER 24
With the absence of two fathers,
the Steiners have invited Rosa
and Trudy Hubermann, and Liesel.
When they arrive, Rudy is still in
the process of explaining his
clothes. He looks at Liesel and his
mouth widens, but only slightly.

The days leading up to Christmas 1942 fell thick and heavy with snow. Liesel went through *The Word Shaker* many times, from the story itself to the many sketches and commentaries on either side of it. On Christmas Eve, she made a decision about Rudy. To hell with being out too late.

She walked next door just before dark and told him she had a present for him, for Christmas.

Rudy looked at her hands and either side of her feet. "Well, where the hell is it?"

"Forget it, then."

But Rudy knew. He'd seen her like this before. Risky eyes and sticky fingers. The breath of stealing was all around her and he could smell it. "This gift," he estimated. "You haven't got it yet, have you?"

"No."

"And you're not buying it, either."

"Of course not. Do you think I have any money?" Snow was still falling. At the edge of the grass, there was ice like broken glass. "Do you have the key?" she asked.

"The key to what?" But it didn't take Rudy long to understand. He made his way inside and returned not long after. In the words of Viktor Chemmel, he said, "It's time to go shopping."

The light was disappearing fast, and except for the church, all of Munich Street had closed up for Christmas. Liesel walked hurriedly to remain in step with the lankier stride of her neighbor. They arrived at the designated shop window. STEINER—SCHNEIDERMEISTER. The glass wore a thin sheet of mud and grime that had blown onto it in the passing weeks. On the opposite side, the mannequins stood like witnesses. They were serious and ludicrously stylish. It was hard to shake the feeling that they were watching everything.

Rudy reached into his pocket.

It was Christmas Eve.

His father was near Vienna.

He didn't think he'd mind if they trespassed in his beloved shop. The circumstances demanded it.

The door opened fluently and they made their way inside. Rudy's first instinct was to hit the light switch, but the electricity had already been cut off.

"Any candles?"

Rudy was dismayed. "*I* brought the key. And besides, this was your idea."

In the middle of the exchange, Liesel tripped on a bump in the floor. A mannequin followed her down. It groped her arm and dismantled in its clothes on top of her. "Get this thing off me!" It was in four pieces. The torso and head, the legs, and two separate arms. When she was rid of it, Liesel stood and wheezed. "Jesus, Mary."

Rudy found one of the arms and tapped her on the shoulder with its hand. When she turned in fright, he extended it in friendship. "Nice to meet you."

For a few minutes, they moved slowly through the tight pathways of the shop. Rudy started toward the counter. When he fell over an empty box, he yelped and swore, then found his way back to the entrance. "This is ridiculous," he said. "Wait here a minute." Liesel sat, mannequin arm in hand, till he returned with a lit lantern from the church.

A ring of light circled his face.

"So where's this present you've been bragging about? It better not be one of these weird mannequins."

"Bring the light over."

When he made it to the far left section of the shop, Liesel took the lantern with one hand and swept through the hanging suits with the other. She pulled one out but quickly replaced it with another. "No, still too big." After two more attempts, she held a navy blue suit in front of Rudy Steiner. "Does this look about your size?"

While Liesel sat in the dark, Rudy tried on the suit behind one of the curtains. There was a small circle of light and the shadow dressing itself.

When he returned, he held out the lantern for Liesel to see. Free of the curtain, the light was like a pillar, shining onto the refined suit. It also lit up the dirty shirt beneath and Rudy's battered shoes.

"Well?" he asked.

Liesel continued the examination. She moved around him and shrugged. "Not bad."

"Not *bad*! I look better than just not bad."

"The shoes let you down. And your face."

Rudy placed the lantern on the counter and came toward her in mock-anger, and Liesel had to admit that a nervousness started gripping her. It was with both relief and disappointment that she watched him trip and fall on the disgraced mannequin.

On the floor, Rudy laughed.

Then he closed his eyes, clenching them hard.

Liesel rushed over.

She crouched above him.

Kiss him, Liesel, kiss him.

"Are you all right, Rudy? Rudy?"

"I miss him," said the boy, sideways, across the floor.

"Frohe Weihnachten," Liesel replied. She helped him up, straightening the suit. "Merry Christmas."

PART NINE

the last human stranger

featuring:

the next temptation—a cardplayer—

the snows of stalingrad—an ageless

brother—an accident—the bitter taste

of questions—a toolbox, a bleeder,

a bear—a broken plane—

and a homecoming

THE NEXT TEMPTATION

This time, there were cookies.

But they were stale.

They were *Kipferl* left over from Christmas, and they'd been sitting on the desk for at least two weeks. Like miniature horseshoes with a layer of icing sugar, the ones on the bottom were bolted to the plate. The rest were piled on top, forming a chewy mound. She could already smell them when her fingers tightened on the window ledge. The room tasted like sugar and dough, and thousands of pages.

There was no note, but it didn't take Liesel long to realize that Ilsa Hermann had been at it again, and she certainly wasn't taking the chance that the cookies might *not* be for her. She made her way back to the window and passed a whisper through the gap. The whisper's name was Rudy.

They'd gone on foot that day because the road was too slippery for bikes. The boy was beneath the window, standing watch. When she called out, his face appeared, and she presented him with the plate. He didn't need much convincing to take it.

His eyes feasted on the cookies and he asked a few questions.

"Anything else? Any milk?"

"What?"

"Milk," he repeated, a little louder this time. If he'd recognized the offended tone in Liesel's voice, he certainly wasn't showing it.

The book thief's face appeared above him again. "Are you stupid? Can I just steal the book?"

"Of course. All I'm saying is . . ."

Liesel moved toward the far shelf, behind the desk. She found some paper and a pen in the top drawer and wrote *Thank you,* leaving the note on top.

To her right, a book protruded like a bone. Its paleness was almost scarred by the dark lettering of the title. *Die Letzte Menschliche Fremde—The Last Human Stranger.* It whispered softly as she removed it from the shelf. Some dust showered down.

At the window, just as she was about to make her way out, the library door creaked apart.

Her knee was up and her book-stealing hand was poised against the window frame. When she faced the noise, she found the mayor's wife in a brand-new bathrobe and slippers. On the breast pocket of the robe sat an embroidered swastika. Propaganda even reached the bathroom.

They watched each other.

Liesel looked at Ilsa Hermann's breast and raised her arm. *"Heil* Hitler."

She was just about to leave when a realization struck her.

The cookies.

They'd been there for weeks.

That meant that if the mayor himself used the library, he must have seen them. He must have asked why they were there. Or—and as soon as Liesel felt this thought, it filled her with a strange optimism—perhaps it wasn't the mayor's library at all; it was hers. Ilsa Hermann's.

She didn't know why it was so important, but she enjoyed the fact that the roomful of books belonged to the woman. It was she who introduced her to the library in the first place and gave her the initial, even literal, window of opportunity. This way was better. It all seemed to fit.

Just as she began to move again, she propped everything and asked, "This is your room, isn't it?"

The mayor's wife tightened. "I used to read in here, with my son. But then . . ."

Liesel's hand touched the air behind her. She saw a mother reading on the floor with a young boy pointing at the pictures and the words. Then she saw a war at the window. "I know."

An exclamation entered from outside.

"What did you say?!"

Liesel spoke in a harsh whisper, behind her. "Keep quiet, *Saukerl*, and watch the street." To Ilsa Hermann, she handed the words slowly across. "So all these books . . ."

"They're mostly mine. Some are my husband's, some were my son's, as you know."

There was embarrassment now on Liesel's behalf. Her cheeks were set alight. "I always thought this was the mayor's room."

"Why?" The woman seemed amused.

Liesel noticed that there were also swastikas on the toes of her slippers. "He's the mayor. I thought he'd read a lot."

The mayor's wife placed her hands in her side pockets. "Lately, it's you who gets the most use out of this room."

"Have you read this one?" Liesel held up *The Last Human Stranger*.

Ilsa looked more closely at the title. "I have, yes."

"Any good?"

"Not bad."

There was an itch to leave then, but also a peculiar obligation to stay. She moved to speak, but the available words were too many and too fast. There were several attempts to snatch at them, but it was the mayor's wife who took the initiative.

She saw Rudy's face in the window, or more to the point, his candlelit hair. "I think you'd better go," she said. "He's waiting for you."

On the way home, they ate.

"Are you sure there wasn't anything else?" Rudy asked. "There must have been."

"We were lucky to get the cookies." Liesel examined the gift in Rudy's arms. "Now tell the truth. Did you eat any before I came back out?"

Rudy was indignant. "Hey, you're the thief here, not me."

"Don't kid me, *Saukerl,* I could see some sugar at the side of your mouth."

Paranoid, Rudy took the plate in just the one hand and wiped with the other. "I didn't eat any, I promise."

Half the cookies were gone before they hit the bridge, and they shared the rest with Tommy Müller on Himmel Street.

When they'd finished eating, there was only one afterthought, and Rudy spoke it.

"What the hell do we do with the plate?"

THE CARDPLAYER

Around the time Liesel and Rudy were eating the cookies, the resting men of the LSE were playing cards in a town not far from Essen. They'd just completed the long trip from Stuttgart and were gambling for cigarettes. Reinhold Zucker was not a happy man.

"He's cheating, I swear it," he muttered. They were in a shed that served as their barracks and Hans Hubermann had just won his third consecutive hand. Zucker threw his cards down in disgust and combed his greasy hair with a threesome of dirty fingernails.

✻ ✻ ✻ SOME FACTS ABOUT ✻ ✻ ✻
REINHOLD ZUCKER
He was twenty-four. When he won a round
of cards, he gloated—he would hold the
thin cylinders of tobacco to his nose and
breathe them in. "The smell of victory,"
he would say. Oh, and one more thing.
He would die with his mouth open.

• • •

Unlike the young man to his left, Hans Hubermann didn't gloat when he won. He was even generous enough to give each colleague one of his cigarettes back and light it for him. All but Reinhold Zucker took up the invitation. He snatched at the offering and flung it back to the middle of the turned-over box. "I don't need your charity, old man." He stood up and left.

"What's wrong with him?" the sergeant inquired, but no one cared enough to answer. Reinhold Zucker was just a twenty-four-year-old boy who could not play cards to save his life.

Had he not lost his cigarettes to Hans Hubermann, he wouldn't have despised him. If he hadn't despised him, he might not have taken his place a few weeks later on a fairly innocuous road.

One seat, two men, a short argument, and me.

It kills me sometimes, how people die.

THE SNOWS OF STALINGRAD

In the middle of January 1943, the corridor of Himmel Street was its dark, miserable self. Liesel shut the gate and made her way to Frau Holtzapfel's door and knocked. She was surprised by the answerer.

Her first thought was that the man must have been one of her sons, but he did not look like either of the brothers in the framed photos by the door. He seemed far too old, although it was difficult to tell. His face was dotted with whiskers and his eyes looked painful and loud. A bandaged hand fell out of his coat sleeve and cherries of blood were seeping through the wrapping.

"Perhaps you should come back later."

Liesel tried to look past him. She was close to calling out to Frau Holtzapfel, but the man blocked her.

"Child," he said. "Come back later. I'll get you. Where are you from?"

More than three hours later, a knock arrived at 33 Himmel Street and the man stood before her. The cherries of blood had grown into plums.

"She's ready for you now."

• • •

Outside, in the fuzzy gray light, Liesel couldn't help asking the man what had happened to his hand. He blew some air from his nostrils—a single syllable—before his reply. "Stalingrad."

"Sorry?" He had looked into the wind when he spoke. "I couldn't hear you."

He answered again, only louder, and now, he answered the question fully. "Stalingrad happened to my hand. I was shot in the ribs and I had three of my fingers blown off. Does that answer your question?" He placed his uninjured hand in his pocket and shivered with contempt for the German wind. "You think it's cold here?"

Liesel touched the wall at her side. She couldn't lie. "Yes, of course."

The man laughed. "This isn't cold." He pulled out a cigarette and placed it in his mouth. One-handed, he tried to light a match. In the dismal weather, it would have been difficult with both hands, but with just the one, it was impossible. He dropped the matchbook and swore.

Liesel picked it up.

She took his cigarette and put it in her mouth. She, too, could not light it.

"You have to suck on it," the man explained. "In this weather, it only lights when you suck. *Verstehst?*"

She gave it another go, trying to remember how Papa did it. This time, her mouth filled with smoke. It climbed her teeth and scratched her throat, but she restrained herself from coughing.

"Well done." When he took the cigarette and breathed it in, he reached out his uninjured hand, his left. "Michael Holtzapfel."

"Liesel Meminger."

"You're coming to read to my mother?"

Rosa arrived behind her at that point, and Liesel could feel the shock at her back. "Michael?" she asked. "Is that you?"

Michael Holtzapfel nodded. "*Guten Tag,* Frau Hubermann. It's been a long time."

"You look so . . ."

"Old?"

Rosa was still in shock, but she composed herself. "Would you like to come in? I see you met my foster daughter. . . ." Her voice trailed off as she noticed the bloodied hand.

"My brother's dead," said Michael Holtzapfel, and he could not have delivered the punch any better with his one usable fist. For Rosa staggered. Certainly, war meant dying, but it always shifted the ground beneath a person's feet when it was someone who had once lived and breathed in close proximity. Rosa had watched both of the Holtzapfel boys grow up.

The oldened young man somehow found a way to list what happened without losing his nerve. "I was in one of the buildings we used for a hospital when they brought him in. It was a week before I was coming home. I spent three days of that week sitting with him before he died. . . ."

"I'm sorry." The words didn't seem to come from Rosa's mouth. It was someone else standing behind Liesel Meminger that evening, but she did not dare to look.

"Please." Michael stopped her. "Don't say anything else. Can I take the girl to read? I doubt my mother will hear it, but she said for her to come."

"Yes, take her."

They were halfway down the path when Michael Holtzapfel remembered himself and returned. "Rosa?" There was a moment of waiting while Mama rewidened the door. "I heard your son was there. In Russia. I ran into someone else from Molching and they told me. But I'm sure you knew that already."

Rosa tried to prevent his exit. She rushed out and held his sleeve. "No. He left here one day and never came back. We tried to find him, but then so much happened, there was . . ."

Michael Holtzapfel was determined to escape. The last thing he wanted to hear was yet another sob story. Pulling himself away, he said, "As far as I know, he's alive." He joined Liesel at the gate, but the girl did not walk next door. She watched Rosa's face. It lifted and dropped in the same moment.

"Mama?"

Rosa raised her hand. "Go."

Liesel waited.

"I said go."

When she caught up to him, the returned soldier tried to make conversation. He must have regretted his verbal mistake with Rosa, and he tried to bury it beneath some other words. Holding up the bandaged hand, he said, "I still can't get it to stop bleeding." Liesel was actually glad to enter the Holtzapfels' kitchen. The sooner she started reading, the better.

Frau Holtzapfel sat with wet streams of wire on her face.

Her son was dead.

But that was only the half of it.

She would never really know how it occurred, but I can tell you without question that one of us here knows. I always seem to know what happened when there was snow and guns and the various confusions of human language.

When I imagine Frau Holtzapfel's kitchen from the book thief's words, I don't see the stove or the wooden spoons or the water pump, or anything of the sort. Not to begin with, anyway. What I see is the Russian winter and the snow falling from the ceiling, and the fate of Frau Holtzapfel's second son.

His name was Robert, and what happened to him was this.

✳ ✳ ✳ A SMALL WAR STORY ✳ ✳ ✳
His legs were blown off at the
shins and he died with his
brother watching in a cold,
stench-filled hospital.

It was Russia, January 5, 1943, and just another icy day. Out among the city and snow, there were dead Russians and Germans everywhere. Those who remained were firing into the blank pages in front of them. Three languages interwove. The Russian, the bullets, the German.

As I made my way through the fallen souls, one of the men was saying, "My stomach is itchy." He said it many times over. Despite his shock, he crawled up ahead, to a dark, disfigured figure who sat streaming on the ground. When the soldier with the wounded stomach arrived, he could see that it was Robert Holtzapfel. His hands were caked in blood and he was heaping snow onto the area just above his shins, where his legs had been chopped off by the last explosion. There were hot hands and a red scream.

Steam rose from the ground. The sight and smell of rotting snow.

"It's me," the soldier said to him. "It's Pieter." He dragged himself a few inches closer.

"Pieter?" Robert asked, a vanishing voice. He must have felt me nearby.

A second time. "Pieter?"

For some reason, dying men always ask questions they know the answer to. Perhaps it's so they can die being right.

The voices suddenly all sounded the same.

Robert Holtzapfel collapsed to his right, onto the cold and steamy ground.

I'm sure he expected to meet me there and then.

He didn't.

Unfortunately for the young German, I did not take him that afternoon. I stepped over him with the other poor souls in my arms and made my way back to the Russians.

Back and forth, I traveled.

Disassembled men.

It was no ski trip, I can tell you.

As Michael told his mother, it was three very long days later that I finally came for the soldier who left his feet behind in Stalingrad. I showed up very much invited at the temporary hospital and flinched at the smell.

A man with a bandaged hand was telling the mute, shock-faced soldier that he would survive. "You'll soon be going home," he assured him.

Yes, home, I thought. For good.

"I'll wait for you," he continued. "I was going back at the end of the week, but I'll wait."

In the middle of his brother's next sentence, I gathered up the soul of Robert Holtzapfel.

Usually I need to exert myself, to look through the ceiling when I'm inside, but I was lucky in that particular building. A small section of the roof had been destroyed and I could see straight up. A meter away, Michael Holtzapfel was still talking. I tried to ignore him by watching the hole above me. The sky was white but deteriorating fast. As always, it was becoming an enormous drop sheet. Blood was bleeding through, and in patches, the clouds were dirty, like footprints in melting snow.

Footprints? you ask.

Well, I wonder whose those could be.

In Frau Holtzapfel's kitchen, Liesel read. The pages waded by unheard, and for me, when the Russian scenery fades in my eyes, the snow refuses to stop falling from the ceiling. The kettle is covered, as is the table. The humans, too, are wearing patches of snow on their heads and shoulders.

The brother shivers.

The woman weeps.

And the girl goes on reading, for that's why she's there, and it feels good to be good for something in the aftermath of the snows of Stalingrad.

THE AGELESS BROTHER

Liesel Meminger was a few weeks short of fourteen.

Her papa was still away.

She'd completed three more reading sessions with a devastated woman. On many nights, she'd watched Rosa sit with the accordion and pray with her chin on top of the bellows.

Now, she thought, it's time. Usually it was stealing that cheered her up, but on this day, it was giving something back.

She reached under her bed and removed the plate. As quickly as she could, she cleaned it in the kitchen and made her way out. It felt nice to be walking up through Molching. The air was sharp and flat, like the *Watschen* of a sadistic teacher or nun. Her shoes were the only sound on Munich Street.

As she crossed the river, a rumor of sunshine stood behind the clouds.

At 8 Grande Strasse, she walked up the steps, left the plate by the front door, and knocked, and by the time the door was opened, the girl was around the corner. Liesel did not look back, but she knew that if she did, she'd have found her brother at the bottom of the steps again, his knee completely healed. She could even hear his voice.

"That's better, Liesel."

It was with great sadness that she realized that her brother would be six forever, but when she held that thought, she also made an effort to smile.

She remained at the Amper River, at the bridge, where Papa used to stand and lean.

She smiled and smiled, and when it all came out, she walked home and her brother never climbed into her sleep again. In many ways, she would miss him, but she could never miss his deadly eyes on the floor of the train or the sound of a cough that killed.

The book thief lay in bed that night, and the boy only came before she closed her eyes. He was one member of a cast, for Liesel was always visited in that room. Her papa stood and called her half a woman. Max was writing *The Word Shaker* in the corner. Rudy was naked by the door. Occasionally her mother stood on a bedside train platform. And far away, in the room that stretched like a bridge to a nameless town, her brother, Werner, played in the cemetery snow.

From down the hall, like a metronome for the visions, Rosa snored, and Liesel lay awake surrounded, but also remembering a quote from her most recent book.

*** *THE LAST HUMAN STRANGER*, PAGE 38 ***
*There were people everywhere on the city
street, but the stranger could not have
been more alone if it were empty.*

473

When morning came, the visions were gone and she could hear the quiet recital of words in the living room. Rosa was sitting with the accordion, praying.

"Make them come back alive," she repeated. "Please, Lord, please. All of them." Even the wrinkles around her eyes were joining hands.

The accordion must have ached her, but she remained.

Rosa would never tell Hans about these moments, but Liesel believed that it must have been those prayers that helped Papa survive the LSE's accident in Essen. If they didn't help, they certainly can't have hurt.

THE ACCIDENT

It was a surprisingly clear afternoon and the men were climbing into the truck. Hans Hubermann had just sat down in his appointed seat. Reinhold Zucker was standing above him.

"Move it," he said.

"*Bitte?* Excuse me?"

Zucker was hunched beneath the vehicle's ceiling. "I said move it, *Arschloch*." The greasy jungle of his fringe fell in clumps onto his forehead. "I'm swapping seats with you."

Hans was confused. The backseat was probably the most uncomfortable of the lot. It was the draftiest, the coldest. "Why?"

"Does it matter?" Zucker was losing patience. "Maybe I want to get off first to use the shit house."

Hans was quickly aware that the rest of the unit was already watching this pitiful struggle between two supposed grown men. He didn't want to lose, but he didn't want to be petty, either. Also, they'd just finished a tiring shift and he didn't have the energy to go on with it. Bent-backed, he made his way forward to the vacant seat in the middle of the truck.

"Why did you give in to that *Scheisskopf*?" the man next to him asked.

Hans lit a match and offered a share of the cigarette. "The draft back there goes straight through my ears."

The olive green truck was on its way toward the camp, maybe ten miles away. Brunnenweg was telling a joke about a French waitress when the left front wheel was punctured and the driver lost control. The vehicle rolled many times and the men swore as they tumbled with the air, the light, the trash, and the tobacco. Outside, the blue sky changed from ceiling to floor as they clambered for something to hold.

When it stopped, they were all crowded onto the right-hand wall of the truck, their faces wedged against the filthy uniform next to them. Questions of health were passed around until one of the men, Eddie Alma, started shouting, "Get this bastard off me!" He said it three times, fast. He was staring into Reinhold Zucker's blinkless eyes.

✳ ✳ ✳ THE DAMAGE, ESSEN ✳ ✳ ✳
Six men burned by cigarettes.
Two broken hands.
Several broken fingers.
A broken leg for Hans Hubermann.
A broken neck for Reinhold
Zucker, snapped almost in line
with his earlobes.

They dragged each other out until only the corpse was left in the truck.

The driver, Helmut Brohmann, was sitting on the ground, scratching his head. "The tire," he explained, "it just blew." Some of the men sat with him and echoed that it wasn't his fault. Others walked around smoking, asking each other if they thought their injuries were bad enough to be relieved of duty. Another small group gathered at the back of the truck and viewed the body.

Over by a tree, a thin strip of intense pain was still opening in Hans Hubermann's leg. "It should have been me," he said.

"What?" the sergeant called over from the truck.

"He was sitting in my seat."

Helmut Brohmann regained his senses and climbed back into the driver's compartment. Sideways, he tried to start the engine, but there was no kicking it over. Another truck was sent for, as was an ambulance. The ambulance didn't come.

"You know what that means, don't you?" said Boris Schipper. They did.

When they resumed the trip back to camp, each man tried not to look down at Reinhold Zucker's openmouthed sneer. "I told you we should have turned him facedown," someone mentioned. A few times, some of them simply forgot and rested their feet on the body. Once they arrived, they all tried to avoid the task of pulling him out. When the job was done, Hans Hubermann took a few abbreviated steps before the pain fractured in his leg and brought him down.

An hour later, when the doctor examined him, he was told it was definitely broken. The sergeant was on hand and stood with half a grin.

"Well, Hubermann. Looks like you've got away with it, doesn't it?" He was shaking his round face, smoking, and he provided a list of what would happen next. "You'll rest up. They'll ask me what we should do with you. I'll tell them you did a great job." He blew some more smoke. "And I think I'll tell them you're not fit for the LSE anymore and you should be sent back to Munich to work in an office or do whatever cleaning up needs doing there. How does that sound?"

Unable to resist a laugh within the grimace of pain, Hans replied, "It sounds good, Sergeant."

Boris Schipper finished his cigarette. "Damn right it sounds good. You're lucky I like you, Hubermann. You're lucky you're a good man, and generous with the cigarettes."

In the next room, they were making up the plaster.

THE BITTER TASTE OF QUESTIONS

Just over a week after Liesel's birthday in mid-February, she and Rosa finally received a detailed letter from Hans Hubermann. She ran inside from the mailbox and showed it to Mama. Rosa made her read it aloud, and they could not contain their excitement when Liesel read about his broken leg. She was stunned to the extent that she mouthed the next sentence only to herself.

"What is it?" Rosa pushed. *"Saumensch?"*

Liesel looked up from the letter and was close to shouting. The sergeant had been true to his word. "He's coming home, Mama. Papa's coming home!"

They embraced in the kitchen and the letter was crushed between their bodies. A broken leg was certainly something to celebrate.

When Liesel took the news next door, Barbara Steiner was ecstatic. She rubbed the girl's arms and called out to the rest of her family. In their kitchen, the household of Steiners seemed buoyed by the news that Hans Hubermann was returning home. Rudy smiled and laughed, and Liesel could see that he was at least trying.

However, she could also sense the bitter taste of questions in his mouth.

Why him?

Why Hans Hubermann and not Alex Steiner?

He had a point.

ONE TOOLBOX, ONE BLEEDER, ONE BEAR

Since his father's recruitment to the army the previous October, Rudy's anger had been growing nicely. The news of Hans Hubermann's return was all he needed to take it a few steps further. He did not tell Liesel about it. There was no complaining that it wasn't fair. His decision was to act.

He carried a metal case up Himmel Street at the typical thieving time of darkening afternoon.

* * * RUDY'S TOOLBOX * * *
It was patchy red and the
length of an oversized shoe box.
It contained the following:
Rusty pocketknife × 1
Small flashlight × 1
Hammer × 2
(one medium, one small)
Hand towel × 1
Screwdriver × 3

(varying in size)
Ski mask × 1
Clean socks × 1
Teddy bear × 1

Liesel saw him from the kitchen window—his purposeful steps and committed face, exactly like the day he'd gone to find his father. He gripped the handle with as much force as he could, and his movements were stiff with rage.

The book thief dropped the towel she was holding and replaced it with a single thought.

He's going stealing.

She ran out to meet him.

There was not even the semblance of a hello.

Rudy simply continued walking and spoke through the cold air in front of him. Close to Tommy Müller's apartment block, he said, "You know something, Liesel, I was thinking. You're not a thief at all," and he didn't give her a chance to reply. "That woman lets you in. She even leaves you cookies, for Christ's sake. I don't call that stealing. Stealing is what the army does. Taking your father, and mine." He kicked a stone and it clanged against a gate. He walked faster. "All those rich Nazis up there, on Grande Strasse, Gelb Strasse, Heide Strasse."

Liesel could concentrate on nothing but keeping up. They'd already passed Frau Diller's and were well onto Munich Street. "Rudy—"

"How does it feel, anyway?"

"How does what feel?"

"When you take one of those books?"

At that moment, she chose to keep still. If he wanted an answer, he'd have to come back, and he did. "Well?" But again, it was Rudy who answered, before Liesel could even open her mouth. "It feels good, doesn't it? To steal something back."

Liesel forced her attention to the toolbox, trying to slow him down. "What have you got in there?"

He bent over and opened it up.

Everything appeared to make sense but the teddy bear.

As they kept walking, Rudy explained the toolbox at length, and what he would do with each item. For example, the hammers were for smashing windows and the towel was to wrap them up, to quell the sound.

"And the teddy bear?"

It belonged to Anna-Marie Steiner and was no bigger than one of Liesel's books. The fur was shaggy and worn. The eyes and ears had been sewn back on repeatedly, but it was friendly looking nonetheless.

"That," answered Rudy, "is the one masterstroke. That's if a kid walks in while I'm inside. I'll give it to them to calm them down."

"And what do you plan to steal?"

He shrugged. "Money, food, jewelry. Whatever I can get my hands on." It sounded simple enough.

It wasn't until fifteen minutes later, when Liesel watched the sudden silence on his face, that she realized Rudy Steiner wasn't stealing anything. The commitment had disappeared, and although he still watched the imagined glory of stealing, she could see that now he was not believing it. He was *trying* to believe it, and that's never a good sign. His criminal greatness was unfurling before his eyes, and as the footsteps slowed and they watched the houses, Liesel's relief was pure and sad inside her.

It was Gelb Strasse.

On the whole, the houses sat dark and huge.

Rudy took off his shoes and held them with his left hand. He held the toolkit with his right.

Between the clouds, there was a moon. Perhaps a mile of light.

"What am I waiting for?" he asked, but Liesel didn't reply. Again, Rudy opened his mouth, but without any words. He placed the toolbox on the ground and sat on it.

His socks grew cold and wet.

"Lucky there's another pair in the toolbox," Liesel suggested, and she could see him trying not to laugh, despite himself.

Rudy moved across and faced the other way, and there was room for Liesel now as well.

The book thief and her best friend sat back to back on a patchy red toolbox in the middle of the street. Each facing a different way, they remained for quite a while. When they stood up and went home, Rudy changed his socks and left the previous ones on the road. A gift, he decided, for Gelb Strasse.

* * * THE SPOKEN TRUTH * * *
OF RUDY STEINER
"I guess I'm better at leaving
things behind than stealing them."

A few weeks later, the toolbox ended up being good for at least something. Rudy cleared it of screwdrivers and hammers and chose instead to store in it many of the Steiners' valuables for the next air raid. The only item that remained was the teddy bear.

On March 9, Rudy exited the house with it when the sirens made their presence felt again in Molching.

While the Steiners rushed down Himmel Street, Michael

Holtzapfel was knocking furiously at Rosa Hubermann's door. When she and Liesel came out, he handed them his problem. "My mother," he said, and the plums of blood were still on his bandage. "She won't come out. She's sitting at the kitchen table."

As the weeks had worn on, Frau Holtzapfel had not yet begun to recover. When Liesel came to read, the woman spent most of the time staring at the window. Her words were quiet, close to motionless. All brutality and reprimand were wrested from her face. It was usually Michael who said goodbye to Liesel or gave her the coffee and thanked her. Now this.

Rosa moved into action.

She waddled swiftly through the gate and stood in the open doorway. "Holtzapfel!" There was nothing but sirens and Rosa. "Holtzapfel, get out here, you miserable old swine!" Tact had never been Rosa Hubermann's strong point. "If you don't come out, we're all going to die here on the street!" She turned and viewed the helpless figures on the footpath. A siren had just finished wailing. "What now?"

Michael shrugged, disoriented, perplexed. Liesel dropped her bag of books and faced him. She shouted at the commencement of the next siren. "Can I go in?" But she didn't wait for the answer. She ran the short distance of the path and shoved past Mama.

Frau Holtzapfel was unmoved at the table.

What do I say? Liesel thought.

How do I get her to move?

When the sirens took another breath, she heard Rosa calling out. "Just leave her, Liesel, we have to go! If she wants to die, that's her business," but then the sirens resumed. They reached down and tossed the voice away.

Now it was only noise and girl and wiry woman.

"Frau Holtzapfel, please!"

Much like her conversation with Ilsa Hermann on the day of the cookies, a multitude of words and sentences were at her fingertips. The difference was that today there were bombs. Today it was slightly more urgent.

✳ ✳ ✳ THE OPTIONS ✳ ✳ ✳
• "Frau Holtzapfel, we have to go."
• "Frau Holtzapfel, we'll die if we stay here."
• "You still have one son left."
• "Everyone's waiting for you."
• "The bombs will blow your head off."
• "If you don't come, I'll stop coming
to read to you, and that means
you've lost your only friend."

She went with the last sentence, calling the words directly through the sirens. Her hands were planted on the table.

The woman looked up and made her decision. She didn't move.

Liesel left. She withdrew herself from the table and rushed from the house.

Rosa held open the gate and they started running to number forty-five. Michael Holtzapfel remained stranded on Himmel Street.

"Come on!" Rosa implored him, but the returned soldier hesitated. He was just about to make his way back inside when something turned him around. His mutilated hand was the only thing attached to the gate, and shamefully, he dragged it free and followed.

They all looked back several times, but there was still no Frau Holtzapfel.

The road seemed so wide, and when the final siren evaporated into the air, the last three people on Himmel Street made their way into the Fiedlers' basement.

"What took you so long?" Rudy asked. He was holding the tool-box.

Liesel placed her bag of books on the ground and sat on them. "We were trying to get Frau Holtzapfel."

Rudy looked around. "Where is she?"

"At home. In the kitchen."

In the far corner of the shelter, Michael was cramped and shivery. "I should have stayed," he said, "I should have stayed, I should have stayed. . . ." His voice was close to noiseless, but his eyes were louder than ever. They beat furiously in their sockets as he squeezed his injured hand and the blood rose through the bandage.

It was Rosa who stopped him.

"Please, Michael, it's not your fault."

But the young man with only a few remaining fingers on his right hand was inconsolable. He crouched in Rosa's eyes.

"Tell me something," he said, "because I don't understand. . . ." He fell back and sat against the wall. "Tell me, Rosa, how she can sit there ready to die while I still want to live." The blood thickened. "Why do I want to live? I shouldn't want to, but I do."

The young man wept uncontrollably with Rosa's hand on his shoulder for many minutes. The rest of the people watched. He could not make himself stop even when the basement door opened and shut and Frau Holtzapfel entered the shelter.

Her son looked up.

Rosa stepped away.

When they came together, Michael apologized. "Mama, I'm sorry, I should have stayed with you."

Frau Holtzapfel didn't hear. She only sat with her son and lifted his bandaged hand. "You're bleeding again," she said, and with everyone else, they sat and waited.

Liesel reached into her bag and rummaged through the books.

✳ ✳ ✳ THE BOMBING OF MUNICH, ✳ ✳ ✳
MARCH 9 AND 10
**The night was long with bombs
and reading. Her mouth was
dry, but the book thief worked
through fifty-four pages.**

The majority of children slept and didn't hear the sirens of renewed safety. Their parents woke them or carried them up the basement steps, into the world of darkness.

Far away, fires were burning and I had picked up just over two hundred murdered souls.

I was on my way to Molching for one more.

Himmel Street was clear.

The sirens had been held off for many hours, just in case there was another threat and to allow the smoke to make its way into the atmosphere.

It was Bettina Steiner who noticed the small fire and the sliver of smoke farther down, close to the Amper River. It trailed into the sky and the girl held up her finger. "Look."

The girl might have seen it first, but it was Rudy who reacted. In his haste, he did not relinquish his grip on the toolbox as he sprinted to the bottom of Himmel Street, took a few side roads, and entered the

trees. Liesel was next (having surrendered her books to a heavily pro-
testing Rosa), and then a smattering of people from several shelters
along the way.

"Rudy, wait!"

Rudy did not wait.

Liesel could only see the toolbox in certain gaps in the trees as he
made his way through to the dying glow and the misty plane. It sat
smoking in the clearing by the river. The pilot had tried to land there.

Within twenty meters, Rudy stopped.

Just as I arrived myself, I noticed him standing there, recovering
his breath.

The limbs of trees were scattered in the dark.

There were twigs and needles littered around the plane like fire
fuel. To their left, three gashes were burned into the earth. The run-
away ticktock of cooling metal sped up the minutes and seconds till
they were standing there for what felt like hours. The growing crowd
was assembling behind them, their breath and sentences sticking to
Liesel's back.

"Well," said Rudy, "should we take a look?"

He stepped through the remainder of trees to where the body of
the plane was fixed to the ground. Its nose was in the running water
and the wings were left crookedly behind.

Rudy circled slowly, from the tail and around to the right.

"There's glass," he said. "The windshield is everywhere."

Then he saw the body.

Rudy Steiner had never seen a face so pale.

"Don't come, Liesel." But Liesel came.

She could see the barely conscious face of the enemy pilot as
the tall trees watched and the river ran. The plane let out a few

more coughs and the head inside tilted from left to right. He said something they obviously could not understand.

"Jesus, Mary, and Joseph," Rudy whispered. "He's alive."

The toolbox bumped the side of the plane and brought with it the sound of more human voices and feet.

The glow of fire was gone and the morning was still and black. Only the smoke was in its way, but it, too, would soon be exhausted.

The wall of trees kept the color of a burning Munich at bay. By now, the boy's eyes had adjusted not only to the darkness, but to the face of the pilot. The eyes were like coffee stains, and gashes were ruled across his cheeks and chin. A ruffled uniform sat, unruly, across his chest.

Despite Rudy's advice, Liesel came even closer, and I can promise you that we recognized each other at that exact moment.

I know you, I thought.

There was a train and a coughing boy. There was snow and a distraught girl.

You've grown, I thought, but I recognize you.

She did not back away or try to fight me, but I know that something told the girl I was there. Could she smell my breath? Could she hear my cursed circular heartbeat, revolving like the crime it is in my deathly chest? I don't know, but she knew me and she looked me in my face and she did not look away.

As the sky began to charcoal toward light, we both moved on. We both observed the boy as he reached into his toolbox again and searched through some picture frames to pull out a small, stuffed yellow toy.

Carefully, he climbed to the dying man.

He placed the smiling teddy bear cautiously onto the pilot's shoulder. The tip of its ear touched his throat.

The dying man breathed it in. He spoke. In English, he said,

"Thank you." His straight-line cuts opened as he spoke, and a small drop of blood rolled crookedly down his throat.

"What?" Rudy asked him. *"Was hast du gesagt?* What did you say?"

Unfortunately, I beat him to the answer. The time was there and I was reaching into the cockpit. I slowly extracted the pilot's soul from his ruffled uniform and rescued him from the broken plane. The crowd played with the silence as I made my way through. I jostled free.

Above me, the sky eclipsed—just a last moment of darkness— and I swear I could see a black signature in the shape of a swastika. It loitered untidily above.

"Heil Hitler," I said, but I was well into the trees by then. Behind me, a teddy bear rested on the shoulder of a corpse. A lemon candle stood below the branches. The pilot's soul was in my arms.

It's probably fair to say that in all the years of Hitler's reign, no person was able to serve the *Führer* as loyally as me. A human doesn't have a heart like mine. The human heart is a line, whereas my own is a circle, and I have the endless ability to be in the right place at the right time. The consequence of this is that I'm always finding humans at their best and worst. I see their ugly and their beauty, and I wonder how the same thing can be both. Still, they have one thing I envy. Humans, if nothing else, have the good sense to die.

HOMECOMING

It was a time of bleeders and broken planes and teddy bears, but the first quarter of 1943 was to finish on a positive note for the book thief.

At the beginning of April, Hans Hubermann's plaster was trimmed to the knee and he boarded a train for Munich. He would be given a week of rest and recreation at home before joining the ranks of army pen pushers in the city. He would help with the paperwork on the cleanup of Munich's factories, houses, churches, and hospitals. Time would tell if he would be sent out to do the repair work. That all depended on his leg and the state of the city.

It was dark when he arrived home. It was a day later than expected, as the train was delayed due to an air-raid scare. He stood at the door of 33 Himmel Street and made a fist.

Four years earlier, Liesel Meminger was coaxed through that doorway when she showed up for the first time. Max Vandenburg had stood there with a key biting into his hand. Now it was Hans Hubermann's turn. He knocked four times and the book thief answered.

"Papa, Papa."

She must have said it a hundred times as she hugged him in the kitchen and wouldn't let go.

Later, after they ate, they sat at the kitchen table long into the night and Hans told his wife and Liesel Meminger everything. He explained the LSE and the smoke-filled streets and the poor, lost, wandering souls. And Reinhold Zucker. Poor, stupid Reinhold Zucker. It took hours.

At 1 a.m., Liesel went to bed and Papa came in to sit with her, like he used to. She woke up several times to check that he was there, and he did not fail her.

The night was calm.

Her bed was warm and soft with contentment.

Yes, it was a great night to be Liesel Meminger, and the calm, the warm, and the soft would remain for approximately three more months.

But her story lasts for six.

PART TEN

the book thief

featuring:

the end of a world—the ninety-eighth day—

a war maker—way of the words—a catatonic girl—

confessions—ilsa hermann's little black book—

some rib-cage planes—and a mountain range of rubble

THE END OF THE WORLD (Part I)

Again, I offer you a glimpse of the end. Perhaps it's to soften the blow for later, or to better prepare *myself* for the telling. Either way, I must inform you that it was raining on Himmel Street when the world ended for Liesel Meminger.

The sky was dripping.

Like a tap that a child has tried its hardest to turn off but hasn't quite managed. The first drops were cool. I felt them on my hands as I stood outside Frau Diller's.

Above me, I could hear them.

Through the overcast sky, I looked up and saw the tin-can planes. I watched their stomachs open and the bombs drop casually out. They were off target, of course. They were often off target.

* * * A SMALL, SAD HOPE * * *
No one wanted to
bomb Himmel Street.
No one would bomb a
place named after

The bombs came down, and soon, the clouds would bake and the cold raindrops would turn to ash. Hot snowflakes would shower to the ground.

In short, Himmel Street was flattened.

Houses were splashed from one side of the street to the other. A framed photo of a very serious-looking *Führer* was bashed and beaten on the shattered floor. Yet he smiled, in that serious way of his. He knew something we all didn't know. But I knew something *he* didn't know. All while people slept.

Rudy Steiner slept. Mama and Papa slept. Frau Holtzapfel, Frau Diller. Tommy Müller. All sleeping. All dying.

Only one person survived.

She survived because she was sitting in a basement reading through the story of her own life, checking for mistakes. Previously, the room had been declared too shallow, but on that night, October 7, it was enough. The shells of wreckage cantered down, and hours later, when the strange, unkempt silence settled itself in Molching, the local LSE could hear something. An echo. Down there, somewhere, a girl was hammering a paint can with a pencil.

They all stopped, with bent ears and bodies, and when they heard it again, they started digging.

* * * PASSED ITEMS, HAND TO HAND * * *
Blocks of cement and roof tiles.
A piece of wall with a dripping
sun painted on it. An unhappy-
looking accordion, peering
through its eaten case.

· · ·

They threw all of it upward.

When another piece of broken wall was removed, one of them saw the book thief's hair.

The man had such a nice laugh. He was delivering a newborn child. "I can't believe it—she's alive!"

There was so much joy among the cluttering, calling men, but I could not fully share their enthusiasm.

Earlier, I'd held her papa in one arm and her mama in the other. Each soul was so soft.

Farther away, their bodies were laid out, like the rest. Papa's lovely silver eyes were already starting to rust, and Mama's cardboard lips were fixed half open, most likely the shape of an incomplete snore. To blaspheme like the Germans—Jesus, Mary, and Joseph.

The rescuing hands pulled Liesel out and brushed the crumbs of rubble from her clothes. "Young girl," they said, "the sirens were too late. What were you doing in the basement? How did you know?"

What they didn't notice was that the girl was still holding the book. She screamed her reply. A stunning scream of the living.

"Papa!"

A second time. Her face creased as she reached a higher, more panic-stricken pitch. "Papa, *Papa!*"

They passed her up as she shouted, wailed, and cried. If she was injured, she did not yet know it, for she struggled free and searched and called and wailed some more.

She was still clutching the book.

She was holding desperately on to the words who had saved her life.

THE NINETY-EIGHTH DAY

For the first ninety-seven days after Hans Hubermann's return in April 1943, everything was fine. On many occasions he was pensive about the thought of his son fighting in Stalingrad, but he hoped that some of his luck was in the boy's blood.

On his third night at home, he played the accordion in the kitchen. A promise was a promise. There was music, soup, and jokes, and the laughter of a fourteen-year-old girl.

"*Saumensch,*" Mama warned her, "stop laughing so loud. His jokes aren't *that* funny. And they're filthy, too. . . ."

After a week, Hans resumed his service, traveling into the city to one of the army offices. He said that there was a good supply of cigarettes and food there, and sometimes he was able to bring home some cookies or extra jam. It was like the good old days. A minor air raid in May. A "*heil* Hitler" here or there and everything was fine.

Until the ninety-eighth day.

* * * A SMALL STATEMENT * * *
BY AN OLD WOMAN
On Munich Street, she said, "Jesus,
Mary, and Joseph, I wish they
wouldn't bring them through. These
wretched Jews, they're rotten luck.
They're a bad sign. Every time I see
them, I know we'll be ruined."

It was the same old lady who announced the Jews the first time Liesel saw them. On ground level, her face was a prune. Her eyes were the dark blue of a vein. And her prediction was accurate.

In the heart of summer, Molching was delivered a sign of things to come. It moved into sight like it always did. First the bobbing head of a soldier and the gun poking at the air above him. Then the ragged chain of clinking Jews.

The only difference this time was that they were brought from the opposite direction. They were taken through to the neighboring town of Nebling to scrub the streets and do the cleanup work that the army refused to do. Late in the day, they were marched back to camp, slow and tired, defeated.

Again, Liesel searched for Max Vandenburg, thinking that he could easily have ended up in Dachau without being marched through Molching. He was not there. Not on this occasion.

Just give it time, though, for on a warm afternoon in August, Max would most certainly be marched through town with the rest of them. Unlike the others, however, he would not watch the road. He would not look randomly into the *Führer*'s German grandstand.

**⁂ A FACT REGARDING ⁂
MAX VANDENBURG
He would search the faces on Munich
Street for a book-thieving girl.**

On this occasion, in July, on what Liesel later calculated as the ninety-eighth day of her papa's return, she stood and studied the moving pile of mournful Jews—looking for Max. If nothing else, it alleviated the pain of simply watching.

That's a horrible thought, she would write in her Himmel Street basement, but she knew it to be true. The pain of watching them. What about *their* pain? The pain of stumbling shoes and torment and the closing gates of the camp?

They came through twice in ten days, and soon after, the anonymous, prune-faced woman on Munich Street was proven absolutely correct. Suffering had most definitely come, and if they could blame the Jews as a warning or prologue, they should have blamed the *Führer* and his quest for Russia as the actual cause—for when Himmel Street woke later in July, a returned soldier was discovered to be dead. He was hanging from one of the rafters in a laundry up near Frau Diller's. Another human pendulum. Another clock, stopped.

The careless owner had left the door open.

**⁂ JULY 24, 6:03 A.M. ⁂
The laundry was warm,
the rafters were firm,
and Michael Holtzapfel
jumped from the chair
as if it were a cliff.**

502

• • •

So many people chased after me in that time, calling my name, asking me to take them with me. Then there was the small percentage who called me casually over and whispered with their tightened voices.

"Have me," they said, and there was no stopping them. They were frightened, no question, but they were not afraid of me. It was a fear of messing up and having to face themselves again, and facing the world, and the likes of you.

There was nothing I could do.

They had too many ways, they were too resourceful—and when they did it too well, whatever their chosen method, I was in no position to refuse.

Michael Holtzapfel knew what he was doing.

He killed himself for wanting to live.

Of course, I did not see Liesel Meminger at all that day. As is usually the case, I advised myself that I was far too busy to remain on Himmel Street to listen to the screams. It's bad enough when people catch me red-handed, so I made the usual decision to make my exit, into the breakfast-colored sun.

I did not hear the detonation of an old man's voice when he found the hanging body, nor the sound of running feet and jaw-dropped gasps when other people arrived. I did not hear a skinny man with a mustache mutter, "Crying shame, a *damn* shame . . ."

I did not see Frau Holtzapfel laid out flat on Himmel Street, her arms out wide, her screaming face in total despair. No, I didn't discover any of that until I came back a few months later and read something called *The Book Thief.* It was explained to me that in the end, Michael Holtzapfel was worn down not by his damaged hand or any other injury, but by the guilt of living.

In the lead-up to his death, the girl had realized that he wasn't

503

sleeping, that each night was like poison. I often imagine him lying awake, sweating in sheets of snow, or seeing visions of his brother's severed legs. Liesel wrote that sometimes she almost told him about her own brother, like she did with Max, but there seemed a big difference between a long-distance cough and two obliterated legs. How do you console a man who has seen such things? Could you tell him the *Führer* was proud of him, that the *Führer* loved him for what he did in Stalingrad? How could you even dare? You can only let him do the talking. The dilemma, of course, is that such people save their most important words for after, when the surrounding humans are unlucky enough to find them. A note, a sentence, even a question, or a letter, like on Himmel Street in July 1943.

* * * MICHAEL HOLTZAPFEL— * * *
THE LAST GOODBYE
Dear Mama,
Can you ever forgive me?
I just couldn't stand it any longer.
I'm meeting Robert. I don't care
what the damn Catholics say about it.
There must be a place in heaven for
those who have been where I have been.
You might think I don't love you
because of what I've done, but I do.
Your Michael

It was Hans Hubermann who was asked to give Frau Holtzapfel the news. He stood on her threshold and she must have seen it on his face. Two sons in six months.

The morning sky stood blazing behind him as the wiry woman made her way past. She ran sobbing to the gathering farther up on Himmel Street. She said the name Michael at least two dozen times, but Michael had already answered. According to the book thief, Frau Holtzapfel hugged the body for nearly an hour. She then returned to the blinding sun of Himmel Street and sat herself down. She could no longer walk.

From a distance, people observed. Such a thing was easier from far away.

Hans Hubermann sat with her.

He placed his hand on hers, as she fell back to the hard ground.

He allowed her screams to fill the street.

Much later, Hans walked with her, with painstaking care, through her front gate, and into the house. And no matter how many times I try to see it differently, I can't pull it off. . . .

When I imagine that scene of the distraught woman and the tall silver-eyed man, it is still snowing in the kitchen of 31 Himmel Street.

THE WAR MAKER

There was the smell of a freshly cut coffin. Black dresses. Enormous suitcases under the eyes. Liesel stood like the rest, on the grass. She read to Frau Holtzapfel that same afternoon. *The Dream Carrier,* her neighbor's favorite.

It was a busy day all around, really.

* * * JULY 27, 1943 * * *
Michael Holtzapfel was buried and the book
thief read to the bereaved. The Allies bombed
Hamburg — and on that subject, it's lucky I'm
somewhat miraculous. No one else could carry close to
forty-five thousand people in such a short amount
of time. Not in a million human years.

The Germans were starting to pay in earnest by then. The *Führer's* pimply little knees were starting to shake.

Still, I'll give him something, that *Führer.*

He certainly had an iron will.

There was no slackening off in terms of war-making, nor was there any scaling back on the extermination and punishment of a Jewish plague. While most of the camps were spread throughout Europe, there were some still in existence in Germany itself.

In those camps, many people were still made to work, and walk. Max Vandenburg was one such Jew.

WAY OF THE WORDS

It happened in a small town of Hitler's heartland.

The flow of more suffering was pumped nicely out, and a small piece of it had now arrived.

Jews were being marched through the outskirts of Munich, and one teenage girl somehow did the unthinkable and made her way through to walk with them. When the soldiers pulled her away and threw her to the ground, she stood up again. She continued.

The morning was warm.

Another beautiful day for a parade.

The soldiers and Jews made their way through several towns and were arriving now in Molching. It was possible that more work needed to be done in the camp, or several prisoners had died. Whatever the reason, a new batch of fresh, tired Jews was being taken on foot to Dachau.

As she always did, Liesel ran to Munich Street with the usual band of onlookers.

"*Heil* Hitler!"

She could hear the first soldier from far up the road and made her way toward him through the crowd, to meet the procession. The voice amazed her. It made the endless sky into a ceiling just above his head, and the words bounced back, landing somewhere on the floor of limping Jewish feet.

Their eyes.

They watched the moving street, one by one, and when Liesel found a good vantage point, she stopped and studied them. She raced through the files of face after face, trying to match them to the Jew who wrote *The Standover Man* and *The Word Shaker*.

Feathery hair, she thought.

No, hair like twigs. That's what it looks like when it hasn't been washed. Look out for hair like twigs and swampy eyes and a kindling beard.

God, there were so many of them.

So many sets of dying eyes and scuffing feet.

Liesel searched them and it was not so much a recognition of facial features that gave Max Vandenburg away. It was how the face was acting—also studying the crowd. Fixed in concentration. Liesel felt herself pausing as she found the only face looking directly into the German spectators. It examined them with such purpose that people on either side of the book thief noticed and pointed him out.

"What's *he* looking at?" said a male voice at her side.

The book thief stepped onto the road.

Never had movement been such a burden. Never had a heart been so definite and big in her adolescent chest.

She stepped forward and said, very quietly, "He's looking for me."

Her voice trailed off and fell away, inside. She had to refind it—reaching far down, to learn to speak again and call out his name.
Max.

"I'm here, Max!"
Louder.
"Max, I'm here!"

He heard her.

> **∗ ∗ ∗ MAX VANDENBURG, AUGUST 1943 ∗ ∗ ∗**
> **There were twigs of hair, just like**
> **Liesel thought, and the swampy eyes**
> **stepped across, shoulder to shoulder**
> **over the other Jews. When they reached**
> **her, they pleaded. His beard**
> **stroked down his face and his mouth**
> **shivered as he said the word,**
> **the name, the girl.**
> **Liesel.**

Liesel shrugged away entirely from the crowd and entered the tide of Jews, weaving through them till she grabbed hold of his arm with her left hand.

His face fell on her.

It reached down as she tripped, and the Jew, the nasty Jew, helped her up. It took all of his strength.

"I'm here, Max," she said again. "I'm here."

"I can't believe . . ." The words dripped from Max Vandenburg's mouth. "Look how much you've grown." There was an intense sadness in his eyes. They swelled. "Liesel . . . they got me a few months ago." The voice was crippled but it dragged itself toward her. "Halfway to Stuttgart."

From the inside, the stream of Jews was a murky disaster of arms and legs. Ragged uniforms. No soldier had seen her yet, and Max gave her a warning. "You have to let go of me, Liesel." He even tried to push her away, but the girl was too strong. Max's starving arms could not sway her, and she walked on, between the filth, the hunger and confusion.

After a long line of steps, the first soldier noticed.

"Hey!" he called in. He pointed with his whip. "Hey, girl, what are you doing? Get out of there."

When she ignored him completely, the soldier used his arm to separate the stickiness of people. He shoved them aside and made his way through. He loomed above her as Liesel struggled on and noticed the strangled expression on Max Vandenburg's face. She had seen him afraid, but never like this.

The soldier took her.

His hands manhandled her clothes.

She could feel the bones in his fingers and the ball of each knuckle. They tore at her skin. "I said get out!" he ordered her, and now he dragged the girl to the side and flung her into the wall of onlooking Germans. It was getting warmer. The sun burned her face. The girl had landed sprawling with pain, but now she stood again. She recovered and waited. She reentered.

This time, Liesel made her way through from the back.

Ahead, she could just see the distinct twigs of hair and walked again toward them.

This time, she did not reach out—she stopped. Somewhere

inside her were the souls of words. They climbed out and stood beside her.

"Max," she said. He turned and briefly closed his eyes as the girl continued. "'There was once a strange, small man,'" she said. Her arms were loose but her hands were fists at her side. "But there was a word shaker, too."

One of the Jews on his way to Dachau had stopped walking now.

He stood absolutely still as the others swerved morosely around him, leaving him completely alone. His eyes staggered, and it was so simple. The words were given across from the girl to the Jew. They climbed on to him.

The next time she spoke, the questions stumbled from her mouth. Hot tears fought for room in her eyes as she would not let them out. Better to stand resolute and proud. Let the words do all of it. "'Is it really you? the young man asked,'" she said. "'Is it from your cheek that I took the seed?'"

Max Vandenburg remained standing.

He did not drop to his knees.

People and Jews and clouds all stopped. They watched.

As he stood, Max looked first at the girl and then stared directly into the sky who was wide and blue and magnificent. There were heavy beams—planks of sun—falling randomly, wonderfully to the road. Clouds arched their backs to look behind as they started again to move on. "It's such a beautiful day," he said, and his voice was in many pieces. A great day to die. A great day to die, like this.

Liesel walked at him. She was courageous enough to reach out and hold his bearded face. "Is it really you, Max?"

Such a brilliant German day and its attentive crowd.

He let his mouth kiss her palm. "Yes, Liesel, it's me," and he held the girl's hand in his face and cried onto her fingers. He cried as the soldiers came and a small collection of insolent Jews stood and watched.

Standing, he was whipped.

"Max," the girl wept.

Then silently, as she was dragged away:

Max.

Jewish fist fighter.

Inside, she said all of it.

Maxi Taxi. That's what that friend called you in Stuttgart when you fought on the street, remember? Remember, Max? You told me. I remember everything. . . .

That was you—the boy with the hard fists, and you said you would land a punch on death's face when he came for you.

Remember the snowman, Max?

Remember?

In the basement?

Remember the white cloud with the gray heart?

The *Führer* still comes down looking for you sometimes. He misses you. We all miss you.

The whip. The whip.

The whip continued from the soldier's hand. It landed on Max's face. It clipped his chin and carved his throat.

Max hit the ground and the soldier now turned to the girl. His mouth opened. He had immaculate teeth.

A sudden flash came before her eyes. She recalled the day she'd wanted Ilsa Hermann or at least the reliable Rosa to slap her, but neither of them would do it. On this occasion, she was not let down.

The whip sliced her collarbone and reached across her shoulder blade.

"Liesel!"

She knew that person.

As the soldier swung his arm, she caught sight of a distressed Rudy Steiner in the gaps of the crowd. He was calling out. She could see his tortured face and yellow hair. "Liesel, get out of there!"

The book thief did not get out.

She closed her eyes and caught the next burning streak, and another, till her body hit the warm flooring of the road. It heated her cheek.

More words arrived, this time from the soldier.

"Steh' auf."

The economical sentence was directed not to the girl but the Jew. It was elaborated on. "Get up, you dirty asshole, you Jewish whore-dog, get up, get up. . . ."

Max hoisted himself upright.

Just another push-up, Max.

Just another push-up on the cold basement floor.

His feet moved.

They dragged and he traveled on.

His legs staggered and his hands wiped at the marks of the whip, to soothe the stinging. When he tried to look again for Liesel, the soldier's hands were placed upon his bloodied shoulders and pushed.

The boy arrived. His lanky legs crouched and he called over, to his left.

"Tommy, get out here and help me. We have to get her up. Tommy, *hurry!*" He lifted the book thief by her armpits. "Liesel, come on, you have to get off the road."

When she was able to stand, she looked at the shocked, frozen-faced Germans, fresh out of their packets. At their feet, she allowed herself to collapse, but only momentarily. A graze struck a match on the side of her face, where she'd met the ground. Her pulse flipped it over, frying it on both sides.

Far down the road, she could see the blurry legs and heels of the last walking Jew.

Her face was burning and there was a dogged ache in her arms and legs—a numbness that was simultaneously painful and exhausting.

She stood, one last time.

Waywardly, she began to walk and then run down Munich Street, to haul in the last steps of Max Vandenburg.

"Liesel, what are you doing?!"

She escaped the grip of Rudy's words and ignored the watching people at her side. Most of them were mute. Statues with beating hearts. Perhaps bystanders in the latter stages of a marathon. Liesel cried out again and was not heard. Hair was in her eyes. "Please, Max!"

After perhaps thirty meters, just as a soldier turned around, the girl was felled. Hands were clamped upon her from behind and the boy next door brought her down. He forced her knees to the road and suffered the penalty. He collected her punches as if they were presents. Her bony hands and elbows were accepted with nothing but a few short moans. He accumulated the loud, clumsy specks of saliva and tears as if they were lovely to his face, and more important, he was able to hold her down.

On Munich Street, a boy and girl were entwined.

They were twisted and comfortless on the road.

Together, they watched the humans disappear. They watched them dissolve, like moving tablets in the humid air.

CONFESSIONS

When the Jews were gone, Rudy and Liesel untangled and the book thief did not speak. There were no answers to Rudy's questions.

Liesel did not go home, either. She walked forlornly to the train station and waited for her papa for hours. Rudy stood with her for the first twenty minutes, but since it was a good half day till Hans was due home, he fetched Rosa. On the way back, he told her what had happened, and when Rosa arrived, she asked nothing of the girl. She had already assembled the puzzle and merely stood beside her and eventually convinced her to sit down. They waited together.

When Papa found out, he dropped his bag, he kicked the *Bahnhof* air.

None of them ate that night. Papa's fingers desecrated the accordion, murdering song after song, no matter how hard he tried. Everything no longer worked.

For three days, the book thief stayed in bed.

Every morning and afternoon, Rudy Steiner knocked on the door and asked if she was still sick. The girl was not sick.

• • •

On the fourth day, Liesel walked to her neighbor's front door and asked if he might go back to the trees with her, where they'd distributed the bread the previous year.

"I should have told you earlier," she said.

As promised, they walked far down the road toward Dachau. They stood in the trees. There were long shapes of light and shade. Pinecones were scattered like cookies.

Thank you, Rudy.

For everything. For helping me off the road, for stopping me . . .

She said none of it.

Her hand leaned on a flaking branch at her side. "Rudy, if I tell you something, will you promise not to say a word to anyone?"

"Of course." He could sense the seriousness in the girl's face, and the heaviness in her voice. He leaned on the tree next to hers. "What is it?"

"Promise."

"I did already."

"Do it again. You can't tell your mother, your brother, or Tommy Müller. Nobody."

"I promise."

Leaning.

Looking at the ground.

She attempted several times to find the right place to start, reading sentences at her feet, joining words to the pinecones and the scraps of broken branches.

"Remember when I was injured playing soccer," she said, "out on the street?"

It took approximately three-quarters of an hour to explain two

517

wars, an accordion, a Jewish fist fighter, and a basement. Not forgetting what had happened four days earlier on Munich Street.

"That's why you went for a closer look," Rudy said, "with the
bread that day. To see if he was there."

"Yes."

"Crucified Christ."

"Yes."

The trees were tall and triangular. They were quiet.

Liesel pulled *The Word Shaker* from her bag and showed Rudy
one of the pages. On it was a boy with three medals hanging around
his throat.

"'Hair the color of lemons,'" Rudy read. His fingers touched the
words. "You told him about me?"

At first, Liesel could not talk. Perhaps it was the sudden bumpi-
ness of love she felt for him. Or had she always loved him? It's likely.
Restricted as she was from speaking, she wanted him to kiss her. She
wanted him to drag her hand across and pull her over. It didn't matter
where. Her mouth, her neck, her cheek. Her skin was empty for it,
waiting.

Years ago, when they'd raced on a muddy field, Rudy was a hastily
assembled set of bones, with a jagged, rocky smile. In the trees this
afternoon, he was a giver of bread and teddy bears. He was a triple
Hitler Youth athletics champion. He was her best friend. And he
was a month from his death.

"Of course I told him about you," Liesel said.

She was saying goodbye and she didn't even know it.

ILSA HERMANN'S LITTLE BLACK BOOK

In mid-August, she thought she was going to 8 Grande Strasse for the same old remedy.

To cheer herself up.

That was what she thought.

The day had been hot, but showers were predicted for the evening. In *The Last Human Stranger,* there was a quote near the end. Liesel was reminded of it as she walked past Frau Diller's.

* * * THE LAST HUMAN STRANGER, * * *
PAGE 211
The sun stirs the earth. Around and
around, it stirs us, like stew.

At the time, Liesel only thought of it because the day was so warm.

On Munich Street, she remembered the events of the previous week there. She saw the Jews coming down the road, their streams and numbers and pain. She decided there was a word missing from her quote.

The world is an *ugly* stew, she thought.

It's so ugly I can't stand it.

Liesel crossed the bridge over the Amper River. The water was glorious and emerald and rich. She could see the stones at the bottom and hear the familiar song of water. The world did not deserve such a river.

She scaled the hill up to Grande Strasse. The houses were lovely and loathsome. She enjoyed the small ache in her legs and lungs. Walk harder, she thought, and she started rising, like a monster out of the sand. She smelled the neighborhood grass. It was fresh and sweet, green and yellow-tipped. She crossed the yard without a single turn of the head or the slightest pause of paranoia.

The window.

Hands on the frame, scissor of the legs.

Landing feet.

Books and pages and a happy place.

She slid a book from the shelf and sat with it on the floor.

Is she home? she wondered, but she did not care if Ilsa Hermann was slicing potatoes in the kitchen or lining up in the post office. Or standing ghost-like over the top of her, examining what the girl was reading.

The girl simply didn't care anymore.

For a long time, she sat and saw.

She had seen her brother die with one eye open, one still in a dream. She had said goodbye to her mother and imagined her lonely wait for a train back home to oblivion. A woman of wire had laid herself down, her scream traveling the street, till it fell sideways like a rolling coin starved of momentum. A young man was hung by a rope made of Stalingrad snow. She had watched a bomber pilot die in a metal case. She had seen a Jewish man who had twice given her the most beautiful pages of her life marched to a concentration camp. And at the center of all of it, she saw the *Führer* shouting his words and passing them around.

Those images were the world, and it stewed in her as she sat with the lovely books and their manicured titles. It brewed in her as she eyed the pages full to the brims of their bellies with paragraphs and words.

You bastards, she thought.

You lovely bastards.

Don't make me happy. Please, don't fill me up and let me think that something good can come of any of this. Look at my bruises. Look at this graze. Do you see the graze inside me? Do you see it growing before your very eyes, eroding me? I don't want to hope for anything anymore. I don't want to pray that Max is alive and safe. Or Alex Steiner.

Because the world does not deserve them.

She tore a page from the book and ripped it in half.

Then a chapter.

Soon, there was nothing but scraps of words littered between her legs and all around her. The words. Why did they have to exist? Without them, there wouldn't be any of this. Without words, the *Führer* was nothing. There would be no limping prisoners, no need for consolation or wordly tricks to make us feel better.

What good were the words?

She said it audibly now, to the orange-lit room. "What good are the words?"

The book thief stood and walked carefully to the library door. Its protest was small and halfhearted. The airy hallway was steeped in wooden emptiness.

"Frau Hermann?"

The question came back at her and tried for another surge to the front door. It made it only halfway, landing weakly on a couple of fat floorboards.

"Frau Hermann?"

The calls were greeted with nothing but silence, and she was tempted to seek out the kitchen, for Rudy. She refrained. It wouldn't have felt right to steal food from a woman who had left her a dictionary against a windowpane. That, and she had also just destroyed one of her books, page by page, chapter by chapter. She'd done enough damage as it was.

Liesel returned to the library and opened one of the desk drawers. She sat down.

* * * THE LAST LETTER * * *

Dear Mrs. Hermann,

As you can see, I have been in your library again and I have ruined one of your books. I was just so angry and afraid and I wanted to kill the words. I have stolen from you and now I've wrecked your property. I'm sorry. To punish myself, I think I will stop coming here. Or is it punishment at all? I love this place and hate it, because it is full of words.

You have been a friend to me even though I hurt you, even though I have been insufferable (a word I looked up in your dictionary), and I think I will leave you alone now. I'm sorry for everything.

Thank you again.

Liesel Meminger

She left the note on the desk and gave the room a last goodbye, doing three laps and running her hands over the titles. As much as she hated them, she couldn't resist. Flakes of torn-up paper were strewn around a book called *The Rules of Tommy Hoffmann*. In the breeze from the window, a few of its shreds rose and fell.

The light was still orange, but it was not as lustrous as earlier. Her hands felt their final grip of the wooden window frame, and there was the last rush of a plunging stomach, and the pang of pain in her feet when she landed.

By the time she made it down the hill and across the bridge, the orange light had vanished. Clouds were mopping up.

When she walked down Himmel Street, she could already feel the first drops of rain. I will never see Ilsa Hermann again, she thought, but the book thief was better at reading and ruining books than making assumptions.

* * * THREE DAYS LATER * * *
The woman has knocked at number
thirty-three and waits for a reply.

It was strange for Liesel to see her without the bathrobe. The summer dress was yellow with red trim. There was a pocket with a small flower on it. No swastikas. Black shoes. Never before had she noticed Ilsa Hermann's shins. She had porcelain legs.

"Frau Hermann, I'm sorry—for what I did the last time in the library."

The woman quieted her. She reached into her bag and pulled out a small black book. Inside was not a story, but lined paper. "I thought if you're not going to read any more of my books, you might like to write one instead. Your letter, it was . . ." She handed the book to Liesel with both hands. "You can certainly write. You write well." The book was heavy, the cover matted like *The Shoulder*

Shrug. "And please," Ilsa Hermann advised her, "don't punish yourself, like you said you would. Don't be like me, Liesel."

The girl opened the book and touched the paper. *"Danke schön, Frau Hermann.* I can make you some coffee, if you like. Would you come in? I'm home alone. My mama's next door, with Frau Holtzapfel."

"Shall we use the door or the window?"

Liesel suspected it was the broadest smile Ilsa Hermann had allowed herself in years. "I think we'll use the door. It's easier."

They sat in the kitchen.

Coffee mugs and bread with jam. They struggled to speak and Liesel could hear Ilsa Hermann swallow, but somehow, it was not uncomfortable. It was even nice to see the woman gently blow across the coffee to cool it.

"If I ever write something and finish it," Liesel said, "I'll show you."

"That would be nice."

When the mayor's wife left, Liesel watched her walk up Himmel Street. She watched her yellow dress and her black shoes and her porcelain legs.

At the mailbox, Rudy asked, "Was that who I think it was?"

"Yes."

"You're joking."

"She gave me a present."

As it turned out, Ilsa Hermann not only gave Liesel Meminger a book that day. She also gave her a reason to spend time in the basement — her favorite place, first with Papa, then Max. She gave her a reason to write her own words, to see that words had also brought her to life.

"Don't punish yourself," she heard her say again, but there would be punishment and pain, and there would be happiness, too. That was writing.

In the night, when Mama and Papa were asleep, Liesel crept down to the basement and turned on the kerosene lamp. For the first hour, she only watched the pencil and paper. She made herself remember, and as was her habit, she did not look away.

"*Schreibe*," she instructed herself. "Write."

After more than two hours, Liesel Meminger started writing, not knowing how she was ever going to get this right. How could she ever know that someone would pick her story up and carry it with him everywhere?

No one expects these things.

They don't plan them.

She used a small paint can for a seat, a large one as a table, and Liesel stuck the pencil onto the first page. In the middle, she wrote the following.

*** *THE BOOK THIEF* ***
a small story
by
Liesel Meminger

THE RIB—CAGE PLANES

Her hand was sore by page three.

Words are so heavy, she thought, but as the night wore on, she was able to complete eleven pages.

PAGE 1
I try to ignore it, but I know this all
started with the train and the snow and my
coughing brother. I stole my first book that
day. It was a manual for digging graves and
I stole it on my way to Himmel Street....

She fell asleep down there, on a bed of drop sheets, with the paper curling at the edges, up on the taller paint can. In the morning, Mama stood above her, her chlorinated eyes questioning.

"Liesel," she said, "what on earth are you doing down here?"

"I'm writing, Mama."

"Jesus, Mary, and Joseph." Rosa stomped back up the steps.

"Be back up in five minutes or you get the bucket treatment. *Verstehst?*"

"I understand."

Every night, Liesel made her way down to the basement. She kept the book with her at all times. For hours, she wrote, attempting each night to complete ten pages of her life. There was so much to consider, so many things in danger of being left out. Just be patient, she told herself, and with the mounting pages, the strength of her writing fist grew.

Sometimes she wrote about what was happening in the basement at the time of writing. She had just finished the moment when Papa had slapped her on the church steps and how they'd "*heil* Hitlered" together. Looking across, Hans Hubermann was packing the accordion away. He'd just played for half an hour as Liesel wrote.

* * * *PAGE 42* * * *

Papa sat with me tonight. He brought the
accordion down and sat close to where Max
used to sit. I often look at his fingers and
face when he plays. The accordion breathes.
There are lines on his cheeks. They look drawn
on, and for some reason, when I see them,
I want to cry. It is not for any sadness or
pride. I just like the way they move and
change. Sometimes I think my papa is an
accordion. When he looks at me and smiles
and breathes, I hear the notes.

After ten nights of writing, Munich was bombed again. Liesel was up to page 102 and was asleep in the basement. She did not hear the cuckoo or the sirens, and she was holding the book in her sleep when

Papa came to wake her. "Liesel, come." She took *The Book Thief* and each of her other books, and they fetched Frau Holtzapfel.

* * * *PAGE 175* * * *
A book floated down the Amper River.
A boy jumped in, caught up to it, and held
it in his right hand. He grinned. He stood
waist-deep in the icy, Decemberish water.
"How about a kiss, **Saumensch?***" he said.*

By the next raid, on October 2, she was finished. Only a few dozen pages remained blank and the book thief was already starting to read over what she'd written. The book was divided into ten parts, all of which were given the title of books or stories and described how each affected her life.

Often, I wonder what page she was up to when I walked down Himmel Street in the dripping-tap rain, five nights later. I wonder what she was reading when the first bomb dropped from the rib cage of a plane.

Personally, I like to imagine her looking briefly at the wall, at Max Vandenburg's tightrope cloud, his dripping sun, and the figures walking toward it. Then she looks at the agonizing attempts of her paint-written spelling. I see the *Führer* coming down the basement steps with his tied-together boxing gloves hanging casually around his neck. And the book thief reads, rereads, and rereads her last sentence, for many hours.

* * * *THE BOOK THIEF — LAST LINE* * * *
I have hated the words and
I have loved them,
and I hope I have made them right.

Outside, the world whistled. The rain was stained.

THE END OF THE WORLD (Part II)

Almost all the words are fading now. The black book is disintegrating under the weight of my travels. That's another reason for telling this story. What did we say earlier? Say something enough times and you never forget it. Also, I can tell you what happened after the book thief's words had stopped, and how I came to know her story in the first place. Like this.

Picture yourself walking down Himmel Street in the dark. Your hair is getting wet and the air pressure is on the verge of drastic change. The first bomb hits Tommy Müller's apartment block. His face twitches innocently in his sleep and I kneel at his bed. Next, his sister. Kristina's feet are sticking out from under the blanket. They match the hopscotch footprints on the street. Her little toes. Their mother sleeps a few feet away. Four cigarettes sit disfigured in her ashtray, and the roofless ceiling is hot plate red. Himmel Street is burning.

The sirens began to howl.

"Too late *now*," I whispered, "for that little exercise," because everyone had been fooled, and fooled again. First up, the Allies had feigned a raid on Munich in order to strike at Stuttgart. But next, ten planes had remained. Oh, there were warnings, all right. In Molching, they came with the bombs.

✳ ✳ ✳ A ROLL CALL OF STREETS ✳ ✳ ✳
Munich, Ellenberg, Johannson, Himmel.
The main street + three more,
in the poorer part of town.

In the space of a few minutes, all of them were gone.

A church was chopped down.

Earth was destroyed where Max Vandenburg had stayed on his feet.

At 31 Himmel Street, Frau Holtzapfel appeared to be waiting for me in the kitchen. A broken cup was in front of her and in a last moment of awakeness, her face seemed to ask just what in the hell had taken me so long.

By contrast, Frau Diller was fast asleep. Her bulletproof glasses were shattered next to the bed. Her shop was obliterated, the counter landing across the road, and her framed photo of Hitler was taken from the wall and thrown to the floor. The man was positively mugged and beaten to a glass-shattering pulp. I stepped on him on my way out.

The Fiedlers were well organized, all in bed, all covered. Pfiffikus was hidden up to his nose.

At the Steiners', I ran my fingers through Barbara's lovely combed hair, I took the serious look from Kurt's serious sleeping face, and one by one, I kissed the smaller ones good night.

Then Rudy.

• • •

Oh, crucified Christ, Rudy . . .

He lay in bed with one of his sisters. She must have kicked him or muscled her way into the majority of the bed space because he was on the very edge with his arm around her. The boy slept. His candlelit hair ignited the bed, and I picked both him and Bettina up with their souls still in the blanket. If nothing else, they died fast and they were warm. The boy from the plane, I thought. The one with the teddy bear. Where was Rudy's comfort? Where was someone to alleviate this robbery of his life? Who was there to soothe him as life's rug was snatched from under his sleeping feet?

No one.

There was only me.

And I'm not too great at that sort of comforting thing, especially when my hands are cold and the bed is warm. I carried him softly through the broken street, with one salty eye and a heavy, deathly heart. With him, I tried a little harder. I watched the contents of his soul for a moment and saw a black-painted boy calling the name Jesse Owens as he ran through an imaginary tape. I saw him hip-deep in some icy water, chasing a book, and I saw a boy lying in bed, imagining how a kiss would taste from his glorious next-door neighbor. He does something to me, that boy. Every time. It's his only detriment. He steps on my heart. He makes me cry.

Lastly, the Hubermanns.

Hans.

Papa.

He was tall in the bed and I could see the silver through his eyelids. His soul sat up. It met me. Those kinds of souls always do—the best ones. The ones who rise up and say, "I know who you are and I am ready. Not that I want to go, of course, but I will come." Those souls are always light because more of them have been put out. More of them have already found their way to other places. This one was sent out by the breath of an accordion, the odd taste of champagne in summer, and the art of promise-keeping. He lay in my arms and rested. There was an itchy lung for a last cigarette and an immense, magnetic pull toward the basement, for the girl who was his daughter and was writing a book down there that he hoped to read one day.

Liesel.

His soul whispered it as I carried him. But there was no Liesel in that house. Not for me, anyway.

For me, there was only a Rosa, and yes, I truly think I picked her up midsnore, for her mouth was open and her papery pink lips were still in the act of moving. If she'd seen me, I'm sure she would have called me a *Saukerl,* though I would not have taken it badly. After reading *The Book Thief,* I discovered that she called everyone that. *Saukerl. Saumensch.* Especially the people she loved. Her elastic hair was out. It rubbed against the pillow and her wardrobe body had risen with the beating of her heart. Make no mistake, the woman *had* a heart. She had a bigger one than people would think. There was a lot in it, stored up, high in miles of hidden shelving. Remember that she was the woman with the instrument strapped to her body in the long, moon-slit night. She was a Jew feeder without a question in the world on a man's first night in Molching. And she was an arm reacher, deep into a mattress, to deliver a sketchbook to a teenage girl.

* * * THE LAST LUCK * * *
I moved from street to street and
came back for a single man named
Schultz at the bottom of Himmel.

• • •

He couldn't hold out inside the collapsed house, and I was carrying his soul up Himmel Street when I noticed the LSE shouting and laughing.

There was a small valley in the mountain range of rubble.

The hot sky was red and turning. Pepper streaks were starting to swirl and I became curious. Yes, yes, I know what I told you at the beginning. Usually my curiosity leads to the dreaded witnessing of some kind of human outcry, but on this occasion, I have to say that although it broke my heart, I was, and still am, glad I was there.

When they pulled her out, it's true that she started to wail and scream for Hans Hubermann. The men of the LSE attempted to keep her in their powdery arms, but the book thief managed to break away. Desperate humans often seem able to do this.

She did not know where she was running, for Himmel Street no longer existed. Everything was new and apocalyptic. Why was the sky red? How could it be snowing? And why did the snowflakes burn her arms?

Liesel slowed to a staggering walk and concentrated up ahead.

Where's Frau Diller's? she thought. Where's—

She wandered a short while longer until the man who found her took her arm and kept talking. "You're just in shock, my girl. It's just shock; you're going to be fine."

"What's happened?" Liesel asked. "Is this still Himmel Street?"

"Yes." The man had disappointed eyes. What had he seen these past few years? "This is Himmel. You got bombed, my girl. *Es tut mir leid, Schatzi.* I'm sorry, darling."

The girl's mouth wandered on, even if her body was now still. She had forgotten her previous wails for Hans Hubermann. That was years ago—a bombing will do that. She said, "We have to get my papa, my mama. We have to get Max out of the basement. If he's not there, he's in the hallway, looking out the window. He does that sometimes when there's a raid—he doesn't get to look much at the sky, you see. I have to tell him how the weather looks now. He'll never believe me. . . ."

Her body buckled at that moment and the LSE man caught her and sat her down. "We'll move her in a minute," he told his sergeant. The book thief looked at what was heavy and hurting in her hand.

The book.
The words.
Her fingers were bleeding, just like they had on her arrival here.

The LSE man lifted her and started to lead her away. A wooden spoon was on fire. A man walked past with a broken accordion case and Liesel could see the instrument inside. She could see its white teeth and the black notes in between. They smiled at her and triggered an alertness to her reality. We were bombed, she thought, and now she turned to the man at her side and said, "That's my papa's accordion." Again. "That's my papa's accordion."

"Don't worry, young girl, you're safe; just come a little farther."
But Liesel did not come.
She looked to where the man was taking the accordion and followed him. With the red sky still showering its beautiful ash, she stopped the tall LSE worker and said, "I'll take that if you like—it's my papa's." Softly, she took it from the man's hand and began carrying it off. It was right about then that she saw the first body.

The accordion case fell from her grip. The sound of an explosion.
Frau Holtzapfel was scissored on the ground.

∗ ∗ ∗ THE NEXT DOZEN SECONDS ∗ ∗ ∗
OF LIESEL MEMINGER'S LIFE
She turns on her heel and looks as far
as she can down this ruined canal
that was once Himmel Street. She sees two
men carrying a body and she follows them.

When she saw the rest of them, Liesel coughed. She listened momentarily as a man told the others that they had found one of the bodies in pieces, in one of the maple trees.

There were shocked pajamas and torn faces. It was the boy's hair she saw first.

Rudy?

She did more than mouth the word now. "Rudy?"

He lay with yellow hair and closed eyes, and the book thief ran toward him and fell down. She dropped the black book. "Rudy," she sobbed, "wake up. . . ." She grabbed him by his shirt and gave him just the slightest disbelieving shake. "Wake up, Rudy," and now, as the sky went on heating and showering ash, Liesel was holding Rudy Steiner's shirt by the front. "Rudy, please." The tears grappled with her face. "Rudy, please, wake up, Goddamn it, wake up, I love you. Come on, Rudy, come on, Jesse Owens, don't you know I love you, wake up, wake up, wake up. . . ."

But nothing cared.

The rubble just climbed higher. Concrete hills with caps of red. A beautiful, tear-stomped girl, shaking the dead.

"Come on, Jesse Owens—"

But the boy did not wake.

In disbelief, Liesel buried her head into Rudy's chest. She held his limp body, trying to keep him from lolling back, until she needed to return him to the butchered ground. She did it gently.

Slow. Slow.

"God, Rudy . . ."

She leaned down and looked at his lifeless face and Liesel kissed her best friend, Rudy Steiner, soft and true on his lips. He tasted dusty and sweet. He tasted like regret in the shadows of trees and in the glow of the anarchist's suit collection. She kissed him long and soft, and when she pulled herself away, she touched his mouth with her fingers. Her hands were trembling, her lips were fleshy, and she leaned in once more, this time losing control and misjudging it. Their teeth collided on the demolished world of Himmel Street.

She did not say goodbye. She was incapable, and after a few more minutes at his side, she was able to tear herself from the ground. It amazes me what humans can do, even when streams are flowing down their faces and they stagger on, coughing and searching, and finding.

* * * THE NEXT DISCOVERY * * *
The bodies of Mama and Papa,
both lying tangled in the gravel
bedsheet of Himmel Street

Liesel did not run or walk or move at all. Her eyes had scoured the humans and stopped hazily when she noticed the tall man and the short, wardrobe woman. That's my mama. That's my papa. The words were stapled to her.

"They're not moving," she said quietly. "They're not moving."

Perhaps if she stood still long enough, it would be *they* who moved, but they remained motionless for as long as Liesel did. I realized at that moment that she was not wearing any shoes. What an odd thing to notice right then. Perhaps I was trying to avoid her face, for the book thief was truly an irretrievable mess.

She took a step and didn't want to take any more, but she did. Slowly, Liesel walked to her mama and papa and sat down between them. She held Mama's hand and began speaking to her. "Remember when I came here, Mama? I clung to the gate and cried. Do you remember what you said to everyone on the street that day?" Her voice wavered now. "You said, 'What are you assholes looking at?'" She took Mama's hand and touched her wrist. "Mama, I know that you . . . I liked when you came to school and told me Max had woken up. Did you know I saw you with Papa's accordion?" She tightened her grip on the hardening hand. "I came and watched and you were beautiful. Goddamn it, you were so beautiful, Mama."

* * * MANY MOMENTS OF AVOIDANCE * * *
Papa. She would not, and
***could* not, look at Papa.**
Not yet. Not now.

Papa was a man with silver eyes, not dead ones.
Papa was an accordion!
But his bellows were all empty.
Nothing went in and nothing came out.

She began to rock back and forth. A shrill, quiet, smearing note was caught somewhere in her mouth until she was finally able to turn.
To Papa.

At that point, I couldn't help it. I walked around to see her better, and from the moment I witnessed her face again, I could tell that this was who she loved the most. Her expression stroked the man on his face. It followed one of the lines down his cheek. He had sat in the washroom with her and taught her how to roll a cigarette. He gave bread to a dead man on Munich Street and told the girl to keep reading in the bomb shelter. Perhaps if he didn't, she might not have ended up writing in the basement.

Papa—the accordionist—and Himmel Street.

One could not exist without the other, because for Liesel, both were home. Yes, that's what Hans Hubermann was for Liesel Meminger.

She turned around and spoke to the LSE.

"Please," she said, "my papa's accordion. Could you get it for me?"

After a few minutes of confusion, an older member brought the eaten case and Liesel opened it. She removed the injured instrument and laid it next to Papa's body. "Here, Papa."

And I can promise you something, because it was a thing I saw many years later—a vision in the book thief herself—that as she knelt next to Hans Hubermann, she watched him stand and play the accordion. He stood and strapped it on in the alps of broken houses and played the accordion with kindness silver eyes and even a cigarette slouched on his lips. He even made a mistake and laughed in lovely hindsight. The bellows breathed and the tall man played for Liesel Meminger one last time as the sky was slowly taken from the stove.

Keep playing, Papa.

Papa stopped.

He dropped the accordion and his silver eyes continued to rust. There was only a body now, on the ground, and Liesel lifted him up and hugged him. She wept over the shoulder of Hans Hubermann.

Goodbye, Papa, you saved me. You taught me to read. No one

can play like you. I'll never drink champagne. No one can play like you.

Her arms held him. She kissed his shoulder—she couldn't bear to look at his face anymore—and she placed him down again.

The book thief wept till she was gently taken away.

Later, they remembered the accordion but no one noticed the book.

There was much work to be done, and with a collection of other materials, *The Book Thief* was stepped on several times and eventually picked up without even a glance and thrown aboard a garbage truck. Just before the truck left, I climbed quickly up and took it in my hand. . . .

It's lucky I was there.

Then again, who am I kidding? I'm in most places at least once, and in 1943, I was just about everywhere.

EPILOGUE

the last color

featuring:

death and liesel—some

wooden tears—max—

and the handover man

DEATH AND LIESEL

It has been many years since all of that, but there is still plenty of work to do. I can promise you that the world is a factory. The sun stirs it, the humans rule it. And I remain. I carry them away.

As for what's left of this story, I will not skirt around any of it, because I'm tired, I'm so tired, and I will tell it as straightly as I can.

* * * A LAST FACT * * *
I should tell you that
the book thief died
only yesterday.

Liesel Meminger lived to a very old age, far away from Molching and the demise of Himmel Street.

She died in a suburb of Sydney. The house number was forty-five—the same as the Fiedlers' shelter—and the sky was the best blue of afternoon. Like her papa, her soul was sitting up.

In her final visions, she saw her three children, her grandchildren, her husband, and the long list of lives that merged with hers. Among them, lit like lanterns, were Hans and Rosa Hubermann, her brother, and the boy whose hair remained the color of lemons forever.

But a few other visions were there as well.
Come with me and I'll tell you a story.
I'll show you something.

WOOD IN THE AFTERNOON

When Himmel Street was cleared, Liesel Meminger had nowhere to go. She was the girl they referred to as "the one with the accordion," and she was taken to the police, who were in the throes of deciding what to do with her.

She sat on a very hard chair. The accordion looked at her through the hole in the case.

It took three hours in the police station for the mayor and a fluffy-haired woman to show their faces. "Everyone says there's a girl," the lady said, "who survived on Himmel Street."

A policeman pointed.

Ilsa Hermann offered to carry the case, but Liesel held it firmly in her hand as they walked down the police station steps. A few blocks down Munich Street, there was a clear line separating the bombed from the fortunate.

The mayor drove.

Ilsa sat with her in the back.

The girl let her hold her hand on top of the accordion case, which sat between them.

It would have been easy to say nothing, but Liesel had the opposite reaction to her devastation. She sat in the exquisite spare room of the mayor's house and spoke and spoke—to herself—well into the night. She ate very little. The only thing she didn't do at all was wash.

For four days, she carried around the remains of Himmel Street on the carpets and floorboards of 8 Grande Strasse. She slept a lot and didn't dream, and on most occasions she was sorry to wake up. Everything disappeared when she was asleep.

On the day of the funerals, she still hadn't bathed, and Ilsa Hermann asked politely if she'd like to. Previously, she'd only shown her the bath and given her a towel.

People who were at the service of Hans and Rosa Hubermann always talked about the girl who stood there wearing a pretty dress and a layer of Himmel Street dirt. There was also a rumor that later in the day, she walked fully clothed into the Amper River and said something very strange.

Something about a kiss.

Something about a *Saumensch*.

How many times did she have to say goodbye?

After that, there were weeks and months, and a lot of war. She remembered her books in the moments of worst sorrow, especially the ones that were made for her and the one that saved her life. One morning, in a renewed state of shock, she even walked back down to Himmel Street to find them, but nothing was left. There was no recovery from what had happened. That would take decades; it would take a long life.

There were two ceremonies for the Steiner family. The first was immediately upon their burial. The second was as soon as Alex Steiner made it home, when he was given leave after the bombing.

Since the news had found him, Alex had been whittled away.

"Crucified Christ," he'd said, "if only I'd let Rudy go to that school."

You save someone.

You kill them.

How was he supposed to know?

The only thing he truly *did* know was that he'd have done anything to have been on Himmel Street that night so that Rudy survived rather than himself.

That was something he told Liesel on the steps of 8 Grande Strasse, when he rushed up there after hearing of her survival.

That day, on the steps, Alex Steiner was sawn apart.

Liesel told him that she had kissed Rudy's lips. It embarrassed her, but she thought he might have liked to know. There were wooden teardrops and an oaky smile. In Liesel's vision, the sky I saw was gray and glossy. A silver afternoon.

MAX

When the war was over and Hitler had delivered himself to my arms, Alex Steiner resumed work in his tailor shop. There was no money in it, but he busied himself there for a few hours each day, and Liesel often accompanied him. They spent many days together, often walking to Dachau after its liberation, only to be denied by the Americans.

Finally, in October 1945, a man with swampy eyes, feathers of hair, and a clean-shaven face walked into the shop. He approached the counter. "Is there someone here by the name of Liesel Meminger?"

"Yes, she's in the back," said Alex. He was hopeful, but he wanted to be sure. "May I ask who is calling on her?"

Liesel came out.

They hugged and cried and fell to the floor.

THE HANDOVER MAN

Yes, I have seen a great many things in this world. I attend the greatest disasters and work for the greatest villains.

But then there are other moments.

There's a multitude of stories (a mere handful, as I have previously suggested) that I allow to distract me as I work, just as the colors do. I pick them up in the unluckiest, unlikeliest places and I make sure to remember them as I go about my work. *The Book Thief* is one such story.

When I traveled to Sydney and took Liesel away, I was finally able to do something I'd been waiting on for a long time. I put her down and we walked along Anzac Avenue, near the soccer field, and I pulled a dusty black book from my pocket.

The old woman was astonished. She took it in her hand and said, "Is this really it?"

I nodded.

With great trepidation, she opened *The Book Thief* and turned the pages. "I can't believe . . ." Even though the text had faded, she was able to read her words. The fingers of her soul touched the story that was written so long ago in her Himmel Street basement.

She sat down on the curb, and I joined her.

"Did you read it?" she asked, but she did not look at me. Her eyes were fixed to the words.

I nodded. "Many times."

"Could you understand it?"

And at that point, there was a great pause.

A few cars drove by, each way. Their drivers were Hitlers and Hubermanns, and Maxes, killers, Dillers, and Steiners. . . .

I wanted to tell the book thief many things, about beauty and brutality. But what could I tell her about those things that she didn't already know? I wanted to explain that I am constantly overestimating and underestimating the human race—that rarely do I ever simply *estimate* it. I wanted to ask her how the same thing could be so ugly and so glorious, and its words and stories so damning and brilliant.

None of those things, however, came out of my mouth.

All I was able to do was turn to Liesel Meminger and tell her the only truth I truly know. I said it to the book thief and I say it now to you.

* * * A LAST NOTE FROM YOUR NARRATOR * * *
I am haunted by humans.

Acknowledgments

I would like to start by thanking Anna McFarlane (who is as warm as she is knowledgeable) and Erin Clarke (for her foresight, kindness, and always having the right advice at the right time). Special thanks must also go to Bri Tunnicliffe for putting up with me and trying to believe my delivery dates for rewrites.

I am indebted to Trudy White for her grace and talent. It's an honor to have her artwork in these pages.

A big thank-you to Melissa Nelson, for making a difficult job look easy. It hasn't gone unnoticed.

This book also wouldn't be possible without the following people: Cate Paterson, Nikki Christer, Jo Jarrah, Anyez Lindop, Jane Novak, Fiona Inglis, and Catherine Drayton. Thank you for putting your valuable time into this story, and into me. I appreciate it more than I can say.

Thanks also to the Sydney Jewish Museum, the Australian War Memorial, Doris Seider at the Jewish Museum of Munich, Andreus Heusler at the Munich City Archive, and Rebecca Biehler (for information on the seasonal habits of apple trees).

I am grateful to Dominika Zusak, Kinga Kovacs, and Andrew Janson for all the pep talks and endurance.

Lastly, special thanks must go to Lisa and Helmut Zusak—for the stories we find hard to believe, for laughter, and for showing me another side.

THE BOOk THIEf

by markus zusak

A READERS GUIDE

ABOUT THE BOOK

Liesel Meminger is only nine years old when she is taken to live with the Hubermanns, a foster family, on Himmel Street in Molching, Germany, in the late 1930s. She arrives with few possessions, but among them is *The Grave Digger's Handbook,* a book she stole from her brother's burial place. During the years that Liesel lives with the Hubermanns, Hitler becomes more powerful, life on Himmel Street becomes more fearful, and Liesel becomes a full-fledged book thief. She rescues books from Nazi book-burnings and steals from the library of the mayor. Liesel is illiterate when she steals her first book, but Hans Hubermann uses her prized books to teach her to read. This is a story of courage, friendship, love, survival, death, and grief. This is Liesel's life on Himmel Street, told from Death's point of view.

QUESTIONS FOR DISCUSSION

1. Discuss the symbolism of Death as the omniscient narrator of the novel. What are Death's feelings for each victim? Describe Death's attempt to resist Liesel. Death states, "I'm always finding humans at their best and worst. I see their ugly and their beauty, and I wonder how the same thing can be both" (page 491). What is ugly and beautiful about Liesel, Rosa and Hans Hubermann, Max Vandenburg, Rudy Steiner, and Mrs. Hermann? Why is Death haunted by humans?

2. What is ironic about Liesel's obsession with stealing books? Discuss other uses of irony in the novel.

3. *The Grave Digger's Handbook* is the first book Liesel steals. Why did she take the book? What is significant about the titles of the books she steals? Discuss why she hides *The Grave Digger's Handbook* under her mattress. Describe Hans Hubermann's reaction when he discovers the book. What does the act of book thievery teach Liesel about life and death? Explain Rudy's reaction when he discovers that Liesel is a book thief. How does stealing books from the mayor's house lead to a friendship with the mayor's wife? Explain how Liesel's own attempt to write a book saves her life.

4. Liesel believes that Hans Hubermann's eyes show kindness, and from the beginning she feels closer to him than to Rosa Hubermann. How does Hans gain Liesel's love and trust? Debate whether Liesel is a substitute for Hans's children, who have strayed from the family. Why

is it so difficult for Rosa to demonstrate the same warmth toward Liesel? Discuss how Liesel's relationship with Rosa changes by the end of the novel.

5. Abandonment is a central theme in the novel. The reader knows that Liesel feels abandoned by her mother and by the death of her brother. How does she equate love with abandonment? At what point does she understand why she was abandoned by her mother? Who else abandons Liesel in the novel? Debate whether she was abandoned by circumstance or by the heart.

6. Guilt is another recurring theme in the novel. Hans Hubermann's life was spared in France during World War I, and Erik Vandenburg's life was taken. Explain why Hans feels guilty about Erik's death. Guilt is a powerful emotion that may cause a person to become unhappy and despondent. Discuss how Hans channels his guilt into helping others. Explain Max Vandenburg's thought, "Living was living. The price was guilt and shame" (page 208). Why does he feel guilt and shame?

7. Compare and contrast the lives of Liesel and Max Vandenburg. How does Max's life give Liesel purpose? At what point do Liesel and Max become friends? Max gives Liesel a story called "The Standover Man" for her birthday. What is the significance of this story?

8. Death says that Liesel was a girl "with a mountain to climb" (page 86). What is her mountain? Who are her climbing partners? What is her greatest obstacle? At what point does she reach the summit of her mountain?

Describe her descent. What does she discover at the foot of her mountain?

9. Hans Junior, a Nazi soldier, calls his dad a coward because he doesn't belong to the Nazi Party. He feels that you are either for Hitler or against him. How does it take courage to oppose Hitler? There isn't one coward in the Hubermann household. Discuss how they demonstrate courage throughout the novel.

10. Describe Liesel's friendship with Rudy. How does their friendship change and grow throughout the novel? Death says that Rudy doesn't offer his friendship "for free" (page 51). What does Rudy want from Liesel? Discuss Death's statement, "The only thing worse than a boy who hates you [is] a boy who loves you" (page 52). Why is it difficult for Liesel to love Rudy? Discuss why Liesel tells Mr. Steiner that she kissed Rudy's dead body.

11. How does Zusak use the literary device of foreshadowing to pull the reader into the story?

12. Liesel Meminger lived to be an old woman. Death says that he would like to tell the book thief about beauty and brutality, but those are things that she had lived. How does her life represent beauty in the wake of brutality? Discuss how Zusak's poetic writing style enhances the beauty of Liesel's story.

Guide prepared by Pat Scales, retired director of library services, South Carolina Governor's School for the Arts and Humanities

RELATED TITLES

In My Hands: Memories of a Holocaust Rescuer
Irene Gut Opdyke, with Jennifer Armstrong

Milkweed
Jerry Spinelli

The Boy in the Striped Pajamas
John Boyne

Tunes for Bears to Dance To
Robert Cormier

INTERNET RESOURCES

United States Holocaust Memorial Museum
www.ushmm.org
The official site of the museum

Jewish Virtual Library
www.jewishvirtuallibrary.org
Provides a comprehensive Jewish encyclopedia, with
articles about the burning of books by the Nazis and
other related topics

IN HIS OWN WORDS

A CONVERSATION WITH
MARKUS ZUSAK

Q: What inspired you to write about a hungry, illiterate girl who has such a desire to read that she steals books?

A: I think it's just working on a book over and over again. I heard stories of cities on fire, teenagers who were whipped for giving starving Jewish people bread on their way to concentration camps, and people huddled in bomb shelters. . . . But I also had a story about a book thief set in my hometown of Sydney. I just brought the two ideas together and realized the importance of words in Nazi Germany. I thought of Hitler destroying people with words, and now I had a girl who was stealing them back, as she read books with the young Jewish man in her basement and calmed people down in the bomb shelters. She writes her own story—and it's a beautiful story—through the ugliness of the world that surrounds her.

Q: There are many novels set during the Holocaust, but *The Book Thief* offers a different perspective. What do you most want teenage readers to understand about Liesel's story and this dark period in our world's history?

A: I honestly just hope that they'll never forget the characters. This is the first time I've ever missed characters that I've written—especially Liesel and Rudy. I also hope that readers of any age will see another side of Nazi Germany, where certain people *did* hide their Jewish friends to save their lives (at the risk of their own). I wanted them to see people who were unwilling to fly the Nazi flag, and boys and girls who thought the Hitler Youth was boring and ridiculous. If nothing else, there's another side that lives beneath the propaganda reels that are still so effective decades later. Those were the pockets I was interested in.

Q: How did you decide to make Death the narrator of the book?

A: With great difficulty! I thought, "Here's a book set during war. Everyone says war and death are best friends." Death is ever-present during war, so here was the perfect choice to narrate *The Book Thief*. At first, though, Death was too mean. He was supercilious, and enjoying his work too much. He'd say extremely creepy things and delight in all the souls he was picking up . . . and the book wasn't working. So I went to a first-person narration, a simple third-person narration . . . and six months later I came back to Death—but this time, Death was to be exhausted from his eternal existence and his job. He was to be afraid of humans—because, after all, he was there to see the obliteration we've perpetrated on each other throughout the ages—and he would now be telling this story to prove to himself that humans are actually worth it.

Q: Liesel has an uncanny understanding of people and an ability to befriend those who most need companionship. Who do you think is Liesel's most unforgettable friend?

A: For me it's Rudy, but a lot of people will tell me it's Hans Hubermann, Max, the mayor's wife, or even Rosa Hubermann. Rudy is just my favorite character. From the moment he painted himself black and became Jesse Owens, he was my favorite. Liesel kissing his dusty, bomb-hit lips was probably the most devastating part of the book for me to write. . . . I was a mess.

On the other hand, I'm also drawn to all of the relationships Liesel forms, even her reading with Frau Holtzapfel, and the return of her son. Even Ludwig Schmeikl—the boy she beats up on the playground and reconciles with at the book-burning . . . I think the relationship with Rosa is the most unexpected, though. The moment when she sees Rosa with the accordion strapped to her (when Hans is sent to the war) is when she realizes exactly how much love her foster mother is capable of.

Q: **Your use of figurative language seems natural and effortless. Is this something that you have to work to develop, or is it innately a part of your writing style?**

A: I like the idea that every page in every book can have a gem on it. It's probably what I love most about writing—that words can be used in a way that's like a child playing in a sandpit, rearranging things, swapping them around. They're the best moments in a day of writing—when an image appears that you didn't know would be there when you started work in the morning.

At other stages, it takes time. It took three years to write this book, and some images remained from start to finish, but others were considered and reconsidered dozens of times, if not more. Often, to keep the workday flowing, I'll continue writing the story and then come back later to develop an image that hasn't worked from the outset. I might even take it out completely.

Q: **There are numerous details about the setting of the book. Did you have to do extensive research? How long did it take you to prepare for writing this novel?**

A: Research isn't my strong point—I have to be absolutely honest about that. The whole time I was researching, I was thinking, "Come on, hurry up, will you? Get home and start writing. . . ." To a certain extent, the world of Molching was given to me. It was in my mind, dormant from childhood, on account of all the stories I was told by my parents. In terms of getting the details right, that was both a hindrance and a huge advantage. History gave this story its bombings, towns, and people. Getting them in the right time and place in the book was more difficult than people might imagine—but it also gave me a framework to place my story on.

I really did the research in phases, before, during, and after I'd finished the manuscript. It wasn't until the end of the writing that I went to Munich to check all of my facts, especially little things, like the seasonal habits of apple trees! (Liesel and Rudy's apple-stealing needed to occur in the right month.) I guess the little things mean a lot. When they add up, hopefully they make the book complete.

Protect the Diamonds,
Survive the Clubs,
Dig the Spades,
Feel the Hearts...

BECOME THE MESSENGER

"Funny and gripping." —*The Miami Herald*

I AM THE MESSENGER

MARKUS ZUSAK

AUTHOR OF THE *NEW YORK TIMES* #1 BESTSELLER *THE BOOK THIEF*

A 2005 MICHAEL L. PRINTZ HONOR BOOK

A Printz Honor Book

"Funny and gripping."

—*The Miami Herald*

Ed Kennedy is 19 and aimlessly lurching into adulthood when he thwarts a bank robbery. His 15 minutes of fame set his life in a new direction: he begins receiving playing cards with strange clues— addresses and unfamiliar names. These clues lead him to intervene in the lives of others . . . and become the messenger.

Read & Discuss

MarkusZusak.com

692

Alfred A. Knopf   RHCB